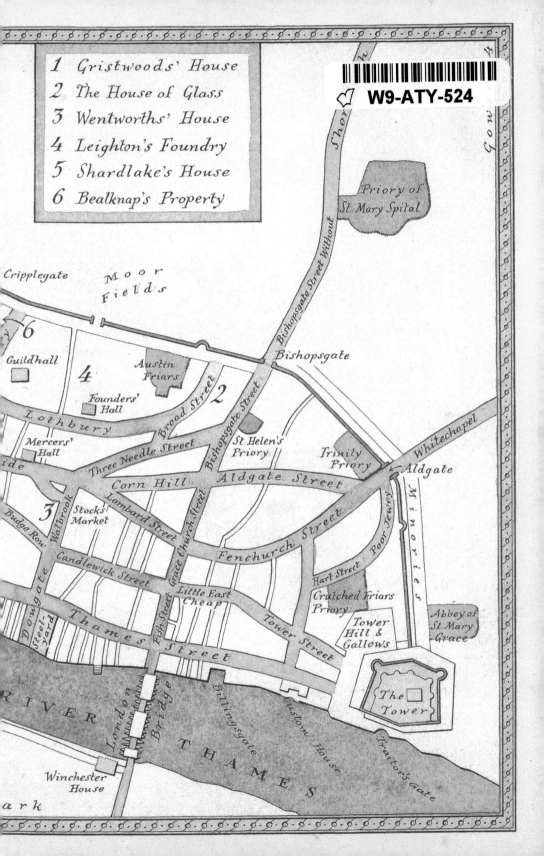

**Key**

1. Gristwoods' House
2. The House of Glass
3. Wentworths' House
4. Leighton's Foundry
5. Shardlake's House
6. Bealknap's Property

Priory of St Mary Spital

Shor...

Cripplegate

M o o r F i e l d s

Bishopsgate Street Without

Bishopsgate

6

Guildhall

Austin Friars

Founders' Hall

Broad Street

2

Bishopsgate Street

St Helen's Priory

Trinity Priory

Aldgate

Whitechapel

L o t h b u r y

Mercers' Hall

Three Needle Street

Corn Hill

Bishopsgate Church Street

Aldgate Street

Minories

...ide

3

Watbrook

Stocks Market

Lombard Street

Grace Church Street

Fenchurch Street

Poor Jewry

Hart Street

Budge Row

Candlewick Street

Fish Street

Little East Cheap

Crutched Friars Priory

Abbey of St Mary Grace

Dowgate

Steel-yard

T h a m e s   S t r e e t

Tower Street

Custom House

Tower Hill & Gallows

The Tower

R I V E R

London Bridge

Billingsgate

Traitor's Gate

T H A M E S

Winchester House

...ark

# Dark Fire

Also by C. J. Sansom

*Dissolution*

C. J. SANSOM

# Dark Fire

§

VIKING

VIKING
Published by the Penguin Group
Penguin Group (USA) Inc., 375 Hudson Street,
New York, New York 10014, U.S.A.
Penguin Group (Canada), 10 Alcorn Avenue, Toronto, Ontario, Canada M4V 3B2
(a division of Pearson Penguin Canada Inc.)
Penguin Books Ltd, 80 Strand, London WC2R 0RL, England
Penguin Ireland, 25 St. Stephen's Green, Dublin 2, Ireland (a division of Penguin Books Ltd)
Penguin Books Australia Ltd, 250 Camberwell Road, Camberwell,
Victoria 3124, Australia (a division of Pearson Australia Group Pty Ltd)
Penguin Books India Pvt Ltd, 11 Community Centre, Panchsheel Park, New Delhi – 110 017, India
Penguin Group (NZ), Cnr Airborne and Rosedale Roads, Albany, Auckland 1310, New Zealand
(a division of Pearson New Zealand Ltd)
Penguin Books (South Africa) (Pty) Ltd, 24 Sturdee Avenue,
Rosebank, Johannesburg 2196, South Africa

Penguin Books Ltd, Registered Offices:
80 Strand, London WC2R 0RL, England

First American edition
Published in 2005 by Viking Penguin,
a member of Penguin Group (USA) Inc.

10  9  8  7  6  5  4  3  2  1

Publisher's Note
This is a work of fiction. Names, characters, places, and incidents either are the product of the author's imagi-nation or are used fictitiously, and any resemblance to actual persons, living or dead, business establishments, events, or locales is entirely coincidental.

Library of Congress Cataloging-in-Publication Data

Sansom, C. J.
  Dark fire / C. J. Sansom.
    p.  cm.
  ISBN 0-670-03372-3
  1. Great Britain—History—Henry VIII, 1509–1547—Fiction. 2. Cromwell, Thomas, Earl of Essex,
1485? –1504—Fiction. 3. Attorney and client—Fiction. 4. Trials (Murder)—Fiction. I. Title.

PR6119.A57D37 2005
823'.92—dc22          2004057180

This book is printed on acid-free paper. ∞

Printed in the United States of America
Set in Poliphilus MT with Clairvaux

# Chapter One

I HAD LEFT MY HOUSE in Chancery Lane early, to go to the Guildhall to discuss a case in which I was acting for the City Council. Although the far more serious matter I would have to deal with on my return weighed on my mind, as I rode down a quiet Fleet Street I was able to take a little pleasure in the soft airs of early morning. The weather was very hot for late May, the sun already a fiery ball in the clear blue sky, and I wore only a light doublet under my black lawyer's robe. As my old horse Chancery ambled along, the sight of the trees in full leaf made me think again of my ambition to retire from practice, to escape the noisome crowds of London. In two years' time I would be forty, in which year the old man's age begins; if business was good enough I might do it then. I passed over Fleet Bridge with its statues of the ancient kings Gog and Magog. The City wall loomed ahead, and I braced myself for the stink and din of London.

At the Guildhall I met with Mayor Hollyes and the Common Council serjeant. The council had brought an action in the Assize of Nuisance against one of the rapacious land speculators buying up the dissolved monasteries, the last of which had gone down in this spring of 1540. This particular speculator, to my shame, was a fellow barrister of Lincoln's Inn, a false and greedy rogue named Bealknap. He had got hold of a small London friary, and rather than bringing down the church, had converted it into a hotchpotch of unsavoury tenements. He had excavated a common cesspit for his tenants, but it was a botched job and the tenants of the neighbouring houses, which the council owned, were suffering grievously from the penetration of filth into their cellars.

The assize had ordered Bealknap to make proper provision but the wretch had served a writ of error in King's Bench, alleging the friary's original charter excluded it from the City's jurisdiction and that he was not obliged to do anything. The matter was listed for hearing before the judges in a week's time. I advised the mayor that Bealknap's chances were slim, pointing out that he was one of those maddening rogues whom lawyers encounter, who take perverse pleasure in spending time and money on uncertain cases rather than admitting defeat and making proper remedy like civilized men.

✝

I PLANNED TO RETURN home the way I had come, via Cheapside, but when I reached the junction with Lad Lane I found Wood Street blocked by an overturned cart full of lead and roof tiles from the demolition of St Bartholomew's Priory. A heap of mossy tiles had spilled out, filling the roadway. The cart was big, pulled by two great shire horses, and though the driver had freed one, the other lay helpless on its side between the shafts. Its huge hooves kicked out wildly, smashing tiles and raising clouds of dust. It neighed in terror, eyes rolling at the gathering crowd. I heard someone say more carts were backed up almost to Cripplegate.

It was not the first such scene in the City of late. Everywhere there was a crashing of stone as the old buildings fell: so much land had become vacant that even in overcrowded London the courtiers and other greedy men of spoil into whose hands it had fallen scarce knew how to handle it all.

I turned Chancery round and made my way through the maze of narrow lanes that led to Cheapside, in places scarce wide enough for a horse and rider to pass under the overhanging eaves of the houses. Although it was still early, the workshops were open and people crowded the lanes, slowing my passage, journeymen and street traders and water carriers labouring under their huge conical baskets. It had hardly rained in a month, the butts were dry and they were doing good business. I thought again of the meeting to come; I had been dreading it and now I would be late.

I wrinkled my nose at the mighty stink the hot weather drew from the sewer channel, then cursed roundly as a rooting pig, its snout smeared with some nameless rubbish, ran squealing across Chancery's path and made him jerk aside. A couple of apprentices in their blue doublets, returning puffy-faced from some late revel, glanced round at my oath and one of them, a stocky, rough-featured young fellow, gave me a contemptuous grin. I set my lips and spurred Chancery on. I saw myself as he must have, a whey-faced hunchback lawyer in black robe and cap, a pencase and dagger at my waist instead of a sword.

It was a relief to arrive at the broad paved way of Cheapside. Crowds milled round the stalls of Cheap Market; under their bright awnings the peddlers called 'What d'ye lack?' or argued with white-coifed goodwives. The occasional lady of wealth wandered around the stalls with her armed servants, face masked with a cloth vizard to protect her white complexion from the sun.

Then, as I turned past the great bulk of St Paul's, I heard the loud cry of a pamphlet seller. A scrawny fellow in a stained black doublet, a pile of papers under his arm, he was howling at the crowd. 'Child murderess of Walbrook taken to Newgate!' I paused and leaned down to pass him a farthing. He licked his finger, peeled off a sheet and handed it up to me, then went on bawling at the crowd. 'The most terrible crime of the year!'

I stopped to read the thing in the shadow cast by the great bulk of St Paul's. As usual the cathedral precincts were full of beggars – adults and children leaning against the walls, thin and ragged, displaying their sores and deformities in the hope of charity. I averted my eyes from their pleading looks and turned to the pamphlet. Beneath a woodcut of a woman's face – it could have been anybody, it was just a sketch of a face beneath disordered hair – I read:

*Terrible Crime in Walbrook; Child Murdered by His Jealous Cousin*

On the evening of May 16th last, a Sabbath Day, at the fair house of Sir Edwin Wentworth of Walbrook, a member of the Mercers' Company, his only son, *a boy of twelve*, was found at the bottom of the garden well with his *neck broken*. Sir Edwin's *fair daughters*, girls of fifteen and sixteen, told how the boy had been attacked by their cousin, *Elizabeth Wentworth*, an *orphan* whom Sir Edwin had taken into his house from charity on the death of her father, and had been pushed by her into the deep well. She is taken to *Newgate*, where she is to go before the Justices the *29th May* next. She refuses to plead, and so is likely to be *pressed*, or if she pleads to be found *guilty* and to go to *Tyburn* next *hanging day*.

The thing was badly printed on cheap paper and left inky smears on my fingers as I thrust it into my pocket and turned down Paternoster Row. So the case was public knowledge, another half-penny sensation. Innocent or guilty, how could the girl get a fair trial from a London jury now? The spread of printing had brought us the English Bible, ordered the year before to be set in every church; but it had also brought pamphlets like this, making money for backstreet printers and fodder for the hangman. Truly, as the ancients taught us, there is nothing under the moon, however fine, that is not subject to corruption.

✝

IT WAS NEARLY NOON when I reined Chancery in before my front door. The sun was at its zenith and when I untied the ribbon of my cap it left a line of sweat under my chin. Joan, my housekeeper, opened the door as I dismounted, a worried expression on her plump face.

'He is here,' she whispered, glancing behind her. 'That girl's uncle—'

'I know.' Joseph would have ridden through London. Perhaps he too had seen the pamphlet. 'What case is he in?'

'Sombre, sir. He is in the parlour. I gave him a glass of small beer.'

'Thank you.' I passed the reins to Simon, the boy Joan had

recently employed to help her about the house, and who now scampered up, a stick-thin, yellow-haired urchin. Chancery was not yet used to him and pawed at the gravel, nearly stepping on one of the boy's bare feet. Simon spoke soothingly to him, then gave me a hasty bow and led the horse round to the stable.

'That boy should have shoes,' I said.

Joan shook her head. 'He won't, sir. Says they chafe his feet. I told him he should wear shoes in a gentleman's house.'

'Tell him he shall have sixpence if he wears them a week,' I said. I took a deep breath. 'And now I had better see Joseph.'

✝

JOSEPH WENTWORTH was a plump, ruddy-cheeked man in his early fifties, uncomfortable in his best doublet of sober brown. It was wool, too hot for this weather, and he was perspiring. He looked like what he was; a working farmer, owner of some poor lands out in Essex. His two younger brothers had sought their fortunes in London, but Joseph had remained on the farm. I had first acted for him two years before, defending his farm against a claim by a large landowner who wanted it to put to sheep. I liked Joseph, but my heart had sunk when I received his letter a few days before. I had been tempted to reply, truthfully, that I doubted I could help him, but his tone had been desperate.

His face brightened as he saw me, and he came over and shook my hand eagerly. 'Master Shardlake! Good day, good day. You had my letter?'

'I did. You are staying in London?'

'At an inn down by Queenhithe,' he said. 'My brother has forbidden me his house for my championing of our niece.' There was a desperate look in his hazel eyes. 'You must help me, sir, please. You must help Elizabeth.'

I decided no good would be done by beating round the bushes. I took the pamphlet from my pocket and handed it to him.

'Have you seen this, Joseph?'

'Yes.' He ran a hand through his curly black hair. 'Are they allowed to say these things? Is she not innocent till proven guilty?'

'That's the technical position. It doesn't help much in practice.'

He took a delicately embroidered handkerchief from his pocket and mopped his brow. 'I visited Elizabeth in Newgate this morning,' he said. 'God's mercy, it's a terrible place. But she still won't talk.' He ran his hand over his plump, badly shaven cheeks. 'Why won't she talk, why? It's her only hope of saving herself.' He looked across at me pleadingly, as though I had the answer. I raised a hand.

'Come, Joseph, sit down. Let us start at the beginning. I know only what you told me in your letter, which is little more than is in this foul pamphlet.'

He took a chair, looking apologetic. 'I'm sorry; I've no good hand at writing.'

'Now, one of your two brothers is the father of the boy who died – is that right? – and the other was father to Elizabeth?'

Joseph nodded, making a visible effort to pull himself together.

'My brother Peter was Elizabeth's father. He took himself to London as a boy and got himself apprenticed as a dyer. He did moderately well, but since the French embargo – well, trade has gone right down these last few years.'

I nodded. Since England's break with Rome the French had banned the export of alum, which was essential for the dyeing trade. It was said even the king wore black hose now.

'Peter's wife died two years ago.' Joseph went on. 'When the bloody flux took Peter last autumn there was barely enough left to pay for his funeral and nothing for Elizabeth.'

'She was their only child?'

'Yes. She wanted to come and live with me, but I thought she'd be better off with Edwin. I've never married, after all. And he's the one with the money and the knighthood.' A note of bitterness entered his voice.

'And he is the mercer the pamphlet mentions?'

Joseph nodded. 'Edwin has a good business head. When he

followed Peter to London as a boy he went straight into the cloth trade. He knew where the best profits could be made: he has a fine house by the Walbrook now. To be fair, Edwin offered to take Elizabeth in. He's already given a home to our mother – she moved from the farm when she lost her sight through the smallpox ten years ago. He was always her favourite son.' He looked up with a wry smile. 'Since Edwin's wife died five years ago, Mother has run his household with a rod of iron, although she's seventy-four and blind.' I saw he was twisting the handkerchief in one hand; the embroidery was becoming torn.

'So Edwin is also a widower?'

'Yes. With three children. Sabine, Avice and – and Ralph.'

'The pamphlet said the girls are in their teens, older than the boy.'

Joseph nodded. 'Yes. Pretty, fair-haired and soft-skinned like their mother.' He smiled sadly. 'All their talk's of fashions and young men from the Mercers' dances, pleasant girlish things. Or was till last week.'

'And the boy? Ralph? What was he like?'

Joseph twisted the handkerchief again. 'He was the apple of his father's eye; Edwin always wanted a boy to succeed him in his business. His wife Mary had three boys before Sabine, but none lived past the cradle. Then two girls before a boy who lived, at last. Poor Edwin's grief shot. Perhaps he spared the rod too much—' He paused.

'Why do you say that?'

'Ralph was an imp, it must be said. Always full of tricks. His poor mother could never control him.' Joseph bit his lip. 'Yet he had a merry laugh, I brought him a chess set last year and he loved it, learned quickly and soon beat me.' In his sad smile I sensed the loneliness Joseph's rupture with his family would bring him. He had not done this lightly.

'How did you hear of Ralph's death?' I asked quietly.

'A letter from Edwin, sent by fast rider the day after it happened. He asked me to come to London and attend the inquest. He had to view Ralph's body and couldn't bear doing it alone.'

'So you came to London, what, a week ago?'

'Yes. I made the formal identification with him. That was a terrible thing. Poor Ralph laid on that dirty table in his little doublet, his face so white. Poor Edwin broke down sobbing, I've never seen him cry before. He wept on my shoulder, said, "My boykin, my boykin. The evil witch," over and over.'

'Meaning Elizabeth.'

Joseph nodded. 'Then we went to the court and heard the evidence before the coroner. The hearing didn't take long, I was surprised it was so short.'

I nodded. 'Yes. Greenway rushes things. Who gave evidence?'

'Sabine and Avice first of all. It was odd seeing them standing in that dock together, so still: I believe they were rigid from fear, poor girls. They said that the afternoon it happened they had been doing tapestry work indoors. Elizabeth had been sitting in the garden, reading under a tree by the well. They could see her through the parlour window. They saw Ralph go across and start talking to her. Then they heard a scream, a dreadful hollow sound. They looked up from their work and saw that Ralph was gone.'

'Gone?'

'Disappeared. They ran outside. Elizabeth was standing by the well, an angry expression on her face. They were afraid to approach her, but Sabine asked her what had happened. Elizabeth wouldn't reply and, sir, she has not spoken since. Sabine said they looked down the well, but it's deep. They couldn't see to the bottom.'

'Is the well in use?'

'No, the groundwater down at Walbrook's been foul with sewage for years. Edwin got a founder to make a pipe to carry water underground from the conduit to the house not long after he bought it. The year the king married Nan Bullen.'

'That would have been expensive.'

'Edwin is rich. But they should have capped off that well.' He shook his head again. 'They should have capped it.'

I had a sudden picture of a fall into darkness, a scream echoing off dank brick walls. I shivered despite the heat of the day.

'What did the girls say happened next?'

'Avice ran for the house steward, Needler. He got a rope and climbed down. Ralph was at the bottom with his neck broken, his poor little body still warm. Needler brought him out.'

'Did the steward gave evidence at the inquest?'

'Oh, yes. David Needler was there.' Joseph frowned. I looked at him sharply.

'You don't like him?'

'He's an impertinent fellow. Used to give me sneering looks when I visited from the country.'

'So, according to their testimony, neither girl actually saw what happened?'

'No, they only looked up when they heard the shout. Elizabeth often sat out in the garden alone. Her – well, her relations with the rest of the family were – difficult. She seemed to have taken a particular dislike to Ralph.'

'I see.' I looked him in the eye. 'And what is Elizabeth like?'

He leaned back, laying the crumpled handkerchief in his lap. 'She was like Ralph in some ways. They both had the dark hair and eyes of our side of the family. She was another that liked her own way. Her poor parents indulged her, being their only one. She could be malapert, coming forward with opinions in an unmaidenly way, and she preferred book-learning to ladies' concerns. But she played the virginal well, and enjoyed embroidering. She's young, sir, young. And she has a kind nature – she was always rescuing cats and dogs from the street.'

'I see.'

'But she changed after Peter died, I have to admit that. Not surprising, her mother gone then her father and then their house sold. She withdrew into herself, sir, stopped being the eager, talkative girl I knew. I remember after Peter's funeral, when I said it would be better for her future to go to Edwin rather than back to the country with me, she gave me such a look, such anger in it, then turned away without a word.' I saw tears come to the corner of his eyes at the memory. He blinked them away.

'And things did not go well when she moved to Sir Edwin's?'

'No. After her father died I visited them several times. I was concerned for Elizabeth. Each time Edwin and my mother said she was becoming more difficult, impossible.'

'In what ways?'

'Refusing to talk to the family, keeping to her room, missing meals. Not even taking proper care of her clothes. If anyone tried to chide her she'd either say nothing or else fly into a screaming rage, calling on them all to leave her alone.'

'And she was on bad terms with all three of her cousins?'

'I think Sabine and Avice were confused by her. They told the coroner they had tried to interest her in womanly things but Elizabeth just told them to go away. She is eighteen, a little older than them, but they should have been all girls together. And Edwin's children moved in higher social circles, they could have taught Elizabeth much.' He bit his lip again. 'I had hoped for her advancement. And it has led to this.'

'And why do you think she disliked Ralph so much?'

'That I understood least of all. Edwin told me that lately, if Ralph came near Elizabeth, she would give him such looks of hate it was frightening to see. I saw it myself one evening in February. I was at dinner with the family, all of them were there. It was an uneasy meal, sir. We were eating beefsteak, my brother enjoys it very rare and I do not think Elizabeth liked it – she sat toying with her food. My mother chid her but she wouldn't reply. Then Ralph asked her, quite politely, if she was enjoying her nice red meat. She went quite pale, put down her knife and gave him such a savage look I wondered—'

'Yes.'

He whispered, 'I wondered if she were ill in her mind.'

'Elizabeth has no cause to hate the family that you know of?'

'No. Edwin is mystified, he has been mystified by her since she came to them.'

I wondered what had gone on at Sir Edwin's house, whether there were things Joseph knew but would not say, as is common enough in family matters, though he seemed frank enough. He went on, 'After they found the body, David Needler locked Elizabeth in her room and sent a message to Edwin at the Mercers' Hall. He rode home and when she wouldn't answer his questions he called the constable.' He spread his hands. 'What else could he do? He feared for the safety of his daughters and our old mother.'

'And at the inquest? Elizabeth said nothing then? Nothing at all?'

'No. The coroner told her this was her chance to speak in her defence, but she just sat looking at him with this cold, blank look. It made him angry, and the jury too.' Joseph sighed. 'The jury found Ralph had been murdered by Elizabeth Wentworth and the coroner ordered her taken to Newgate to face a murder charge at the assize. He ordered her to be kept in the Hole for her impertinence in court. And then—'

'Yes?'

'Then Elizabeth turned and looked at me. Just for a second. There was such misery in that look, sir, no anger any more, just misery.' Joseph bit his lip again. 'In the old days when she was small she was fond of me, she used to come and stay on the farm. Both my brothers saw me as a bit of a country clod, but Elizabeth loved the farm, always rushing off to see the animals as soon as she arrived.' He gave a sad smile. 'When she was little she'd try and get the sheep and pigs to play with her like her pet dog or cat and cry when they wouldn't.' He smoothed out the torn, creased handkerchief. 'She embroidered a set of these for me, you know, two years ago. What a mess I have made of it. Yet when I visit her in that awful place she is now, she just lies there, filthy, as though waiting only for death. I beg and plead with her to speak, but she stares through me as though I was not there. And she is up for trial on Saturday, in only five days' time.' His voice fell to a whisper again. 'Sometimes I fear she is possessed.'

'Come, Joseph, there is no point in thinking like that.'

He looked at me imploringly. 'Can you help her, Master Shard-lake? Can you save her? You are my last hope.'

I was silent a moment, choosing my words carefully.

'The evidence against her is strong, it would be enough for a jury unless she has something to say in her defence.' I paused, then asked, 'You are sure she is not guilty?'

'Yes,' he said at once. He banged a fist on his chest. 'I feel it here. She was always *kind* at heart, sir, *kind*. She is the only one of my family I have known real kindness from. Even if she is ill in her mind, and by God's son she may be, I cannot believe she could kill a little boy.'

I took a deep breath. 'When she is brought into court she will be asked to plead guilty or not guilty. If she refuses then under the law she cannot be tried by a jury. But the alternative is worse.'

Joseph nodded. 'I know.'

'*Peine forte et dure.* Sharp and hard pains. She will be taken to a cell in Newgate and laid in chains on the floor. They will put a big, sharp stone under her back and a board on top of her. They will put weights on the board.'

'If only she would speak.' Joseph groaned and put his head in his hands. But I went on, I had to; he must know what she faced.

'They will allow her the barest rations of food and water. Each day more weights will be added to the board until she talks or dies of suffocation from the press of the weights. When the weights are heavy enough, because of the pressure of the stone placed underneath her back, her spine will break.' I paused. 'Some brave souls refuse to plead and allow themselves to be pressed to death because if there is no actual finding of guilt one's property is not forfeit to the State. Has Elizabeth any property?'

'Nothing in the world. The sale of their house barely covered Peter's debts. Only a few marks were left at the end and they went on the funeral.'

'Perhaps she did do this terrible thing, Joseph, in a moment of madness, and feels so guilty she wants to die, alone in the dark. Have you thought of that?'

He shook his head. 'No. I cannot believe it. I *cannot* believe it.'

'You know that criminal accused are not allowed representation in court?'

He nodded glumly.

'The reason the law gives is that the evidence needed to convict in a criminal trial must be so clear no counsel is needed. That is all nonsense, I'm afraid; the cases are run through quickly and the jury usually decide merely by preferring one man's word against another's. Often they favour the accused because most juries don't like sending people to hang, but in this case,' – I looked at the wretched pamphlet on the table – 'a child killing, their sympathies will be the other way. Her only hope is to agree to plead and tell me her story. And if she *did* act in a fit of madness, I could plead insanity. It might save her life. She'd go to the Bedlam, but we could try for a pardon from the king.' That would cost more money than Joseph had, I thought.

He looked up and for the first time I saw hope in his eyes. I realized I had said, 'I could plead,' without thinking. I had committed myself.

'But if she won't speak,' I went on, 'no one can save her.'

He leaned forward and clutched my hand between damp palms. 'Oh, thank you, Master Shardlake, thank you, I knew you'd save her—'

'I'm not at all sure I can,' I said sharply, but then added, 'I'll try.'

'I'll pay, sir. I've little enough but I'll pay.'

'I had better go to Newgate and see her. Five days – I need to see her as soon as possible, but I have business at Lincoln's Inn that will keep me all afternoon. I can meet you at the Pope's Head tavern next to Newgate first thing tomorrow morning. Say at nine?'

'Yes, yes.' He stood up, putting the handkerchief back in his pocket, and grasped my hand. 'You are a good man, sir, a godly man.'

A soft-headed man, more like, I thought. But I was touched by the compliment. Joseph and his family were all strong reformers, as I had once been, and did not say such things lightly.

'My mother and brother think her guilty, they were furious when I said I might help her. But I must find the truth. There was such a strange thing at the inquest, it affected me and Edwin too—'

'What was that?'

'When we viewed the body it was two days after poor Ralph died. It has been hot this spring but there is an underground cellar where they store bodies for the coroner to view, which keeps them cool. And poor Ralph was clothed. And yet the body *stank*, sir, stank like a cow's head left out in the Shambles in summer. It made me feel sick, the coroner too. I thought Edwin would pass out. What does that mean, sir? I have been trying to puzzle it out. What does it *signify?*'

I shook my head. 'My friend, we do not know what half the things in the world signify. And sometimes they signify nothing.'

Joseph shook his head. 'But God wants us to find the true meaning of things. He gives us clues. And, sir, if this matter is not resolved and Elizabeth dies, the real murderer goes free, whoever he is.'

# Chapter Two

EARLY NEXT MORNING I RODE into the City again. It was another hot day; the sunlight reflecting from the diamond panes of the Cheapside buildings made me blink.

In the pillory by the Standard a middle-aged man stood with a paper cap on his head and a loaf of bread hung round his neck. A placard identified him as a baker who had sold short weight. A few rotten fruits were spattered over his robe but the passers-by paid him little attention. The humiliation would be the worst of his punishment, I thought, looking up at where he sat, then I saw his face contort with pain as he shifted his position. With his head and arms pinioned and his neck bent forward, it was a painful position for one no longer young; I shuddered to think of the pain my back would have given me were I put in his place. And yet it gave me far less trouble these days, thanks to Guy.

Guy's was one of a row of apothecaries' shops in a narrow alley just past the Old Barge. The Barge was a huge, ancient house, once grand but now let out as cheap apartments. Rooks' nests were banked up against the crumbling battlements and ivy ran riot over the brickwork. I turned into the alley, welcoming the shade.

As I pulled to a halt in front of Guy's shop, I had the uneasy sensation of being watched. The lane was quiet, most of the shops not yet open for business. I dismounted slowly and tied Chancery to the rail, trying to look unconcerned but listening out for any movement behind me. Then I turned swiftly and looked up the lane.

I caught a movement at an upper storey of the Old Barge. I looked up, but had only the briefest glimpse of a shadowy figure at a window before the worm-eaten shutters were pulled closed. I stared for a moment, filled with a sudden uneasiness, then turned to Guy's shop.

It had only his name, 'Guy Malton', on the sign above the door. The window displayed neatly labelled flasks, rather than the stuffed alligators and other monsters most apothecaries favour. I knocked and went in. As usual the shop was clean and tidy, herbs and spices in jars lining the shelves. The room's musky, spicy smell brought Guy's consulting room at Scarnsea monastery back to my mind. Indeed the long apothecary's robe he wore was so dark a shade of green that in the dim light it looked almost black and could have been mistaken for a monk's robe. He was seated at his table, a frown of concentration on his thin, dark features as he applied a poultice from a bowl to an ugly burn on the arm of a thickset young man. I caught a whiff of lavender. Guy looked up and smiled, a sudden flash of white teeth.

'A minute more, Matthew,' he said in his lisping accent.

'I am sorry, I am earlier than I said I would be.'

'No matter, I am nearly done.'

I nodded and sat down on a chair. I looked at a chart on the wall, showing a naked man at the centre of a series of concentric circles, Man joined to his creator by the chains of nature. It reminded me of somebody pinned to an archery target. Underneath, a diagram of the four elements and the four types of human nature to which they correspond: earth for melancholic, water for phlegmatic, air for cheerful and fire for choleric.

The young man let out a sigh and looked up at Guy.

'By God's son, sir, that eases me already.'

'Good. Lavender is full of cold and wet properties, it draws the dry heat from your arm. I will give you a flask of this and you must apply it four times a day.'

The young man looked curiously at Guy's brown face. 'I have never heard of such a remedy. Is it used in the land you come from, sir? Perhaps there everyone is burned by the sun.'

'Oh, yes, Master Pettit,' Guy said seriously. 'If we did not wear lavender there we should all burn and shrivel up. We coat the palm trees with it too.' His patient gave him a keen look, perhaps scenting mockery. I noticed that his big square hands were spotted with pale scars. Guy rose and passed him a flask with a smile, raising a long finger. 'Four times a day, mind. And apply some to the wound on your leg made by that foolish physician.'

'Yes, sir.' The young man rose. 'I feel the burning going already, it has been an agony even to have my sleeve brush against it this last week. Thank you.' He took his purse from his belt and passed the apothecary a silver groat. As he left the shop Guy turned to me and laughed softly.

'When people made remarks like that at first I would correct them, tell them we have snow in Granada, which we do. But now I just agree with them. They are never sure if I joke or not. Still, it keeps me in their minds. Perhaps he will tell his friends in Lothbury.'

'He is a founder?'

'Ay, Master Pettit has just finished his apprenticeship. A serious young fellow. He spilt hot lead on his arm, but hopefully that old remedy will ease him.'

I smiled. 'You are learning the ways of business. Turning your differences to advantage.'

Apothecary Guy Malton, once Brother Guy of Malton, had fled Spain with his Moorish parents as a boy after the fall of Granada. He had trained as a physician at Louvain. He had become my friend on my mission to Scarnsea three years before, helped me during that terrible time, and when the monastery was dissolved I had hoped to set him up as a physician in London. But the College would not have him, with his brown face and papist past. With a little bribery, however, I had got him into the Apothecaries' Guild and he had managed to build up a good trade.

'Master Pettit went to a physician first.' Guy shook his head. 'He stitched a clyster thread into his leg to draw the pain down from his arm, and when the wound became inflamed insisted that showed the clyster was working.' He pulled off his apothecary's cap, revealing a head of curly hair that had once been black but now was mostly white. It still seemed odd to see him without his tonsure. He studied me closely with his keen brown eyes.

'And how have you been this last month, Matthew?'

'Still better. I do my exercises twice a day like a good patient. My back troubles me little unless I have to lift something heavy, like the great bundles of legal papers that mount in my room at Lincoln's Inn.'

'You should get your clerk to do that.'

'He gets them out of order. You've never seen such a noddle as Master Skelly.'

He smiled. 'Well, I will have a look at it if I may.'

He rose, lit a sweet-smelling candle, then closed the shutters as I removed my doublet and shirt. Guy was the only one I allowed to see my twisted back. He got me to stand, move my shoulders and arms, then stood behind me and gently probed my back muscles. 'Good,' he said. 'There is little stiffness. You may get dressed. Keep on with your exercises. It is good to have a conscientious patient.'

'I would not like to go back to the old days, fearing ever-worsening pain.'

He gave me another of his keen looks. 'And you are still melancholy? I see it in your face.'

'I have a melancholy nature, Guy. It is settled in me.' I looked at the chart on the wall. 'Everything in the world is made of a mixture of the four elements, and I have too much of earth. The imbalance is fixed in me.'

He inclined his dark head. 'There is nothing under the moon that is not subject to change.'

I shook my head. 'I seem to take less and less interest in the stirs of politics and the law, though once they were the heart of my life. It has been so since Scarnsea.'

'That was a terrible time. You do not miss being close to the centre of power?' He hesitated. 'To Lord Cromwell?'

I shook my head. 'No, I dream of a quiet life in the country somewhere, perhaps near my father's farm. Maybe then I will feel like taking up painting again.'

'Yet I wonder if that is the life for you, my friend. Would you not become bored without cases to sharpen your wits on, problems to solve?'

'Once I might have. But London now – ' I shook my head – 'fuller of fanatics and cozeners every year. And my profession has enough of both.'

He nodded. 'Ay, in matters of religion opinions get more extreme. I tell people nothing of my past, as you may imagine. Dun's the mouse as the proverb has it; colourlessness and stillness keep one safe.'

'I have no patience with any of it these days. Sometimes I think all that matters is faith in Christ and all else is no more than a jangle of words.'

He smiled wryly. 'That is not what you would have said once.'

'No. Yet sometimes even that essential faith eludes me, and I can believe only that man is a fallen creature.' I laughed sadly. 'That I can believe.' I pulled the crumpled pamphlet from my pocket and laid it on the table. 'See there, the girl's uncle is an old client of mine. He wants me to help her. Her trial is on Saturday. That is why I have come early, I am meeting him at Newgate at nine.' I told him of my meeting with Joseph the day before. Strictly it was breaching a confidence, but I knew Guy would say nothing.

'She refuses to speak at all?' he asked when I had finished, stroking his chin thoughtfully.

'Not one word. You'd think she'd be startled out of that when she learned she'd be pressed, but she hasn't been. It makes me think her wits must be affected.' I looked at him seriously. 'Her uncle begins to fear possession.'

He inclined his head. 'It is easy to cry "possession". I have sometimes wondered if the man from whom Our Lord cast out a devil was not merely a poor lunatic.'

I gave him a sidelong look. 'The Bible is quite clear he was possessed.'

'And today we must believe all that is said in the Bible and only that. Master Coverdale's translation of it, that is.' Guy smiled wryly. Then his face became thoughtful and he began pacing the room, the hem of his robe brushing the clean rushes on the floor.

'You can't assume she is mad,' he said. 'Not yet. People have many reasons for silence. Because there are things one is too ashamed or frightened to reveal. Or to protect someone else.'

'Or because one has ceased to care what happens to one.'

'Yes. That is a terrible state, near to suicide.'

'Whatever her reasons, I'll have to persuade the girl out of it if I'm to save her life. The press is a horrible death.' I stood up. 'Oh, Guy, why did I let myself get drawn into this? Most lawyers don't touch criminal cases, the accused not being allowed representation. I've advised one or two before their trials, but I don't enjoy it. And I hate the stink of death around the assizes, knowing in a few days the carts will roll to Tyburn.'

'But the carts go to Tyburn whether you see them or no. If you can make an empty space in one of those carts—'

I smiled wryly. 'You still have a monk's faith in salvation through good works.'

'Should not we all believe in the righteousness of charity?'

'Yes, if we have the energy for it.' I stood up. 'Well, I am due at Newgate.'

'I have a potion,' he said, 'that can sometimes lift a man's spirits. Reduce the black bile in his stomach.'

I raised a hand. 'No, Guy, I thank you but so long as my wits are not dulled, I will stay in the state God has called me to.'

'As you wish.' He extended a hand. 'I will say a prayer for you.'

'Beneath that big old Spanish cross of yours? You still have it in your bedroom?'

'It was my family's.'

'Beware the constable. Just because evangelicals are being arrested now it doesn't mean the government's any easier on Catholics.'

'The constable's a friend. Last month he drank some water he bought from a carrier and an hour later staggered into my shop clutching his stomach in agony.'

'He drank *water*? Unboiled? Everyone knows it is full of deadly humours.'

'He was very thirsty; you know how hot the weather has been. He was badly poisoned – I made him swallow a spoonful of mustard to make him sick.'

I shuddered. 'I thought salted beer was the best emetic.'

'Mustard is better, it works at once. He recovered and now he stumps merrily around the ward calling my praises.' His face became serious. 'Just as well: with all this talk of invasion foreigners are not popular these days. I get insults called after me in the streets more frequently; I always cross the street if there is a gang of apprentices around.'

'I am sorry. The times get no easier.'

'The City is full of rumours the king is unhappy with his new marriage,' he said. 'That Anne of Cleves may fall and Cromwell with her.'

'Are there not always new rumours, new fears?' I laid a hand on his shoulder. 'Keep courage. And come to dinner next week.'

'I shall.' He led me to the door. I turned back to him. 'Don't forget that prayer.'

'I won't.'

I unhitched Chancery and rode up the lane. As I passed the Old Barge I looked up at the window where I had seen the figure. It was still shuttered. But as I turned back into Bucklersbury I had the feeling of being watched again. I turned my head abruptly. The streets were getting busy, but I saw a man in a doublet of lusty-gallant red leaning against a wall with his arms folded, staring straight at me. He was in his late twenties, with a strong-featured face, comely but hard, under untidy brown hair. He had a fighter's build, broad shoulders and a narrow waist. As he met my gaze his wide mouth twisted into a mocking grin. Then he turned away and walked with a quick, light step towards the Barge, disappearing into the crowds.

# Chapter Three

As I rode back to Newgate I reflected anxiously on my watcher. Could the man have some connection with the Wentworth case? I had mentioned the case at Lincoln's Inn the afternoon before and gossip travels faster among lawyers than among the washerwomen in Moorgate fields. Or was he some agent of the State, investigating my dealings with the dark-skinned ex-monk? Yet these days I had no connections with politics.

Chancery stirred uneasily and neighed, sensing my worry or perhaps made uneasy by the dreadful smells that assailed us as we passed the Shambles, a foul trail of blood and fluids seeping down the channel from Bladder Street. The stink here was always bad, however much the City might try to regulate the butchers, but on a hot day like this it was unbearable. If this weather went on I should have to buy a nosegay, I thought, noticing that many of the richer-looking passers-by held posies of spring flowers before their faces.

I passed into Newgate Market, still overshadowed by the great monastic church of Greyfriars, behind whose stained-glass windows the king now stored booty taken from the French at sea. Beyond stood the high City wall and, built into it, the chequered towers of Newgate. London's principal gaol is a fine, ancient building, yet it holds more misery than anywhere in London, many of its inhabitants leaving it only for their execution.

I entered the Pope's Head tavern. It was open all hours and did a good trade from visitors to the gaol. Joseph sat at a table overlooking the dusty rear garden, nursing a cup of small beer, the weak beer drunk to quench thirst. A posy of flowers lay beside him. He was looking uneasily at a well-dressed young man who was leaning over him, smiling affably.

'Come, Brother, a game of cards will cheer you up. I am due to meet some friends at an inn nearby. Good company.' He was one of the coneycatchers who infest the City, looking for country people in their dull clothes who were new to town to fleece them of their money.

'Excuse us,' I said sharply, easing myself into a chair. 'This gentleman and I are due to have conference. I am his lawyer.'

The young man raised his eyebrows at Joseph. 'Then you'll lose all your money anyway, sir,' he said. 'Justice is a fat fee.' As he passed me he leaned close. 'Crook-backed bloodsucker,' he murmured softly.

Joseph did not hear. 'I've been to the gaol again,' he said gloomily. 'I told the gaoler I was bringing a lawyer. Another sixpence he charged, to allow the visit. What's more he had a copy of that filthy pamphlet. He told me he's been letting people in to look at Elizabeth for a penny. They call out through the spyhole and insult her. He laughed about it. It's cruel – surely they're not allowed to do that?'

'The gaolers are allowed anything for their own profit. He would have told you in hope of a bribe to keep her free of such pestering.'

He ran a hand through his hair. 'I have had to pay for food for her, water, everything. I can't afford more, sir.' He shook his head. 'These gaolers must be the wickedest men on earth.'

'Ay. But clever enough at turning a profit.' I looked at him seriously. 'I went to Lincoln's Inn yesterday afternoon, Joseph. I learned the judge sitting at Saturday's assize is Forbizer. That is no good news. He's a strong Bible man and incorruptible—'

'But that's good, surely, a Bible man—'

I shook my head. 'Incorruptible, but hard as stone.'

'No sympathy for a young orphan girl half out of her wits?'

'Not for any living creature. I've appeared before him in civil matters.' I leaned forward. 'Joseph, we *must* get Elizabeth to talk or she's as good as dead.'

He bit his lip in that characteristic gesture of his. 'When I took her some food yesterday she just lay there and looked at it. Not a word of thanks, not even a nod. I think she's hardly eaten for days. I've bought her these flowers but I don't know if she'll look at them.'

'Well, let us see what I can do.'

He nodded gratefully. As we got up I said, 'By the way, does Sir Edwin know you have retained me?'

Joseph shook his head. 'I haven't spoken with Edwin in a week, since I suggested that Elizabeth might not be guilty and he ordered me from his house.' A flash of anger crossed his face. 'He thinks that if I do not want Elizabeth to die, I must be against him and his.'

'Nonetheless,' I said thoughtfully, 'he might have heard.'

'What makes you think so, sir?'

'Oh, nothing. Never mind.'

✝

JOSEPH'S WHOLE BODY seemed to slump as we approached the gaol. We passed the begging grille in the wall through which poor prisoners thrust clutching hands, calling to passers-by for charity for God's love. Those without money got little or no food and it was said some prisoners starved to death. I placed a penny in a grubby, frantic hand, then knocked loudly at the stout wooden door. A spy flap opened and a hard face looked out from under a greasy cap, eyes flicking over my black lawyer's robe.

'Lawyer for Elizabeth Wentworth,' I said, 'with her uncle. He's paid for the visit.' The flap slammed shut and the door opened. The gaoler, dressed in a dirty smock and with a heavy stick at his belt, looked at me curiously as we passed through. Despite the heat of the day the prison with its thick stone walls was cold, a dank chill seeming to emanate from the very stones. The gaoler called out, 'Williams!' and a fat turnkey in a leather jerkin appeared, jangling a large ring of keys in one hand.

'Lawyer for the child murderess.' The gaoler smiled evilly at me. 'Seen the pamphlet?'

'Yes,' I answered shortly.

He shook his head. 'She still won't talk; it'll be the press for her.

25

Did you know, lawyer, there's an old rule prisoners should be *naked* when they're laid out chained for the weights to be put on 'em. Shame to get a view of a nice pair of bubbies, then have to squash 'em flat.'

Joseph's face puckered with distress.

'There is no such rule that I know of,' I said coldy.

The gaoler spat on the floor. 'I know the rules for my own gaol, whatever pen gents may say.' He nodded to the turnkey. 'Take 'em down to the Women's Hole.'

We were led down a wide corridor with wards on either side. Through the barred windows in the doors men were visible sitting or lying on straw pallets, their legs fixed to the walls by long chains. The smell of urine was so strong it stung the nostrils. The turnkey waddled along, keys rattling. Unlocking a heavy door, he led us down a flight of steps into semi-darkness. At the bottom another door faced us. The turnkey pulled aside a flap and peered in before turning to us.

'Still lying just where she was yesterday afternoon when I brought those people down to look at her through the hatch. Silent as a stone she was, hiding herself while they called witch and child killer through the door.' He shook his head.

'May we go in?'

He shrugged and opened the door. As soon as we had passed through he shut it quickly behind us, the key rasping in the lock.

The Hole, the deepest and darkest part of the prison, had a men's and a women's dungeon. The Women's Hole was a small, square chamber, lit dimly by a barred window high up near the ceiling, through which I could see the shoes and skirts of passers-by. It was as chill as the rest of the prison, with a miasma of damp that penetrated even the stink of ordure. The floor was covered with foul straw, stained and matted with all manner of filth. Huddled in one corner was a fat old woman in a stained wadmol dress, fast asleep. I stared round, puzzled, for at first I could see no one else, but then I saw that in the furthest corner the straw had been pulled into a pile around a human figure, hiding it save for a face begrimed with dirt and framed by tangled hair as dark and curly as Joseph's. The face stared at us vacantly with large eyes, hazel like his. It was such a strange sight a shiver ran through me.

Joseph walked across to her. 'Lizzy,' he said chidingly, 'why have you piled the straw round yourself like that? It's filthy. Are you cold?'

The girl did not answer. Her eyes were unfocused; she could or would not look at us directly. I saw that under the dirt her face was pretty, delicate, with high cheekbones. A grubby hand was half visible through the straw. Joseph reached for it, but the girl drew it sharply away without altering her gaze. I went and stood directly in front of her as Joseph laid the posy at her side.

'I've brought you some flowers, Lizzy,' he said. She glanced at the posy and then she did return Joseph's gaze and to my surprise her look was full of anger. I saw a plate of bread and stockfish lying on the straw with a flagon of beer. It must be the food Joseph had brought. It was untouched, fat blackbeetles nosing over the dried fish. Elizabeth looked away again.

'Elizabeth – ' there was a tremble in her uncle's voice – 'this is Master Shardlake. He's a lawyer, he has the best mind in London. He can help you. But you must talk to him.'

I squatted on my haunches so I could look into her face without sitting on that disgusting straw. 'Miss Wentworth,' I said gently, 'can you hear me? Why will you not speak? Are you protecting a secret – yours, or perhaps another's?' I paused. She looked right through me, not even stirring. In the silence I heard the tapping of feet from the street above. I felt suddenly angry.

'You know what will happen if you refuse to plead?' I said. 'You will be pressed. The judge you will come before on Saturday is a hard man and that will be his sentence without a doubt. They've told you what pressing means?' Still no response. 'A dreadful slow death that can last many days.'

At these words her eyes came to life and fixed mine, but only for a second. I shivered at the pit of misery I saw in them.

'If you speak, I may be able to save you. There are possible ways, whatever happened that day at the well.' I paused. 'What did happen,

Elizabeth? I'm your lawyer, I won't tell anyone else. We could ask your uncle to leave if you would rather speak to me alone.'

'Yes,' Joseph agreed. 'Yes, if you wish.'

But still she was silent. She began picking at the straw with one hand.

'Oh, Lizzy,' Joseph burst out, 'you should be reading and playing music as you were a year ago, not lying in this terrible place.' He put a fist to his face, biting his knuckles. I shifted my position and looked the girl directly in the eyes. Something had struck me.

'Elizabeth, I know people have come down here to look at you, to taunt. Yet though you hide your body you show your face. Oh, I know that straw is vile but you could hide your head, it would be a way of preventing people from seeing you, the turnkey would not be permitted to let them in. It is almost as though you wanted them to see you.'

A shudder ran through her and for a moment I thought she would break down, but she set her jaw hard; I saw the muscles clench. I paused a moment, then got painfully to my feet. As I did so, there was a rustle from the straw on the other side of the cell and I turned to see the old woman raising herself slowly on her elbows. She shook her head solemnly.

'She won't speak, gentlemen,' she said in a cracked voice. 'I've been here three days and she's said nothing.'

'What are you here for?' I asked her.

'They say my son and I stole a horse. We're for trial on Saturday too.' She sighed and ran her tongue over her cracked lips. 'Have you any drink, sir? Even the most watery beer.'

'No, I'm sorry.'

She looked over at Elizabeth. 'They say she has a demon inside her, that one, a demon that holds her fast.' She laughed bitterly. 'But demon or no, it's all one to the hangman.'

I turned to Joseph. 'I don't think there's any more I can do here now. Come, let us go.' I led him gently to the door and knocked. It opened at once: the gaoler must have been outside listening. I glanced back; Elizabeth still lay quite still, unmoving.

'The old beldame's right,' the turnkey said as he locked the door behind us. 'She has a devil inside her.'

'Then have a care when you bring people down to goggle at her through that spy hatch,' I snapped. 'She might turn herself into a crow and fly at their faces.' I led Joseph away. A minute later we were outside again, blinking in the bright sunlight. We returned to the tavern and I set a beer in front of him.

'How many times have you visited since she was taken?' I asked.

'Today's the fourth. And each time she sits there like a stone.'

'Well, I can't move her. Not at all. I confess I've never seen anything like it.'

'You did your best, sir,' he said disappointedly.

I tapped my fingers on the table. 'Even if she were found guilty, there may just be ways of stopping her from being hanged. The jury might be persuaded she was mad, she could even claim she was pregnant, then she couldn't be hanged till the baby was born. It would buy us time.'

'Time for what, sir?'

'What? Time to investigate, find what really happened.'

He leaned forward eagerly, nearly knocking over his tankard. 'Then you believe she is innocent?'

I gave him a direct look. 'You do. Though her treatment of you, in all honesty, is cruel.'

'I believe her because I know her. And because, when I see her there, I see—' He struggled for words.

'A woman whose air is of one who has been done a great wrong, rather than one who has committed a great crime?'

'Yes,' he said eagerly. 'Yes. That is it exactly. You feel it too?'

'Ay, I do.' I looked at him evenly. 'But what you or I feel is not evidence, Joseph. And we may be wrong. It is not good for a lawyer to base his work on instinct. He needs detachment, reason. I speak from experience.'

'What can we do, sir?'

'You must go and see her every day between now and Saturday. I don't think she can be persuaded to speak, but it will show her she is not forgotten and I feel that is important, for all that she ignores us. If she says anything, if her manner changes at all, tell me and I will come again.'

'I'll do it, sir,' he said.

'And if she still does not speak, I will appear in court on Saturday. I don't know if Forbizer will even hear me, but I'll try and argue that her mind is disturbed—'

'God knows, it must be. She has no reason to treat me so. Unless – ' he hesitated – 'unless the old woman is right.'

'There's no profit in thinking that way, Joseph. I'll try to argue that the issue of her sanity should be remitted to a jury. I am sure there are precedents, though Forbizer doesn't have to follow them. Again, that would buy us time.' I looked at him seriously. 'But I am not optimistic. You must prepare your mind for the worst, Joseph.'

'No, sir,' he said. 'While you are working for us, I have hope.'

'Prepare for the worst,' I repeated. It was all very well for Guy to talk of the merit of good works. He did not have to come before Judge Forbizer on gaol-delivery day.

# Chapter Four

I RODE FROM NEWGATE TO my chambers at Lincoln's Inn, just up the road from my house in Chancery Lane. When King Edward III ordered that no lawyers should be allowed to practise within the precincts of London, necessitating our removal outside its walls, he did us great service for the Inn was semi-rural, with wide orchards and the space of Lincoln's Inn Fields beyond.

I passed under the high square towers of the Great Gate, left Chancery at the stables and walked to my chambers across Gatehouse Court. The sun shone brightly on the red-brick buildings. There was a pleasant breeze; we were too far from the City walls here for London smells to penetrate.

Barristers were striding purposefully around the precincts; the Trinity law term began the following week and there were cases to set in order. Among the black robes and caps there were also, of course, the usual young gentlemen in bright doublets and exaggerated cod-pieces strutting around, sons of gentry who joined the Inns only to learn London manners and make social contacts. A pair of them walking by had evidently been rabbiting in Coney Garth, for a pair of hounds frisked at their heels, their eyes on the furry bodies dripping blood from poles slung over their masters' shoulders.

Then, ambling down the path from Lincoln's Inn Hall with his customary amiable smile on his beaky features, I saw the tall, thin figure of Stephen Bealknap, against whom I would be pleading in King's Bench in a few days. He halted in front of me and bowed. The courtesies require that barristers, even when opponents in the bitterest of cases, must observe the civilities, but Bealknap's friendly manner always had something mocking in it. It was as though he said: you know I am a great scamp, but still you must be pleasant to me.

'Brother Shardlake!' he declaimed. 'Another hot day. The wells will be drying up at this rate.'

Normally I would have made a curt acknowledgement and moved on, but it struck me there was a piece of information he could help me with. 'So they will,' I said. 'It has been a dry spring.'

At my unaccustomed civility, a smile appeared on Bealknap's face. It seemed quite pleasant until you came close and saw the meanness in the mouth, and realized the pale-blue eyes would never quite meet yours no matter how you tried to fix them. Beneath his cap a few curls of wiry-looking blond hair strayed.

'Well, our case is on next week,' he said. 'June the first.'

'Ay. It has come on very quick. It was only in March you lodged your writ. I am still surprised, Brother Bealknap, that you have taken this up to King's Bench.'

'They have a proper respect for the rights of property law there. I shall show them the case of *Friars Preachers* v. *the Prior of Okeham.*'

I laughed lightly. 'I see you have been ferreting in the Assize of Nuisance Rolls, Brother. That case is on a different point and it is two hundred years old.'

He smiled back, his eyes darting around. 'It is still relevant. The prior pleaded that matters of nuisance such as his faulty gutter were beyond the council's jurisdiction.'

'Because his priory came directly under the king's authority. But St Michael's priory comes under yours now. You are the freeholder and you are responsible for the nuisance your priory causes. I hope you have better authority than that to hand.'

He would not be drawn, bending to examine the sleeve of his robe. 'Well, Brother,' I said lightly, 'we shall see. But now we are met, I would ask a question on another matter. Will you be at the gaol delivery on Saturday?' I knew that running compurgators in the bishop's court was one of Bealknap's disreputable sidelines, and he often lurked around the Old Bailey justice hall looking for clients. He flicked a curious glance at me.

'Perhaps.'

'Judge Forbizer is on, I believe. How quickly does he deal with the cases?'

Bealknap shrugged. 'Fast as he can. You know the King's Bench judges; they think dealing with common thieves and murderers beneath them.'

'But Forbizer has good knowledge of the law for all his hardness. I wondered how open he would be to legal argument for the accused.'

Bealknap's face lit up with interest and his eyes, bright with curiosity, actually met mine for a moment. 'Ah, I had heard you were retained for the Walbrook murderess. I said I didn't believe it, you're a property man.'

'The *alleged* murderess,' I replied flatly. 'She comes up before Forbizer on Saturday.'

'You won't get far with him,' Bealknap said cheerfully. 'He has a Bible man's contempt for the sinful, wants to hasten them to their just desserts. She'll have little mercy from Forbizer. He'll want a plea or a kill.' His eyes narrowed and I guessed he was thinking whether he might turn this to his advantage. But there was no way, or I should not have asked him.

'So I thought. But thank you,' I added, as lightly as I could. 'Good morning!'

'I shall look out for you on Saturday, Brother,' he called after me. 'Good luck: you will need it!'

✝

IT WAS IN NO GOOD temper that I entered the small set of ground-floor rooms I shared with my friend Godfrey Wheelwright. In the outer office my clerk, John Skelly, was studying a conveyance he had just drawn up, a lugubrious expression on his thin face. He was a small, weazened fellow with long rats' tails of brown hair. Although not yet twenty he was married with a child and I had taken him on last winter partly from pity at his obvious poverty. He was an old pupil of St Paul's cathedral school and had good Latin, but he was a hopeless fellow, a poor copier and forever losing papers as I had told Guy. He looked up at me guiltily.

'I have just finished the Beckman conveyance, sir,' he mumbled. 'I'm sorry it is late.'

I took it from him. 'This should have been done two days ago. Is there any correspondence?'

'It is on your counting table, sir.'

'Very well.'

I passed into my room. It was dim and stuffy; dust motes danced in the beam of light from the little window giving onto the courtyard. I removed my robe and cap and sat at my table, breaking the seals on my letters with my dagger. I was surprised and disappointed to find I had lost another case. I had been acting on the purchase of a warehouse down at Salt Wharf, but now my client wrote curtly to say the seller had withdrawn and he no longer required my services. I studied the letter. The purchase was a curious one: my client was an attorney from the Temple and the warehouse was to be conveyed into his name, which meant the purchaser must want his own name kept secret. This was the third case in two months where the client had suddenly withdrawn his instructions without reason.

Frowning, I put the letter aside and turned to the conveyance. It was clumsily written and there was a smudge at the bottom of the page. Did Skelly think such a mess would pass? He would have to do it again, with more time wasted that I was paying for. I tossed it aside and, sharpening a new quill, took up my commonplace book, which held years of notes from moots and readings. I looked at my old notes on criminal law, but they were scanty and I could find nothing about *peine forte et dure*.

There was a knock at the door and Godfrey came in. He was of an age with me. Twenty years before we had been scholars and ardent young reformers together, and unlike me he had retained his zealous belief that following the break with Rome a new Christian commonwealth might dawn in England. I saw that his narrow, delicate-featured face was troubled.

'Have you heard the rumours?' he asked.

'What now?'

'Yesterday evening the king rowed down the Thames to dinner at the Dowager Duchess of Norfolk's house with Catherine Howard beside him under the canopy. In the royal barge, for all London to see. It's the talk of the City. He meant to be seen – it's a sign the Cleves marriage is over. And a Howard marriage means a return to Rome.'

I shook my head. 'But Queen Anne was beside him at the May Day jousts. Just because the king has his eye on a Howard wench doesn't mean he'll put the queen aside. God's wounds, he's had four wives in eight years. He can't want a fifth.'

'Can't he? Imagine the Duke of Norfolk in Lord Cromwell's place.'

'Cromwell can be cruel enough.'

'Only when it is necessary. And the duke would be far harsher.' He sat down heavily opposite me.

'I know,' I said quietly. 'None of the privy councillors has a crueller reputation.'

'He is a lunch guest of the benchers here on Sunday, is he not?'

'Yes.' I made a face. 'I shall see him for myself for the first time. I do not greatly look forward to it. But, Godfrey, the king would never turn the clock back. We have the Bible in English and Cromwell's just got an earldom.'

He shook his head. 'I sense trouble coming.'

'When has there not been trouble these last ten years? Well, if London has a new topic that may take the heat from Elizabeth Wentworth.' I had told him yesterday that I had taken on the case. 'I've been to see her in Newgate. She won't say a word.'

He shook his head. 'Then she'll be pressed, Matthew.'

'Listen, Godfrey, I need a precedent to say someone who won't speak because they're mad can't be pressed.'

He stared at me with his large blue-grey eyes, strangely innocent for a lawyer's. 'Is she mad?'

'She may be. There's a precedent somewhere in the yearbooks, I'm sure.' I looked at him; Godfrey had an excellent memory for cases.

'Yes,' he said. 'I think you're right.'

'I thought I might try the library.'

'When's gaol delivery – Saturday? You've little time. I'll help you look.'

'Thank you.' I smiled gratefully; it was like Godfrey to forget his own worries and come to my aid. His fears, I knew, were real enough; he knew some of the evangelicals in the circle of Robert Barnes, who had recently been put in the Tower for making sermons with too Lutheran a flavour.

I walked with him to the library and we spent two hours among the great stacks of case law, where we found two or three cases which might be helpful.

'I'll send Skelly over to copy these,' I said.

He smiled. 'And now you can buy me lunch as a reward for my help.'

'Gladly.'

We went outside into the hot afternoon. I sighed. As ever, among the law books in the magnificent library I had felt a momentary sense of security, of order and reason; but out in the harsh light of day I recalled that a judge could ignore precedent and remembered Beal-knap's words.

'Courage, my friend,' Godfrey said. 'If she is innocent, God will not allow her to suffer.'

'The innocent suffer whilst rogues prosper, Godfrey, as we both know. They say that churl Bealknap has a thousand gold angels in the famous chest in his rooms. Come, I'm hungry.'

As we crossed the courtyard to the dining hall I saw a fine litter with damask curtains standing outside a nearby set of chambers, carried by four bearers in Mercers' Company livery. Two attendant ladies, carrying posies, stood at a respectful distance while a tall woman in a high-collared gown of blue velvet stood talking to Gabriel Marchamount, one of the serjeants. Marchamount's tall, plump figure was encased in a fine silk robe, and a cap with a swan's feather was perched on his head. I remembered Bealknap had been under his patronage once until he tired of Bealknap's endless crookery; Marchamount liked his reputation as an honest man.

I studied the woman, noting the jewelled pomander that hung at her bosom from a gold chain, and as I did so she turned and met my eye. She murmured something to Marchamount and he raised his arm, bidding me to halt. He gave the woman his arm and led her across the courtyard to us. Her attendants followed, their skirts making a whispering noise on the stone flags.

Marchamount's companion was strikingly attractive, in her thirties, with a direct, open gaze. She wore a round French hood about her hair, which was blonde and very fine; little wisps slipped out, stirring in the breeze. I saw the hood was faced with pearls.

'Master Shardlake,' Marchamount said in his deep, booming voice, a smile on his rubicund face, 'may I introduce my client and good friend, Lady Honor Bryanston? Brother Matthew Shardlake.'

She extended a hand. I took the long white fingers gently and bowed. 'Delighted, madam.'

'Forgive my intrusion on your business,' she said. Her voice was a clear contralto with a husky undertone, the accent aristocratic. Her full-lipped mouth made girlish dimples in her cheeks as she smiled.

'Not at all, madam.' I was going to introduce Godfrey but she continued, ignoring his presence. 'I have been in conference with Master Marchamount. I recognized you from a description the Earl of Essex gave when we dined last. He was singing your praises as one of the best lawyers in London.'

The Earl of Essex. Cromwell. I had thought, and hoped, that he had forgotten me. And I realized she would have been told to look out for a hunchback.

'I am most grateful,' I said cautiously.

'Yes, he was quite effusive,' Marchamount said. His tone was light, but his prominent brown eyes studied me keenly. I recalled he was known as an opponent of reform and wondered what he had been doing dining with Cromwell.

'I am ever on the lookout for fine minds to strike their wits against each other around my dining table,' Lady Honor continued. 'Lord Cromwell suggested you as a candidate.'

I raised a hand. 'You compliment me too highly. I am a mere jobbing lawyer.'

She smiled again and raised a hand. 'No, sir, I hear you are more than that. A bencher, who may be a serjeant one day. I shall send you an invitation to one of my sugar banquets. You live further down Chancery Lane, I believe.'

'You are well informed, madam.'

She laughed. 'I try to be. New information and new friends stave off a widow's boredom.' She looked round the quadrangle, studying the scene with interest. 'How marvellous it must be to live beyond the foul airs of the City.'

'Brother Shardlake has a fine house, I hear.' There was a slight edge to Marchamount's voice, a glint in his dark brown, protuberant eyes. He laughed, showing a full set of white teeth. 'Such are the profits of land law, eh, Brother?'

'Justly earned, I am sure,' Lady Honor said. 'But now you must excuse me, I have an appointment at the Mercers' Hall.' She turned away, raising a hand. 'Expect to hear from me shortly, Master Shardlake.'

Marchamount bowed to us, then led Lady Honor back to her litter, making a great fuss of helping her inside before walking back to his chambers, stately as a full-rigged ship. We watched as the litter made its swaying way to the gate, her ladies walking sedately behind.

'Forgive me Godfrey,' I said. 'I was going to introduce you, but she gave me no chance. That was a little rude of her.'

'I would not have welcomed the introduction,' he said primly. 'Do you know who she is?'

I shook my head. London society did not interest me.

'Widow to Sir Harcourt Bryanston. He was the biggest mercer in London when he died three years ago. He was far older than her,' he added disapprovingly. 'They had sixty-four poor men in attendance at his funeral, one for every year of his age.'

'Well, what's so wrong with that?'

'She's a Vaughan, an aristocrat fallen on hard times. She married Bryanston for his money, and since his death she's set herself up as the greatest hostess in London. Trying to build up her family name again, which was trampled down in the wars between Lancaster and York.'

'One of the old families, eh?'

'Ay. She specializes in setting reformers against papists over her dinner table, takes a perverse pleasure in it.' He looked at me earnestly. 'She's invited Bishops Gardiner and Ridley and started a conversation about transubstantiation before now. Matters of religious truth are not to be toyed with like that.' A sudden hardness entered his voice. 'They are for hard reflection, on which the fate of our eternal souls depend. As you used to say yourself,' he added.

'Ay, I did.' I sighed, for I knew my loss of religious enthusiasm these last few years troubled my friend. 'So she's in with both factions then?'

'She has both Cromwell and Norfolk at her table, but she's no loyalty to either side. Don't go, Matthew.'

I hesitated. There was strength, a sophistication about Lady Honor that stirred something in me that had been quiet a long time. And yet being in the middle of such arguments as Godfrey described would not be comfortable, and for all he might have kind words for me I had no wish to see Cromwell again. 'I'll see,' I said.

Godfrey looked over to Marchamount's chambers. 'I'll wager the good serjeant would give much to have a lineage like hers. I hear he is still pestering the College of Arms for a shield, though his father was but a fishmonger.'

I laughed. 'Ay, he likes mixing with those of breeding.'

The unexpected meeting had lifted me from the concerns of work, but they returned as we entered the dining hall. Under the great vaulted beams I saw Bealknap sitting alone at one end of a long table. He was shovelling food into his mouth with his spoon while reading a large casebook. *Friars Preachers* v. *the Prior of Okeham*, no doubt, to quote against me at Westminster Hall in a week's time.

# Chapter Five

The Old Bailey Court is a small, cramped building set against the outer side of the City wall opposite Newgate. There is nothing of the panoply of the civil courts in Westminster Hall, although judgements here deal not with money and property, but maiming and death.

On Saturday morning I arrived in good time. The court did not usually sit on Saturdays, but with the civil-law term starting the following week the judges would be heavily occupied and the London assize had been brought forward to get the criminal business out of the way. I passed inside the courtroom, clutching my file of precedents, and bowed to the bench.

Judge Forbizer sat on his dais working on papers, his scarlet robes a slash of colour among the dull clothes of the rabble crowding the benches, for the assize was ever a popular spectacle and the Wentworth case had aroused much interest. I looked for Joseph and saw him sitting at the end of a bench, squashed against a window by the press of people, biting his lip anxiously. He raised a hand in greeting and I smiled, trying to show a confidence I did not feel. He had visited Elizabeth every day since Tuesday, but she had still not uttered a word. I had met him the evening before and told him I would try for a plea of madness, which was all that was left to us.

Some distance away I saw a man who looked so like Joseph it could only be his brother Edwin. He wore a fine green robe with a fur trim; his face was drawn with care. He met my look and glared, pulling his robe closer around him. So he knew who I was.

And then, in the row in front of Edwin Wentworth, I saw the

young man who had been watching me near Guy's shop. Today he wore a sober doublet of dark green. He sat resting his chin on an elbow placed insolently on the rail separating the spectators' benches from the court. He stared at me speculatively, large dark eyes keen with interest. I frowned and he smiled briefly, settling himself more comfortably. So I was right, I thought, they've set this ruffian to watch me, try to put me off my stride. Well, that will not work. I hitched my gown and stepped away to the lawyers' bench. As this was a criminal trial it was empty, but as I sat down I noticed Bealknap in a doorway. He was talking with an official in clerical dress, the bishop's ordinary.

At that time there was still much corrupt use of benefit of clergy. If a man was found guilty of a crime, then by claiming he was a clerk in holy orders he had the right to be handed over to the bishop for punishment. All one had to do to claim benefit was to prove one was literate by reading aloud the opening verse of psalm 51. King Henry had restricted the use of benefit to non-capital crimes but the rule still stood. Those who satisfied the test were taken to Bishop Bonner's gaol until he decided they had repented; a repentance verified by twelve compurgators, men of good standing who attested to the convict's truthfulness. Bealknap had a ring of compurgators who for a fee would happily vouch for anyone. His sideline was well known throughout Lincoln's Inn, but no barrister would ever inform against another member of the profession.

As I took my place, Forbizer stared at me. It was impossible to gauge his mood; his thin, choleric face always wore the same expression of cold disgust at human sinfulness. He had a long, tidily clipped grey beard and hard coal-black eyes that stared at me coldly. A barrister appearing at a criminal trial meant troublesome legal interruptions.

'What do you want?' he asked.

I bowed. 'I am here to represent Mistress Wentworth, your honour.'

'Are you now? We'll see.' He lowered his head to his papers again.

There was a stir and everyone turned as the jury, twelve well-fed London merchants, were escorted into the jury box. Then the door from the cells opened and the tipstaff led in a dozen ragged prisoners. The more serious cases were heard first, the ones that carried the death penalty; murder, burglary and thefts valued at more than a shilling. The accused were manacled together at the ankles and their chains made a clanking noise as they were led to the dock. They brought a mighty stink with them and some spectators produced nosegays, though the smell did not seem to trouble Forbizer. Elizabeth was at the end of the line next to the fat woman, the alleged horse thief. The woman was tightly grasping the hand of a ragged young man who was trembling and fighting back tears, her son no doubt. I had only seen Elizabeth's face before; now I saw she had a comely figure. She wore a grey indoor dress, crumpled and filthy through being worn over a week at Newgate. I tried to catch her eye but she kept her head bowed. There was a murmur among the spectators, and I saw the sharp-faced young man studying her with interest.

The prisoners shuffled into the dock. Most had frightened, drawn expressions and the young horse thief was shaking like a leaf now. Forbizer gave him a hard look. The clerk stood and asked the prisoners, one by one, how they pleaded. Each replied, 'Not guilty.' Elizabeth was last.

'Elizabeth Wentworth,' the clerk asked solemnly, 'you are charged with the foul murder of Ralph Wentworth on May sixteenth last. How say you – guilty or not guilty?'

I felt the courtroom tense. I did not rise yet, I must wait and see whether she took this final chance to speak, but I looked at her beseechingly. She bowed her head, the long tangled hair falling forward and hiding her face. Forbizer leaned across his desk.

'You are being asked to plead, Mistress,' he said coldly and evenly. 'You had better.'

She lifted her head and looked at him, but it was the same look she had given me in her cell: unfocused, blank, as though looking through him. Forbizer reddened slightly.

'Mistress, you stand accused of one of the foulest crimes imaginable against God and man. Do you or do you not accept trial by a jury of your peers?'

Still she did not speak or move.

'Very well, we will address this at the end of the session.' He looked at her narrowly a moment more, then said, 'Bring on the first case.'

I took a deep breath. Elizabeth stood motionless as the clerk read the first indictment. She stood thus all through the next two hours, only occasionally moving her weight from one hip to the other.

I had not attended a criminal trial for years and was surprised anew at the careless speed of the proceedings. After each accusation was read witnesses were brought on and put under oath. The prisoners were allowed to question their accusers or bring on their own witnesses and several matters descended to exchanges of abuse, which Forbizer silenced in a clear, rasping voice. The horse thieves were accused by a stout innkeeper; the fat woman insisted over and again she had never been there, although the innkeeper had two witnesses; her son only sobbed and shook. At length the jury were sent out; they would be kept in the jury room without meat or drink until they reached their verdicts and would not be long. The prisoners shuffled their feet anxiously, chains clanking, and a buzz of conversation rose from the spectators.

Everyone had been penned in the hot room all morning and the stench by now was dreadful. A shaft of sunlight from the window had settled on my back and I felt myself begin to perspire. I cursed; judges never like a sweating advocate. I looked around. Joseph sat with his head in his hands, while his brother studied Elizabeth's still, frozen form through half-closed eyes, his mouth set hard. My watcher leaned back on his bench, arms folded.

The jury returned. The clerk handed Forbizer the sheaf of

informations annotated with their verdicts. I felt the tension in the box as the prisoners stared at the strips of paper holding their fates; even Elizabeth glanced up briefly.

Five men were found innocent of theft and seven guilty, including the old woman and her son, whose name was Pullen. As the verdict on them was read out the old woman called out for the judge to be merciful and to spare her son, who was but nineteen.

'Goodwife Pullen —' Forbizer's lower lip curled slightly, red amid his neat beard, his habitual gesture of contempt — 'You took the horse together, you have both been found guilty of larceny and so there will be a-pullen at both your necks.' Someone among the spectators laughed and Forbizer glared at them; he did not like levity in court, even at his own jokes. The old woman gripped her son's arm as he began to weep again.

The constable released those found innocent from their shackles and they scurried off. The condemned were led back to Newgate and the clattering of their chains faded away. Now Elizabeth alone remained in the dock.

'Well, Miss Wentworth,' Forbizer rasped, 'will you plead now?'

No reply. There was a murmuring in court: Forbizer silenced it with a look. I rose, but he waved me to sit down again.

'Wait, Brother. Now, Mistress. Guilty or not guilty, it takes little effort to say.' Still she stood like a stone. Forbizer set his lips. 'Very well, the law is clear in these cases. You will suffer *peine forte et dure*, crushing beneath weights until you plead or die.'

I rose again. 'Your honour—'

He turned to me coldly. 'This is a criminal trial, Brother Shardlake. Counsel may not be heard. Do you know so little law?' There was a titter along the benches; these people wanted Elizabeth dead.

I took a deep breath. 'Your honour, I wish to address you not on the murder but regarding my client's capacity. I believe she does not plead because her wits are gone, she is insane. She should not therefore suffer the press. I ask for her to be examined—'

'The jury can consider her mental state when she is tried,' Forbizer said shortly, '*if* she condescends to plead.' I glanced at Elizabeth. She was looking at me now, but still with that dead, dull stare.

'Your honour,' I said determinedly, 'I would like to cite the precedent of *Anon* in the Court of King's Bench in 1505, when it was held that an accused who refuses to plead and whose sanity is put in question should be examined by a jury.' I produced a copy. 'I have the case—'

Forbizer shook his head. 'I know that case. And the contrary case of *Beddloe*, King's Bench, 1498, which says only the trial jury may decide on sanity.'

'But in deciding between the cases, your honour, I submit consideration must be given to my client's weaker sex, and the fact she is below the age of majority—'

Forbizer's lip curled again, a moist fleshy thing against his grey beard. 'And so a jury has to be empanelled now to determine her sanity, and you buy more time for your client. No, Brother Shardlake, no.'

'Your honour, the truth of this matter can never be determined if my client dies under the press. The evidence is circumstantial, justice calls for a fuller investigation.'

'You are addressing me now on the matter itself, sir. I will not allow—'

'She may be pregnant,' I said desperately. 'We do not know, as she will say nothing. We should wait to see if that may be so. The press would kill an unborn child!'

There was more muttering among the spectators. Elizabeth's expression had changed; she was looking at me with angry outrage now.

'Do you wish to plead your belly, madam?' Forbizer asked. She shook her head slowly, then lowered it, hiding her face in her hair once more.

'You understand English then,' Forbizer said to her. He turned back to me. 'You are clutching at any excuse for delay, Brother Shardlake. I will not allow that.' He hunched his shoulders and addressed Elizabeth again. 'You may be below the age of majority, Mistress, but you are above that of responsibility. You know what is right and wrong before God, yet you stand accused of this hideous crime and refuse to plead. I order you to *peine forte et dure*, the weights to be pressed on you this very afternoon.'

I jumped up again. 'Your honour—'

'God's death, man, be quiet!' Forbizer snapped, banging a fist on his desk. He waved at the constable. 'Take her down! Bring up the petty misdemeanours.' The man stepped into the dock and led Elizabeth away, her head still bowed. 'The press is slower than the noose,' I heard one woman say to another. 'Serve her right.' The door closed behind them.

I sat with my head bowed. There was a babble of conversation and a rustling of clothes as the spectators rose. Many had come only to see Elizabeth; the petty thefts worth under a shilling were of little interest, those guilty would just be branded or lose their ears. Only Bealknap, still lurking in the doorway, looked interested, for those convicted of lesser crimes could claim benefit of clergy. Edwin Wentworth went with the rest; I saw the back of his robe as he walked out. Joseph remained alone on his bench, looking disconsolately after his brother. The sharp-faced young man had already gone, with Sir Edwin perhaps. I went over to Joseph.

'I am sorry,' I said.

He clutched my hand. 'Sir, come with me, come now to Newgate. When they show her the weights, the stone to go beneath her back, it may frighten her into speech. That could save her, could it not?'

'Yes, she'd be brought back for trial. But she won't do it, Joseph.'

'Try, sir, please – one last try. Come with me.'

I closed my eyes for a moment, 'Very well.'

As we walked into the vestibule of the court, Joseph gave a gasp and clutched his stomach. 'Agh, my guts,' he said. 'This worry has put them out of order. Is there a jakes here?'

'Round the back. I'll wait for you. Hurry. They'll take her to the press straight away.'

He shouldered a way through the departing crowd. Left alone in the hall, I sat down on a bench. Then I heard a rapid patter of footsteps from the court. The door was flung open and Forbizer's clerk, a round little man, ran up to me, his face red, robes billowing around him. 'Brother Shardlake,' he puffed. 'Thank goodness. I thought you had gone.'

'What is it?'

He handed me a paper. 'Judge Forbizer has reconsidered, sir. He asked me to give you this.'

'What?'

'He has reconsidered. You are to have another two weeks to persuade Mistress Wentworth to plead.'

I stared at him uncomprehendingly. No one could have looked less like reconsidering than Forbizer. There was something shifty, uneasy, in the clerk's face. 'A copy of this has gone to Newgate already.' He thrust the paper at me and vanished back into the courtroom.

I looked at it. A brief order above Forbizer's spiky signature, stating Elizabeth Wentworth was to be detained in the Newgate Hole for another twelve days, until the tenth of June, to reconsider her plea. I sat staring around the hall, trying to work it out. It was an extraordinary thing for any judge to do, let alone Forbizer.

There was a touch on my arm. I looked up to find the sharp-faced young man at my elbow. I frowned and he smiled again, a cynical smile that turned up one corner of his mouth, showing white even teeth.

'Master Shardlake,' he said, 'I see you have the order.' His voice was as sharp as his face, with the burr of a London commoner.

'What do you mean? Who are you?'

He gave a small bow. 'Jack Barak, sir, at your service. It was I persuaded Judge Forbizer to grant the order just now. You did not see me slip behind the bench?'

'No. But — what is this?'

His smile vanished and again I saw the hardness in his face. 'I serve Lord Cromwell. It was in his name I persuaded the judge to give you more time. He didn't want to, stiff-necked old arsehole, but my master is not refused. You know that.'

'Cromwell? Why?'

'He would see you, sir. He is nearby, at the Rolls House. He asks me to take you there.'

My heart began pounding with apprehension. 'Why? What does he want? I haven't seen him in close on three years.'

'He has a commission for you, sir.' Barak raised his eyebrows and stared at me insolently with those large brown eyes. 'Two weeks' more life for the girl is your fee, paid in advance.'

# Chapter Six

BARAK LED ME at a brisk pace to the courthouse stables. My heart still banged against my ribs and the skin on my face had a tight, drawn feeling. I knew Lord Cromwell was not above bullying judges, but he always liked to observe the legal niceties and would not have done this lightly. And Barak was a strange person to use to confront a judge. But though he had risen to be chief minister, Cromwell was the son of a Putney alehouse keeper and was happy to work with men of low birth so long as they were intelligent and ruthless enough. But what in Christ's name did Cromwell want from me? His last mission had plunged me into a hell of murder and violence I still shuddered to recall.

Barak's horse was a beautiful black mare, its coat shining with health. He cantered out while I was still saddling Chancery, pausing in the stable doorway to look back impatiently. 'Ready?' he asked. 'His lordship wants to see you this morning, you know.'

I studied him again as I climbed on the vaulting block and eased myself onto Chancery's back. A hard eye and a fighter's build, as I had observed before. A heavy sword at his hip and a dagger too at his belt. But there was intelligence in his eyes and in the wide, sensual mouth, whose upturned corners seemed made for mockery.

'Wait a moment,' I said, seeing Joseph running across the yard to us, his plump face bright, clutching his cap in his hand. When he had returned from the jakes I told him Forbizer had changed his mind: I said I did not know why. 'Your advocacy, sir,' he had said. 'Your words moved his conscience.' Joseph was ever a naive man.

Now he laid a hand on Chancery's side, beaming up at me. 'I

have to go with this gentleman, Joseph,' I said. 'There is another urgent case I must attend to.'

'Some other poor wretch to save from injustice, eh? But you will be back soon?'

I glanced at Barak; he gave a brief nod.

'Soon, Joseph. I will contact you. Listen, now we have some time to investigate Ralph's murder there is something I would have you do for me, if you can. It will be difficult—'

'Anything, sir, anything.'

'I want you to go to your brother Edwin and ask if he will see me at his house. Say I am unsure of Elizabeth's guilt and wish to hear his side of things.'

A shadow came over his face. 'I need to meet the family, Joseph,' I told him gently. 'And see the house and garden. It is important.'

He bit his lip, then nodded slowly. 'I will do what I can.'

I patted his arm. 'Good man. And now I must go.'

'I shall tell Elizabeth!' he called after me as we rode out into the road. 'I shall tell her, thanks to you, she is spared the press!' Barak looked at me, raising an eyebrow cynically.

✝

WE RODE DOWN Old Bailey Street. The Rolls House was not far, directly opposite Lincoln's Inn in fact. A sprawling complex of buildings, it had once been the Domus Conversorum, where Jews who wished to convert to Christianity were instructed. Since the expulsion of all Jews from England centuries before, the building had been used to house the Court of Chancery Rolls, though one or two foreign Jews, who had washed up in England somehow and agreed to convert to Christianity, were still housed there from time to time. The Six Clerks' Office, which administered the Court of Chancery, was located there too. The office of Keeper of the Domus was still combined with the Mastership of the Rolls.

'I thought Lord Cromwell had given up the mastership,' I said to Barak.

51

'He still keeps an office in the Rolls House. Works there sometimes when he wants to be undisturbed.'

'Can you tell me what this is about?'

He shook his head. 'My master is to tell you himself.'

We rode up Ludgate Hill. It was another hot day; the women bringing produce into town were wearing cloths over their faces to protect them from the dust thrown up by passing carts. I looked down over the red-tiled rooftops of London, and the broad shining band of the river. The tide was out and the Thames mud, stained yellow and green with the refuse that poured every day from the northern shore, lay exposed like a great stain. People said that recently will o'the wisps of flame had been seen at night dancing over the rubbish and wondered uneasily what it portended.

I made another attempt to get information. 'This must be import-ant to your master. Forbizer's not intimidated lightly.'

'He's a care for his skin like all men of the law.' There was an edge of contempt in Barak's voice.

'This sore puzzles me.' I paused, then added, 'Am I in trouble?'

He turned. 'No, not if you do as you're told. It's as I said, my master has a commission for you. Now come: time is important.'

We entered Fleet Street. The dust hung over the Whitefriars' monastic buildings in a pall, for the great friary was in the course of demolition. The gatehouse was covered in scaffolding, men hacking away at the decoration with chisels. A workman stepped into our path, raising a dusty hand.

'Halt your horses, please, sirs,' he called out.

Barak frowned. 'We're on Lord Cromwell's business. Piss off.'

The man wiped his hand on his grubby smock. 'I'm sorry, sir. I only wished to warn you, they're about to blow up the Whiteys' chapter house, the noise could startle the horses—'

'Look—' Barak broke off suddenly. A flash of red light appeared over the wall, followed by a tremendous explosion, louder than a clap of thunder. A heavy crash of falling stone, accompanied by cheers, sounded as a surging cloud of dust rolled over us. Hot-blooded as it looked, Barak's mare only neighed and jerked aside, but Chancery let out a scream and reared up on his hind legs, nearly unseating me. Barak reached across and grabbed the reins.

'Down, matey, down,' he said firmly. Chancery calmed at once, dropping to his feet again. He stood trembling; I was shaking too.

'All right?' Barak asked.

'Yes.' I gulped. 'Yes. Thank you.'

'God's death, the dust.' The powdery cloud, filled with the acrid tang of gunpowder, swirled round us and in a moment my robe and Barak's doublet were spotted with grey. 'Come on, let's get out of this.'

'I'm sorry, sirs,' the workman called after us anxiously.

'So you should be! Arsehole!' Barak called over his shoulder.

We turned up Chancery Lane, the horses still nervous and troubled by the heat and flies. I was perspiring freely but Barak seemed quite cool. I was reluctantly grateful to him; but for his quick action I could have had a bad fall.

I looked longingly for a moment at the familiar Lincoln's Inn gatehouse as Barak led the way through the gate of the Rolls House directly opposite. At the centre of a complex of houses stood a large, solidly built church. A guard in the yellow and blue quarters of Cromwell's livery stood outside the door with a pike. Barak nodded to him and the man bowed and snapped his fingers for a boy to lead our horses away.

Barak pushed open the heavy door of the church and we stepped in. Rolls of parchment bound in red tape lay everywhere, stacked against the walls with their faded paintings of biblical scenes and piled up along the pews. Here and there a black-robed law clerk stood picking among them, seeking precedents. More clerks waited in a queue beside the door to the Six Clerks' Office, seeking writs or dates for hearings.

I had never visited the office, for on the rare occasions I did have a case on in Chancery I would send a clerk to deal with the notoriously lengthy paperwork. I stared at the endless rolls. Barak followed my gaze.

'The ghosts of the old Jews have poor reading,' he said. 'Come on, through here.' He led me towards a walled-off side chapel; another guard in bright livery stood outside the door. Did Cromwell take armed guards everywhere nowadays? I wondered. Barak knocked softly and entered. I took a deep breath as I followed him, for my heart was thumping powerfully against my ribs.

The wall paintings of the side chapel had been whitewashed over, for Thomas Cromwell hated idolatrous decoration. The chapel had been converted into a large office, with cupboards against the walls and chairs drawn up before an imposing desk lit incongruously by a stained-glass window above. There was no one behind it; Cromwell was not there. In a corner, behind a smaller desk, sat a short, black-robed figure I knew: Edwin Grey, Lord Cromwell's secretary. He had been at Cromwell's side for fifteen years, since the time the earl had worked for Wolsey. When I was in favour I had had much legal business through him. Grey rose and bowed to us. His round, pink face under the thinning grey hair was anxious.

He shook my hand; the fingers of his own were black from years of ink. He nodded at Barak; I caught distaste in his look.

'Master Shardlake. How do you fare, sir? It has been a long time.'

'Well enough, Master Grey. And you?'

'Well enough, given the times. The earl had to deal with a message, he will be back in a moment.'

'How is he?' I ventured.

Grey hesitated. 'You will see.' He turned abruptly as the door was thrown open and Thomas Cromwell strode into the room. My old master's heavy features were frowning, but at the sight of me he smiled broadly. I bowed low.

'Matthew, Matthew!' Cromwell said enthusiastically. He shook my hand with his powerful grip, then went and sat behind his desk. I studied him. He was dressed soberly in a black gown, though the

Order of the Garter awarded to him by the king swung from his dark blue doublet. Looking at his face, I was shocked by the change in his appearance since I last saw him three years before. His hair was far greyer, and his strong, coarse features seemed pulled tight with strain and anxiety.

'Well, Matthew,' he said, 'how are you? Your practice prospers?'

I hesitated, thinking of my lost cases. 'Well enough, thank you, my lord.'

'What's that on your robe? It's on your doublet too, Jack.'

'Dust, my lord,' Barak replied. 'They're bringing down the Whiteys' chapter house and nearly brought us down with it.'

Cromwell laughed, then gave Barak a sharp look. 'Is it done?'

'Ay, my lord. Forbizer gave no trouble.'

'I knew he wouldn't.' Cromwell turned back to me. 'I was interested to learn of your involvement in the Wentworth case, Matthew. It occurred to me then we might be of help to each other for old times' sake.' He smiled again. I wondered uneasily how he had heard; but he had eyes and ears everywhere and certainly at Lincoln's Inn.

'I am most grateful, my lord,' I said carefully.

He smiled wryly. 'These little crusades of yours, Matthew. The girl's life matters to you?'

'Ay, it does.' I realized that these past days I had thought of little but Elizabeth's case. I wondered why for a moment. It was something to do with her wounded helplessness, lying there in that filthy Newgate straw. If Cromwell wished to use her life as a rope to bind me to him, he had chosen well.

'I believe she is innocent, my lord.'

He waved a beringed hand. 'I'm not concerned with that,' he said bluntly. He fixed me with a serious look; once again I felt the power of those dark eyes. 'I need your help, Matthew. It's an important matter, and secret. The bargain is I'll keep the girl alive for twelve days. We have only that for my task. Less than a fortnight.' He nodded abruptly. 'Sit down.'

I did as bidden. Barak went and stood against the wall, folding his hands across a large gold-coloured codpiece. Glancing at Cromwell's desk, I saw among the papers a miniature painting in a tiny silver frame, an exquisite portrait of the head and shoulders of a woman. Following my gaze, Cromwell frowned and turned it over. He nodded to Barak.

'Jack's a trusted servant. He's one of only eight that know this story, including myself and Grey here and his majesty the king.' My eyes widened at that name. I still held my cap, which I had removed on entering the church, and involuntarily began twisting it in my hands.

'One of the other five is an old acquaintance of yours.' Cromwell smiled again, cynically. 'It's not a matter to irk your conscience this time – you needn't crush your cap into a rag.' He leaned back and shook his head indulgently. 'I was impatient with you over Scarnsea, Matthew. I saw that later. None of us could have known how complex that affair would turn out. I have always admired your mind, your skills at teasing out the truth in men's affairs. Ever since the old days when we were all young reformers. Do you remember?' He smiled, but then a shadow crossed his face. 'Days with more hope and less care.' He sat silent for a moment and I thought of the rumours of his troubles over the Cleves marriage.

'May I ask who this old acquaintance is, my lord?' I ventured.

He nodded. 'You remember Michael Gristwood?'

Lincoln's Inn is a small world. 'Gristwood the attorney, who used to work for Stephen Bealknap?'

'The same.'

I remembered a small, scurrying fellow, with bright sharp eyes. Gristwood had once been friendly with Bealknap and, like him, forever on the lookout for new money-making schemes. But he had none of Bealknap's calculating coldness and his schemes never came to anything. I remembered he had once come to me for help in a property case he had taken on. A mere unqualified solicitor, he had got hopelessly out of his depth. The case was in a dreadful tangle, and he had been fulsomely grateful for my help. He had bought me a dinner in hall, where I had listened, half-amused, as he offered to involve me in a number of hare-brained schemes by way of thanks.

'He had a falling out of some sort with Bealknap,' I said. 'He hasn't been around Lincoln's Inn a long time. Didn't he go to work for the Court of Augmentations?'

Cromwell nodded. 'He did. To help Richard Rich pull in the proceeds of the dissolution.' He made a steeple of his fingers and looked at me over them.

'Last year, when St Bartholomew's priory in Smithfield surrendered to the king, Gristwood was sent to supervise the taking of the inventory of chattels to go to the king.'

I nodded. The hospital priory had been a large monastic house. I recalled the prior had been in league with Cromwell and Rich, and as a reward had been granted most of the priory lands. So much for vows of poverty. Yet they said Prior Fuller was dying, of a wasting disease God had laid on him for closing the hospital. Others said that Richard Rich, who had moved into the prior's fine house himself, was slowly poisoning him.

'Gristwood took some Augmentations men with him,' Cromwell continued, 'to quantify the furniture, the plate to be melted down and so on. He took the monastery librarian to show him what books might be worth keeping. The Augmentations men are thorough: they poke into nooks and crannies the monks themselves have often forgotten.'

'I know.'

'And in the crypt under the church, in a cobwebby corner, they found something.' He leaned forward, the hard dark eyes seeming to bore into mine. 'Something that was lost to man centuries ago, something that has become little more than a legend and a diversion for alchemists.'

I stared at him in astonishment. I had not expected this. He laughed uneasily. 'Sounds like a mummers' tale, eh? Tell me, Matthew, have you ever heard of Greek Fire?'

'I'm not sure.' I frowned. 'The name is vaguely familiar.'

'I knew nothing of it myself until a few weeks ago. Greek Fire was an unknown liquid that the Byzantine emperors used in warfare against the infidel eight hundred years ago. They fired it at enemy ships and it would set them ablaze from end to end, a rushing inextinguishable fire. It could burn even on water. The formula for its creation was kept a close secret, passed down from one Byzantine emperor to another till in the end it was lost. The alchemists have been after it for hundreds of years but they've never fathomed it. Here, Grey.' He snapped his fingers and the clerk rose from his desk and put a piece of parchment in his master's hands. 'Handle it carefully, Matthew,' Cromwell murmured. 'It is very old.'

I took the parchment from him. It was frayed at the edges and torn at the top. Above some words in Greek was a richly painted picture without perspective, such as the old monks used to illustrate their books. Two oared ships of ancient design faced each other across a stretch of water. At the front of one ship a golden pipe was belching red tongues of fire, engulfing the other.

'This looks like a monkish thing,' I said.

He nodded. 'So it is.' He paused, collecting his thoughts. I glanced at Barak. His face was sober, nothing mocking in it now. Grey stood beside me, looking at the parchment, his hands folded.

Cromwell spoke again, quietly though there were only the three of us to hear. 'Friend Gristwood was at St Bartholomew's one day last autumn when he was called to the church by one of the Augmentations clerks. Among the old lumber in the crypt they had found a large barrel, which, when they opened it, proved to be full of a thick, dark liquid with a terrible smell, like the stench of Lucifer's privy Gristwood said. Michael Gristwood had never seen anything remotely like it before and he was curious. There was a plaque on the barrel, with a name, Alan St John. And some Latin words. *Lupus est homo homini.*'

'Man is wolf to man.'

'Those monks could never use plain English. Well, friend Gristwood thought to set the librarian to search for the name St John in the library. They found it in the catalogue and it led them to an ancient box of manuscripts about Greek Fire, deposited there by one Captain St John, who died in St Bartholomew's hospital a century ago. He was old soldier, a mercenary who was at Constantinople when it fell to the Turks. He left a memoir.' Cromwell raised his eyebrows. 'He told how a Byzantine librarian fleeing with him to the boats gave him the barrel, which he claimed contained the last of Greek Fire, together with the formula to make the substance. The librarian had found it when clearing out the emperor's library and gave it to St John so that at the last a Christian should have the secret, not the heathen Turks. You see the page is torn?'

'Yes.'

'Gristwood tore off the formula that was written in Greek above that picture, together with instructions for constructing the throwing apparatus used to project it. Of course, he should have brought it to me − it was monastic property and it belongs to the king now − but he didn't.' Cromwell frowned and his heavy jaw set. There was a moment's silence, and I realized I was twisting at my cap again. He went on in the same quiet voice.

'Michael Gristwood has an older brother. Samuel. Also known as Sepultus Gristwood the alchemist.'

'Sepultus,' I repeated. 'Latin for buried.'

'As in the buried knowledge only alchemists can divine. Yes, like most of those rogues he gave himself a fancy Latin name. But when Sepultus heard Michael's story, he realized the formula could be worth a fortune.'

I swallowed hard. I realized now how great this matter was.

'If it's genuine,' I said. 'Alchemists' formulae for the creation of wonders are ten a penny.'

'Oh, it's genuine,' he said. 'I've seen it used.'

Godless gesture though it was, I felt a sudden urge to cross myself.

'The Gristwoods must have spent some time making more of the stuff, for it was March this year before Michael Gristwood came to me. Not directly, of course, someone of his standing couldn't do that, but through intermediaries. One of whom brought me that parchment and the other documents from the convent. Everything but the formula. With a message from the Gristwood brothers that they had made Greek Fire, they were offering a demonstration and if I decided I wanted the formula they'd give it to me. In return for a licence on its development, so they'd have the exclusive right of manufacture.'

I looked at the parchment. 'But it didn't belong to him. As you said, as it was monastic property it is now the king's.'

He nodded. 'Yes. And I could have had the brothers brought to the Tower and the information forced out of them. That was my first reaction. But what if they fled before they could be arrested? What if they sold the formula to the French or the Spaniards? They're a tricky pair. I decided to play along at least until I'd seen what they could do; once I'd found out if there was anything in it I could promise them a licence, then have them arrested for theft when they were least expecting it.' He set his thin lips. 'That was my mistake.' He looked at Grey, still hovering beside me. 'Sit down, master clerk,' he snapped. 'You make me uneasy hovering there. Matthew can keep the parch-ment.'

Grey bowed and returned to his desk, where he sat expressionless. He must be used to bearing the brunt of Cromwell's temper. I saw Barak's eyes on his master, a look of almost filial concern in them. Cromwell leaned back again.

'England has lit a fire across Europe, Matthew, the first large state to break from Rome. The pope wants the French and Spanish to com-bine and overthrow us. They won't trade with us, there's undeclared war with the French in the Channel and we're having to plough half the revenues from the monasteries into defence. If you knew how much we've spent it would make your hair curl. The new forts along the coast, the building of ships and guns and cannon—'

'I know, my lord. Everyone is frightened of invasion.'

'Those who are loyal to reform, at least. You haven't turned papist since last we met, have you?' His stare took on a terrible intensity.

I squeezed the cap tightly. 'No, my lord.'

He nodded slowly. 'No, that's what I've been told. You've lost the fire for our cause but you've not turned enemy, which is more than can be said for some. So a new weapon, something that could make our ships invincible, you can see how important that could be.'

'Yes, but—' I hesitated.

'Go on.'

'My lord, sometimes in desperate times we clutch at desperate remedies. The alchemists have promised us wonders for hundreds of years, but precious few have actually appeared.'

He nodded approvingly. 'Good, Matthew, you could ever put your finger on a weak point in an argument. But, remember, I've seen it. I met the Gristwoods here and told them I'd arrange for an old crayer to be floated up to an abandoned jetty at Deptford early one morning and, if they could destroy it with Greek Fire in front of me, I'd make a deal with them. Jack arranged it all, and only he and I and they were present early one morning at the start of the month. And they did it.' He spread his arms wide and shook his head. I could see that he was still amazed by what he had seen.

'They brought some strange device of steel they'd made with them, with a pipe on a pivot. They operated a pump on the device – and then a great sheet of liquid flame shot out and consumed the old boat in minutes. When I saw it I nearly fell in the water. It wasn't an explosion, like gunpowder, just' – he shook his head again – 'an inextinguishable fire, more fast and furious than any fire I've seen. Like a dragon's breath. And with no incantations, Matthew, no magic words. This is no trick, it's something new; or, rather, something ancient rediscovered. I had a second demonstration a week later; they did it again. So now I've told the king.'

I glanced at Grey, who nodded at me seriously. Cromwell took a deep breath.

'He was more enthusiastic than I'd dared to hope. You should have seen his eyes light up. He clapped me on the shoulder, and he's not done that in a long while. He asked for a demonstration before him. There's an old warship, the *Grace of God*, in Deptford for breaking up. I've arranged for it to be there on the tenth of June, in twelve days' time.' The tenth of June, I thought, the day Elizabeth's period of grace expires.

'I've been caught unawares,' he went on. 'I didn't think the king would jump at it so quickly. I can't fence with the Gristwoods any more. I must have that formula in my hands, and the Greek Fire they've made, before the king sees that demonstration. I want you to get it from them.'

I breathed heavily. 'I see.'

'It's only a matter of persuasion, Matthew. Michael Gristwood knows you and respects you. If you remind him the formula is legally the king's and tell him the king is personally involved, I think you can make him believe you, and give you the formula. I want it done then and there. Jack has a hundred pounds in gold angels about him that Gristwood is to have as a reward. And you can warn him that if he doesn't cooperate I can call the Tower's rack to my aid.'

I looked up at him. My head swam at the thought of becoming involved in a matter that concerned the king himself, but Cromwell had Elizabeth's life in his hands. I took a deep breath.

'Where does Gristwood live?'

'Sepultus and Michael live with Michael's wife in a big old house in Wolf's Lane, in the parish of Allhallows the Less in Queenhithe. Sepultus works from there. I want you to go there today. Jack will accompany you.'

'I beg this may be all. I live quietly these days, that is all I wish to do.'

I expected harsh words for my weakness, but Cromwell only smiled wryly. 'Yes, Matthew, after this you may go back to your quiet.' He looked at me fixedly. 'Be grateful you have the chance.'

'Thank you, my lord.'

He stood up. 'Then go now, ride to Queenhithe. If the Gristwoods are not there, find them. Jack, I want you back here by the end of the day.'

'Yes, my lord.'

I rose and bowed. Barak rose and opened the door. Before I followed him I turned back to my old master.

'May I ask, my lord: why did you choose me for this?' From the corner of my eye, I saw Grey give me a slight shake of the head.

Cromwell inclined his head. 'Because Gristwood knows you for an honest man and will trust you. As I do because I know you are one of the few who would not seek to make advantage for themselves from this. You are too honest.'

'Thank you,' I said quietly.

His face hardened. 'And because you care too much for the fate of the Wentworth girl and, finally, you are too afraid of me to dare cross me.'

# Chapter Seven

OUTSIDE, BARAK TOLD ME brusquely to wait while he fetched the horses. I stood on the steps of the Domus, looking out across Chancery Lane. For a second time Cromwell had casually dropped me into an affair with dangerous ramifications. But there was nothing I could do; even if I had dared defy him, there remained Elizabeth.

Barak reappeared, riding his black mare and leading Chancery. I mounted and we rode to the gate. His expression was closed, serious. Barak, I thought, what sort of a name was that? It wasn't English, though he seemed English enough.

We had to pause in the gateway as a long procession of sulky looking apprentices wearing the blue and red badges of the Leather-sellers' Company marched past. Longbows were slung over their shoulders, and a few carried long matchlock guns. Because of the invasion threat, all young men now had to undertake compulsory military practice. They passed up towards Holborn Fields.

We rode downhill to the City. 'So you were at the scene of this demonstration of Greek Fire, Barak?' I said, adopting a deliberately haughty tone; I had decided I was not going to be intimidated by this rude young fellow.

'Keep your voice down.' He gave me a frowning look. 'We don't want that name bandied abroad. Yes, I was there. And it was as the earl said. I would not have believed it had I not seen it.'

'Many wonderful tricks may be performed with gunpowder. At the last mayor's procession there was a dragon that spat balls of exploding fire—'

'D'you think I don't know a gunpowder trick when I see one? What happened at Deptford was different. It wasn't gunpowder: it was like nothing that's been seen before, in England, anyway.' He turned away, steering his horse through the crowds going through the Ludgate.

We rode along Thames Street, our progress slow through the lunchtime crowds. It was the hottest time of the day and Chancery was sweating and uncomfortable. I felt sunburn prickling on my cheeks and coughed as a swirl of dust went into my mouth.

'Not far now,' Barak said. 'We turn down to the river soon.'

I voiced a thought which had occurred to me. 'I wonder why Gristwood did not approach Lord Cromwell through Sir Richard Rich. He's Chancellor of Augmentations.'

'He wouldn't trust Rich. Everyone knows what a rogue he is. Rich would have kept the formula and bargained with it himself, and probably dismissed Gristwood into the bargain.'

I nodded. Sir Richard was a brilliant lawyer and administrator, but he was said to be the most cruel and unscrupulous man in England.

We entered the maze of narrow streets leading down to the Thames. I glimpsed the river, its brown waters alive with wherries and white-sailed tilt boats, but the breeze that came from it was tainted; the tide was still out, the filth-strewn mud stewing in the sun.

Wolf's Lane was a long narrow street full of old houses, decayed-looking cheap shops and lodging places. Outside one of the larger houses I saw a brightly painted sign which showed Adam and Eve standing on either side of the philosopher's egg, the legendary sealed vase in which base metal could be turned to gold, an alchemist's sign. The place was in dire need of repair, plaster was peeling from the walls and the overhanging roof lacked several tiles. Like many houses built on Thames mud, it had a pronounced tilt to one side.

The front door was open, and I saw to my surprise that a woman in a plain servant's dress was hanging onto the jamb with both hands, as though afraid of falling.

'What's this?' Barak asked. 'Drunk at one in the afternoon?'

'I don't think it's that.' I had a sudden feeling of dread. Then, seeing us, the woman let out a screeching wail.

'Help! For Jesu's sake, help me! Murder!'

Barak jumped down and ran towards her. I threw the horses' reins quickly over a rail, and ran over. Barak had the woman by the arms; she was staring wildly at him, sobbing loudly.

'Come on, girl,' he said with surprising gentleness. 'What ails you?'

She made an effort to calm herself. She was young and plump-cheeked, a country girl by the look of her.

'The master,' she said. 'Oh, God, the master—'

I saw that the wood of the doorframe was splintered and broken. The door, which hung from one hinge, had been battered in. I looked past her and down a long dim corridor hung with a faded tapestry showing the three kings bearing gifts to the infant Jesus. Then I gripped Barak's arm. The rushes on the wooden floor were criss-crossed with footprints. They were dark red.

'What has happened here?' I whispered.

Barak shook the girl gently. 'We're here to help. Come on now, what's your name?'

Whoever smashed their way in could still be here. I gripped the dagger at my waist.

'I'm Susan, sir, the servant,' the girl said tremulously. 'I'd been shopping in Cheapside with my mistress, we – we came back and found the door like this. And upstairs my master and his brother—' She gulped and looked within. 'Oh, God, sir—'

'Where is your mistress?'

'In the kitchen.' She took a deep, whooping breath. 'She went stiff as a board when she saw them, she couldn't move. I sat her down and said I'd go for help, but when I got to the door I felt faint, I couldn't go another step.' She clung to Barak.

'You're a brave girl, Susan,' he said. 'Now, can you take us to your mistress?'

The girl let go of the door. She shuddered at the sight of the bloody footsteps inside, then swallowed and, clutching Barak's hand tightly, led the way down the corridor.

'Two people, by the look of those prints,' I said. 'A big man and a smaller one.'

'I think we're in the shit here.' Barak murmured.

We followed Susan into a large kitchen with a view onto a stone-flagged yard. The room was dingy, the fireplace black with dirt and stains of rats' piss on the whitewashed ceiling. It struck me that Gristwood's schemings had brought him little profit. A woman sat at a big table worn with years of use. She was small and thin, older than I would had expected, wearing a white apron over a cheap dress. Straggles of grey hair were visible under her white coif. She sat rigidly, her hands clutching the table edge, her head trembling.

'She's shocked out of her wits, poor soul,' I whispered.

The servant crossed to her. 'Madam,' she said hesitantly. 'Some men have come. To help us.'

The woman jerked and stared at us wildly. I raised a soothing hand. 'Goodwife Gristwood?'

'Who are you?' she asked. Something sharp and watchful came into her face.

'We came on some business with your husband and his brother. Susan said you came home and found the place broken into—'

'They're upstairs,' Goodwife Gristwood whispered. 'Upstairs.' She clutched her bony hands together so hard the knuckles whitened.

I took a deep breath. 'May we see?'

She closed her eyes. 'If you can bear it.'

'Susan, stay here and look after your mistress. Barak?'

He nodded. If he was feeling the same shock and fear as I, he gave no sign. As we turned to the door, Susan sat down and hesitantly took her mistress's hand.

We passed the tapestry, which I saw from the style was very ancient, and mounted a narrow wooden staircase to the first floor. The house's lopsidedness was noticeable here, some of the stairs were warped and a large crack ran down the wall. There were more bloody footsteps, wet and glinting – this blood had been shed very recently.

At the top of the stairs a number of doors gave off the hallway. They were closed except for the one straight ahead of us. Like the front door it hung off one hinge, the lock smashed in. I took a deep breath and stepped inside.

The chamber was large and well lit, running the whole length of the house. There was an odd, sulphurous smell in the air. I saw the ceiling's large beams were painted with Latin texts. '*Aureo hamo piscari,*' I read. To fish with a golden hook.

No one would fish here again. A man in a stained alchemist's robe lay sprawled on his back over an upturned bench amid a chaos of broken glass pipes and retorts. His face had been completely smashed in; one blue eyeball glared at me from the hideous pulpy mess. I felt my stomach heave and turned quickly to study the rest of the room.

The whole workshop was in chaos, more overturned benches, broken glass everywhere. Next to a large fireplace lay the remains of a large iron-bound chest. It was little more than a heap of broken spars now, the metal bands smashed right through. Whoever had wielded the axe here – and everything pointed to an axe – must have had unusual strength.

Beside the chest Michael Gristwood lay on his back, his body half-covered by a blood-soaked chart of the astral planes that had fallen from the wall. His head was almost severed from his neck; a great spray of arterial blood had stained the floor and even the walls. I blenched again.

'That the lawyer?' Barak asked.

'Ay.' Michael's eyes and mouth were wide open in a last scream of astonished terror.

'Well, he won't be needing Lord Cromwell's bag of gold,' Barak said. I frowned. He shrugged. 'Well, he won't, will he? Come on, let's go back downstairs.'

With a last glance at the butchered remains, I followed him down to the kitchen. Susan seemed to have recovered herself somewhat and was boiling a pan of water on the filthy range. Goodwife Gristwood still sat with her hands clenched.

'Anyone else live here, Susan?' Barak asked.

'No, sir.'

'Is there anyone that could come and sit with you?' I asked Goodwife Gristwood. 'Any other relatives?' Again a momentary sharpness came into her face, then she answered, 'No.'

'Right,' Barak said bluntly. 'I'm going to the earl. He must say what's to be done here.'

'The constable should be told—'

'Pox on the constable. I'm going to the earl now.' He pointed at the women. 'Stay here with them, make sure they don't leave.'

Susan looked up anxiously. 'Do you mean Lord Cromwell, sir? But, sir – but we've done nothing.' Her voice rose in fear.

'Do not worry, Susan,' I said gently. 'He must be told. He—' I hesitated.

Goodwife Gristwood spoke, her voice cold and hard. 'My husband and Sepultus were working for him, Susan. I know that much, I told them they were fools, that he's dangerous. But Michael would never listen to me.' She fixed us with pale blue eyes that were suddenly full of anger. 'Now see what's become of him and Sepultus. The fools.'

'God's bones, woman,' Barak burst out. 'Your husband's lying slain in his gore upstairs. Is that all you have to say about him?' I looked at him in surprise, then realized that under his bravado he too was shocked by what we had seen. Goodwife Gristwood merely smiled bitterly and turned her head away.

'Stay here,' Barak told me again. 'I'll be back soon.' He turned and left the kitchen. Susan gave me a scared look; Goodwife Gristwood had retreated into herself.

'It's all right, Susan,' I said with an attempt at a smile. 'You're not in any trouble. There may be a few questions for you, that's all.' She still looked frightened: that was the effect Cromwell's name had on most people. I set my teeth. What in God's name had I got involved in? And who was Barak to give me orders?

I crossed to the window and looked out at the yard, surprised to see that both the flagstones and the high walls were stained black. 'Has there been a fire here?' I asked Susan.

'Master Sepultus did experiments out there sometimes, sir. Terrible bangs and hissings there were.' She crossed herself. 'I was glad he wouldn't let me see.'

Goodwife Gristwood spoke again. 'Yes, we were kept out of our own kitchen when he and my husband were at their foolery.'

I looked again at the scorch marks. 'Did they go out there often?'

'Only recently, sir,' Susan said. She turned to her mistress. 'I'll make an infusion, madam, it might ease us. Would you like some, sir? I have some marigolds—'

'No, thank you.'

We sat together in silence for a while. My mind was racing. It struck me that the formula might still be in the workshop, perhaps even with some samples of this Greek Fire. Now was a chance to look before the room was disturbed further, though I shrank from returning there. I bade the women stay in the kitchen and mounted the stairs again.

I stood in the doorway for a moment, steeling myself to look again at those terrible carcasses. Poor Michael had been in his mid-thirties, I recalled, younger than me. The afternoon sun was shining into the room, a sunbeam illuminating his dead face. I remembered that dinner in Lincoln's Inn Hall, how I had thought he had the questing, nosy look of an amiable rodent. I turned away from his look of terror.

There was a terrible casualness about the way the two men had been smashed down. It seemed the killers had simply staved in the doors and then felled the brothers like animals, with an axe blow each. They had probably been watching the house, waiting for the women to leave. I wondered if Michael and Sepultus, hearing the front door broken in, had locked themselves in the workshop in a vain attempt to save themselves.

I noticed Michael was wearing a rough smock over his shirt. Perhaps he had been helping his brother. But with what? I looked around. I had never been in an alchemist's workshop – I gave such people a wide berth, for they were known as great frauds, but I had seen pictures of their laboratories and something was missing. Frowning, I walked over to a wall lined with shelves, my feet crunching on broken glass. One shelf was full of books but the others were empty. From round marks in the dust I guessed jars and bottles had been stored there. That was what I had seen in the pictures, alchemists' chambers full of bottles of liquids and powders. There was nothing like that here. In the pictures there had also been benches with oddly shaped retorts for distillation – that would explain all the broken glass on the floor. 'They took his potions,' I murmured.

I took one of the books from the shelves, *Epitome Corpus Hermeticum*, and flicked through it. A marked passage read: 'Distillation is the elevation of the essence of a dry thing, by fire, thus by fire we come to the essence of things, even while all else be consumed.' I shook my head and put it down, turning to the remains of the chest. I saw that the fireplace and the wall behind it were fire-blackened like the yard.

The contents of the chest lay scattered all over the floor – letters and documents, one or two with bloody thumb prints on them. So the killers had searched through the contents. There was a document dated three years ago, conveying the house to Sepultus and Michael Gristwood, and a marriage contract between Michael Gristwood and Jane Storey drawn up ten years earlier. Under it Jane's father contracted to leave all his property to his son-in-law on his death, an unusually generous provision.

Something else on the floor caught my eye. I bent down and picked up a gold angel; it had fallen from a leather bag nearby that contained twenty more. The brothers' money had been left behind. Well, I thought, that was not what the killers were after. I rose, pocketing the coin. Another smell was beginning to overlay the sulphurous stink in the room, the sweet, rich smell of decay. I stepped on something that crunched under my heel and, looking down, saw I had broken a delicate set of scales. Sepultus's alchemist's balance. Well, he would not be needing it now. With a last glance at the bloody remains, I left the room.

✝

JANE GRISTWOOD sat where I had left her, Susan beside her sipping something from a wooden cup. Susan looked up nervously as I came in. I took the gold coin and laid it in front of her mistress. She looked up at me.

'What's this?'

'I found it upstairs, in the remains of your husband's chest. There is a whole purse of angels there, together with the deeds to the house and other papers. You should keep them safe.'

She nodded. 'The deeds to the house. I suppose it's mine now. Great broken-down place; I never wanted it.'

'Yes, it will come to you now unless Michael had sons.'

'He had no sons.' She spoke with sudden bitterness, then looked up at me. 'You know the law then. You know about inheritance.'

'I am a barrister, madam.' I spoke sharply, for her coldness was beginning to repel me as it had Barak. 'You may care to fetch the gold and those papers; there will be others poking around this house soon.'

She stared at me for a moment. 'I can't go up there,' she whispered. Then her eyes widened and her voice rose to a shriek. 'Don't make me go up there; for pity's sake, don't make me see them again!' She began sobbing, a desperate howling like an animal caught in a trap. The girl took her hand again.

'I will fetch them,' I said, ashamed of my earlier curtness. I went back upstairs and drew the papers and the gold purse together. In the hot afternoon the smell of death was growing stronger. As I stood up I nearly slipped. I looked down, fearing I had slithered in the blood, but saw there was a patch of something else by the fireplace; a little pool of viscous, colourless liquid that had spilled from a small glass bottle that lay on its side on the floor. I bent down and dipped my finger in it. I rubbed my fingers together, it had a slippery feel. I sniffed. The stuff was odourless, like water. I righted the bottle and replaced the stopper that had fallen off in the struggle and lay nearby. There was no label to identify the thick, clear liquid inside. Hesitantly, I touched the tip of my tongue to it, then jerked back as a stinging, bitter taste filled my mouth, making me gasp and cough.

I heard footsteps outside and crossed to the window, dabbing at my burning mouth. Barak was outside with half a dozen men in Cromwell's livery carrying swords. I hastened downstairs as they marched in, their feet clumping heavily on the boards as they hurried to the kitchen. As I ran downstairs I heard Susan give a little scream. The men had crowded in; Goodwife Gristwood was frowning at them. Barak saw the little pile of papers I carried. 'What are those?' he asked sharply.

'Family papers and some gold. They were in the chest upstairs. I fetched them for Goodwife Gristwood.'

'Let me see.'

I frowned as he grabbed the papers. At least, I thought, the churl can read. He opened the bag of gold and examined the contents. Satisfied, he laid the gold and papers before Goodwife Gristwood. She clutched them to her. Barak looked at me.

'Any sign of the formula up there?'

'Not that I can see. If it was in that chest they took it.'

He turned to Jane Gristwood. 'Do you know anything about a paper your husband and his brother had, a formula they were working on?'

She shook her head wearily. 'No. They told me nothing of what they did. Only that they were engaged on some work for Lord Cromwell. I didn't want to know.'

'These men are going to have to search your house from top to bottom,' he said. 'It's important we find that paper. Afterwards two of them will stay here with you.'

She looked at him narrowly. 'Are we prisoners, then?'

'They are for your protection, madam. You may still not be safe.'

She removed her coif and ran her fingers though her grey hair, then gave Barak a hard stare. 'What about my front door? Anyone could get in.'

'It will be repaired.' He spoke to one of the retainers, a hard-looking fellow. 'See to that, Smith.'

'Yes, Master Barak.'

He turned back to me. 'Lord Cromwell wants a meeting now. He's gone to his house in Stepney.'

I hesitated. Barak stepped closer. 'That's an order,' he said quietly. 'I have told my master the news. He is not a happy man.'

# Chapter Eight

RIDING THROUGH the City again after being in that silent house of death, I felt strangely disconnected from the jostling, noisy crowds. We had a long way to go, for Lord Cromwell's house at Stepney was far beyond the City wall. We paused only to allow a procession past – a cleric in white robes leading a man dressed in sackcloth, ashes strewn over his face and carrying a faggot, the church congregation following behind. Someone whose reformist opinions had been deemed heretical but who had repented, the ashes and the faggot reminders of the burning that awaited him if he relapsed. The man was weeping – perhaps it had been a reluctant recantation – but if he sinned again his body would be weeping blood as the fire shrivelled it.

I glanced at Barak, who was eyeing the scene with distaste. I wondered what his religious opinions were. It had been quite a feat for him to reach Cromwell, collect these men and get back to Queenhithe so quickly. Yet he did not look tired, though I felt exhausted. The procession shuffled past and we moved on. Thankfully the afternoon shadows were lengthening, the overhanging houses bringing a welcome shade to the streets.

'What's that in your pocket?' Barak asked as we rode up Bishopsgate.

I put my hand to my robe and realized that I had slipped Sepultus's book there without thinking.

'It's a book on alchemy.' I looked at him fixedly. 'How you watch me. You thought the formula might have been with those papers I gave to Goodwife Gristwood?'

He shrugged. 'Can't trust anyone these days, not if you're in the earl's service. Besides,' he added with an insolent smile, 'you're a lawyer and everyone knows you have to keep an eye on lawyers. Not to do so would be *crassa neglegentia*, as you people say.'

'Gross negligence. You have some Latin then?'

'Oh yes. I have Latin, and know men of law. Many lawyers are great reformers, are they not?'

'Ay,' I replied cautiously.

'Is it not amusing, then, now that the monks and friars have gone, how the lawyers are the only ones to walk around in black robes, calling each other brother and trying to part people from their money?'

'There have been jokes against lawyers time out of mind,' I said shortly. 'They become tiring.'

'And they take oaths of obedience, though not of chastity or poverty.' Barak smiled mockingly again. His mare wove quickly through the crowds and I had to spur poor Chancery to keep up. We passed under the Bishopsgate and soon the chimneys of Cromwell's impressive three-storey house came into view.

The last time I had been there, on a bitter winter's day three years before, a crowd of people had been waiting at the side gate. Another crowd was there this hot afternoon. The outcasts of London, shoeless and in rags. Some supported themselves on makeshift crutches, others had the pits and marks of disease on their faces. The number of workless poor in London was growing beyond control; the dissolution had cast hundreds of servants from the London monasteries, and the unhappy patients from the hospitals and infirmaries too, out onto the streets. And pitiful as the doles given by the Church had been, now even those were gone. There was talk of charitable schools and hospitals, and schemes for state works, but nothing had been done yet. Cromwell, meanwhile, had adopted the wealthy landowner's custom of distributing his own doles; it strengthened his standing in London.

We rode past the beggars and through the main gate. At the front door a servant met us. He asked us to wait in the hallway, then a few minutes later John Blitheman, Lord Cromwell's steward, appeared.

'Master Shardlake,' he said, 'welcome. It has been a long time. Does the law keep you busy?'

'Busy enough.'

Barak, who had untied his sword and handed it with his cap to a servant boy, came over.

'He's waiting for us, Blitheman.' The steward smiled at me apologetically and led us into the house. A minute later we were outside Cromwell's study. Blitheman knocked softly and his master called, 'Enter,' in a snapping tone.

The chief minister's study was as I remembered, full of tables covered with reports and drafts of bills, a forbidding place despite the sunlight streaming in. Cromwell sat behind his desk. His manner was different from what it had been that morning; he sat crouched in his chair, head sunk between his shoulders, and gave us a look so baleful it made me shiver.

'So,' he said without preliminaries, 'you found them murdered.' His voice was cold, intense.

I took a deep breath. 'Yes, my lord. Most brutally.'

'I've got men searching for the formula,' Barak said. 'They'll take the place apart if need be.'

'And the women?'

'They'll be kept there. They're both scared out of their wits. They know nothing. I've told the men to ask round the neighbouring houses to see if anyone saw the attack, but Wolf's Lane looks like a place where people take care to mind their own business.'

'Who betrayed me?' Cromwell whispered intently. 'Which of them?' He stared at me fixedly. 'Well, Matthew, what did you make of what you saw?'

'I think there were two men involved and that they broke in with axes. They killed the brothers at once in the alchemist's workshop, where they were working, then went to a chest that was kept there and smashed it in. There was a bag of gold inside, but they left it untouched.' I hesitated. 'My guess is that the formula was there and they knew it.'

There was a grey tinge to Cromwell's face. He set his thin lips.

'You can't be sure,' Barak interjected.

'I'm not sure of anything,' I replied with sudden heat. I made my voice calm. 'But no search was made of the rest of the room. The books on the shelves were undisturbed and would they not have been an obvious place to look for a hidden paper? Also, I believe some bottles were taken from the shelves. I think the people who murdered those poor men knew exactly what they were looking for.'

'So there will be no physical traces left of their experiments,' Cromwell said.

'That would be my guess, my lord.' I looked anxiously at him, but he only nodded reflectively.

'See, Jack,' he said suddenly, nodding at me. 'Learn from a master of observation.' He turned bleak eyes on me again. 'Matthew, you must help me solve this.'

'But, my lord——'

'I can't tell anyone else,' he said with sudden passion. 'I daren't. If it got to the king——' He sighed, a shuddering sound. It was the first time I had seen Thomas Cromwell afraid.

'You must solve this,' he repeated. 'You can have any authority, any resources.'

I stood on the fine carpet, my heart thudding. Once before he had sent me to investigate a killing, pitching me into horrors beyond imagining. Not again, I thought. Not again.

He seemed to read my mind and sudden anger flashed in his eyes. 'Christ's wounds, man,' he snapped. 'I've saved that girl's life for you. Or at least I'll save it if you help me; Forbizer can be made to change his mind again if need be. My own life could be at stake here as well as everything you once believed in.' I had a momentary vision of Elizabeth, lying blank-eyed in her cell. And I knew that at a word from Cromwell I could be flung in gaol too, for knowing too much.

'I will help, my lord,' I said quietly.

He looked at me for a long moment, then gestured to Barak. 'Jack, the Bible. Before I tell you more, Matthew, I must have your oath to keep this matter secret.'

Barak laid a luxury edition of the new Great Bible, which had been ordered to be set in every church, upon the desk. I looked at the brightly coloured title page: King Henry on his throne, handing copies of God's Word to Cromwell on one side, Archbishop Cranmer on the other, who in turn passed them down to the people. I swallowed and touched the book.

'I swear I will keep the matter of Greek Fire privy,' Cromwell said. I repeated the words, feeling I was turning a key in a set of fetters that bound me to him again.

'And help me to the best of your ability.'

'To the best of my ability.'

Cromwell gave a satisfied nod, though he still sat hunched over his desk like some great beast at bay. He picked something up and turned it over in his big hands: it was the miniature portrait he had had at the Domus.

'The reformist cause is tottering, Matthew.' He spoke quietly. 'It's even worse than the rumours say. The king's afraid and grows more afraid every day as Norfolk and Bishop Gardiner tip their poison in his ear. Afraid of common people reading the Bible, fearing they'll end by overthrowing the social order in bloody chaos like the Anabaptists at Münster. Radical reformers stand in danger of the fire – you know Robert Barnes is under arrest?'

'I had heard.' I took a deep breath; I did not want to hear this.

'The Act of Six Articles the king forced through last year takes us halfway back to Rome and now he wants the lower classes forbidden from reading the Bible. And he's afraid of invasion.'

'Our defences—'

'Could never withstand a combined onslaught by France and Spain. King Francis and Emperor Charles have quarrelled and the threat's over for now, but things could change again.' He took the miniature and laid it on top of the Bible. 'Do you still paint, Matthew, for a pastime?'

I looked at him, puzzled by his change of tack. 'Not for some time, my lord.'

'Give me your opinion of this portrait.'

I studied it. The woman was young, with attractive if vacuous features. The image was so clear you could imagine you were looking through a window at her. From the jewels set in her elaborate hood and in the collar of her high-cut dress she was someone of wealth.

'This is beautiful,' I said. 'It could almost be by Holbein.'

'It *is* by Holbein. It is the Lady Anne of Cleves, now our queen. I kept it when the king threw it in my face.' He shook his head. 'I thought I could shore up our defences and our reformed faith at the same time by marrying the king to the daughter of a German duke.' He gave a short, bitter laugh. 'I spent two years after Queen Jane died trying to find a foreign princess for him. It wasn't easy. He has a certain reputation.'

He was interrupted by a gentle cough. Barak was looking at his master anxiously.

'Jack warns me I am going too far. But you've given your oath, haven't you, Matthew, to keep your mouth *tight shut*?' His hard brown eyes bored into mine as he emphasized the words.

'Yes, my lord.' I felt sweat forming on my brow.

'Eventually the Duke of Cleves agreed we could have one of his daughters. The king wanted to see the Lady Anne before agreeing to marry her, but the Germans took that as an affront. So I sent Master Holbein to make a picture. After all, his genius is to make exact representations, is it not?'

'No one in Europe does that better.' I hesitated. 'And yet—'

'Yet what is an *exact* representation, eh, Matthew? We all look different in different lights, can never be caught completely in one glance. I told Holbein to paint her in the best light. And he did. That was another mistake. Can you see?'

I thought a moment. 'It is full face—'

'Not till you see her in profile do you realize how long her nose is. Nor does it show her high body odour, nor how she didn't speak a word of English.' His shoulders slumped. 'When she landed at Rochester in January the king disliked her on sight. And now the Duke of Norfolk's dangled his niece before the king, schooled her to catch his fancy. Catherine Howard is pretty, not yet seventeen, and he's caught. He drools over her like an old dog over a fine joint of meat and blames me for saddling him with the Cleves mare. But if he marries Norfolk's niece, the Howards will have me dead and England back under Rome.'

'Then all that's happened these ten years,' I said slowly, 'all the suffering and death, it would have been for nothing.'

'Worse than nothing, there'll be a cull of reformers that would make Thomas More's inquisitions seem mild.' He clenched his big fists, then got up and walked over to the window, staring out over the lawn. 'I'm doing all I can to discredit them, find papist plots. I've had Lord Lisle arrested, and Bishop Sampson; he's in the Tower, I had him shown the rack. But I can find nothing – nothing.' He turned and faced me. 'Then I told the king about Greek Fire. He can't wait for the demonstration; he loves weapons of war, and warships above all. He sees us making England's navy the greatest on the seas, clearing the French from the south coast. He's my friend again.' Cromwell clenched his fists. 'A foreign power would pay much for that formula. I'm setting extra spies in the ambassadors' houses, all the ports are being watched. Matthew, I must have that formula back safe before the demonstration. Today is the twenty-ninth of May. We have only twelve full days.'

Then, to my surprise, I felt an alien emotion towards Thomas Cromwell: I felt sorry for him. But I reminded myself that a creature at bay is at its most dangerous.

He sat up, slipping the miniature into the pocket of his robe. 'Michael Gristwood had to use three intermediaries to get to me. They are the only others who know about Greek Fire. Two of them are lawyers, men of Lincoln's Inn that you know. The first was Stephen Bealknap—'

'Not Bealknap. Dear God, he's the last one any man should trust. And they'd had a falling out.'

'So I hear. They must have mended it.'

'I've a case on against Bealknap.'

Cromwell nodded. 'Will you win?'

'Ay, if there's any justice.'

He grunted. 'Talk to him, find if he told anyone else. I doubt he did, for I told Gristwood to order him from me to sew up his mouth.'

'Bealknap has a care for his safety. But he's a greedy rogue.'

'Find out.' He paused. 'When Gristwood told Bealknap about Greek Fire, he gave thought as to who might have access to me. He went to Gabriel Marchamount.'

'Did he? They had some dealings in the past, I know, but Bealknap was too shady for Marchamount's liking.'

'Marchamount moves in semi-papist circles. That worries me. Question him too. Threaten him or flatter him or offer him gold, I don't care so long as you loosen his tongue.'

'I'll try, my lord. And the third—'

'Marchamount took the story to a mutual acquaintance of ours. Lady Bryanston.'

My eyes widened in surprise. 'I met her only a few days ago. She invited me to dinner.'

'Yes, I dropped your name at her table last week, when I was thinking of employing you to get the formula from Gristwood. That is good, you must go. Talk to her too.'

I reflected a moment. 'I shall, my lord. But if I am to get to the root of this matter—'

'Yes?'

'I need to know more about Greek Fire. Retrace the steps from its discovery to the demonstrations you held.'

'If you think fit. But remember, time presses. Barak here can tell you all about the demonstrations, he can take you out to Deptford to see where they took place.'

'And I could talk to the monastery librarian. Perhaps visit St Bartholomew's to see where the stuff was found.'

He smiled coldly. 'You don't believe in Greek Fire yet, do you? You will. As for Bernard Kytchyn, Brother Bernard the librarian as he used to be, I've been trying to trace him since Lady Honor first came to me. To make sure he kept his mouth shut too. But like half these ex-monks he's disappeared without trace.'

'Perhaps I could try the Court of Augmentations; he must have arrangements to collect his pension.'

Cromwell nodded. 'That's Richard Rich's territory. But you could say it was in connection with a case.' He looked at me sharply. 'I don't want Rich getting a whiff of this. I raised him to the king's council, but he knows about the plots against me and will change sides in a moment to protect himself. If he went to the king and said I'd lost Greek Fire—' He raised his eyebrows.

'I would like to talk to Goodwife Gristwood again,' I said. 'I had a feeling she was keeping something back.'

'Good, good.'

'And finally, there is a man of learning I would like to consult. An apothecary.'

He frowned. 'Not that black monk from Scarnsea?'

'He is a learned man. I would only like to ask him, if need be, for advice about alchemy. I would not wish to involve him further than necessary.'

'So long as he is not told of Greek Fire. There were rumours of its rediscovery three hundred years ago and the Lateran Council banned its use. They said it was too dangerous. An ex-monk might feel himself bound by that. Or might want to give it to France or Spain, where the monkish brethren still flourish.'

'He would not do that. But I do not wish to place him in danger.'

Cromwell smiled suddenly. 'I see this matter intrigues you, Matthew.'

'I will bend my mind to it.'

He nodded. 'Come to me if you need anything. But time is all. You must move fast. You'll have Jack to help you. I'm setting him to work with you.'

I stared at Barak. What I felt must have shown in my face, for he smiled sarcastically.

'I work alone these days,' I said.

'You need help with this. Jack will lodge with you. You'll get used to his rough ways.'

I had already learned Barak did not trust me. It occurred to me that perhaps Cromwell did not either, not wholly, and was setting Barak to keep an eye on me.

I hesitated. 'My lord,' I ventured, 'I must also give some time to Mistress Wentworth's case.'

He shrugged. 'Very well. And Jack will help you with that. But this business comes first.' He fixed me with those hard brown eyes. 'If you fail, all those associated with me will be at risk. Your lives could be at stake too.'

He rang a little bell and Grey stepped in from an inner room. He looked worried.

'Grey's been told. Keep me informed of progress every day. Any news, anything you want, send it via Grey. No one else.'

I nodded.

'I can't trust anyone now,' he growled. 'Not the people I raised to the council, not even my own staff, whom Norfolk pays to spy on me. But Grey's been with me since I was a nobody, haven't you, Edwin?'

'Ay, my lord.' He hesitated. 'Is Master Barak to be involved in this too?'

'He is.'

Grey pursed his lips. Cromwell looked at him.

'Matthew can do anything that requires diplomacy.'

'That – er – might be best.'

'Jack can deal with anything that requires a strong hand, eh?'

I glanced at Barak. He was studying his master's face. One again I caught that look of concern, and I realized that he feared deeply for Cromwell. And perhaps for his own fate too.

# Chapter Nine

WHEN WE LEFT THE ROOM Barak told me he had things to collect. I went outside, fetched Chancery and led him into the front yard. From a little distance a murmuring was audible, and I heard a shout of 'Don't shove there!' The doles were being distributed.

My mind was in a whirl. Cromwell and reform about to fall? I remembered Godfrey's distress a few days ago, the mutterings everywhere about the queen. Though my faith had reached a low ebb, I felt a clutch of dread at the thought of the papists back in charge, the bloodshed and return to superstition that must follow.

I began walking distractedly about the yard. Now I was saddled with this churl Barak. What was he doing? 'A pox on it all!' I burst out aloud.

'Ho there, what's this?' I whirled round to see Barak grinning at me. I reddened with embarrassment.

'Don't worry,' he said. 'Things affect me like that sometimes. But I've a choleric temperament. His lordship said you were a man of melancholy humour, who keeps his feelings to himself.'

'Usually I do,' I said curtly. I saw that Barak carried a big leather satchel slung over his shoulder. He inclined his head to it. 'The papers from the abbey and some material my master has gathered about Greek Fire.'

He fetched the black mare and we rode out again. 'I'm starving hungry,' he said conversationally. 'Does your housekeeper keep a good table?'

'Good plain fare,' I replied shortly.

'Will you see the girl's uncle soon?'

'I'll send him a note when I get back.'

'His lordship has saved her the press,' he said. 'It's a nasty death.'

'Twelve days. We don't have long, either for Elizabeth or this other business.'

'It's all a fog to me.' Barak shook his head. 'You're right to question Mother Gristwood again.'

'Mother? She's childless.'

'Is she? Not surprised. I wouldn't want to tup her. Nasty old stoat.'

'I don't know why you dislike her so, but that's no basis for suspicion.' I spoke shortly. Barak grunted. I turned and looked at him. 'Your master seems very concerned Sir Richard Rich should not be involved.'

'If he learned about Greek Fire and its loss he'd use it against the earl. My master raised Rich up, as he said, but he's a man who'd betray anyone for his own advantage. You know his reputation.'

'Yes. He founded his career by perjuring himself at Thomas More's trial. Many say that was at your master's bidding.'

Barak shrugged. We rode on in silence for a while, up towards Ely Place. Then Barak drew his horse in close. 'Don't look round,' he said quietly, 'but we're being followed.'

I looked at him in surprise. 'Are you sure?'

'I think so. I've taken a quick look back once or twice and the same man's been there. Odd-looking arsehole. Here, turn in by St Andrew's Church.'

He led the way through the gate, behind the high wall enclosing the church, and jumped quickly down from his horse. I dismounted more slowly. 'Hurry now,' he said impatiently, leading the mare behind the wall. I joined him where he stood peering round the gateway.

'See,' he breathed, 'here he comes. Don't stick your head out too far.'

There were plenty of pedestrians around and a few carts, but the only rider was a man on a white colt. He was about Barak's age, tall and thin, with a thatch of untidy brown hair. His pale face had a scholarly look, though it was pitted as an old cheese with the scars of smallpox. As we watched the man halted, shading his eyes against the sun as he looked up the road to Holborn Bar. Barak pulled me back. 'He's missed us. He'll be looking round in a moment. What a face, he looks as if he's just been dug up.' I frowned at his presumption in grabbing at me, but he only smiled back cheerily, pleased to have bested the white-faced man.

'Come on, we'll lead the horses round the church and go back by Shoe Lane.' He took the mare's reins. I followed him on the path through the churchyard.

'Who was that?' I asked as we halted on the far side of the church – somewhat breathlessly, for he had led a brisk pace.

'Don't know. He must have been following us since we left his lordship's house. There's not many would have the nerve to set watch there.' He heaved himself deftly into the saddle, and I lifted myself onto Chancery's back more slowly; after my day of riding hither and thither my back was sore. Barak looked at me curiously.

'You all right?'

'Yes,' I snapped, settling myself in the saddle.

He shrugged. 'Well just ask, any time, if you want a hand. It's nothing to me you're a hunchback, I'm not superstitious.' I stared after him, speechless, as he turned and led the way into Shoe Lane, whistling tunelessly.

As we rode on to Chancery Lane I was too offended by his insolence to speak, but then I thought I should find out what I could about the wretched man. 'That's twice I've been watched this last week,' I said. 'By that man and before by you.'

'Ay,' Barak answered cheerfully. 'His lordship set me to see what sort of case you were in, whether you might stand up to this job. I told him you had a determined look about you.'

'Did you? And have you worked for the earl a long time?'

'Oh, ay. My father came from Putney, where the earl's father kept his tavern. When he died I was asked to enter Lord Cromwell's service. I had my own contacts round London then, doing this and that' – he raised an eyebrow and gave that cynical smile again – 'and he's found me useful enough.'

'What did your father do?'

'He was a gong-screwer, cleaned out people's cesspits. Silly old arsehole, he fell into one of the pits he was digging out and drowned.' Despite the lightness of his tone a brief shadow passed across his face.

'I am sorry.'

'I've no family now,' Barak said cheerfully. 'Free of all ties. What about you?'

'My father is still alive. He has a farm in Lichfield, in the Midlands.' My conscience pricked me. He was getting old, but I had not been back to see him in a year.

'Son of carrot crunchers, eh? Where did you get your education? Do they have schools up there?'

'They do. I went to Lichfield cathedral school.'

'I've an education too,' Barak replied. 'Know some Latin.'

'Oh?'

'I went to St Paul's school, got a scholarship for a clever lad, but I had to fend for myself after my father died.' Again that brief shadow of sadness, or was it anger? He tapped his satchel. 'Those Latin papers my master gave me for you, I can read them. Well, just about.'

As we turned in at my gate Barak studied my house; I could see he was impressed by the mullioned windows and tall chimneys. He turned to me, raising that eyebrow again. 'Fine place.'

'Now we are here,' I said, 'we had better have our story clear. I suggest we tell my servants you are the agent of a client and are helping me on a case.'

He nodded. 'All right. What servants have you?'

'My housekeeper, Joan Woode, and a boy.' I gave him a fixed stare. 'You should also look to how you address me. Given our respective stations, "sir" would be appropriate; "Master Shardlake" would at least be civil. All the way here it has been "you" as though I were your brother or your dog. That will not do.'

'Right you are.' He grinned cheekily. 'Need a hand down, sir?'

'I can manage.'

As we dismounted, the boy Simon appeared from behind the house. He stared at Barak's mare in admiration.

'That's Sukey,' Barak told him. 'Look after her well and there'll be something for you.' He winked. 'She likes a carrot now and then.'

'Yes, sir.' Simon bowed and led the horses away. Barak watched him go.

'Shouldn't he have shoes? He'll be cutting his feet on ruts and stones this dry weather.'

'He won't wear them. Joan and I have tried.'

Barak nodded. 'Ay, shoes are uncomfortable at first. They rub on your calluses.'

Joan appeared in the doorway. She gave Barak a look of surprise. 'Good afternoon, sir. May I ask how it went at the court?'

'We've got twelve days' grace for Elizabeth,' I said. 'Joan, this is Master Jack. He will be staying with us a short while, to help me with a new matter on behalf of his master. Could you make a room ready for him?'

'Yes, sir.'

Barak bowed and gave her a smile, as charming as his earlier ones had been mocking. 'Master Shardlake did not tell me his housekeeper was so attractive.'

Joan's plump face reddened and she pushed some greying hairs under her cap. 'Oh, please, sir—'

I stared, surprised my sensible housekeeper should fall for such nonsense, but she was still red-faced as she led Barak in. I supposed women would find him good-looking if they were susceptible to rough charm. She led him upstairs. 'The room hasn't been slept in for a while, sir,' she said, 'but it's clean.'

I went into my parlour. Joan had opened the window and the

tapestry on the wall showing the story of Joseph and his brothers stirred in the warm breeze. There was new rush matting on the floor, giving off the harsh tang of the wormwood Joan put on it to discourage fleas.

I remembered I must write to Joseph arranging to meet. I climbed the stairs to my study. As I passed Barak's room I heard my housekeeper clucking like an old hen about the state of the blankets. That room, I remembered, had once belonged to my former assistant, Mark. I shook my head in puzzlement at how the wheel of fortune turned.

✝

JOAN PREPARED an early supper. It was a fish day so we had trout and afterwards a bowl of strawberries. The good weather that spring had brought them on early. Barak joined me at table, and I said grace, though I no longer did that when I was alone. 'For the food the Lord has provided, let us be thankful. Amen.' Barak closed his eyes and bowed his head, raising it as soon as I had finished intoning. He tucked happily into his fish, lifting his food to his mouth with his knife in an ill-bred way. I wondered what his religious views were, if any.

He interrupted my train of thought. 'I'll give you those books and papers later,' he said. 'By Jesu, they're strange reading.'

I nodded. 'And I should consider how to proceed.' It was time to try and stamp my authority on the matter. 'Let me get it right. The first person involved in point of time was the friar, the librarian.' I ticked names off on my fingers. 'Then the Gristwoods went to Bealknap and he went to Marchamount. Marchamount told Lady Honor, who told Cromwell. Three of them, then. We can discount the friar as the moving force behind this.'

'Why?'

'Because someone hired two ruthless rogues to kill the Gristwoods. I can't see Lady Honor or either of the lawyers charging in there with an axe, can you? But any of those three could have afforded to hire killers, though it would cost much more than a pensioned-off friar could raise. I still want to talk to him – he saw the stuff discovered. I'll see Bealknap and Marchamount tomorrow at Lincoln's Inn; there's a lunch in hall. For the Duke of Norfolk,' I added.

He screwed up his face in distaste. 'That arsehole. How he hates my master.'

'I know. We can use tomorrow morning to go to the jetty where you saw that ship burned up, and I'll try to see Joseph then too. We can also go to Augmentations – they're so busy these days they keep open on Sundays. I can miss church for once. What about you?'

'My parish in Cheapside is so full of people coming and going the vicar scarce keeps note of who's there or not.'

Pleased at the brisk way I had formulated my plan of action, I gave Barak a satirical half-smile to match his own. 'You don't feel the need to humble yourself before God then, ask forgiveness of your sins?'

He raised his eyebrows. 'I serve the king's vicar-general and the king is God's anointed representative on earth. If I am on his business, how can I be doing other than God's will?'

'Do you really believe that?'

He gave his mocking grin 'About as much as you do.'

I took some strawberries and passed the bowl to Barak. He spooned half the dish onto his plate and added cream. 'Then there is Lady Honor,' I continued.

He nodded. 'She usually has these sugar banquets of hers on a Tuesday. If you haven't heard by Monday morning I'll ask his lordship to give her a nudge.'

I looked at him levelly. 'Doing what you can do to assist, eh?'

'Ay.'

'And is that what you are? My assistant?'

'Assist and facilitate,' he replied briskly. 'That's what his lordship asked me to do. I know what I'm about. Don't mind that fussy old arsehole Grey; he doesn't like my rough ways. He thinks he knows my master's business better than my master, but he doesn't. Sniffling old pen gent.'

I would not be diverted. 'You started as my watcher.'

He changed the subject. 'That Wentworth case — there's more to it than meets the eye, if you ask me. That girl in court, y'know what she reminded me of? John Lambert's burning. Remember that?'

I remembered only too well. Lambert was the first Protestant preacher to go too far for the king. Eighteen months earlier he had been tried for the heresy of denying transubstantiation, before the king himself as head of the Church, judge and inquisitor, dressed in the white robes of theological purity. It had been the first major reversal for reform. 'That was a cruel burning,' I said, looking at him sharply.

'Were you there?'

'No. I avoid these spectacles.'

'My master likes his people to go, show loyalty to the king.'

'I remember. He made me go to Anne Boleyn's execution.' I closed my eyes for a moment against that memory.

'It was a slow burning, the fire fairly sweated the blood out of him.'

I was relieved to see a look of distaste cross Barak's face. Burning was a terrible death, and in those days of accusation and counter-accusation it was the one everyone feared. I shuddered, passing my hand across my brow. It felt red and sore, I had a touch of the sun.

Barak leaned his elbows on the table. 'The way Lambert walked to the stake with head bowed, refusing to answer the taunts of the crowd, that was what reminded me of the girl. His demeanour. Later, of course, he was screaming.'

'You think Elizabeth seemed like a martyr, then?'

Barak nodded. 'Ay, a martyr. That's the word.'

'But for what?'

He shrugged. 'Who can say? But you're right to talk to the family; I'll warrant the answer's there.'

The idea of Elizabeth's manner as martyrlike had not occurred to me, but it rang true. I looked again at Barak. Whatever else he was, he was no fool. 'I've sent Simon with a note asking Joseph to call here tomorrow at twelve.' I got up. 'We can go to the jetty first thing, we should start early. Where is it exactly?'

'Downriver, out beyond Deptford.'

'And now I should look at these papers of yours. Could you bring them to me?'

'Ay.' As he got up he nodded. 'You're getting to grips with the matter, I see. Planning everything out. My master said you were like that, didn't let go once you were started.'

✝

THE SUN WAS BEGINNING to set as I took Barak's satchel out into the garden. I had had much work done there these last two years and often sat outside enjoying its calm and fine scents. Its design was simple; squares of flower beds divided by trellised paths shaded by climbing roses. No knot gardens with complex designs in the form of puzzles for me; there were puzzles in my work and my garden was a place of quiet order. Once I had thought reform might similarly order the world, but that hope was long gone. More recently I had hoped that the peace of my garden might be a foretaste of a quiet life away from London, but that too now seemed very far off. I sat on a bench, glad simply to be alone at last, and opened the satchel.

I sat reading for two hours as the sun sank gradually and the first moths appeared, flickering towards the candles Simon lit in the house. I turned first to the papers Michael Gristwood had brought from the monastery. There were four or five illustrated manuscripts written by old monastic writers, giving vivid descriptions of the use of Greek Fire. Sometimes they called it Flying Fire, sometimes the devil's tears, fire from the dragon's mouth, Dark Fire: I puzzled over that last name. How could fire be dark? An odd image came into my head of black flames rising from black coals. It was absurd.

There was a page in Greek torn from the biography of the Byzantine emperor Alexios I who reigned four hundred years ago.

Each of the Byzantine galleys was fitted in the prow with a tube ending with the head of a lion made of brass, and gilded, frightful to behold, through the open mouth of which it was arranged that fire should be projected by the soldiers through a flexible apparatus. The Pisans fled, having no previous experience of this device and wondering that fire, which usually burns upwards, could be so directed downward or towards either side according to the will of the engineer who discharges it.

I laid down the paper. What happened to the apparatus? I wondered. Had that been taken from Wolf's Lane too? If it was metal it would be heavy. Had the killers brought a cart there? I turned to another account, of a giant Arab fleet sent to invade Constantinople and utterly destroyed by flying fire in AD 678, fire that burned even on the very surface of the sea. I stared out over the lawn. Fire that burned downwards, that could burn on water itself? I knew nothing about the mysteries of alchemy, but surely such things were impossible?

I turned next to the only paper in the collection in English. It was written in a round, clumsy hand.

*I, Alan St John, late soldier of the Emperor Constantine Palaiologos of Byzantium, do make this testament in the hospital of St Bartholomew's in Smithfield, this eleventh day of March 1454.*

The year after Constantinople fell to the Turks, I remembered.

*I am told I am like to die and have confessed my sins, for I followed the rough ways of a soldier of fortune all my life. The friars of this blessed place have treated and comforted me these last months since I returned from the fall of Constantinople sore wounded, which wounds grow infected again. The friars' care is proof of the love of God, and to them I leave my papers, that tell of the old secret of Greek Fire the Byzantines knew, that was passed down secretly from emperor to emperor and lost at last, together with the last barrel of distilled Greek Fire itself, that I brought back from the East. The secret was found by a librarian of Constantinople as he cleared the library to rescue the books from the approaching Turks, and he gave the papers and the barrel into my care before we fled the city in the ships the Venetians sent. I do not understand the Greek and Latin and meant to consult with alchemists*

*in England, but then my illness disabled me. May God forgive me: I*
*meant to make a profit from this thing, but no money can aid me now.*
*The friars say it is God's will, for this is a terrible secret that could*
*bring much ruin and bloodshed to unhappy humanity. It is no surprise*
*they called the principal element in Greek Fire Dark Fire. I leave*
*it all to the friars to do with as they will, for they are close to the*
*Grace of God.*

I put it down. So the friars had hidden the papers, and the barrel,
away, realizing the potential for danger and destruction they had in
their hands: not knowing that ninety years later King Henry and
Cromwell would come and clear them all out. As I sat there, I had a
vision of the fall of Constantinople, that great tragedy of our age;
soldiers and officials and citizens fleeing the doomed city, making for
the dock and the boats to Venice to the sound of booming artillery
and the roars of the Turks outside.

I picked the paper up again, and sniffed it. It had a faint scent,
pleasant and musky. I turned to the remaining papers, the same odour
lingered on some of the others. I frowned; the smell was nothing like
incense: surely it had not come from a monastery cellar. I had never
smelt anything like it before. I laid the papers down again, then started
as a moth flew into my face. The sun was touching the top of the trees
over in Lincoln's Inn Fields, and cows were lowing in the distance. I
turned to the books.

These were mostly Latin and Greek works that told stories of
Greek Fire. I read old Athenian legends of magic garments that could
burst into fire when worn, read Pliny's description of pools by the
Euphrates that discharged inflammable mud. It was clear the writers
were merely repeating stories, with no real idea of how Greek Fire was
actually made. There were also a couple of alchemical works, which
discussed the matter in terms of the philosopher's stone, the precepts of
Hermes Trismegistus, and analogies between metals, stars and living
things. Like the book I had taken from Sepultus's workshop, I found
them incomprehensible.

I turned back finally to the old parchment Cromwell had shown me in his room, the picture of the ship spouting Greek Fire, with the top part torn off. I ran my fingers along the torn edge. That act had cost Michael Gristwood his life.

'Better the monks had destroyed everything,' I whispered aloud.

I heard footsteps and looked up to see Barak approaching. He glanced over the flower beds.

'This is a fine-smelling place.' He nodded at the documents surrounding me. 'Well,' he said, 'what d'you make of it all?'

'Not much. For all this great jangle of words no one seems to have any clue what Greek Fire really was. As for the alchemical works, they are incomprehensible riddles and obscure words.'

Barak grinned. 'I tried to read a law book once, it made me feel like that.'

'Guy may be able to make some sense of them.'

'That old black monk of yours? He's well known round where I lodge. By God, he's a strange-looking one.'

'He's a very knowledgeable man.'

'Ay, so they say round the Old Barge.'

'That is where you live?' I remembered those shutters closing.

'Ay, it's not a fine place like this but it's in the middle of London – useful as my business takes me all over the City.' He sat beside me and gave me a sharp look. 'You're to say as little as possible to the black monk, remember.'

'I'll ask him to elucidate these alchemy books, say it's something I've to look into for a client. He won't press me more than that, he knows I have to keep clients' confidences.'

'Guy Malton, the black apothecary calls himself,' Barak said thoughtfully. 'I'll wager that's not the name he was born with.'

'No, he was born Mohammed Elakbar; his parents converted to Christianity after the fall of Granada. Your own name's unusual, come to that. Barak, it is like Baruch, one of the Old Testament names reformers are giving their children now. But you're too old for that.'

He laughed and stretched long legs in front of him. 'You're a scholar, aren't you? My father's family was descended from Jews who converted to Christianity in old times. Before they were all kicked out of England. I think of it whenever I have to visit my master at the Domus. So maybe it was Baruch once. I've a funny little gold box my father left me that he said had been passed down from those days. It was all he had to leave me, poor old arsehole.' Again that sombre look passed quickly across his face. He shrugged. 'Anything else those old papers reveal?'

'No. Except I think the monks hid the formula and the barrel for fear of the destruction Greek Fire could cause.' I looked at him. 'They were right. The devastation such a weapon could wreak would be terrible.'

He returned my look. 'But if it could save England from invasion. Surely anything is worth that.'

I did not reply. 'Tell me what it was like. At the demonstration.'

'I will, but tomorrow at the wharf. I came to tell you I'm going out. I have to fetch some clothes from the Old Barge. And I am going to ask around the taverns, see if any of my contacts know of that pock-faced man. Then afterwards I've a girl to see, so I'll be back late. Got a key?'

I looked at him disapprovingly. 'Ask Joan for hers. We must start very early tomorrow.'

He smiled at my look. 'Don't worry, you won't find me wanting in diligence.'

'I hope not.'

'Nor will the girl.' He gave me a lubricious wink and turned away.

# Chapter Ten

THAT NIGHT I COULD NOT SLEEP, from the heat and from the tangle of images that chased each other through my mind: Elizabeth in her cell, Cromwell's drawn, anxious look, that pair of dreadful corpses. Far into the night I heard Barak come in, footsteps creeping quietly upstairs to his room. I rose and knelt by the bed in the sticky darkness to pray for rest and guidance on the morrow. I was praying less and less these days, feeling often that my words did not ascend to God but merely dissolved inside my head like smoke, but when I returned to bed I fell at once into slumber and woke with a start to the light of early morning, a warm breeze wafting through the open window and Joan calling me down to breakfast.

Despite his night of rousting, Barak seemed fresh as a new pin, eager to be off. He told me he had been unable to trace the man who had followed us, but had set enquiries in train among his acquaintances. Straight after breakfast we walked down to catch a boat at Temple Stairs. It was not yet seven; I was seldom abroad at such an hour on a Sunday and it was strange to see everywhere deserted. The river, too, was quiet, the wherrymen waiting idly at the stairs pleased to have our business. The tide was at low ebb and we had to walk to the boat across a wooden catwalk laid over the thick, rubbish-strewn mud. I turned my head from the smell given off by the bloated carcass of a dead donkey. I was glad to step into the boat. The wherryman steered us into the middle of the river.

'D'you want to shoot the rapids under London Bridge?' he asked. 'It'll be an extra half-groat.' He was an ill-favoured young fellow with the scar of some old fight running down his face; the Thames boatmen were ever a battlesome crew. I hesitated, but Barak nodded. 'Ay, the water's at its lowest, there won't be much pull under the piers.'

I gripped the sides of the boat as the great bridge, crowded with houses, loomed up, but the wherryman steered us deftly through and we floated on downriver past Billingsgate, where the big seagoing ships lay docked, past the looming mass of the Tower of London. Then we passed the new naval docks at Deptford, and I stared in wonder at the king's great warship *Mary Rose*, in for repair, her enormous masts and rigging soaring high as steeples above the surrounding buildings.

Beyond Deptford signs of habitation ended and the river broadened, the far bank growing distant to the view. Wastes of marsh and reeds crowded to the water's edge. The occasional wharves we passed were mostly abandoned, for shipworking was concentrated upriver now.

'That's it,' Barak said at length, leaning over the side. A little way off I saw a crumbling jetty rising on wooden piers. Behind, a space of weed-strewn earth cleared from the surrounding reed beds fronted a large, tumbledown wooden shed.

'I expected something larger,' I said.

'My master chose it because it was out of the way.'

The wherryman guided the little boat to the jetty, grasping at a ladder fixed to the end. Barak climbed nimbly up. I followed more carefully.

'Come back for us in an hour,' Barak told the boatman, passing him his fare. He nodded and cast off, leaving us alone. I looked round. Everything was silent and still, the surrounding reeds whisper-ing in the light breeze, richly coloured butterflies flitting among them.

'I'll just check the shed,' Barak said, 'in case some vagabond has made a home there.'

As he went to peer through the warped boards of the shed, something dangling from a ring in an iron bollard caught my eye. A thick, knotted hemp rope, such as might be used to tie up a boat, hung over the end of the jetty. I drew it up. There were only about two feet of rope; the end was charred. It had been burnt right through.

Barak rejoined me. 'All clear.' He passed me a leathern bottle. 'A drink?'

'Thank you.' I unstoppered it and took a draught of small beer. Barak nodded at the rope which I still held. 'That's all that's left of the boat I tied up there.'

'Tell me,' I said quietly.

He led me into a patch of shade cast by the shed. He looked out over the river for a moment, then took another draught of beer and began his tale. He told the story with more fluency than I would have expected, a sense of wonder overcoming his usual brashness.

'Back in March my master told me to buy an old crayer, in my own name, and have it brought down here. I found one, a big thirty-foot tub, and had it rowed down and moored here.'

'I travelled from Sussex to London in a crayer once.'

'You know what they're like then. Long, heavy barges. This one was a big solid thing, with sail and oars, that used to carry coal down the coast from Newcastle. *Bonaventure*, she was called.' He shook his head. 'She was to have an adventure all right.

'Like I said, my master chose this place because it was out of the way. He asked me to be here at first light on a March morning, when hopefully there wouldn't be any river traffic, and wait for him. He told me I might see something strange. "More likely, though," he said, "you won't."

'Anyway, I rode down here before dawn, and damned difficult it was, following the trackways through these marshes in the dark. The old crayer was where I'd moored her, for she wasn't worth anyone stealing. I tied Sukey up and walked about, stamping my feet to keep warm as the sun came up. The strange noises those river birds make as the day starts, they made me jump a few times.

'Then I heard horses' hooves, and a creaking sound, and through the reeds I saw my master approaching on horseback. It was strange seeing him out there. He had a lowering look on him, kept glaring at the two men accompanying him. They were on horseback and one of the horses was pulling a cart with something heavy hidden under a pile of sacking.

'They got to the wharf at last and dismounted. I got a good look at the Gristwoods for the first time. I thought them poor folk, God rest them.'

I nodded. 'Michael was an unqualified attorney. The sort who deals with small cases, pushes business for the barristers.'

'Ay, I know that sort,' Barak said with a sudden sharpness that made me glance at him. 'They were both small, skinny men, kept glancing at my master with apprehensive looks. I could see he thought all this beneath his dignity; I thought if they didn't satisfy him they'd smart for it. One of the brothers wore a skullcap and a long alchemist's robe, the complete paraphernalia, for all that it was spattered with mud from his trip through the marshes. My master had on a simple black cloak, as he does when he travels alone. He introduced me to the Gristwoods and the pair doffed their caps and scraped to me like I was an earl.' He laughed. 'I thought they were the crookedest-looking pair of arseholes I'd ever seen.

'My master ordered me to tie the horses to posts by the shed, where I'd put Sukey. When I got back, the brothers were unloading their cart. I'd never seen such a pile of strange stuff: a long thin brass pipe and a big metal handpump like some of the conduits have. The earl came over and said quietly, "Look over that boat with me, Jack. I want to be sure there's no trickery." I dared to ask him what it was all about, and he looked dubiously to where the brothers were unloading an iron tank of some sort; by the way they were sweating and grunting there was something heavy inside. He told me then that Sepultus was an alchemist and had promised to show us a great wonder with that apparatus. He raised an eyebrow, then walked over to the boat.

'I helped him in and he looked the ship over from end to end. We even went down to the hold and walked about, coughing for there was a little coal dust. He said to look for trickery, anything strange.

But there was nothing; it was just the empty old tub I'd bought cheap from the ship merchant.

'When we got back on deck the brothers had set up their apparatus on the jetty. The metal tank had been attached to the pump at one end and to the pipe at the other. I caught a whiff of something from the tank. It was like nothing I'd ever smelt before, a harsh tang that seemed to go right up your nostrils into your skull.'

'Tell me more about how the apparatus looked.'

'The pipe was about twelve feet long, and hollow, like a gun barrel. Under the end they'd fixed a wick, a pot of string greased with candle wax. The other end was fixed to the tank, as I said.'

'How big was the tank? Enough to hold, say, a large barrelful of liquid?'

He frowned. 'Yes. Though I don't know how full it was.'

'No. I'm sorry, go on.'

'When my master and I got back on land we saw they'd heaved the tank onto a big iron tripod. To my surprise, they were trying to light a fire of sticks underneath it now, fussing about with flints.

'Then Michael Gristwood gave a great shout of excitement. "It's lit!" he cried. "It's lit! Move away, my lord, away from the pipe!" My master looked scandalized at being addressed so familiarly, but went to stand behind the brothers. I went with him, wondering what on earth was to happen.'

Barak paused a moment. He looked out over the water, swirling with little gurgling eddies as the tide swept in again.

'It happened very quickly then. Michael took a twig from the fire and lit the wick, then ran back, and he and Sepultus worked the pump up and down. I saw a movement at the front of the pipe and then a great sheet of yellow flame, a dozen feet long, shot out with a roaring sound, flew through the air and hit the boat amidships. It seemed to twist in the air like a live thing.'

'Like fire from a dragon's mouth.'

He shivered. 'Ay. The wood caught light immediately, the flames seemed to stick to it and devour it like an animal eating its way along a carcass. Some of the flames fell down on the water and by the throat of God I saw *the water burning*. Saw it with my own eyes, a patch of flames leaping up and down on the river. For a minute I was terrified the whole river might burn up, fire leaping all the way to London.

'Then the brothers turned the pipe round at an angle, pumped again, and another long gout of flame, too bright to look at, shot out and hit the stern. It seemed to leap at it like something alive. The boat was burning merrily now. The heat from that flying fire was tremen-dous. I was twenty feet away but my face felt scorched. Another burst of fire, and another, and then the poor old crayer was blazing from end to end. Everywhere birds were clattering up from the marshes and flying off. By Jesu, I was frightened, I'm no godly man but I was praying to Our Lady and all the saints to protect me and if my master allowed rosaries I'd have been fondling the beads till they broke.

'We watched the boat, just a mass of flame now, clouds of thick black smoke rising into the sky. I looked at my master. He wasn't afraid, he just stood watching with his arms folded, a gleam of excitement in his eyes.

'Then I heard the screaming. I think it had been going on for a while but I hadn't noticed. It was the horses, they'd seen those huge gouts of leaping fire and they were terrified. I ran to them and they were kicking and flailing, trying to escape from the posts. I managed to calm them before they did themselves real harm, for I've a way with horses, and thank God there were no more sheets of flame; what was left of the boat was sinking now. When I went back to the jetty it had gone, even the rope holding it had burned away as you can see. My master was talking with the Gristwoods, who were looking pleased with themselves for all that their clothes clung to them with sweat. They began packing up their stuff.' He laughed and shook his head. 'The river was quiet again, the boat had sunk and the fire on the water had gone out, thank Christ. It was like nothing had ever happened: except a thirty-ton crayer had been burned to nothing in moments.' Barak took a deep breath and raised his eyebrows. 'And that's it, that's what I saw with my own eyes. Afterwards, when the

Gristwoods had driven off again, my master told me that what I had seen was called Greek Fire, told me how Michael Gristwood had found the formula at Barty's, and swore me to secrecy.'

I nodded. I walked to the end of the jetty, Barak following. I looked down into the dark, heaving waters.

'Were you at the second demonstration?'

'No. My master commissioned me to find another, larger, ship, an old balinger, and have it taken here, but he attended that one alone. He told me the second ship was destroyed in exactly the same way.' He looked into the river. 'So there's the remains of two of them down there.'

I nodded thoughtfully. 'So to get Greek Fire to work you need that apparatus. Who built it for them, I wonder, and where did they keep it?'

Barak looked at me quizzically. 'You believe in it now that you've heard what I saw?'

'I believe you saw something very extraordinary.'

A merchantman came into view, sailing up the middle of the river, a huge carrack returning home to London from some far corner of the world. Its sails were unfurled to catch the light breeze, the high castellated prow riding the waves proudly. The seamen on deck, seeing us, shouted and waved; probably we were the first Englishmen they had seen in months. As the ship passed up to London, I had a terrible vision of it aflame from end to end, the sailors screaming, no time to escape.

'You know there are many who say the last days of the world are upon us,' I said quietly. 'That soon the world will be destroyed, Christ will return and the Last Judgement will come.'

'Do you believe that?' Barak asked.

'Not until now,' I said. I saw another boat, tiny by comparison, pass the carrack and approach us. 'Here's our boatman, we must get back to London, look for that librarian.'

☨

WE GOT THE WHERRYMAN to take us on to Westminster, for the Court of Augmentations' offices were housed in a room off Westminster Hall. We climbed Westminster Stairs and paused in New Palace Yard to get our breath. The sun was high now; it was another hot day. The water in the fountain was low; I thought of pumps, siphons, tanks.

'So this is where the lawyers come to argue,' Barak said, staring with interest at the high north face of the hall with its enormous stained-glass window.

'Ay, this is where the civil courts sit. Have you never been here?'

'Like most honest people I keep clear of the place.'

He followed me up the steps to the north door. The guard, seeing my lawyer's robe, nodded and we passed inside. In winter the interior of the giant stone building is icy, everyone shivering except for the judges in their furs. Even today it felt chilly. Barak looked up at the giant carved ceiling and the statues of ancient kings by the high windows. He whistled, the sound echoing as every noise did there.

'Bit different from the Old Bailey.'

'Yes.' I looked down the hall, beyond the empty shop counters to the courts behind their low partitions, King's Bench and Common Pleas and Chancery, the benches and tables deserted and silent. Tomorrow the law term would begin and every inch of the place would be thronged. I remembered I was to argue against Bealknap here next week: somehow I would have to find time to prepare. I looked across to a door in a far corner, from behind which a murmur of voices was audible. 'Come on,' I said and led Barak to the Court of Augmentations' office.

It was no surprise that Augmentations had obtained a dispensation to open on a Sunday. Responsible for the sale of hundreds of monastic buildings and for the pensions of the former monks, there was no busier place in the land. Inside there were counters on two sides of the room where clerks dealt with enquiries. A gaggle of anxious women in sober dresses stood arguing with a harassed-looking clerk.

'Our abbess was promised the High Cross,' one of the women

was saying plaintively. 'That she might have it to treasure, sir, a memory of our life.'

The clerk gestured impatiently at a paper. 'It's not mentioned in the surrender deed. Why d'you want it anyway? If you ex-nuns are still meeting together for papist services, that's against the law.'

I led Barak on past a little group of well-dressed men poring over a ground plan which showed the familiar shape of a monastic church and cloisters. 'It's not worth a thousand if we've to bring the building down,' one was saying.

We came to a counter marked 'Pensions'. There was nobody there. I rang a little bell and an elderly clerk appeared from behind a door, looking cross to be disturbed. I told him we wished to trace the address of a former monk. The man began to say that he was busy, we should call back later, but Barak delved in his doublet and produced a seal with Cromwell's coat of arms. He slapped it on the table. The clerk looked at it and at once became servile.

'I'll do anything I can, of course. To help the earl—'

'I'm looking for one Bernard Kytchyn,' I said. 'Former librarian at St Bartholomew's Priory, Smithfield.'

The clerk smiled. 'Ah yes, Barty's — that'll be easy. He'll collect his pension from here.' He opened a drawer and, producing a massive ledger, began leafing through it. After a minute he stabbed at an entry with an inky finger.

'There it is, sirs. Bernard Kytchyn, six pounds and two marks a year. He's listed as chantry priest at St Andrew's Church, Moorgate. It's a wicked scandal, sir, the chantries being allowed to stay open, priests still mumming Latin prayers for the dead day after day. They should bring the chantries down too.' He smiled at us brightly; as we were Cromwell's men he would expect us to agree. I only grunted, however, and turned the ledger round to check the entry.

'Barak,' I said, 'when I go back to Chancery Lane, I suggest you go and find Kytchyn, tell him—'

I broke off, as the door behind the clerk opened. To my astonishment Stephen Bealknap stepped out, a frown on his thin face.

'Master clerk, we had not finished. Sir Richard Rich requires—' He broke off in turn as he saw me. He looked surprised, his eyes meeting mine for a second before angling away.

'Brother Shardlake—'

'Bealknap, I did not know you had an interest in Augmentations pensions.'

He smiled. 'I don't usually. But there . . . there is a corrodian, a pensioner with right of residence, attached to my property at Moorgate. It seems I have taken on responsibility for him too. An interesting legal problem, is it not?'

'Yes.' I turned to the clerk. 'We are finished now. Well, Brother, I shall see you the day after tomorrow.' I bowed to Bealknap. The clerk replaced his book and ushered Bealknap back to his room. The door closed behind them.

I frowned. 'Corrodies are attached to monasteries, not friaries. What's he really doing here?'

'He mentioned Rich.'

'Yes.' I hesitated. 'Could Cromwell have the clerk questioned?'

'That would be difficult, it would mean Sir Richard Rich would get to hear of it.' Barak ran a hand through his thatch of brown hair. 'I've seen that pinch-faced old arsehole before somewhere.'

'Bealknap? Where?'

'I'll have to think. It was a long time ago, but I swear I know him.'

'We must go,' I said. 'Joseph will be waiting for me.'

I had arranged for Simon to bring Chancery and Sukey down to Westminster so that we could ride back from Westminster to Chancery Lane, and he was waiting by one of the buttresses by the east wall, sitting on Chancery's broad back and swinging his newly shod feet. We mounted, leaving him to walk back at his own pace, and set off.

As we passed Charing Cross, I noticed a well-dressed woman on a fine gelding, her face covered from the sun by a vizard. She was attended by three mounted retainers, with two ladies walking behind carrying posies and looking hot. The woman's horse had stopped to piss and the party was waiting till it had finished. As we passed she turned and stared at me. Her vizard, framed by an expensive hood, was a striped cloth mask with eyeholes and the blank, masked stare was oddly disconcerting. Then she lifted the mask and smiled and I recognized Lady Honor. She looked quite cool, though the mask must have been stifling and women's corsetry is an unkind thing in hot weather. She raised a hand in greeting.

'Master Shardlake! We are met again.'

I reined Chancery in. 'Lady Honor. Another hot day.'

'Is it not?' she replied feelingly. 'I am pleased to have met with you. Will you come and dine with me next Tuesday?'

'I should be delighted,' I said.

I was conscious of Barak at my side, his eyes cast down as befitted a servant.

'The House of Glass in Blue Lion Street, anyone will tell you. Be there at five. It's a sugar banquet only, it won't go on late. There will be interesting company.'

'I shall look forward to it.'

'By the way, I hear you are representing Edwin Wentworth's niece.'

I smiled wryly. 'It seems all London knows, my lady.'

'I've met him at Mercers' Company dinners. Not as clever as he thinks he is, though good at making money.'

'Really?'

She laughed. 'Ah, your face went sharp and lawyerly then, sir. I have piqued your interest.'

'I have the girl's life in my hands, Lady Honor.'

'A responsibility.' She grimaced. 'Well, I must get on, I am visiting my late husband's relatives.'

She lowered her vizard and the party moved off. 'A fine-looking piece.' Barak said as we rode on.

'A lady of natural distinction.'

'Bit too pert for me. I like a woman who keeps her place. Rich widows are the devil for pertness.'

'Know many, do you?'

'I might do.'

I laughed. 'She is out of your league, Barak.'

'Out of yours too.'

'I would not be so impertinent as to think otherwise.'

'*She'll* never fall to beggary.'

'The great families don't have the assured places they once held.'

'Whose fault's that?' he said roundly. 'They fought each other in the wars of York and Lancaster till they near wiped each other out. I say we're better off under new men like the earl.'

'He still likes his earldom, Barak. A coat of arms is everyone's dream. Marchamount has made a joke of himself round Lincoln's Inn trying to persuade the College of Heralds he has people of gentle birth in his background.' A thought struck me. 'I wonder if that's why he is cultivating Lady Honor. Marriage to someone of birth—' At the thought I felt an unexpected pang.

'Got his eye on her?' Barak said. 'That could be interesting.' He shook his head. 'This chasing after status among the high-ups, it makes me laugh.'

'If one aims for gentlemanly status one aims for a higher way of life. Better than a lower.'

'I have my own lineage,' he said with a mocking laugh.

'Ah, yes. Your father's trinket.'

'Ay, though I keep quiet about my blood. They say the Jews were great bloodsuckers and gatherers of gold. And killers of children. Come on,' he said abruptly. 'I've to find this Kytchyn fellow.'

'If you find him, ask him to meet with me tomorrow. At St Bartholomew's.'

Barak turned in the saddle. 'At Barty's? But Sir Richard Rich lives there now. My master wants him kept out of this. And your friend Bealknap mentioning his name worries me.'

'I must see where the stuff was found, Barak.'

He raised his eyebrows. 'Very well. But we have to be careful.'

'God's death, d'you think I don't realize that?'

At the bottom of Chancery Lane we parted. As I rode up the lane alone I felt suddenly nervous, remembering how we had been followed yesterday and seeing again those bodies in the Queenhithe house. I was relieved to approach my gate. As I did so I saw Joseph approaching from the other end of the lane. His shoulders were slumped, his face sad and preoccupied, but as he saw me he smiled and raised his hand in greeting. That heartened me; it was the first friendly gesture I had had since the trial.

# Chapter Eleven

A S I REINED IN BESIDE HIM I saw that Joseph looked tired and
hot. Simon had not yet returned, so I bade Joseph go indoors
while I led the horses to the stables.

Returning to the hall, I removed my cap and robe. It was cooler
indoors and I stood a moment, savouring the air on my sweat-coated
face, then went into the parlour. Joseph had taken a seat in my
armchair and he jumped up, embarrassed. I waved a hand.

'Don't worry, Joseph, it's a cursed hot day.' I took a hard chair
opposite him. Despite his tiredness I saw there was an excited gleam
in his eyes, a new look of hope.

'Sir,' he said, 'I have been successful. My brother will see you.'

'Well done.' I poured us some beer from a pot Joan had left on
the table. 'How did you manage it?'

'It wasn't easy. I went to the house; they had to let me in or else
cause a scene in front of the servants. I told Edwin you were uncertain
of Elizabeth's guilt and wanted to talk to the family before deciding
whether you could continue to represent her. Edwin was very hostile
at first, angry at my interference. And I'm no good hand at lying; I
feared I would become confused.'

I smiled. 'No, Joseph, you are too honest for that trade.'

'I don't like it. But for Lizzy's sake – anyway, my mother
persuaded him. That surprised me because she was against the poor
girl most of all, though she's her own granddaughter. But Mother said
if we could convince you it must have been Elizabeth that killed
Ralph, you would leave them alone to grieve. Sir, they'll see us
tomorrow morning at ten. They will all be at home then.'

'Good. Well done, Joseph.'

'I fear I let them believe you have doubts about Lizzy's innocence.' He gave me an imploring look. 'But it was not an unchristian thing, was it, to lie for her sake?'

'Often the world does not allow us to be too pure, I fear.'

'God sets us hard dilemmas.' He shook his head sadly.

I looked at the clock on the mantelpiece. I should have to hurry. 'I am sorry, Joseph, but I must leave you again. I have an engagement at Lincoln's Inn. Meet me at the Walbrook conduit tomorrow, just before ten.'

'I will, sir. You are good to give me your time when you are so busy.'

'Have you eaten? Stay here, my housekeeper will fetch you something.'

'Thank you, sir.'

I bowed quickly and left him. I told Joan to fetch him some food, then hurriedly donned my robe again; it had been washed the day before but already had a City stink. I wanted to catch both Marchamount and Bealknap before the dinner. As I hurried out to the street, I thought: poor honest Joseph, if he knew the nightmare tangle of deceptions Cromwell had involved me in he would flee the house. But no, he would not; while I was his only hope of setting Elizabeth free he would stand fast, like a much-battered rock.

✠

I REFLECTED ON WHAT Barak had told me at the wharf. With my naturally sceptical temperament it was hard for me to believe Greek Fire could be real, and as for 'Sepultus' Gristwood, no class of persons is more associated with trickery than alchemists. Yet I had no doubt Barak had truthfully described what he saw. And he and Cromwell were hardly people to be taken in easily. There were new wonders and terrors every day in this world, which many prophets said was coming to its end; but I could not quite believe in it all yet. It was too fantastical.

And if it *was* real? The Byzantines might have kept the secret so well they ended by losing it, but in this our Europe of spies and religious quarrels England could not keep such a secret for long. It would be stolen sooner or later, and then what? The seas empty of ships, whole navies devoured by fire? I shook my head in troubled perplexity; how bizarre it seemed to me, thinking of such things and all the while trudging through the dust of staid, familiar Chancery Lane. I must put such thoughts from my head, I told myself, concentrate on the task ahead. And after being followed yesterday I had an eye out for my own security. I cast a quick glance round, but the only others in the lane were more robed lawyers riding to the Inn. An acquaintance waved and I returned his salute. With a dark glance at the Domus opposite, I turned under the Lincoln's Inn gate, the guard in his box bowing as I passed.

I went first to my chambers, for I needed to leave a note for Godfrey. I had expected them to be empty but when I entered Skelly was there copying, slouched so low over his quill his nose almost touched the papers. He peered up at me.

'In on a Sunday, John? You should not bend your head so close to the paper, the humours will rush to your brain.'

'It took me so long to rewrite the Beckman conveyance, sir, I got behind. I came in to copy the arbitration agreement for the Salters' Company.'

'Well, this shows application,' I said. I leaned over to have a look, then caught my breath. He had failed to ensure his ink was well mixed and a pale dribble of words ran across the page. 'This is no good.'

He looked up at me tremulously, his eyes red. 'What's wrong with it, sir?'

'The ink is watery.' His miserable stare made me suddenly angry. 'Look, can't you see? This will fade in a year. A legal document is no good unless it be written in thick black ink.'

'I'm sorry, sir.'

My irritation spilled over. 'It'll have to be done again. That's more good paper you've cost me, Skelly. The cost will come from your wages.' I frowned at his anxious face. 'Oh, just start again.'

Godfrey's door opened. 'What's afoot? I thought I heard raised voices.'

'John Skelly would make an angel in the heavenly spheres raise its voice. I didn't think you'd be in, Godfrey. You're not going to the lunch with Norfolk surely?'

He grunted. 'I thought I should see what the papist rogue looked like in the flesh.'

'Now that we are met, may I ask a favour? Come into my room.'
'Certainly.'

I closed the door on Skelly, and bade my friend sit down. 'Godfrey, I have a – a new matter. Something urgent. Together with the Wentworth case it will take much of my time this next fortnight. Can you deal with some of my work? For a share of the fee, of course.'

'I would be happy to. Including the Bealknap hearing?'

'No, I had better keep that. But everything else.'

He studied me carefully. 'You look troubled, Matthew.'

'I hate losing my temper. But between Skelly and this new affair—'

'Something interesting?'

'I can't speak of it. Now – ' I lifted a heap of papers from a table – 'I will show you what cases I have.' I spent half an hour going through my matters with him, relieved that, apart from the Bealknap case next week, I should not have to appear in court for a fortnight.

'I am in your debt again,' I said when we were done. 'Any news of your friend Robert Barnes?'

He sighed heavily. 'Still in the Tower.'

'Barnes is a friend of Archbishop Cranmer's. Surely he'll protect him.'

'I hope so.' He brightened. 'The archbishop is to give the sermons at St Paul's Cross next week now Bishop Sampson is in the Tower.' He clenched his fist, reminding me that for all his mild ways he was fierce in his religion. 'With God's help we *will* prevail over the papist troop.'

'Listen, Godfrey, I'll try to get into chambers when I can. Keep an eye on Skelly, try and get him to produce work that's at least presentable. I have another appointment now, but I will see you at the lunch. Thank you, my friend.'

I went out again, crossing the courtyard to Marchamount's rooms. Over by the Great Hall servants were bustling in and out, getting everything ready for the dinner. The four Inns of Court vied for the patronage of those near to the king and Norfolk's presence was something of a coup, for all that his politics would be unpopular with many members of Lincoln's Inn.

I knocked and entered Marchamount's outer office. It was impressive, books and documents lining the shelves and, even on Sunday, a clerk labouring busily over papers. He looked up enquiringly.

'Is the serjeant in?'

'He's very busy, sir. Has a big case starting in Common Pleas tomorrow.'

'Tell him it is Brother Shardlake, on Lord Cromwell's business.'

His eyes widened at that and he disappeared through a door. A moment later he was back and bowed me through.

Gabriel Marchamount, like many barristers, lived as well as worked in Lincoln's Inn. His receiving room was as opulent as any I had seen. Expensive wallpaper in bright reds and greens lined the walls. Marchamount sat in a high-backed chair that would not have shamed a bishop, behind a wide desk strewn with papers. His broad figure was encased in an expensive yellow doublet with a pea-green belly that emphasized his choleric colour; his thin reddish hair was combed carefully over his pate. A robe edged with fur lay on a cushion nearby together with his white serjeant's coif, the mark of his rank: the highest position a barrister can reach short of a judgeship. A silver goblet of wine stood at his elbow.

Marchamount was known as a man who lived and breathed the

law and loved the status it brought him; since his admission to the Order of the Coif three years before his patrician manner and habits had expanded to the extent that they were the subject of mocking jokes about the Inn. It was said he hoped to rise further, to a judgeship. Though the gossips said his advancement owed much to his cultivation of contacts among the antireform party at the king's court, I knew his intelligence was not to be underrated.

He rose and greeted me with a smile and a small bow. I saw his dark eyes were sharp and wary.

'Brother Shardlake. Are you here for my lunch with the duke?' He smiled with false modesty. I had not realized he had arranged the meal. 'My lunch' was typical of him.

'I might look in.'

'How goes business?'

'Well enough, thank you, Serjeant.'

'Wine, Brother?'

'Thank you, it is a little early for me.'

He sat down again. 'I hear you are retained to advise in the Wentworth case. An unpleasant business. Not much *unguentum auri* there, I'd guess.'

I smiled tightly. 'No. A small fee. In fact, it is another killing I have called to see you about. Michael Gristwood and his brother have been brutally murdered.'

I watched carefully for his reaction, but he only nodded sadly and said, 'Yes, I know. A dreadful business.'

'How did you know, sir?' I asked sharply. 'This has been kept quiet on Lord Cromwell's orders.'

He spread his arms. 'His widow came to see me yesterday. Said you had told her the house was hers, asked for my help in getting it transferred into her name since I knew her husband.' His eyes narrowed. 'Is the Greek Fire formula gone?'

I paused; the words seemed to hang in the stuffy air for a moment. 'Yes, Serjeant. That is why Lord Cromwell wants the matter investigated quickly and secretly. She was quick off the mark,' I added. 'I wonder she didn't go to Bealknap. He was nearer her husband in station.'

'She has no money. Bealknap would turn her away in a second if she couldn't pay him, but she knew I do charitable work some' times.' He gave a self-satisfied smile. 'I've long since stopped doing minor estate work myself, but I know a junior fellow who will help her.'

Yes, I thought, Marchamount was the sort to do charitable work in the hope it would bring him merit with God, in accordance with the old religion's tenets. He would enjoy having the old ways back, too, the rich ceremonial and sonorous Latin.

'Tell the barrister nothing about the circumstances,' I told him. 'Lord Cromwell doesn't want this news leaking.'

He bridled a little at my peremptory manner. 'I could work that out for myself. I said nothing of Greek Fire to Goodwife Gristwood. Of course, she merely said her husband and his brother had been murdered. Not that that is unusual in these times.' He paused. 'There is to be no inquest?'

'The matter is to stay in Lord Cromwell's hands. And I am instructed to talk to all who knew about Greek Fire. I have to ask you to tell me everything about your involvement, Serjeant.'

Marchamount settled himself in his chair, linking his hands together. Square strong hands, yet soft and as white as his face was red. A gold ring containing an enormous emerald glinted on one middle finger. He adopted a look of judicious consideration, yet I sensed fear there. Goodwife Gristwood's news would have been a shock – Marchamount would guess Cromwell would be making enquiries and know that if he did not satisfy him he could find himself in the Tower, for all his airs.

'I did not know Michael Gristwood well,' he said. 'He approached me to see if I needed a solicitor's assistance a couple of years ago. He had been working with Brother Bealknap, but they had quarrelled.'

'I had heard. What was that about? Do you know?'

He raised an eyebrow. 'Michael was not above a little sharp dealing, but he found the way Bealknap cheated everyone as a matter of daily routine hard to stomach. I told him there'd be no sharp practice if he dealt with me.'

I nodded, acknowledging his point.

'I farmed some small pieces of work out to him, but to be frank they were not well done and I gave him no more. I heard he'd gone to Augmentations and that did not surprise me, for there are easy profits there. God have mercy on his soul,' he added sonorously.

'Amen,' I said.

Marchamount sighed. 'Then one day last March Brother Bealknap came to my office asking to see me. He told me what Michael had found at St Bartholomew's. He wanted an introduction to Lord Cromwell.' He spread his hands. 'I thought it was all some mare's nest and I laughed at Bealknap. But when he brought me the papers I could see there was something here that should at least –' he hesitated – 'be taken further.'

'Yes, I have the papers now.' I frowned. 'March, you said. But Michael Gristwood found those papers last autumn. What happened in the six months between?'

'I wondered about that. Michael told me he and his brother had spent the winter building the apparatus used to project the stuff from old plans and experimenting to make more of the Greek Fire.'

I remembered the burn marks in the Gristwoods' yard. 'Had they succeeded?'

He shrugged. 'They said so.'

'So, you helped Michael Gristwood to a meeting with Lord Cromwell. Did Gristwood offer to pay you?'

He gave me a haughty look. 'I had no need of their money. I helped them get the papers to the earl because it was right and proper. Of course, I could not approach the chief secretary myself.' He waved a hand self-deprecatingly. 'My contacts do not quite reach his circles. But I know Lady Honor, a fine woman and discreet as any female in

England, and she does know the earl. A fine woman,' he repeated with a smile. 'I asked her to take the papers to him.'

It would be another foot in the doors of power for you, I thought. 'But you could not give her the formula itself?'

'That was not in my gift. I do not think anyone apart from the brothers has seen it since they tore it from that parchment. Michael told me they had done that, but not where it was kept. And the pair wanted money for it. Michael was quite open about that.'

'But as monastic property those papers belonged to the king. Gristwood should have taken them to Sir Richard Rich, as Chancel-lor of Augmentations, to pass to Lord Cromwell.'

Marchamount spread his hands. 'I know that, of course, but what could I do? I could not *make* Gristwood give me the formula, Brother Shardlake. Naturally I told him he should have given it straight to the proper authorities.' He raised his chin and looked down his nose at me.

'So you gave the papers to Lady Honor with a message.'

'I did. And a message came back through her, from the earl, for me to give to Gristwood. Afterwards two or three further messages passed through my hands. They were sealed, of course, so I knew nothing of what they said.' He spread his hands. 'I am afraid that is all I know, Brother. I was a mere messenger, I know nothing about this Greek Fire, nor even whether it was genuine.'

'Very well. Serjeant, I must repeat you are to speak to nobody about this.'

He spread his hands. 'Of course. I am at the service of Lord Cromwell's investigation.'

'Tell me if you are approached in any way, or if you remember anything that could be useful.'

'Naturally. I believe we shall be meeting again on Tuesday, by the way; we are both invited to Lady Honor's banquet.'

'Yes.'

'A lady of distinction,' he said again, then looked at me sharply. 'Will you be questioning her?'

'At some point. And I shall probably wish to speak to you once more.' I rose. 'I will leave you to your business for now. I look forward to Tuesday.'

He nodded, then leaned back and smiled, showing his white teeth. 'Is Greek Fire genuine, then?' he asked suddenly.

'I am afraid that is a question I may not answer.'

He inclined his head, then gave me a penetrating look. 'So you are working for Lord Cromwell again,' he said quietly. 'You know, many think you deserve the coif of a serjeant: you should be pleading before Common Pleas, not oafs like Forbizer. Yet you have been passed over a few times. Some say it was because you were out of favour with those that matter.'

I shrugged. 'I cannot help what people say.'

He smiled again. 'Many say Lord Cromwell may soon be out of office. If the king puts Queen Anne away.' He shook his head sadly.

'Again, I cannot help what people say.'

Marchamount was sounding me out, I knew, wondering if I was one of the many who, hearing the rumours, might switch to the religious conservatives. I said nothing, merely folded my hands in front of me.

Marchamount made a little moue. 'Well, I must not keep you.' He rose and bowed.

I smiled inwardly at the way he had made the dismissal his. But looking in his eyes I felt again that he was afraid.

# Chapter Twelve

O UTSIDE IN THE COURTYARD black-robed barristers were heading towards the hall from all directions. I saw Bealknap among them, walking alone as usual, for he had few if any friends – though he never seemed to care. It was too late to talk to him now, I would have to wait till after the lunch. Joining the crowd filing into hall, I saw Godfrey a little ahead of me and tapped him on the shoulder.

Lincoln's Inn Hall looked its very best. Beneath the vaulting hammerbeam roof the richly coloured tapestries glowed in the light of many candles. The dark oak floorboards gleamed with polish. A throne-like chair had been set for the duke in the centre of the High Table at the north end of the hall. Other long tables, set with the Inn's best silver, had been placed at right angles to High Table. People were finding their places; a few students selected for their good backgrounds, short black robes over their gaudy doublets, took the places furthest from High Table. The serjeants, sweating under the white coifs tied around their faces, sat nearest and the benchers and barristers in between.

As benchers Godfrey and I were entitled to places next to the serjeants, and to my surprise Godfrey shouldered his way to a place as near as possible to where the duke would sit. I sat next to him. On my other side was an aged bencher called Fox. As he never tired of telling people, he had been a student at Lincoln's Inn during the reign of King Richard III and had watched the hall being built. As we took our places, I saw Bealknap arguing with a bencher over a place nearly opposite me. Although he had fifteen years at the Bar,

Bealknap's unsavoury reputation meant he had never been called to read, yet he was disputing crossly for the place. Perhaps thinking such an argument beneath him, the bencher allowed Bealknap to take the place. He sat down with a smile of satisfaction on his thin features.

A servant banged his staff. Everyone rose as the officers of the Inn marched up the hall. Among the black robes was one man in the rich scarlet of a peer, his wide collar trimmed with black fur; Thomas Howard, third Duke of Norfolk. I was surprised to see how small he was. How old, too, for his long face was deeply lined and the hair beneath the wide jewelled cap was thin and grey. He looked, I thought, insignificant; in ordinary clothes one would not have glanced at him twice. A dozen retainers in the red and gold quarters of the Howard livery spread out and stood against the walls.

The Inn's officers bowed and smiled as they bade the duke take his seat. I saw Marchamount take a place at High Table. He was not an officer, but from what he said had been instrumental in organizing the lunch. He beamed at the crowd, in his element. I wondered how well he knew Cromwell's, and reform's, greatest enemy. Curious, I studied the duke's lined face. It was as hard as any man's I had seen, the thin mouth under the prominent nose pursed with severity. Small black eyes surveyed the crowd with lively calculation. The duke's gaze met mine for a second and I dropped my eyes.

The first course was brought in, steaming dishes of vegetables carved into the shapes of stars and half-moons, richly sauced with sugar and vinegar and accompanied by cold meat. As this was a lunch there would be none of the spectacular fare of an evening supper, but much effort had been put into the preparation of the food. I turned appreciatively to Godfrey.

'This fare is almost worth the company,' I whispered.

'Nothing is worth this company.' Godfrey was staring at the duke, a bitter look on his normally amiable features.

'Don't let him catch you giving him foul looks,' I whispered, but he shrugged and went on staring. The duke was talking to the treasurer, Serjeant Cuffleigh.

'Our defences couldn't stand a combined assault by the French and Spaniards,' I heard the duke tell Cuffleigh in a deep voice.

Cuffleigh smiled. 'Few have as much military experience as you, your grace. You hammered the Scots for us at Flodden.'

'I'm afraid of fighting nobody, but the balance of forces needs to be right. When I faced the northern rebels three years ago I hadn't enough men to meet them, so the king and I got them to disband their forces with sweet words. *Then* we hammered the churls.' He smiled coldly.

Marchamount leaned across. 'And we can't do that with the French and Spaniards.'

'I dare say not,' Cuffleigh agreed hesitantly.

'That's why we need peace. A half-baked alliance with a bunch of squabbling Germans is no use.'

Old Brother Fox leaned across to me. 'I see his grace is talking to the treasurer,' he said. 'You know, Thomas More refused the treasurer-ship and was fined a pound. Ah, the king exacted a higher penalty when More refused to recognize Nan Bullen as queen.'

'Brother Cuffleigh looks a trifle anxious,' I said, to divert Brother Fox before he began his reminiscences of More's time at the Inn.

'Cuffleigh is a reformer and the duke loves baiting evangelicals.' Fox, a traditionalist, spoke with satisfaction. The duke was smiling coldly at the treasurer now. 'Not just apprentices,' I heard him say loudly. 'Even silly little women fancy they can read the Bible now and understand God's Word.' He laughed.

'It is permitted, your grace,' Cuffleigh replied weakly.

'It won't be for long. The king plans to restrict Bible-reading to heads of households. I'd restrict it further – I'd only permit it for the clergy. I've never read it and never will.'

All along the upper part of the tables, where the duke's words could be heard, men were looking at him, some approvingly and others with set faces. He glanced over the assembly with those bright, hard eyes and smiled cynically.

Then, before I could stop him, Godfrey rose in his place. All eyes turned to him as he took a deep breath, faced the duke, and said loudly, 'God's Word is for all to read. It is the bringer of the sweetest light there is, the light of truth.'

His words rang and echoed round the hall. All along the tables eyes widened. Norfolk leaned over, resting his chin on a beringed hand, and stared at Godfrey with cold amusement. I grabbed at the sleeve of his robe and tried to pull him down but he shook me off.

'The Bible brings us from error to truth, to the presence of Jesus Christ,' he continued. A couple of students clapped until furious glares from the Inn's officers scared them into silence. Godfrey reddened, as though he suddenly realized what an unforgivably bold thing he had done, but he went on. 'Were I to be killed for my beliefs, I would rise from the grave to proclaim the truth once more,' he said and then, to my relief, sat down.

The duke rose in his place. 'No, sir, you would not,' he said evenly. 'You would not, you would be screaming in hell with all the other Lutheran heretics. You should have a care, sir, that your tongue does not lose you your head and put you in the pit before your time.' He sat down again. Leaning over to Marchamount, who was glaring at Godfrey as though he could have slain him, he began whispering in his ear.

'Jesu, man, what were you thinking of?' I asked Godfrey. 'You'll be disciplined for this.'

He looked at me. His normally soft features had taken on a steely expression. 'I care not.' He almost spat the words. 'Jesus Christ is my Saviour, through grace, and I will not have His Word made mock of.' His eyes gleamed with self-righteous anger. I turned away. When his emotions were roused by his faith Godfrey could sometimes change into a different person, a dangerous one.

✝

AT LAST THE MEAL ended. The duke and his retinue filed out and at once a buzz of conversation erupted. Godfrey sat there, taking satisfaction, it seemed to me, from a myriad stares. Some barristers, the traditionalists mostly, got up and left. Old Brother Fox, looking much disturbed, rose from his bench. I stood up too. Godfrey gave me a reproachful look.

'Will you stay a moment?' he asked. 'Or do you not wish to be associated with me any more?'

'God's wounds, Godfrey,' I snapped, 'I've work to do, a cartload of it. There are others in the world besides you. I have to see Bealknap before he disappears.' And indeed he was even now heading for the door. I hurried after him, catching him as he stepped into the sunny quadrangle, blinking in the light.

'Brother Bealknap,' I said crisply, 'I need to talk to you.'

'About the case?' He smiled. 'Your friend made a monkey of himself in there, by the way. He'll be disciplined—'

'It is not about the case, Bealknap. I have a commission, from Lord Cromwell. To investigate the murder yesterday of Michael Gristwood.'

His eyes widened and his jaw dropped. If he was acting ignorance, it was a good performance. But lawyers can act better than any mummer in a mystery play.

'Your chambers, I think.'

Bealknap nodded, stunned into silence, and led the way across Gatehouse Court. He had a room on the first floor of a corner building, up a narrow flight of creaking stairs. His chamber was plainly furnished, a poor-looking desk and a couple of battered tables heaped untidily with papers. The room was dominated by a huge iron-bound chest that stood in one corner, made of thick boards and secured by iron bands and padlocks. It was said about the Inns that all the gold Bealknap earned went in there and that he passed his evenings running it through his fingers and counting it. He hardly spent any, though; it was known that tailors and innkeepers had been chasing him through the courts for years for money he owed.

Bealknap looked at the chest and seemed momentarily to relax. Many lawyers would have been embarrassed to have such stories of miserliness spread about them, but Bealknap seemed not to mind. Keeping the chest in his office was safe enough for he lived in rooms next door, and with its guards and watchmen the Inn was as safe a place as anywhere in London. Yet I remembered what the Gristwoods' killers had made of the chest in Sepultus's workshop.

Bealknap took off his cap and ran a hand through his wiry blond hair. 'Will you take a seat, Brother?'

'Thank you.' I sat by his desk, casting an eye over the papers. To my surprise I saw the crest of the Hanseatic League on one document, French writing on another.

'You have business with French merchants?' I asked.

'They pay well. The French are having problems with the Custom House these days.'

'Not surprising as they threaten war on us.'

'That won't happen. The king knows the dangers, as the duke was saying at lunch.' He waved the subject away. 'In God's name, Brother, what is this about Michael Gristwood?'

'He was found dead yesterday morning at his home. His brother was murdered too. The formula is gone. You know what I am talking about.'

'My poor friend. This is very shocking.' His eyes darted all over the room, avoiding mine.

'Did you tell anyone apart from Serjeant Marchamount about the formula?' I asked.

He shook his head firmly. 'No, sir, I did not. When Michael brought me the papers he found at Bart's I said he should get them to Lord Cromwell.'

'For payment, though they were the king's by right. Was that your idea, or his?'

He hesitated, then looked at me directly. 'His. But I didn't quarrel with him about that, Brother. It was an opportunity, and only a fool passes those up. I offered to go to Marchamount for him.'

'For a fee?'

'Naturally.' He raised a hand. 'But – but Lord Cromwell accepted the position, and I was only a poor intermediary—'

'You are a shameless fellow, Bealknap.' I looked at the papers again. 'You could have taken them to the French, perhaps. They might have offered more to keep this secret out of Cromwell's hands.'

He jumped up, agitated. 'God's death, that would have been treason! D'ye think I'd take the risk of being gutted alive at Tyburn? You have to believe me.'

I said nothing. He sat down again, then laughed nervously. 'Besides, I thought the whole thing was nonsense. After I took Michael to Marchamount he paid me and I heard no more till just now.' He jabbed a finger at me. 'Don't try to involve me in this, Shardlake. I'd no part in it, on my oath!'

'When did Michael first bring you the papers?'

'In March.'

'He waited six months after finding them?'

'He said he and his brother the alchemist had been experimenting with the formula, making more, building some sort of apparatus to fire the stuff at ships. It made no sense to me.'

It was a similar tale to Marchamount's. 'Ah yes,' I said, 'the apparatus. Did they build that it themselves, I wonder?'

Bealknap shrugged. 'I've no idea. Michael said only that it had been made. I tell you, I know nothing.'

'They said nothing of where the apparatus, or the formula, were kept?'

'No. I didn't even study their papers. Michael showed them to me, but half of them were in Greek and what I could read sounded like nonsense. You know some of those old monks were jesters? They'd forge documents to pass the time.'

'Is that what you thought those papers were? A jest, a forgery?'

'I didn't know. I introduced Michael to Marchamount and then I was glad to be shot of the matter.'

'Back to your compurgators, eh?'

'Back to business.'

'Very well.' I rose. 'That will do for now. You will tell no one Michael is dead, Bealknap, or that we have spoken, or you will answer to Lord Cromwell.'

'I've no wish to tell anyone, I don't want to be involved at all.'

'I am afraid you are.' I gave him a tight smile. 'I will see you at Westminster Hall on Tuesday for the case. By the way,' I added with apparent casualness, 'did you resolve the problem with your corrodiary?'

'Oh, yes.'

'Strange, I did not think friaries took on pensioners living in.'

'This one did,' he said with a glare. 'Ask Sir Richard Rich if you don't believe me.'

'Ah, yes, you mentioned his name at Augmentations. I did not know you had his patronage.'

'I don't,' he answered smoothly, 'but I knew the clerk had a meeting with Sir Richard Rich. That was why I urged him to hurry.'

I smiled and left him. I was sure I was right about corrodians, I would check. I frowned. There was something about Bealknap's response to my question about the corrodian that did not ring true. He had been frightened, but had seemed suddenly confident when he mentioned Richard Rich. Somehow that worried me very much.

# Chapter Thirteen

I WALKED TIREDLY DOWN Chancery Lane to my house. Barak would be back by now. I had enjoyed the respite from his company. I would have liked nothing better than to rest, but I had said I would go to Goodwife Gristwood's that day. Another trip across London. But we had only eleven days left now. The words seemed to echo in time with my footsteps; eleven days, eleven days.

Barak had returned and was sitting in the garden, his feet up on a shady bench and a pot of beer beside him. 'Joan is looking after you, then,' I said.

'Like a prince.'

I sat down and poured myself a mug of beer. I saw he had found time to visit the barber's, for his cheeks were smooth; I was conscious of my own dark stubble and realized I should have had a shave before such an important dinner. Marchamount would have mentioned it had I come on less serious business.

'What luck with the lawyers?' Barak asked.

'They both say they just acted as middlemen. What about you? Did you find the librarian?'

'Ay.' Barak squinted against the afternoon sun. 'Funny little fellow. I found him saying Mass in a side chapel in his church.' He smiled wryly. 'He wasn't pleased to hear what I wanted, started trembling like a rabbit, but he'll meet us outside Barty's gatehouse at eight tomorrow morning. I said if he didn't turn up the earl would be after him.'

I took off my cap and fanned myself. 'Well, I suppose we had better be off to Wolf's Lane.'

Barak laughed. 'You look hot.'

'I am hot. I've been working while you've been resting your arse on my bench.' I stood up wearily. 'Let's get it done.'

We went round to the stables. Chancery had travelled further than he was used to the day before and was unhappy at being led into the sun again. He was old; it was time to think of putting him out to pasture. I mounted, nearly catching my robe in the saddle. I had kept it on as it lent me a certain gravitas that would be useful in dealing with Goodwife Gristwood, but it was a burden in this weather.

As we rode out, I went over what I should say. I must find out if she knew anything of the apparatus for projecting Greek Fire; there had been something, I was sure, she had been keeping back yesterday.

Barak interrupted my reflections. 'You lawyers,' he said, 'what's the mystery of your craft?'

'What do you mean?' I replied wearily, scenting mockery.

'All trades have their mysteries, the secrets their apprentices learn. The carpenter knows how to make a table that won't collapse, the astrologer how to divine a man's fate, but what mysteries do lawyers know? It's always seemed to me they know only how to mangle words for a penny.' He smiled at me insolently.

'You should try working at some of the legal problems the students have at the Inns. That would stop your mouth. England's law consists of detailed rules, developed over generations, that allow men to settle their disputes in an ordered way.'

'Seems more like a great thicket of words to keep men from justice. My master says the law of property's an ungodly jumble.' He gave me a keen look and I wondered if he was watching to see whether I would contradict Cromwell.

'Have you any experience with the law then, Barak?'

He looked ahead again. 'Oh, ay, my mother married an attorney after my father died. He was a fine sophister, flowing with words. No qualifications at all, though, like friend Gristwood. Made his money by tangling people up in legal actions he'd no knowledge how to solve.'

I grunted. 'The law's practitioners aren't perfect. The Inns are trying to control unqualified solicitors. And some of us try honourably to gain each man his right.' I knew my words sounded prosy even as I spoke them, but the sardonic smile that was Barak's only reply still irked me.

As we passed down Cheapside we had to halt at the Great Cross to let a flock of sheep pass on their way to the Shambles. A long queue of water carriers was waiting with their baskets at the Great Conduit. I saw there was only a dribble of water from the fountain.

'If the springs north of London are drying up,' I observed, 'the City will be in trouble.'

'Ay,' Barak agreed. 'Normally we keep buckets of water to hand in summer in the Old Barge in case there's a fire. But there's not enough water.'

I looked at the buildings around me. Despite the rule they should be made of stone to avoid fires, many were wooden. The City was a damp place in winter – sometimes the smell of damp and mould in a poor dwelling was enough to make one retch – but summer was the dangerous time, when people feared hearing the warning shout of 'Fire' almost as much as the other summer terror, plague.

I jerked round at the sound of a high-pitched yell. A beggar girl, no more than ten and dressed only in the filthiest rags, had just been thrown out of a baker's shop. People stopped to look as she turned and banged on the door of the shop with tiny fists.

'You took my little brother! You made him into pies!'

Passers-by laughed. Sobbing, the girl slid down the door and crouched weeping at its foot. Someone laid a penny at her feet before hurrying on.

'What in God's name is that about?' I asked.

Barak grimaced. 'She's mazed. She used to beg round Walbrook and the Stocks Market with her young brother. Probably kicked out of a monastery almshouse. Her brother disappeared a few weeks ago and now she runs up to people screaming they've killed him. That's not the only shopkeeper she's accused. She's become a laughing stock.' He frowned. 'Poor creature.'

I shook my head. 'More beggars every year.'

'There go many of us if we're not careful,' he said. 'Come on, Sukey.'

I looked at the girl, still crouched against the door, arms like sticks wrapped round her thin frame.

'Are you coming?' Barak asked.

I followed him down Friday Street, then down to Wolf's Lane. Even on this hot sunny day the narrow street had a sinister look, the overhanging top storeys cutting out much of the sun. Many houses leaned over at such an angle they looked as though they could collapse at any moment. Under the alchemist's sign I saw a crude repair had been made to the door with planks and nails. We dismounted and Barak knocked on the door. I brushed a layer of brown dust from my robe.

'Let's see what the pinched old crow has to say for herself this time,' Barak grunted.

'For Jesu's sake, she's just lost her husband.'

'Fat lot she cares. All she wants is to get her name on the deeds of this place.'

The door was opened by one of Cromwell's men. He bowed. 'Good day, Master Barak.'

'Good day, Smith. All quiet?'

'Yes, sir. We've had the bodies taken away.'

I wondered where. Did the earl have a place kept aside for inconvenient corpses?

The girl Susan appeared, looking composed now.

'Hello, Susan,' Barak said. He gave the girl a wink, making her blush. 'How's your mistress?'

'Better, sir.'

'We would talk with her again,' I said.

She curtseyed and led us in. I touched the old tapestry in the hall. It was heavy and smelled of dust. 'Where did your master get this?' I asked curiously. 'It's a fine piece of work. Very old.'

Susan gave it a look of distaste. 'It came from the mother superior's house at St Helen's nunnery, sir. Augmentations didn't want it – it was so faded it had no value. Great ugly thing, it flaps in the breeze and makes you jump.'

Susan took us into a parlour with another view of the strangely blackened yard, and went to fetch her mistress. It was a large room with fine oak beams, but the furniture was cheap and there was only a little poor silver on display in the cupboard. I wondered if the Gristwoods had gone beyond their means in buying this house. Michael would not have earned much as an Augmentations clerk and an alchemist's income, I guessed, could be uncertain.

Goodwife Gristwood came in. She wore the same cheap dress as yesterday, and her face was stiff with strain. She curtseyed to us perfunctorily.

'I'm afraid I have some more questions for you, Goodwife,' I said gently. 'I hear you have been to see Serjeant Marchamount.'

She gave me a fierce look. 'I have to look to my own future now. There's nobody else. I only told him Michael was dead. Which he is,' she added bitterly.

'Very well, but you must tell as few people as possible about what happened here. For now.'

She sighed. 'Very well.'

'And now I would ask you more about yesterday's events. Please, sit down.'

Reluctantly she took a chair. 'Did your husband and brother seem as normal when you and Susan left the house to shop?'

She looked at me wearily. 'Yes. We left before the markets opened and returned at noon. Michael hadn't gone to Augmentations yesterday – he went up to help his brother with one of his vile-smelling experiments. When we got back we saw the front door had been staved in and then those – those red footprints. Susan didn't want to come in, but I made her.' She hesitated. 'Somehow I knew there wasn't anybody here, not living.' Her tightly held features seemed to sag a little. 'We went upstairs and found them.'

I nodded. 'Is Susan your only servant?'

'She's all we could afford, silly lump though she is.'

'And none of the neighbours saw or heard anything?'

'The goodwife next door told your man she heard a great banging and clattering, but that was nothing unusual when his brother was at his work.'

'I would like to look at the workshop again. Do you feel able to come with me?' I recalled her terror at the notion the day before, but now she only shrugged apathetically.

'If you wish. They've taken them away. After you've seen it, can I get it cleared? If I'm to keep myself fed, I'll have to let it out.'

'Very well.'

She led me up the twisting staircase, still complaining about the need to let the room and how she had no money coming in now. Barak followed; behind her back he worked his mouth in a silent gobble in imitation of her. I gave him a stern look.

At the top of the stairs she fell silent. The door still hung off its hinges. I looked at the other doors leading off the corridor. 'What are these?' I asked.

'Our bedroom, my brother-in-law's, and that third one is where Samuel kept his rubbish.'

'Samuel?'

She grimaced. 'Sepultus. Samuel was his real name, his Christian name. *Sepultus*,' she said again, with mocking emphasis.

I went to the door she had indicated and threw it open. I had wondered if I might find the Greek Fire apparatus in there, but there was nothing but a jumble of broken chairs, bottles, cracked flasks and, staring up from a corner, a large toad preserved in a vinegar bottle. Barak peered in over my shoulder. I picked up an enormous, curved horn that lay on a cloth. Little pieces had been cut out of it.

'What in heaven's name is this?'

Goodwife Gristwood snorted again. 'A unicorn's horn, so Samuel said. He'd bring it out to impress people, powder up bits of it in his messes. I'll be reduced to boiling it for soup if I can't let some rooms.'

I closed the door and looked around the hall with its bare boards, its dried-up old rushes in the corner and the big crack in the wall. Goodwife Gristwood followed my gaze. 'Yes, the house is falling down. This whole street's built on Thames mud. It's drying out in this hot weather. Creaks all the time, makes me jump. Maybe the whole place will fall on my head and that'll be an end to all my problems.'

Barak raised his eyebrows to the ceiling. I coughed. 'Shall we go into the workshop?'

The bodies had gone but the floor was still covered with blood, its faint tang mixed with the sulphurous stink. Goodwife Gristwood looked at the spray of blood on the wall and went pale.

'I want to sit down,' she said.

I felt guilty at having brought her; lifting a chair from the wreckage, I helped her sit. After a minute some colour returned to her face and she looked at the smashed chest. 'Michael and Samuel bought that last autumn. Heaved it up here. They'd never let me know what was in it.'

I nodded at the empty shelves. 'Do you know what was kept on those?'

'Samuel's powders and chemicals. Sulphur and lime and God knows what. The smells I had to put up with, the noises.' She nodded at the fireplace. 'When he was heating potions there I was sometimes afraid he'd blow the house up as high as a monastery church. Whoever killed them took Samuel's bottles as well, God knows why. This is where all the great knowledge Samuel claimed to have brought him in the end,' she said wearily. 'And Michael with him.' There was a sudden catch in her voice; she swallowed and made her face severe again. I studied her. She was holding in some powerful emotions. Grief? Anger? Fear?

'Has anything else been taken that you can see?'

'No. But I came up here as little as I could help.'

'You did not think much of your brother-in-law's trade?'

'Michael and I were happy enough on our own till Samuel sug-gested we all buy a large house together when the lease ran out on his old workshop. Samuel was all right purifying lime for the gunpowder makers, but when he tried anything more ambitious he'd come unstuck. He was greedy beyond his knowledge, like all alchemists.' She sighed. 'A couple of years ago he fancied he'd found a way to strengthen pewter, some formula he'd teased out of one of his old books, but he never managed it and the Pewtermasters' Guild sued him. And Michael was always so easily led, was sure one day his brother would make their fortune. These last few weeks Michael and Samuel spent half their time up here. They told me they'd found out a marvellous secret.' She looked at the bloody doorway again. 'Men's greed.'

'Did they ever mention the term Greek Fire?' I watched her face. She hesitated before replying.

'Not to me. I tell you, I wasn't interested in what they did up here.' She shifted uneasily in her chair.

'You spoke of experiments, sometimes out in the yard. Did they have an apparatus, a large thing of tanks and pipes? Did you ever see anything like that?'

'No, sir. I'd have noticed. All they took out to the yard were flasks of liquid and powder. That's not what the earl's men have turned my house upside down looking for, is it? I thought it was some papers.'

'Yes, it was,' I said mildly. Her eyes had narrowed warily when I mentioned the apparatus. 'But there was a big metal construction as well. You are sure you know nothing of that?'

'Nothing, sir, I swear.' She was lying, I was sure. I nodded and stepped to the fireplace. The stoppered bottle lay where I had left it, but to my surprise the thick liquid on the floorboards seemed to have evaporated; there was nothing left but the barest stain on the floor. I touched it; the floor was quite dry. I hesitated, then picked up the little bottle, still half-full of the stuff.

'Might you have any idea what this liquid is, madam?'

'No, I haven't.' Her voice rose. 'Greek Fire, formulae, books, I don't know what any of it means! God's wounds, I don't care either!' Her voice rose to a shout and she covered her face with her hands.

I picked up the bottle and wrapped it carefully in my handkerchief, then slipped it into my pocket, suppressing a momentary stab of fear that it might be Greek Fire itself, that it might explode into flames.

Goodwife Gristwood wiped her face and sat looking at the floor. When she spoke again it was in a cold whisper. 'If you want to find who might have told the killers about my husband, you should go to her.'

'Who?'

'His whore.' Barak and I looked at each other in surprise as she continued, her voice like a thin stream of icy water. 'The woman that keeps the brewery told me in March she'd seen Michael in Southwark, going into one of the whorehouses. She enjoyed telling me too.' She looked at me bitterly. 'I asked him and he admitted it. He said he wouldn't go again but I didn't believe him. Some days he'd come home drunk, smelling like a stewhouse, goggle-eyed with sated lust.'

Barak laughed aloud at the words. Goodwife Gristwood rounded on him. 'Shut up! You churl, laughing at a woman's shame!'

'Leave us,' I told him curtly. For a moment I thought he would argue, but he shrugged and left. The goodwife looked up at me, her eyes fierce. 'Michael was besotted with that vile tart. I raged and shouted at him but still he went to her.' She bit her lip hard. 'I'd always been able to manage him before, stop him getting too involved with mad schemes, but then Samuel came and between him and that whore I lost him.' She looked again at the awful spray of blood then stared at me, her eyes fierce. 'I asked him once if his lusts were all he cared about and he said the tart was kind to him and he could talk to her. Well, *you* talk to her, sir. Bathsheba Green at the Bishop's Hat brothel at Bank End.'

'I see.'

'They do what they like over in Southwark, outside the City's jurisdiction. This side of the river she'd have her cheeks branded, and I'd do it for them.'

Despite her vicious words I felt sorry for Jane Gristwood, alone now with nothing but this big decaying house. I wondered what she had felt for her husband. Something more than the contempt and bitterness she expressed, I was sure. Certainly she would make what trouble she could for the whore.

I looked into her eyes and again had the sense of something held back. I would return when I had found this Bathsheba Green.

'Thank you, Goodwife Gristwood,' I said. I bowed to her.

'Is that all?' She looked relieved.

'For now.'

'Talk to *her*,' she repeated fiercely. Talk to *her*.'

✝

AS I WALKED DOWNSTAIRS I heard voices from the back regions; a man's murmur then a woman's sudden giggle. 'Barak!' I called sharply. He appeared, sucking an orange. 'Susan gave me this,' he said, tucking the half-eaten fruit away in his codpiece. 'Fresh off the boat.'

'We should go,' I said curtly, leading the way outside. I blinked in the afternoon sun, bright after the gloomy house.

'What did Madam Sour-face have to say?' Barak asked as we untied the horses.

'More without you there baiting her. She told me Michael was seeing a whore. Bathsheba Green, of the Bishop's Hat in Southwark.'

'I know the Bishop's Hat. It's a rough place. I would have thought an Augmentations man could have afforded a better class of nip.' We mounted the horses; I adjusted my cap so some shade might fall on my neck.

'I was asking Susan about the family,' Barak said as we rode away. 'Goodwife Gristwood tried to rule the roost, but her husband and his brother paid little heed, apparently. They were thick as thieves. Both after a quick fortune, she said.'

'Did she know of Michael's dalliance at Southwark?'

'Yes. Said it turned the goodwife bitter. But you could see that, pinched old raven.'

'She's lost her husband, has nothing in the world now except that ruin of a house.'

Barak grunted. 'Apparently Gristwood married her for her money when she was nearly thirty. There was some scandal in her family, Susan didn't know what.'

I turned to look at him. 'Why do you dislike her so?'

He laughed, in a tone as bitter as Jane Gristwood's own. 'She reminds me of my mother, if you must know. The way she was after you for information about the house the moment we were in the door, and her husband lying in his gore upstairs. My ma was like that, married our lodger not a month after my father died. I quit the house then.'

'A poor widow must look to her future.'

'They do that all right.' He pulled his horse a little ahead of me, ending the conversation, and we rode on in silence. I kept raising my hand to remove the sweat that was falling into my eyes. I was not used to criss-crossing London like this. The heat was baking the rubbish in the streets, releasing all its vile humours. Beneath my doublet my armpits were damp with sweat and my breeches felt as though they were stuck to Chancery's saddle. This was a trial for him too: he was finding it hard to keep up with Barak's mare. I resolved that in future we would travel by water when we could. It was all very well for Barak and his horse – each was a decade younger than Chancery and me.

☩

BY THE TIME we arrived back at Chancery Lane the sun was low. I told Joan to fetch us some food In my parlour I dropped gratefully into my armchair; Barak collected some cushions together and sprawled inelegantly on the floor.

'Well, where are we now?' he asked. 'This day's nearly done. Then only ten more.'

'We've had more new leads than answers so far. But that's what

I'd expect at the start of an investigation as complicated as this. We must visit that whore. And I think the goodwife is still holding something back. Is your man Smith staying with her?'

'Till otherwise instructed.' He retrieved his orange and sucked it noisily. 'I told you she was a nasty old crow.'

'It's something to do with the apparatus. I don't think they kept it the house.'

'Then where?'

'I don't know. Some warehouse? But there was nothing about any other property among their papers.'

'You looked?'

'Yes.'

I took the bottle from my pocket and handed it carefully to Barak. 'There was a pool of this stuff on the floor. It's almost colourless, has no smell, but if you taste it you get a kick like a mule.'

He unstoppered the bottle and sniffed the contents carefully, then put a little on his fingers. He touched it to his tongue and made a grimace, as I had. 'Jesu, you're right!' he said. 'It's not Greek Fire, though. I told you, that had a fearsome stink.'

I took the bottle back, stoppered it and shook it gently, watching the colourless liquid swirl within. 'I want to take this to Guy.'

'So long as you're careful what you tell him.'

'God's wounds, how many times do I have to tell you I will be?'

'I'll come with you.'

'As you will.'

'What exactly did you get out of the two lawyers?'

'Marchamount and Bealknap both insist they were just middlemen. I'm not sure about Bealknap. He's involved with Richard Rich in some way, though I don't know whether it relates to Greek Fire. Incidentally, he has dealings with foreign merchants, says he represents them in negotiations with the Custom House. I saw some papers on his desk. Lord Cromwell will have access to the records of trade. Could someone in his office check them? I've too little time.'

Barak nodded. 'I'll send a note. I've been trying to remember where I've seen that arsehole Bealknap's face before, but it hasn't come to me. It was a long time ago, I'm sure.'

There was a knock and Joan entered with a tray. She clucked at the dusty state of our clothes and I asked her to lay out new ones upstairs. I winced at a spasm from my back as I bent to pour some beer.

'You shouldn't overtire yourself, sir,' she said.

'I'll be all right when I've had some rest.'

As she left us, we both took welcome draughts of beer.

'The Duke of Norfolk was in a confident mood today,' I said. 'Baiting reformers at the lunch. A friend of mine baited him back, he'll be in trouble now.'

'I thought lawyers were all reformers.'

'Not all. And they'll turn to follow the wind, just like everyone else in London, if Cromwell falls. From fear and hope of advancement.'

'We've so little time,' Barak said. 'Are you sure we need to go to Barty's with that librarian tomorrow? I agree you need to talk to him, but you could see him at his chantry.'

'No. I need to see the roots of this, to go back to where it all started. Tomorrow we'll go to Barty's, then to see Guy and to the whorehouse in Southwark to see if that girl has anything to say. I've my interview with the Wentworths as well.' I sighed.

'Ten days.' He shook his head.

'Barak,' I said, 'I may be a melancholy man, but you have all the marks of a sanguine humour. You would rush at things too much if it was left to you.'

'We need this finished. And don't forget how we were followed yesterday,' he added gloomily. 'We might be in danger too.'

'I know that only too well.' I stood up. 'And now I am going to look at more of those old papers.'

I left him and went up to my bedroom, reflecting how I had felt afraid when I walked alone to the Inn earlier. I had to admit that when I was out I felt safer with Barak, the man of the streets, around. But I wished I did not have the necessity.

# Chapter Fourteen

NEXT MORNING, the thirty-first of May, was hotter than ever. Again we left early on horseback; the way to St Bartholomew's lay due northward so we could not use the river. The sun was still low in the sky, turning a bank of thin cloud on the horizon to bright pink. Barak had gone out again the evening before and I had been asleep when he returned. At breakfast he seemed in a surly mood; perhaps he had a hangover, or a girl had sent him packing and dented his vanity. I packed a couple of the alchemical books into the battered old leather satchel my father had given me when first I came to London. I wanted Guy to look at them later.

The City was coming to life after the Sunday rest; shutters and shelves clattered as the shopkeepers made ready for the new week, shifting beggars from their doorways with curses. The homeless ones stumbled into the street, faces red and chapped with constant exposure to the sun. One, a little girl, almost stumbled into Chancery.

'Careful there,' I called.

'Careful yourself, shitting hunchback bastard!' Furious eyes stared at me from a filthy face, and I recognized the girl who had caused the commotion at the baker's shop. I watched her limp away, dragging one leg. 'Poor creature,' I said. 'When people say that beggars lick the sweat from the true labourers' brows, I wonder if they think of waifs like that?'

'Ay.' Barak paused. 'Did you manage to ferret any more out of those old papers last night?'

'There is a lot about the Greek wars in those manuscripts. There was much trickery in them. Once, to deceive their opponents into thinking they had more troops than they did, Alexander tied torches to the tails of a flock of sheep. The Persians, looking at his camp at night, thought he had far more men than was true.'

Barak grunted. 'Sounds like balls. The sheep would have bolted. Anyway, what's that to do with our business?'

'The story stuck in my head for some reason. There is reference as well to some sort of liquid being used in Rome's wars in Babylonia. There are a few books on the Roman wars at Lincoln's Inn; I'll try to find them.'

'So long as it doesn't take too much time.'

'Did you write to Lord Cromwell about Bealknap and the customs?'

'Ay. And last night I tried to find some more about that man who followed us. No luck.'

'We haven't seen him again. Perhaps he's given up.'

'Maybe, but I'll keep my eyes open.'

We passed a dead mastiff in an alleyway, its bloated carcass stinking to heaven. Why did people flock to the City, I wondered, to the ratlike scrabble for subsistence that so often ended in begging on the streets? The lure of money, I supposed; hopes of scraping a living and dreams of becoming rich.

St Sepulchre's was one of a number of streets giving onto the wide open space of Smithfield. It was quiet this morning, for it was not one of the fair days when drovers brought hundreds of cattle in to market. To one side the hospital of St Bartholomew's stood silent and empty behind its high wall, an Augmentations guard at the gate. When the monastery went down the year before, the patients had been turned out to fend for themselves as best they could; talk of a new hospital paid for by subscriptions from the rich had come to nothing yet.

The monastery itself stood at right angles to the hospital, its high buildings dominating the square, although some of those had gone now. Here too a guard stood outside the gatehouse. I saw workmen were bringing out boxes and stacking them against the wall, where a group of blue-robed apprentices buzzed around them.

'Can't see Kytchyn anywhere,' Barak said. 'We'll have to ask the guard.'

We rode across the open space, where paths led between clumps of scrubby grass. There was one large patch of earth where no grass grew and the earth was mixed with blackened cinders; the site where heretics were burned. I remembered Lord Cromwell once telling me he longed to burn a papist using his own images for fuel and two years ago he had: a wooden saint had fed the pyre when Father Forest was burned there, suspended above the fire in chains to prolong his agony before ten thousand spectators. Forest had denied the king's supremacy over the Church, so legally he should have been executed as a traitor, not burned, but Cromwell could afford to ignore such niceties. I had not been there, but as I averted my eyes from the spot I could not help reflecting on that terrible death; the flames making the skin shrivel away, the blood beneath hissing as it dropped into the fire. I shook my head to clear it as I pulled Chancery to a halt before the gatehouse and dismounted.

I saw the boxes were full of bones, brown and ancient. A group of apprentices was delving inside them, casting pieces of tattered winding sheets onto the pavement, hauling out skulls and carefully scraping away the greenish moss that clung to some of them. The watchman, a huge fat fellow, watched indifferently. We tied the horses to a post. Barak went over to the watchman and nodded at the apprentices. 'God's teeth, what are they at?'

'Scraping off the grave moss. Sir Richard is clearing out the monks' graveyard.' The big man shrugged. 'The apothecaries say the moss on the skulls of the dead is good for the liver and they've sent their apprentices up here.' He delved in his pocket and pulled out a little golden trinket in the shape of a crescent. 'There's some strange things buried with them – this monk had been on the Crusades.' He winked. 'My little bonus for letting the boys scavenge.'

'We have business here,' I said. 'We are due to meet a Master Kytchyn.'

'Lord Cromwell's business,' Barak added.

The doorman nodded. 'The fellow you want is here already, I allowed him into the church.' He studied us closely, eyes alert with curiosity.

I walked up to to the gateway. The guard hesitated a moment, then stepped aside and let us through.

The scene that met my eyes on the other side of the gatehouse made me stop dead. The nave of the great church had been pulled down, leaving only a gigantic pile of rubble from which spars of wood protruded. The north end of the church still stood and a huge wooden wall had been erected to seal it from the elements. Most of the neighbouring cloisters had been pulled down too, and the chapter house stripped of its lead. I could see beyond to the prior's house, the fine dwelling Sir Richard Rich had bought. Washing hung from lines in the back garden and three little girls ran and played among the flapping sheets, oddly incongruous amid the destruction. I had seen monastic houses brought down before – who had not in those days? – but not on this scale. A sinister quietness hung over the wreckage.

Barak laughed and scratched his head. 'Not much left, is there?'

'Where are the workmen?' I asked.

'They start late if it's Augmentations work. They know it's a good screw.'

I followed Barak as he picked his way through the rubble towards a door in the wooden barrier. I had a lifetime's contempt for these huge, rich monastic churches kept for the enjoyment of perhaps a dozen monks; when the purpose of the foundation was to serve a hospital the waste of resources seemed even more obscene. Yet as I followed Barak through the door, I had to admit that what was left of the interior of St Bartholomew's Church was magnificent. The walls soared a hundred and fifty feet in a series of pillared arches, richly painted in greens and ochres, up to a row of stained-glass windows. Because of the wooden barrier at the south end, what remained of the interior was gloomy, but I could see that the niches where saints' shrines had stood were empty now and that the side chapels had been stripped of all their images. Near the top of the church, however, one large canopied tomb remained. A candle burned before it, the only one in that building, which once would have been lit by thousands. A figure stood before the tomb, head bent. We walked towards him, our footsteps ringing on the tiled floor. I caught a faint tang in the air; the incense of centuries.

The figure turned as we drew near. A tall, thin man of about fifty in a white clerical cassock, a tangle of grey hair framing a long, anxious face. The look he gave us was wary and fearful. He leaned back as though wishing he might melt into the shadowed wall.

'Master Kytchyn?' I called.

'Ay. Master Shardlake?' His voice was unexpectedly high. He cast a nervous look at Barak, making me wonder if he had been rough with Kytchyn the day before.

'I'm sorry about the candle, sir,' he said quickly. 'I – it was a moment of weakness, sir, when I saw our old founder's tomb.' He leaned forward quickly and pinched out the flame, wincing as the hot wax burned his fingers.

'No matter,' I said. I glanced at the tomb, where a remarkably lifelike effigy of a friar in Dominican black lay in the dimness, arms folded in prayer.

'Prior Rahere,' Kytchyn mumbled. 'Our founder.'

'Yes. Well, never mind that. I wanted to see the place where a certain Master Gristwood discovered something last year.'

'Yes, sir.' He swallowed, still looking frightened. 'Master Grist-wood said to say no word of what we found, on pain of death, and I haven't, I swear. Sir, is it true what this man told me? Master Gristwood has been murdered?'

'It is, Brother.'

'I am not brother,' Kytchyn mumbled. 'I am not a friar any more. No one is.'

'Of course. I am sorry – a slip of the tongue.' I looked around the church. 'Are they to bring the rest of this place down?'

'No.' His face cheered a little. 'The local people have asked to keep what is left as their own church. They are fond of the place. Sir Richard has agreed.'

And their support will be useful to Rich when the prior dies, I thought. I looked around. 'I gather all this began when the Augmentations men found something in the church crypt, last autumn.'

Kytchyn nodded. 'Yes. When the priory surrendered, the Augmentations men came to take an inventory. I was in the library when Master Gristwood came in. He asked if there was any record that might help with something strange they had found down in the crypt.'

'The crypt was used for storage?'

'Yes, sir. It's a big place, there's stuff that's been there hundreds of years. I knew of nothing kept there apart from old lumber, though I'd been librarian twenty years. I swear it, sir.'

'I believe you. Go on, Master Kytchyn.'

'I asked Master Gristwood if he might show me what they had found. They brought me here to the church. It was still whole then, the nave hadn't been taken down.' He looked sadly at the barrier.

'Which part of the church was the crypt in?'

'Over by yonder wall.'

I smiled reassuringly. 'Come, I would have a look. Light your candle again.'

Kytchyn did so with much nervous fumbling, then led us to an iron-studded door. He walked slowly and sedately, the way he would have learned to walk as a young friar. The door creaked mightily as he opened it, the sound echoing through the cavernous church.

He led us down a flight of stone stairs into a long crypt running the length of the church. It was quite dark, with a dank smell. As he led the way, the candle illuminated pieces of lumber and broken statuary. A huge abbot's throne, richly decorated but pitted with woodworm, rose up before us and then I almost cried out as a face loomed out of the gloom. I jumped back, stumbling into Barak, then reddened as I realized it was a statue of the Virgin with an arm broken off. I caught a flash of white teeth as Barak smiled in amusement.

Kytchyn came to a halt by a wall. 'They brought me here, sir,' Kytchyn said. 'There was a barrel standing by the wall, a heavy old wooden barrel.'

'How big?'

'You can see the mark in the dust.'

He lowered the candle and I saw a wide circle in the dust on the stone flags. The barrel had been as large as a wine cask, big enough but not enormous. I nodded and stood up again. Kytchyn held the candle near his chest, making his lined face appear disembodied.

'Had it been opened?' I asked.

'Yes. One of the Augmentations men was there, holding a chisel he'd used to prise the lid off. He looked relieved to see us. Master Gristwood said, "Look in here, Brother Librarian" – I was still brother then – "and tell me if you recognize what's inside. I warn you, though, it stinks." Master Gristwood laughed, but I saw the other Augmentations man cross himself before he lifted the lid for me.'

'And what was inside?' I asked.

'Blackness,' he replied. 'Nothing but blackness, deeper than the blackness of the crypt. And a dreadful smell, like nothing I'd ever known before. Sharp, with a strange sweetness, like something rotting yet lifeless too. It caught my throat and made me cough.'

'That's what I smelt,' Barak said. 'You've caught it well, fellow.'

Kytchyn swallowed. 'I lifted the candle I carried and held it over the barrel. The darkness inside reflected the light. It was so strange I nearly dropped the candle into it.'

Barak laughed. 'God's death, it's as well you didn't.'

'I saw it was a liquid. I touched my finger to it.' Kytchyn shuddered. 'It had a horrible feel, thick and slimy. I told them I'd no idea what it was. Then they pointed to the plaque with St John's name on, that showed it had been there a hundred years. I said there might be some record of it in the library. I tell you, sir, I wanted to get away.' He looked round him fearfully.

'I can understand,' I said. 'So it was dark, black. That explains why one of the names the ancients had was Dark Fire.'

'Dark as the pit of hell. Master Gristwood agreed, ordered his man to seal the barrel up again, then came back to the library with me.'

'Let's go there too,' I said. 'Come, I can see you would like to be out of here.'

'Thank you, yes.'

We made our way back to the church, then out into the sunlight. Kytchyn stood looking at the rubble, tears at the corners of his eyes. In the old days, when a monk or friar entered the cloister he ceased to have a separate legal personality, he died to the world. An act had just gone through parliament restoring their legal status as individuals. In Lincoln's Inn people joked about them being 'restored to life' by Cromwell. But to what life? 'Come, Master Kytchyn,' I said gently, 'the library.'

He led us through the roofless chapter house and I realized we would have to pass across the garden. The children were still playing there; a maid taking in the washing gave us a curious look.

We were halfway across when a door opened and a small man in a fine silk shirt came out. I drew a sharp breath, for I recognized Sir Richard Rich at once. I had been introduced to him at a function at the Inn. 'Shit,' Barak murmured under his breath, then bowed low as Rich came over. I bowed too, as did Kytchyn, whose eyes had widened with fear.

Rich halted before us. There was a puzzled frown on his handsome, delicately pointed features. Piercing grey eyes surveyed us.

'Brother Shardlake,' he said in a tone of amused surprise.

'You remember me, sir?'

'I never forget a hunchback.' His smile reminded me of his reputation for cruelty; it was said he had sometimes operated the rack himself in his days investigating heresy. To my surprise the little girls ran towards him, arms outstretched. 'Daddy, Daddy!' they cried.

'Now, girls, I am busy. Mary, take them indoors.'

The servant gathered the children together. Rich looked after them as they were led away. 'My brood,' he said indulgently. 'My wife says I don't whip them enough. Now then, what are you three doing in my garden? Ah, the former Brother Bernard, is it not? White suits you better than Dominican black.'

'Sir – I – sir—' Poor Kytchyn was tongue-tied.

I spoke up, trying to make my tone as light as Sir Richard's. 'Master Kytchyn is showing us the library. Lord Cromwell said I might see it as a favour.'

Rich inclined his head. 'There are no books left, Brother, my Augmentations men have burned them all.' He smiled mockingly at poor Kytchyn.

'It was the design of the building, my lord,' I said. 'I am thinking of building a library.'

He chuckled. 'You'd be better looking at one with the roof still on. By God's wounds, you must be doing well at Lincoln's Inn. Or does your wealth come from Lord Cromwell? Back in favour, eh?' Rich's penetrating eyes narrowed. 'Well, if the earl says you may look at the library I suppose you may. Watch the crows nesting on the roofbeams don't shit on you. From papist shit to birdshit, eh, Brother?' He smiled again at Kytchyn, who hung his head. Rich's mouth set hard as he turned his eyes to me.

'But ask permission if you wish to walk though my garden again, Shardlake.' Without another word he followed his children indoors. Kytchyn turned and led us rapidly away to a gate in the wall.

'I knew it was a bad idea to come here,' Barak said. 'My master said Rich was to know nothing.'

'We didn't tell him anything,' I said uncomfortably.

'He's curious. Don't look round, but the arsehole's watching us through the window.'

Kytchyn led us through the gate onto a trampled lawn surrounded on three sides by roofless buildings. He pointed. 'The library's there, next to the infirmary.'

We followed him into what must once have been a large, imposing library. Empty shelving covered the walls to a height of two storeys, and the floor was strewn with broken cupboards and torn manuscripts. It saddened me even more than the church had. I looked up to where a few skeletal roofbeams still stood, casting lines of shadow on the floor. A flock of crows took off, cawing. They circled and settled again. Through a glassless window I caught a glimpse of a lawned close with houses beyond. A fountain in the middle was dry. Kytchyn stood looking around miserably.

'So,' I asked quietly, 'when you came here with Master Gristwood, what did you find?'

'He wanted me to look for references to that soldier St John. Any papers of note left by those who died in the hospital were filed away. There were some under St John's name and Master Gristwood took them all. Then the next day he came back and spent a whole afternoon here, looking up any references to Byzantium or Greek Fire.'

'How did you know that was what he was after?'

'He got me to help him, sir. He took some more papers and some books. He never brought them back and soon after all the shelves were cleared, everything burned.' He shook his head. 'Some of the books were very beautiful, sir.'

'Well, it's all done now.'

There was a sudden clatter of wings as the crows took off again. They circled above, cawing noisily. 'What made them do that?' Barak muttered.

'You helped Master Gristwood search for papers. Did you look at any of them?'

'No, sir. I didn't want to know.' He looked at me seriously. His face was covered in sweat; it was hot in there, the sun shining down on us. 'I am not a bold man, sir. All I want is to be left to my prayers.'

'I understand. Do you know what happened to the barrel?'

'Master Gristwood had it taken away on a cart. I don't know where, I didn't ask.' Kytchyn took a deep breath, and lifted his hand to open the collar of his surplice. 'Excuse me, sir, it's so hot—' As he spoke he took a sideways step. From somewhere I heard a faint click.

Kytchyn's gesture saved my life. Suddenly he jerked forward with a high-pitched scream, and to my horror I saw a crossbow bolt embedded in his upper arm, blood welling red over his white surplice. He staggered against the wall, looking at his arm in horror.

Barak drew his sword and ran leaping to the window. The pock-faced man who had followed us from Cromwell's house was standing there, glittering blue eyes fixed on Barak as he fitted a new bolt to his crossbow. Barak, though, was almost on him and the man paused, then dropped the weapon with a clatter and fled across the yard. Barak threw himself over the window sill, regardless of broken glass, but the man was already at the abbey wall, clambering up. Barak grabbed at a flailing foot, but he was just too late; the assailant disappeared over the wall. Barak clambered up and, his elbows on the wall, looked down at the street for a moment before letting himself down. He picked up his sword, walked back to the window and climbed through again. His face was like thunder.

I bent to comfort Kytchyn. He had crumpled to the floor, clutching his arm and sobbing as the blood welled between his fingers. 'I wish I'd never seen those papers,' he moaned. 'I know nothing, sir, nothing. I swear.'

Barak knelt down, lifting Kytchyn's hand from his wound with surprising gentleness. 'Come, fellow, let's see.' He studied the arm. 'It's all right, the head of the bolt's come out the other side. You need a surgeon to snap it off, that's all. Here, lift your arm.' Trembling, Kytchyn obeyed. Barak took a handkerchief from his pocket and made a tourniquet, binding the arm above the wound.

'Come on, friend, there's a surgeon across the way that tends to injuries among the drovers. I'll take you there. Keep your arm raised.' He lifted the trembling Kytchyn to his feet.

'Who's trying to kill me?' the clerk squealed. 'I know nothing, sir, nothing.'

'I think that bolt was aimed at me,' I said slowly. 'It would have hit me if Kytchyn had not moved when he did.'

Barak's face was serious, his joking manner gone. 'Ay, you're right. God's pestilence, how did he know we were here?'

'Perhaps we were followed from the house.'

'There's someone who will be able to tell us,' he said grimly. 'I'll take Kytchyn to the surgeon, then I'll have a little word. Pock-face won't come back, but stand away from the window just in case. I'll not be long.'

I was too shocked to do anything but nod obediently. I leaned back against the wall as Barak helped the moaning Kytchyn outside. My heart was thudding as though it would leap from my throat, my whole body cold with sweat. The place suddenly seemed deathly quiet; it was too far from Sir Richard's house for him to have heard anything. I groaned involuntarily. Cromwell had put my life in danger a second time. I looked at the crossbow lying where Barak had left it on the floor, squat and deadly. I jumped at a sudden clatter, but it was only the crows returning to their perches.

A few minutes later I heard voices, Barak's and another's. The big doorkeeper was propelled through the doorway, protesting loudly. Large as the man was, Barak had his arm pinned behind him in a vice-like grip. He released him and sent him spinning across the room. He fell with a crash among the debris.

'You've no right!' the gatekeeper shouted. 'When Augmentations hear about this—'

'Pox on shitting Augmentations!' Barak shouted. Grabbing the man's dirty robe, he hauled him to his feet again. He had sheathed his sword but now pulled a wicked-looking dagger from his belt and held it to the doorkeeper's flabby throat. 'Listen to me, arsehole. I serve the Earl of Essex and I've authority to take what measures I like. Like slitting your weasen-pipe, see?' The man gulped, his eyes wide. Barak took the doorkeeper's head and jerked it round to face me. 'That priest I brought out just now was struck by a crossbow bolt intended for my master there, Lord Cromwell's lawyer. And the only person who could have let him in was you, you fat whore's cunny. So talk.'

'I didn't,' he babbled, 'There are other ways in—'

Barak reached down and gave the man's balls a hard squeeze, making him roar.

'I'll tell,' he shouted, 'I'll tell!'

'Get on with it then!'

The doorkeeper gulped. 'Shortly after you arrived, sir, another man came up to me. A strange-looking fellow, looking like a clerk; he's had the smallpox. He held up a gold angel and asked what the two of you were doing here. I – I told him you were meeting someone. He offered me the angel to let him in too. It was a gold angel, sir, and I'm poor.'

'Let's see it.'

The watchman fumbled in his belt and produced the big gold coin. Barak grabbed it. 'Right, I'll have that. It'll pay for our friend's surgeon. Now, this man. Was he carrying anything? A crossbow, for example?'

'I didn't see a crossbow!' the man howled. 'He had a big satchel, I didn't know what was in it!'

Barak stepped away from him. 'Get out, then, you great bag of guts. Go on. And don't say a word. Gabble about this and Lord Cromwell will be after you.'

He cringed at that. 'I'd not do anything against Crum, sir, I mean the earl—'

'Get out! Arsehole!' Barak twirled him round and helped him through the doorway with a kick. He turned to me, breathing heavily.

'I'm sorry I let pock-face get so close,' he said. 'I dropped my guard.'

'You can't be watching all the time.'

'He must have been somewhere among that rabble in the church. By Jesu, he's good. Are you all right?'

I took a deep breath and dusted down my robe. 'Yes.'

'I'll have to get word of this to the earl. Now. He's at Whitehall. Come with me.'

I shook my head. 'I can't, Barak. I have my appointment with Joseph. I can't miss that, I'm still responsible for Elizabeth. Then I want to see Guy.'

'All right. I'll meet you outside the apothecary's in four hours and we can go on to Southwark. It was nine by the church clock as I came in – say, at one.'

'Very well.'

He looked at me dubiously. 'You sure you'll be all right on your own?'

'God's death,' I snapped irritably, 'if we have to stay together every minute we'll double the time this takes. Come,' I said more gently, 'we can ride together as far as Cheapside.'

He looked worried. I wondered what Cromwell's reaction would be when he learned a third killing had been attempted.

# Chapter Fifteen

W E WERE AT Aldersgate before Barak spoke again. 'I knew we should never have gone to Barty's,' he said crossly. 'What did we achieve except for that poor arsehole being shot and Rich put on the alert?'

'We got confirmation that Greek Fire was discovered in the way the Gristwoods said it was. That there really was a barrel of − something − and a formula.'

'So you believe it now. Well, we have made a step,' he said sarcastically.

'When I was learning law,' I said, 'one of my teachers said that there is a question that applies in every case. The question is: what circumstances are relevant?'

'And the answer?'

'*All* the circumstances are relevant. One must know all the facts, the whole history, before proceeding. And I have learned much, downriver and again today, for all it nearly cost me. I have some leads that I would like to pick over with Guy.'

Barak shrugged, evidently still feeling the visit had been a dangerous waste of time. As we rode on it occurred to me that all who knew about Greek Fire might be in danger: Marchamount, Bealknap, Lady Honor.

'I'll have to tell the earl we met Rich,' Barak said. 'He'll not be pleased.'

'I know.' I bit my lip. 'It worries me that all of our three suspects are linked to some of the highest and most dangerous people in the land. Marchamount to Norfolk and Bealknap, apparently, to Rich.

And Lady Honor, it seems, to almost everyone.' I frowned. 'What *is* the connection between Rich and Bealknap? I'm sure Bealknap was lying.'

Barak grunted. 'That's for you to find out.' We had reached Cheapside. 'I'll leave you here,' he said. 'Meet you at the old Moor's shop at one.'

He rode off south, and I turned down Cheapside. As I rode between the rows of busy stalls I kept a careful eye out. I told myself no one would dare assault me among such a crowd – anyone would surely be seized before he could get away. But I was glad to see a number of constables with their staffs among the crowd. I turned up Walbrook Road, where many imposing merchants' houses stood. A little way up the street I saw Joseph pacing up and down. I dismounted and shook his hand. He looked strained and tired.

'I have been to see Elizabeth again this morning.' He shook his head. 'Still she says nothing, just lies there, paler and thinner each time.' He studied me. 'You look out of sorts yourself, Master Shardlake.'

'This new case I have is a troubling matter.' I took a deep breath. 'Well, shall we face your family?'

He set his jaw. 'I am ready, sir.'

Then so must I be, I thought. Taking Chancery's reins, I followed him to an imposing new house. He knocked at the front door. It was answered by a tall, dark-haired fellow of about thirty, dressed in a new jerkin and a fine white shirt. He raised his eyebrows.

'You! Sir Edwin said you would be calling.'

Joseph reddened at his insolent manner. 'Is he in, Needler?'

'Ay.'

I did not like the steward on his looks. He had a broad sly face under long black hair and a stocky frame starting to run to fat. An impertinent servant, I thought, allowed to get above himself. 'Can someone stable my horse?' I asked.

The steward called to a boy to take the animal, then led us through a wide hallway and up an imposing staircase, the banisters carved with heraldic beasts. We followed him into a richly appointed parlour hung with tapestries. Through the window I could see a garden, large for a town house. Flower beds with trellised walkways between ran down to a stretch of lawn; the grass was browning at the edges from lack of rain. There was a bench under an oak tree and, nearby, a circular brick well. I saw its top was sealed.

Four people sat on cushioned chairs. All were dressed in black, to my surprise for it was nearly a fortnight since Ralph had died and few wear mourning so long. Sir Edwin Wentworth was the only man among them; seeing him close I saw the resemblance to Joseph not only in his plump red face but in something fussy about his manner. He fumbled with the hem of his robe as he stared at me, eyes hard with anger.

His two daughters sat together: they were as pretty as Joseph had described, both with fair hair falling over the shoulders of their black dresses, milk-white complexions and with startlingly large cornflower-blue eyes. They had been embroidering, but as I entered they laid their needles on their cushions and gave me quick, demure smiles before lowering their heads and sitting with a well-brought-up stillness that was decorous but also a little unnerving, their hands unmoving in their laps.

The third female in the room could not have been more different. Joseph's mother sat ramrod straight in her chair, snow-white hair gathered under a black cap, veiny hands folded over a stick. She was thin, the planes of her skull visible beneath pale skin that was a patchwork of lines and smallpox scars. Wrinkled eyelids were closed for ever over her decayed eyes. She should have been a pitiful figure, but somehow she dominated the room.

She was the first to speak, turning her head towards me and thrusting out a lantern jaw. 'Is that the lawyer come with Joseph?' she asked in a clear voice with a trace of a country accent, showing pearl-white teeth I knew must be false. I shuddered involuntarily, for having dead people's teeth fixed in your jaw by a wooden plate was a conceit I disliked.

'Yes, Mother.' Edwin cast me a look of distaste.

She smiled crookedly. 'The seeker after truth. Come here, master lawyer, I would know your face.' She raised a beringed claw and I realized she wanted to feel my features as blind people sometimes will with their social inferiors. I approached slowly, for this was presumption from a woman who had once been a mere farmer's wife, but bent down. I felt all the eyes in the room upon me as her hands flickered lightly over my head and face with surprising gentleness.

'A proud face,' she said. 'Angular, melancholic.' She ran her hands lightly over my shoulders. 'Ah, a satchel of books and the slip and slide of a lawyer's robe.' She paused. 'They say you are a hunchback.'

I took a deep breath, wondering if she intended to humiliate me or just spoke as she liked out of age.

'Yes, madam,' I replied.

She smiled, giving me a glimpse of wooden gums. 'Well, you can take solace in having a distinguished face,' she said. 'Are you a Bible Christian? I hear you were once associated with the Earl of Essex himself, God protect him from his enemies.'

'When I was younger, I knew him.'

'Edwin will have no papist in this house. He even gives the girls religious books, encourages them to study the Bible. Such ideas are a little advanced for me.' She waved a hand at her son. 'Answer his questions, Edwin,' she said brusquely. 'Tell him everything. You too, girls.'

'Sabine and Avice have had enough, Mother, surely?' Edwin's voice was pleading.

'No. The girls, too.' Sir Edwin's daughters cast identical wide blue gazes at their grandmother, apparently as much under the old woman's spell as their father.

'We must have all this finished,' she continued. 'Perhaps you can imagine, Master Shardlake, the misery Ralph's death at Eliza-beth's hands has brought our small family. Three weeks ago we were happy, with fine expectations. Look at us now. And Joseph taking

Elizabeth's part makes matters worse. Perhaps you may imagine our feelings about him. We will not have Joseph in our house again after today.' She spoke calmly, evenly, without turning her head to her oldest son. Joseph lowered his head like a naughty child. I thought what inner courage it must have taken to defy this beldame.

'Am I right,' Sir Edwin asked, in a deep voice very like his brother's, 'that if you think Elizabeth is guilty you will cease to represent her? That those are the rules of your trade?'

'Not quite, sir,' I replied. 'If I *know* she is guilty, then I must and shall cease my representation.' I paused. 'May I tell you how the matter seems to me?'

'Very well.'

I went over the circumstances as I knew them: the girls hearing the scream, looking from the window, then rushing into the garden; Needler coming out and finding Ralph's body in the well. I felt sorry for the two girls having to listen to the terrible story once more. They cast their heads down again, kept their faces expressionless.

'But you see,' I concluded, 'no one actually *saw* Elizabeth push the boy into the well. It seems to me he might have slipped.'

'Then why does she not say so?' the old woman snapped.

'Because she knows questioning would bring the truth from her,' Edwin said with sudden fierceness. 'Of course she killed Ralph! You didn't have her in your house nine months, sir; you didn't see the viciousness she was capable of!' His mother leaned across and put a hand on his arm and he sat back, sighing angrily.

'Can you tell me more about that?' I asked. 'I only know what Joseph has told me.'

Sir Edwin shot an angry glance at his brother. 'She was malapert, disobedient and violent. Yes, sir, violent, though she was but a girl.'

'From the very start?'

'She was surly from the day she came, after my brother's funeral. We were prepared to make allowances as she'd lost everything. I was prepared to share all I had and I am not a poor man, though when I came to London I'd no more than Joseph has.' Sir Edwin's chest swelled momentarily with pride, even in the midst of his grief and anger. 'I told the girls to make her welcome, teach her the lute and virginal, take her out visiting. Much thanks they got. Tell him, Sabine.'

The older girl lifted her head and turned her doll-like eyes on me. 'She was horrible to us, sir,' she said quietly. 'She said she had more to do than tinkle on a music box.'

'We offered to take her to call on our friends,' Avice added. 'To banquets, to meet young gentlemen, but after one or two visits she said she didn't want to come again, called our friends mannered fools.'

'We did *try*, sir,' Sabine said earnestly.

'I know you did, girls,' their grandmother said. 'You did all you could.'

I remembered what Joseph had told me about Elizabeth's bookish interests, her love of the farm. She was clearly a girl of independent spirit, different from her cousins, who I guessed would happily limit themselves to womanly interests, aiming only for good marriages. But lack of common interests could scarcely have led to murder.

'After a while she'd barely speak to us,' Avice added sadly.

Her sister nodded. 'Yes, she took to staying in her room.'

'She had her own room?' That surprised me. In most households unmarried girls would sleep together in the maidens' chamber.

'This is a large house,' Sir Edwin said haughtily. 'I am able to provide separate rooms for all my family. In Elizabeth's case that was just as well.'

'She'd never have slept with us,' Sabine said. 'Why, soon it got so that if either of us went to ask her to join in things, she'd shout at us to go away.' She flushed. 'As time went on she started using bad words to us.'

'She lost all decorum,' Sir Edwin said. 'She was scarce like a girl at all.'

The old woman leaned forward, dominating the room again. 'More and more she seemed to hate us. At meals you couldn't get a civil word from her. In the end she said she'd take her food in her room and we let her; her presence at table spoiled our meals. When you are blind, Master Shardlake, you are more sensitive to atmospheres, and the atmosphere around Elizabeth grew dark with unreasoning hate for us. As dark as sin.'

'She hit me once,' Sabine said. 'That was in the garden. She took to sitting out on the bench on her own when the weather grew warm. One day she was sitting reading one of her books there and I went and asked her if she would like to come picking mayflowers outside the City walls. And she just picked up her book and started hitting me about the head with it, using terrible words. I ran away to the house.'

'I saw that myself,' Sir Edwin said. 'I was working in my study and I saw Elizabeth fly at my poor daughter from the window. I told Elizabeth to keep to her room for the rest of the day. I should have known then what she might do. I blame myself.' Suddenly he buried his head in his hands and his voice broke. 'My Ralph, my boykin. I saw him lying there, dead and stinking——' He sobbed, a heartbreaking sound.

The girls lowered their heads again and the old woman's jaw set hard. 'You see the horrors you raise for us, Master Shardlake.' She turned to Sir Edwin. 'Come, my son, fortitude. Tell him how Elizabeth treated Ralph.'

The mercer wiped his face with a handkerchief. He glared at Joseph, who seemed near to tears again himself, then at me. 'I thought at first she might like Ralph better than my daughters. He was another one who went his own way, bless the imp. And he did try to befriend her, he was pleased to have someone new in the house. To begin with they seemed to get on well: she went for a couple of country walks with him, they played chess together. But then she turned against him too. One evening, about a month after she came, I remember we were in here before dinner and Ralph asked Elizabeth to play a game of chess. She agreed, though in a surly way. He was soon winning, forward boy that he was. He leaned forward and took her rook, and said, "There. I have him, that rook will peck out no more eyes from my men." And Elizabeth threw the board up in the air with a great cry of anger, sending the pieces all over the room, and landed Ralph a great clout on the head. She left him sobbing and ran to her room.'

'It was a terrible scene,' the old woman said.

'We told Ralph to keep out of her way after that,' Sir Edwin went on. 'But the boy loved the garden, as why should he not, and she often sat there.'

'They may say Elizabeth is mad,' the old woman said. 'If she won't speak, no one can be sure. But I say it was wicked jealousy, jealousy because her cousins were more accomplished than her and our household a better one than the home she'd lost.' She turned her face to me. 'I felt and heard it all, the growth of her unreasoning hatred and violence, for I stay at home while Edwin is in the City and the girls go visiting.' She paused with a sigh. 'Well, Master Shardlake, you have heard us. Do you still doubt Elizabeth threw Ralph down that well?'

I avoided a reply. 'You were here on that day, madam?'

'I was in my room. Needler ran up and told me what had happened. It was I ordered him to go down the well. I felt Ralph's poor dead face when he brought him up.' She waved a bony hand in the air, as though touching that dead face again. Her harsh features softened for a moment.

I turned to the girls. 'You agree with what your father and grandmother have said?'

'Yes, sir,' Avice said.

'I wish to God it were not so,' Sabine added. She passed a hand over her eyes. 'Grandam,' she said meekly, 'my vision is blurred. Do I have to use the nightshade?'

'Belladonna is good, child. By expanding your pupils, it makes you look more comely. But perhaps a smaller dose.'

I looked at the old woman with distaste. I had heard of drops of deadly nightshade being used in this way for cosmetic purposes, but it was poisonous stuff.

I thought a moment, then stood up. 'I wonder if I might see

Elizabeth's room, and perhaps the garden, before I go? I will only take a few minutes.'

'This is too much—' Sir Edwin began, but once more his mother interrupted.

'Get Needler to take him. Take Joseph too, then afterwards they can both leave.'

'Mother—' Joseph had risen and taken a step towards the old woman. She tightened her grip on her stick and for a moment I thought she might strike him, but she only turned her head abruptly away. Joseph stepped back, his face working. Sir Edwin gave him an angry look, then rang a bell. The steward appeared, so quickly I wondered if he had been listening at the door, and bowed low to his master.

'Needler,' Sir Edwin said heavily, 'Master Shardlake wishes to visit the room that was Elizabeth's and then the garden. Show them, then show them out.'

'Yes, Sir Edwin.' Needler's manner was obsequious. 'And cook says he has a dish of blackbirds for tonight, if that pleases you.'

'Not too much sauce in it this time,' the old lady said sharply.

'Yes, madam.'

Neither Sir Edwin nor his mother made any move to say farewell, and the girls lowered their heads, though not before I saw Sabine glance at Needler and redden. I wondered if she could have a fancy for the boor: there was no accounting for young girls' fancies.

The steward led us out, closing the door with a snap. I was glad to be out of that room. Joseph was pale. Needler looked at us enquiringly.

'The murderess's bedroom, is it?'

'The accused's room,' I replied coldly. 'And mind your tongue, fellow.' Needler shrugged and led us up a further flight of stairs. He unlocked a door and we passed inside.

Whatever else had happened to her in that house, Elizabeth had had a fine room. There was a four-poster bed with a feather mattress, a dressing table with a mirror of glass, and chests for her clothes.

There was good rush matting on the floors that gave off a pleasant scent in the warm air. Several books stood on a shelf above the dressing table. I read the titles with surprise: Tyndale's *Obedience of a Christian Man*, the Coverdale New Testament, and several devotional works as well as *The Castel of Health* and Latin poetical works by Virgil and Lucan. A learned little library.

'Is Elizabeth a religious girl?' I asked Joseph.

'A good Bible Christian like all the Wentworths. She liked to read.'

I examined the Testament. It was much thumbed. I turned to Needler. 'Did Elizabeth speak much of religion?'

He shrugged. 'Perhaps she reflected on her sins, the way she was treating her family, and asked for God's help.'

'She does not seem to have received it.'

'There is still time,' Joseph murmured.

'Did Elizabeth have a maidservant? A woman to help her wash and dress?'

Needler raised his eyebrows. 'Wouldn't have one, sir. Said the servants mocked her.'

'And did they?'

'Perhaps – at her odd ways.'

'What happened to Grizzy?' Joseph asked suddenly. He pointed at a basket in the corner, filled with straw. 'Elizabeth's old cat,' he explained. 'She brought it from Peter's house.'

'It ran away,' Needler said. 'Cats do when they come to a strange house.'

Joseph nodded sadly. 'She was devoted to it.' So she was deprived even of that company, I thought. I opened one of the chests; it was full of dresses, neatly arranged. I indicated I had seen enough and we left the chamber. The smell of the warm rushes clung to my nostrils; I thought of the contrast with the foul stink in Newgate Hole.

Needler led us downstairs again, through a side door and into the garden. It was a peaceful place in the sunshine, insects buzzing lazily round the flowers. He led us across the lawn, the grass dry under our feet. He paused at the well and pointed to the bench, shaded by the large oak. 'That's where she was sitting when I came out after I heard the young mistresses screaming. Mistress Sabine and Mistress Avice were standing by the well, wringing their hands. "Ralph's gone," Mistress Sabine screamed at me. "Elizabeth's put him in the well." '

'And Elizabeth said nothing?'

'Just sat there with her head bowed, a dark look on her face.'

I went over to the well. Joseph hung back. A round wooden board was fixed over it, secured by padlocks to metal rings driven into the brickwork.

'This looks newly done.'

'Yes, sir. The master had the cap put on last week. Bit late really: it should have been done before.'

'I would like to see inside. Do you have keys to those locks?'

He looked at me evenly. 'Sir Edwin ordered them thrown away, sir. Nobody will be using that well again. The water's been poisoned for years. Not that there was any when I climbed down, we've had so little rain this spring.'

I bent down. There was a space of an inch or so between the wood and the rim on one side. I bent close and then pulled back at the smell that came from the gap; it was the stench of something dead, rotting. I remembered what Joseph had said about the smell on Ralph's body — like a cow's head left out in the Shambles a week. I looked across at him; he had taken a seat on the bench and was staring up at the window of the room we had left. His treatment from his family must have upset him greatly. I turned to Needler, who stood looking on impassively.

'There's a mighty stink coming from that well.'

'Like I said, the water's poisoned.'

'How did it smell when you went down there?'

'Bad enough.' He shrugged. 'But I wasn't worrying about smells, I was feeling for poor Master Ralph's body and hoping the rope ladder I'd let down wouldn't break. If that's all, I ought to be supervising the lunch.'

I stared at him a moment, then smiled. 'Yes, thank you, I have seen all I need.'

His eyes narrowed. 'Is there anything you'd like me to tell the master? Perhaps you won't be representing the girl now?'

'If I've anything to tell him I'll contact him myself, Needler. Now, Joseph, we should go.'

He rose wearily and followed me back to the hall. Needler opened the front door and we went out to the street. Needler said he would have my horse brought round, then closed the door with a snap. As we stood waiting on the step, Joseph gave me a direct look.

'Do you believe Elizabeth is guilty now, as my mother said?'

'No, Joseph, I think more and more that she is innocent.' I frowned 'There is something wrong in that house.'

'My mother is an uncommon woman. Stronger than most men. She was beautiful when she was young, though you wouldn't think it now. She always loved Edwin most, thought me a poor creature to be content with the farm.'

I touched his arm. 'It was a brave thing you did, subjecting yourself to that for Elizabeth's sake.'

'It was hard for me.'

'I saw. Tell me, when she was younger, did Elizabeth ever show any signs of trouble in her mind?'

'None, sir. Never. She was merry before she came to this house.'

'It is interesting she only seems to have become hostile if a family member approached her. Otherwise she wished only to be left alone.' I hesitated, then said, 'Joseph, I think there is something down that well.'

'What? What do you mean?'

'I don't know yet. But I remembered what you said about how Ralph's body smelt. I smelt something similar, coming from down the well. A sewage smell you might expect if there was bad water at the bottom, but Needler said there was no water at all when he went down.' I hesitated. 'I think there is something else down there. Something dead.'

His eyes were wide. 'What? What could it be?'

'I don't know, Joseph. I don't know. I'll have to think.' I put a hand on his arm.

'Oh, dear God, what has happened to us?'

I saw from a church clock it was well past twelve and touched his arm again. 'Once again I fear I must leave you, my friend. Another appointment I cannot miss. I will think what to do next. Can I reach you at your lodging house?'

'Ay, I'll be there until this matter is resolved,' he said firmly.

'What about your farm?'

'I have an arrangement with my neighbour. Things are in a poor way, there has been so little rain, but I cannot make it rain in Essex by being there, can I?'

The boy appeared round the side of the house, leading Chancery. He looked at us nosily as I gave him a farthing. I straightened my satchel and mounted.

'I will be in touch, Joseph, very soon.'

Joseph shook my hand. I looked after him as he walked away down Walbrook Road, something oddly indomitable in his big, heavy figure. Well, I must be indomitable too. I mounted Chancery for the short ride to Guy's. As I did so my heart jumped for a moment at the sight of a tall, pale figure among the people passing, but it was only an old man. He entered a shop. I shuddered slightly, then turned the horse south.

# Chapter Sixteen

WHEN I ARRIVED AT Guy's shop there was no sign of Barak's horse outside. Wondering whether he was still with Cromwell, I tied Chancery to the rail and went in.

Guy was at his table, grinding herbs in a pestle, and looked up in surprise. 'Ho, Matthew. I did not expect to see you today.'

'Guy, I have a favour to ask, some information. By the way, I am due to meet someone here. A young fellow with brown hair and an insolent grin. I don't suppose you've seen him?'

He shook his head. 'I have seen no one. It is my morning for preparing my herbs. Is this to do with the Wentworth case? How goes it?'

'We have a stay of execution. I have just come from the family's house, in fact. But it is something else I wanted to ask you about. I am sorry I have not asked you to dinner as I promised, but another matter has stolen up on me; between that and the Wentworth case I have scarce had time to breathe.'

'It does not matter.' He smiled, though I knew he was lonely and looked forward to coming to my house; with his dark skin he got few invitations to company. I slipped the satchel from my back, wincing a little at a stab of pain.

'Have you been doing your exercises?' he asked.

'These past few days, no. As I said, I've scarce had time to turn around.'

'You seem strung tight as a bowstring, Matthew.'

I sat down, rubbing sweat from my brow. 'Not surprising, as someone has just tried to kill me.'

C. J. SANSOM

'What?'

'You'd get it out of me in the end. I can't tell you all, but Lord Cromwell has spared Elizabeth Wentworth from the press for two weeks provided I undertake a mission for him. Nothing to do with the monasteries this time, but murder again and roguery—' I broke off, looking through the window. 'Young Barak, who I see tying his horse up outside, has been deputed by Cromwell to assist me.'

'Then the help you want is for Cromwell?' Guy looked at me seriously.

'To help to catch a brutal killer. I am not allowed to say more – I should not even have mentioned Cromwell's name. It is too dangerous.' I sighed. 'I will not press you if you feel you cannot in conscience help.'

The door opened and Barak came in. He looked uneasily at the bottles and jars lining the walls, then at Guy with his dark face and apothecary's robes. Guy bowed.

'Master Barak, I pray you are well.' He mispronounced the W in his lisping accent as he always did. I realized how strange and foreign he must seem to Barak.

'Thank you, master apothecary.' Barak stared around. I guessed he had never been in an apothecary's shop before; he looked like he had always known rude health.

'Would you like a little beer?' Guy asked him.

'Thank you,' Barak answered. 'It is a hot day.'

Guy went out to fetch it and Barak came over to me. 'The earl's worried. He's had Kytchyn taken to a place of safety till this is over.'

'Thank God for that.'

'He says you're being too slow. He's concerned you won't be seeing Lady Honor till tomorrow. There are only ten days till the demonstration, and the king's told him he's looking forward to it.'

'Perhaps he should seek a miracle worker then.'

Barak stepped away as Guy returned, bearing two cups of small beer. I drank gratefully, for I was very thirsty. Guy stood at the end of his table and studied Barak carefully a moment; I was pleased to see Barak look uncomfortable under that penetrating gaze.

'Well, then,' Guy said quietly. 'What help do you both wish from me?'

'We have to deal with alchemists,' I said. 'I know nothing of their trade, and would welcome your advice.' I opened the satchel and laid the alchemical books on the table. Then I carefully took the bottle from my pocket and held it out. 'Have you any idea what this strange stuff might be?'

He opened it carefully, then poured some on his finger and sniffed. 'Be careful, it burns like fire,' I warned as he bent and touched his tongue to it.

To my surprise, he laughed. 'There's nothing to worry about,' he said. 'There's no mystery here. This is aqua vitae, though distilled to a very high concentration.'

'Aqua vitae?' I laughed with astonishment. 'This new stuff that is distilled from bad wine and prescribed for sore eyes and melancholia?'

'The same. I think its value overrated, it just makes people drunk.' He rubbed the stuff between his fingers. 'A cupful, they say, will blind a horse. Where did you get it?'

'On the floor of an alchemist's workshop that had been — abandoned.' He looked at me sharply.

'Never mind where we got it, apothecary,' Barak cut in. 'Are you sure that's what it is?'

Guy gave him a long look, and I feared he would order him from his shop, but he turned to me with a smile. 'I believe so. Though the thickness of the liquid and the fiery taste suggest the concentration is very strong. I believe I may even be able to tell you where it came from. But first, there is a way of proving what it is. I will show you. It is quite spectacular, Master Barak. Wait a moment.'

He put the bottle down carefully, then left the room.

'Listen to me, Barak,' I said. 'Guy is a friend: have a care how you speak to him. And he is not one to be bullied like that doorkeeper. You will only anger him.'

'I don't trust him, on his looks.'

'I think that's mutual.'

Guy returned, carrying a candle and a small glazed dish. He closed the shutters, then carefully tipped a little of the liquid into the dish. Then he touched the candle to it.

I gasped, and Barak stepped back, as a blue flame flared in the bowl, rising two inches into the air.

'You'll burn the shop down!' Barak exclaimed. Guy only laughed again.

'The flame is too weak to set anything alight and it will die in a moment.' Sure enough, as we watched, the blue flame sank as quickly as it had risen, turned yellow, guttered and went out. Guy smiled at us. 'There. That is a characteristic of aqua vitae, that blue flame. It was certainly a very strong mixture.' He opened the shutters again. 'Note there is no smell or smoke.'

'You said you might know where it came from,' Barak said, his tone more respectful now.

'I did. We apothecaries are ever on the lookout for new herbs, new concoctions, from the strange parts of the world Englishmen voyage to nowadays. It is the constant topic at the Apothecaries' Hall. A few months ago we heard of a cargo that had been landed at Billingsgate from a ship that had ventured into the Baltic trade, to the lands of endless snow. They brought back a cargo of a colourless liquid they say men drink there. When people tried quaffing it here, as they would beer, it made them very sick. This sounds like the stuff.'

'What happened to the cargo?'

'That I do not know. I think one or two of my brethren went after it as a curiosity, but were told it had been sold. You would need to enquire among the sailors' taverns to find more.'

I nodded thoughtfully. A thick, viscous liquid that burned in a strange way. In some ways it sounded like Greek Fire, but in others quite unlike. The liquid in the monastery had been black, with a strong smell, Kytchyn said, and the flame we had just seen could never have set light to a ship. But what if this stuff was part of the formula, what if it changed its behaviour if other things were added?

'What do you know of alchemy, Guy?' I asked. I took the

alchemy books from my satchel and laid them on the table. 'These books are so full of mysteries and jargon I can scarce understand a word.'

He picked one up and leafed through it. 'Alchemy has given itself a bad name. Perhaps worse than it deserves. The alchemists like to keep their trade cloaked in secrecy and fill their books with references only they can understand.' He laughed. 'Some of the old books I think nobody understands.'

'And it impresses people, makes them think there must be a great mystery there to be uncovered.'

Guy nodded. 'But in that they are no worse than some physicians with their ancient remedies and secret formulae. Or lawyers, for that matter: in some courts you plead in old French no ordinary mortal could comprehend.'

There was a bark of laughter from Barak. 'He has you there.'

Guy raised a hand. 'And yet alchemy is part of natural science, the study of the world around us. God has left signs and clues in the world, that by struggling we might come to understand things: cure diseases, grow better crops—'

'Turn lead into gold?' I hesitated. 'Set water on fire?'

'Perhaps. And the task of alchemy, like astrology and medicine for that matter, is to read those clues.'

'As rhinoceros horn is supposed to bring virility, the clue being its resemblance to the male organ. But, Guy, so much of this looking for signatures and correspondences is mere fraud.'

'Yes, it is. I agree that the manner in which alchemists profess secret, arcane knowledge is often no more than a trick to keep their trade inaccessible.'

'So you think, like most, that alchemy's a suspect trade?'

'Not altogether. There are plenty of rogues who claim to have found the philosopher's stone that can turn base metal into gold, but for each one of them there is another who has striven to make real achievements by careful observation, by study of how substances are made up and how they change. How the four elements of earth, air, fire and water interact to make all the things we know. How heat can change one thing into another — wine into aqua vitae, for example.

'And everything comes from the four elements. Earth, air, fire and water. Any new material that appears, like that strange stuff, can be broken down into those essential elements and reconfigured.'

He smiled. 'There is nothing truly new in the world. No new elements, at least. But a good alchemist may, for example, discover by careful observation how to melt down ores in the furnace in such a way as to produce better iron, as they are doing in the Weald now.'

'Or how to make a finer form of pewter,' I said, remembering Goodwife Gristwood's story of Sepultus's failed experiments.

'Exactly. It is usually a matter of separating out some impurity of an earthy nature.' He smiled. 'I am with those thinkers who consider God means us to uncover the secrets of the earth by the slow, sure path of observation rather than mystical formulae in ancient books. Even if they do come up with some strange notions, like the man in Poland who says the earth goes round the sun.'

'Yes.' Something had stirred a memory. 'A furnace, you said. You remind me that metals are forged in furnaces. So alchemists must often work with founders, as they all have furnaces.'

'Of course,' Guy agreed. 'I make do with a fire here to distil my herbs, but to melt ores and metals a furnace would be needed.' He frowned. 'This is a strange discussion, Matthew. What has it to do with this — ' he glanced at Barak — 'this case of yours?'

'I'm not sure.' I frowned in thought. 'A founder would also be needed to make, say, a large metal tank with a pump and pipes.'

'Yes. Alchemists often have arrangements with the Lothbury founders to assist them. It has to be someone they trust, of course, if they're to share their secrets.'

'Guy,' I said excitedly, 'do you remember that young founder I met last week? Would he know who might work with alchemists up there? And perhaps one who works with the City on the water conduits, works with pumps and valves?'

He hesitated. 'Perhaps. That would be a specialized trade. But Matthew, if this is a dangerous matter, I would not involve him.'

'Lord Cromwell may command it,' Barak said.

Guy turned to him. 'He may command what he wishes,' he said imperturbably.

Barak glared. 'Yes, my Spanish friend, he may.'

'God's death, Barak, be quiet,' I said angrily. 'I understand, Guy. I can find what I need as easily from the City records, see whom they employ on the conduits.'

Guy nodded. 'I would prefer that.' He turned back to Barak. 'And by the way, sir, I am not Spanish. I come from Granada, which was conquered by Spain fifty years ago. My parents were Moslems who were expelled from Spain by Ferdinand and Isabella. Along with the Jews – yours is a Jewish name, I think.'

Barak reddened. 'I am English, apothecary.'

'Are you now?' He raised an eyebrow. 'Ah well. Thank you for your understanding, Matthew. I wish you safe in your quest.' He shook my hand, then looked at me wryly. 'Your eyes are alight, Matthew, alight with the prospect of progress in your chase. May I keep those books, by the way? I should be interested to look through them.'

'Please do.'

'If you want to talk more, I am here.' He gave Barak a cold look. 'So long as foreigners are allowed to remain.'

✝

OUTSIDE I TURNED angrily on Barak. 'Well done,' I said. 'Your manners really helped our enquiries.'

He shrugged. 'Insolent old Moor. God's teeth, he's an ugly creature.'

'And you,' I snapped, 'you are what you call everyone else – an arsehole.'

Barak only grinned.

'Since you probably lost us Guy's help in finding the founder, you can go up to the Guildhall and ask for details of all the founders they employ on the conduits. I am going to Wolf's Lane to ask Good-wife Gristwood a few more questions. If Michael and Sepultus were visiting the founders, she must have known about it.'

'I thought we were going across to Southwark to find the whore.'

'I'll meet you at the Steelyard steps in an hour and a half. Who knows, I may even have time to grab a pie from a stall.' I wiped sweat from my brow, the heat of the afternoon was punishing. Barak hesitated and I wondered if he were going to argue: I felt so angry I would almost have welcomed it. But he only smiled, mounted his black mare and cantered away.

☦

As I RODE THROUGH the narrow streets to Queenhithe my anger ebbed. I found myself once more watching fearfully for dangerous movements in the shadows. The streets were empty, people indoors avoiding the heat if they could. I felt my cheek prickle with sunburn and pulled my cap lower. I jumped as a rat scurried from a doorway and ran down the street, hugging the wall.

The Gristwoods' house was unchanged, the split and broken front door still in place. I knocked, the sound echoing within. Jane Gristwood herself opened the door. She wore the same white coif and grey dress and there was a new unkemptness about her appearance; I saw food stains on the dress. She stared at me wearily.

'You again?'

'Yes, madam. May I come in?'

She shrugged and held the door open. 'That stupid girl Susan's gone,' she said.

'Where's the watchman?'

'Drinking and farting in the kitchen.' She led me past the ancient tapestry into the dowdy parlour and stood there waiting for me to speak.

'Any more news on the house?' I asked.

'Yes, it's mine. I've seen Serjeant's Marchamount's lawyer.' She laughed bitterly. 'For what it's worth. I'll need to take in lodgers – a fine class of tenant I'll get in this mouldy hole. He had my money, you know.'

'Who?'

'Michael. When we married he got a big dowry from my father, to get me off his hands. That's all gone and this is how I'm left. He couldn't even bring any decent furniture from the monasteries, just that ugly old wall hanging. Did you see that whore?' she concluded bluntly.

'Not yet. But I have a query, madam. I believe Sepultus may have worked with a founder in his recent experiments.'

The frightened look that came into her face told me I had hit the mark. Her voice rose.

'I've told you: I'd no interest in his mad doings beyond worrying he'd blow up the house. Why are you asking me these questions? I'm a poor widow alone!'

'You are keeping something back, madam,' I said. 'I must know what it is.'

But she had stopped listening. She was staring out at the garden, her eyes wide. 'It's him again,' she whispered.

I whirled round. A gate in the wall was open and a man was standing there. I dreaded seeing the pockmarked man but it was a stocky, dark-haired young fellow who stood there. Seeing us looking, he turned and fled. I stepped to the door, then paused. Even if I caught him, what then? He could overpower me easily. I turned back to Goodwife Gristwood. She had sat down at the table and was crying, her thin body wrenched with sobs. I waited until she calmed down.

'You know who that man was, madam?' I asked sternly.

She raised a piteous face to me. 'No! No! Why do you try to catch me in these coils? I saw him watching the house yesterday. He was there all afternoon, just watching, he near scared the wits from me. He's one of the men who killed Michael, isn't he?'

'I don't know, madam. But you should tell your watchman.'

'This is punishment for my sin,' she whispered. 'God is punishing me.'

'What sin?' I asked sharply.

She took a deep breath, then looked me hard in the eye. 'When I was young, Master Shardlake, I was a plain girl. Plain, but full of base lusts and when I was fifteen I romped with an apprentice.'

I had forgotten how coarse her tongue was.

'I had a child.'

'Ah.'

'I had to give him away and do hard penance, confessing my sin in church before the congregation, saying how unclean I was Sunday after Sunday. The old religion was no gentler than the new when it came to sins of the flesh.'

'I am sorry.'

'I was thirty before I found anyone to marry me. Or rather, my father did. Father was a master carpenter and Michael advised him once over an unpaid debt. Michael had a few unpaid bills himself, he'd been involved in one of his crazy money-making schemes and my dowry saved him from the debtors' prison.' She sighed. 'But God does not forget a sin, does he? He goes on punishing, *punishing*.' She balled her work-roughened hands into fists.

'The founder,' I said.

She sat there a few seconds more, her fists clenched. When she spoke again there was tense resolution in her voice.

'They made me give my son away to the nuns at St Helen's. The nuns wouldn't let me near, but I bribed a washerwoman to give me news. When he was fourteen the nuns got him an apprenticeship as a founder.

'And then, when he was free of the nuns, I made myself known to David. I've visited with him every week since then.' She smiled then, a triumphant little smile.

'And then Sepultus took house with you and was looking for a founder to help in his work?'

Her eyes widened. 'How do you know that?'

'I guessed.'

'I didn't tell you because I didn't want David involved in this terrible thing.'

'Madam, your son could be in danger if others know of his involvement. And he has nothing to fear if all he has been doing is honest work.'

She half rose. 'Danger? David in danger?'

I nodded. 'But if you tell me where he is, Lord Cromwell will protect him as he has you.'

She spoke quickly. 'His name is David Harper. It was my maiden name. He is junior to another man, Peter Leighton of Lothbury. It was Leighton that Sepultus worked with.'

'Does Master Leighton work on repairing the conduits?'

She looked at me sharply. 'How did you know?'

'Another guess.'

She stood up. 'I'll go to David now. Warn him. I'll have to prepare him before he'll see you – the founders are a close bunch.'

'Very well, but I must see him and this man Leighton.'

'Can I send word to you?'

I nodded and gave her my address.

'You will help us, sir?' she asked tremulously, an anxious mother, all her harshness gone.

'I will do all I can, I promise. And I will see that watchman of yours, make sure he stays alert. Take him to Lothbury with you. Keep all your doors locked.' I remembered the crossbow. 'And shutter the windows.'

'But it's so hot—'

'It would be safer.' Pock-face and now this young man; I remembered the two sets of bloody footsteps. I had known there were two of them.

# Chapter Seventeen

IT WAS A RELIEF TO reach the river stairs. The tide was full, temporarily drowning the stinking mud, and a welcome breeze came off the river. There was no sign of Barak, so I left Chancery at the stables and stood looking at the high warehouses of the merchants of the Hanseatic League, for whom Brother Bealknap acted. The ancient privileges to trade with Baltic ports of these German merchants were increasingly flouted by English merchant adventurers, such as the one who had brought the strange drink from the far reaches of that cold sea. Bealknap could have known about the Polish stuff from his mercantile contacts, it could have been through him that it came to the Gristwoods.

I hitched my satchel over my shoulder. The river was crowded, not only with passengers going up and down and across to Southwark but with people of the wealthier sort who had hired tilt boats to ride upon the water and enjoy the breeze. Everywhere brightly coloured sails passed to and fro. I glanced over them, wondering if Lady Honor and her maids might be among them.

There was a touch at my shoulder; I turned to see Barak there.

'Did you find anything at the Guildhall?' I asked curtly, for I was still annoyed by his treatment of Guy.

'Ay, I got a list of names of founders who work on the conduit.' He looked shamefaced and I wondered whether he was beginning to realize that his rough ways with people were not suited to the delicacy of this investigation.

'And I was able to get the information I needed from Goodwife Gristwood.' I told him all she had said. He passed me the list and I nodded. Peter Leighton's name was prominent.

'Good, that's useful. It confirms we're on the right track.'

'I called in at the Old Barge, too,' Barak said. 'I've asked for any messages to be sent both there and to your house. There's a note from Cromwell's clerk. Bealknap does do a little work for the Hanse merchants and also some French ones – routine stuff declaring imports at the Custom House.'

'I wonder how much he rakes off.'

'The link with the French is dangerous.' He looked at me seriously. 'Imagine French fireships sailing up the Thames.'

'I'd rather not.'

'I've remembered where I saw Bealknap before, by the way.'

I looked at him with interest. 'Where?'

'Remember I told you the man my mother married after my father died was a law clerk? He was one of friend Bealknap's compurgators. I remember Bealknap coming to the house and telling him to pretend he knew some rogue who'd pleaded his clerkship at the assizes and been locked up in the bishop's palace.'

'You remember that clearly?' I asked eagerly. 'Clearly enough to swear in court?'

'Ay, now my memory's been jogged.'

'How old were you?'

'Ten perhaps.'

I stroked my chin. 'Then a court might not accept your evidence. Are you still in touch with your mother and stepfather?'

'No.' Barak reddened and his lips set. 'I haven't seen them in years.' The corners of his wide mouth, usually upturned ready for mockery, were pushed down.

'Even so, this gives us a hold over the rogue. Well done.' I studied him to see how he would react to words of praise such as an employer might use to an employee, but he only nodded. I decided to venture further. 'You know I visited the Wentworths earlier?'

'Ay.'

'Are you any good at picking locks?'

He raised his eyebrows. 'Passing fair.'

'I thought you might be.' I told him what had passed at Sir Edwin's. He whistled when I told him of the stink coming from the well.

'I want us to break into the garden at night and get those locks off. Then I'd like you to climb down and take a look. We'll need a rope ladder.'

He laughed. 'God's death, you don't ask much, do you?'

'Less than the earl has asked of me. Well? It was part of the bargain, Barak, that you'd help me with the Wentworths.'

'All right. I owe you a favour; I suppose I put you out of sorts with your friend.' I realized this was the nearest he would come to an apology.

Just then a wherry with a canopy pulled up at the wharf, depositing a pair of well-dressed Flemish merchants on the steps. Barak and I took their places and the boatman pulled away. It was pleasant to be out on the smooth brown water. I watched the stately swans bobbing by the banks. Shouts of laughter came from the tilt boats around us and the gulls cried overhead.

'You've got your case against Bealknap tomorrow, haven't you?' Barak asked.

'Don't remind me. I'll have to spend tonight preparing. But it will be a chance to quiz him again.'

'These serjeants, like Marchamount, what does their rank signify?'

'Only serjeants have the right to be heard in the Court of Common Pleas. There aren't many, they're appointed by the Crown and the other judges. The judges themselves are always appointed from the Serjeancy.'

'You ever been considered for it?'

I shrugged. 'These things are all decided by murmurings behind the scenes.'

I jumped at the sudden, piercing sound of a trumpet. The boats in the middle of the river rowed frantically out of the way as an enormous canopied barge painted in bright gold appeared, a dozen oarsmen in the king's livery making rapid sweeps through the water

in time to the beating of a drum. Our little wherry bobbed wildly in
the royal barge's wake as, like everyone else in the boats, we doffed
our caps and bowed our heads. The king's canopy was drawn shut,
protecting him from the sun. I wondered if Cromwell was in there
with him, or perhaps Catherine Howard. The barge swept upriver to
Whitehall.

The boatman spoke. 'They say if Queen Anne goes down there'll
be more religious changes.'

'Perhaps,' I replied noncommittally.

'It's hard for common folk to keep track of it all.' He lowered his
head to the oars.

✝

THE WHERRY DROPPED US at St Mary Overy steps on the
Southwark side. I followed Barak up to the wharf. Winchester Palace
came into view as we mounted the slippery stairs. I paused a moment
to catch my breath and looked at the facade of the forbidding Norman
building, the glass in its enormous rose window glinting in the midday
sun. The Bishop of Winchester owned most of Southwark, including
the brothels; the palace was his London residence and the king was
said to have dined there with Catherine Howard many times that
spring. I wondered what plots against Cromwell had been hatched
within its walls.

Barak made off along the side of the high palace wall towards the
warren of poor houses that lay to the east. I followed.

'Have you visited Southwark before?' he asked me.

'No.' I had travelled the main road to Surrey many times but
never ventured into the streets beyond, haunts of whores and criminals.
Barak walked along confidently. He favoured me with one of his
mocking grins.

'Ever been to a whorehouse?'

'Yes,' I said shortly. 'But a better class of one.'

'Ah, with gardens and shady nooks?'

'When I was a student and knew no better.'

'The Winchester geese can be shy birds if they think you're anything official. If we let out even a hint we're on any business other than trugging before we're well inside they'll fly off down the alleys faster than you could believe. You need to follow my lead here.' He looked at me seriously.

'Very well.'

'Take off your robe – it'll scare them. We'll pretend we're customers, all right? I'm your servant that's brought you over the river for a bit of fun. The madam will invite us to have a drink with the whores; if she offers you food, take it, no matter how much it costs. It's one way they make money if the whores are cheap, which these will be.'

I took off my robe and stuffed it in my satchel. It was a relief to be rid of it.

'When we're inside I'll ask for Bathsheba Green, say she's been recommended, then you get her alone and question her. I wouldn't get too familiar, though. These houses are famous for the French pox.'

'How do you know she's there?'

'I've contacts among the street urchins, I've paid them to watch a house for me before.' He smiled and lowered his voice. 'A member of the conservative faction, a most holy cleric, used to frequent one of the boy-houses down here. That information was very useful to my master.'

I shook my head. 'Is there nothing he won't do?'

'Not much. The lads know Bathsheba's working times – she'll be there this afternoon.'

We passed into a warren of small timber-framed houses, the unpaved lanes stinking with refuse, among which pigs and skinny dogs grubbed for food. The cloying stink of the Southwark tanneries rose in the hot air. In accordance with the Southwark regulations all the brothels were painted white, standing out against the dingy plaster of the other houses. Each had a sign with a lewd reference outside the door, a naked Adam and Eve or a bed or a nightshirt. We stopped before a poor-looking house where the paint was flaking, a bishop's hat crudely painted on the sign outside. Shutters were drawn over the windows. I heard a raucous burst of male laughter from within. Kicking away a couple of hens rooting outside, Barak knocked confidently on the door.

It was opened by a middle-aged woman. She was short and stocky, with a square ugly face surrounded by curly red hair. She had been branded as a whore in London at some point for a dark 'W' stood out on her white cheek. She looked at us suspiciously.

'Good day, Mistress.' Barak smiled. 'I've brought my master over from the City, he's a taste for a quiet house.'

She looked me over, then nodded. 'Come in.'

We followed her into a dark room that was even hotter than the street, with a fug of unwashed bodies and cheap tallow candles barely disguised by the cheap incense burning in a corner. The smoky candles lit a table where two middle-aged men sat, shopkeepers by the look of them. One was fat and merry-looking, the other thin and ill at ease. They nodded to us. A pippin pie was set on the table and the men had plates of food before them. A whore sat beside each, a buxom creature for the fat man and a nervous-looking girl of about sixteen for the other. Both women had opened their bodices so their breasts spilled out. Sitting thus at table, they looked bizarre rather than erotic.

The madam indicated a cupboard, where a thin boy in a greasy jerkin stood by a jar of beer. 'Will you eat with us, sir?'

'Yes, thank you.'

She nodded to the boy, who poured two mugs of beer and set them on the table. The plump whore leaned across and whispered something in her client's ear, making him laugh throatily.

'Half a groat each that'll be, sirs,' the madam said. I passed across the money. She peered closely at the coins before slipping them into a purse at her belt and smiling at us, a red slash in her face, showing decayed teeth.

'Make yourselves comfortable. I'll get a couple more girls to join us, we'll make a merry lunch.'

'Only a girl for my master,' Barak said. 'He's a shy fellow, wants a girl to gentle him, treat him softly. We've heard of a girl called Sheba, or Bathsheba, who works here.'

Her eyes narrowed at once. 'Who told you that?'

'Someone at the Guildhall,' I replied.

'Which company?'

'I can't remember, it was at one of the dinners.' I forced a smile. 'Only I like a gentle girl and he said Bathsheba was kindly. I'd pay more for a gentle girl.'

'I'll see.' She disappeared through an inner door.

'My one's sweet and plump enough,' the fat shopkeeper said. 'Eh, Mary?' The woman winked at me and laughed, her large, veined breasts wobbling as she put an arm around his neck.

I heard the madam calling from somewhere within the house. 'Daniel, here!' The boy ran out of the room. I heard a muted whisper and a minute later the madam returned. She smiled again.

'Bathsheba will see you in her room, sir. Bring your drink if you like.'

'Thank you, I'll leave it.' I rose from the table, trying to look enthusiastic.

'You don't want to waste time in there drinking, eh?' The fat shopkeeper chuckled.

The madam led me down a dark corridor with several closed doors, her heavy feet stumping on the uneven floorboards. I was suddenly afraid, very conscious that I was alone. I jumped as a door opened, but it was only a faded whore who looked out quickly then slammed the door shut. The madam knocked at another. 'Here's Bathsheba,' she said, smiling her horrible smile as she ushered me inside. She closed the door behind her, but I heard no retreating footsteps and realized she was standing outside, listening.

The room was small and mean, the only furniture a cheap trunk and a large old truckle bed. The shutters were half-open, but the room still had a sweaty stink. A girl lay on the bed. For some reason I had expected Bathsheba to be pretty, but although young she had pasty, heavy features and a swarthy complexion. There was something familiar about her face, though I could not place it. She had made no effort to pretty herself and lay there in a stained old dress, without rouge, her black hair disordered on the greyish pillow. Her best feature was her large, intelligent brown eyes but they stared at me not in welcome but, I saw, with fear. She had a large bruise and a half-healed cut on one cheekbone.

'Well, Bathsheba,' I said quietly, 'I am told you are a gentle girl.'

'Who told you that, sir?' Her voice was scared, faltering.

'Someone I met at the Guildhall.'

'I've only had one customer of your class,' she said. 'And he is dead.' To my surprise I saw tears in the corners of her eyes. It seemed Michael Gristwood's feelings for her had not been one-sided. She continued to look at me fearfully. How had they realized so quickly I was not an ordinary customer? I studied her scared face a moment, then laid my satchel on the edge of the bed and sat down carefully.

'I swear I mean you no harm,' I said soothingly, 'but I am here to enquire into the death of Master Gristwood. I am a lawyer.'

'I know nothing of his death,' she said quickly.

'I didn't think you did. I only want to know what he talked about with you. Did he mention his work?'

I saw her glance at the door and lowered my voice.

'You will be paid, I'll see to that.' I paused, then said, 'You cared for each other?'

'Yes.' Defiance entered her face. 'We both needed kindness and we gave it to each other. Madam Neller didn't like me getting close to a client but it happens.'

'How did you meet?' I felt pleased with my quick progress.

'He came here one day with some Augmentations clerks. They'd come on a roist south of the river and ended up here. Michael pleasured me, he made me laugh and he visited again on his own. He had a hard time with his wife. He said she had no laughter in her.'

'I've met her. Not a merry soul.'

'But he told me nothing of his work.' She looked at the door again, her bruise showing livid. I wondered if the madam had given it to her.

'He didn't say anything about some papers he had, or anything he was working on with his brother?' I asked gently.

'I know nothing,' she said, her voice trembling. 'I told the others—'

'What others?' I asked quickly.

Bathsheba pointed to her cheek. 'The ones who gave me this.'

Heavy footsteps sounded outside. I heard someone whispering to the madam, then started back as the door was flung open. Two men stepped into the room. One was a bald, hulking fellow carrying a club and the other a stocky young man whose features were so like Bathsheba's he could only be her brother. I recognized him at once: he was the man I had seen in the Gristwoods' yard. He held a long dagger, which he pointed at my throat as I jumped up from the bed. I caught a glimpse of the madam's worried face before the big man shut the door and stood against it.

'He hasn't hurt you, Sheba?' the young man asked, never taking his eyes from my face.

'No, George, but I was afraid the boy wouldn't find you in time.'

'Has he hurt you?'

'No. I kept him talking. About Michael again.'

'Pox on Madam Neller, letting these shits in at all.' He turned to me. 'We've got you this time, matey. You won't get away with hitting a defenceless woman.'

I lifted my hands. 'There's a mistake, I swear. I never met this girl before today.'

'No, but your pock-faced mate did that came and beat her last week. He'd have killed her if one of the other girls hadn't run for me.' He turned to his sister, clenching his fists. 'Is it him in the other room? The pock-faced man? Or that lump of a confederate of his, with the wens on his nose?'

'Madam Neller says no. She's keeping him occupied.'

'A pock-faced man?' I asked. 'Tall and very pale? Asking about Michael Gristwood?'

'Ay, your confederate.'

I considered shouting for Barak, but Bathsheba's brother had a desperate look and could slit my throat in a moment. I forced myself to speak calmly. 'Please listen. That man is after me as well – he tried to kill me yesterday. I mean no harm, I wished only to ask Bathsheba about Master Gristwood—'

'He was asking the same questions,' Bathsheba said. 'About Michael's papers, his brother's work. He says he's a lawyer.'

The young man's eyes flashed angrily. 'I didn't know they allowed hunchbacks to be lawyers.' He stepped closer and held the dagger to my neck. 'If you're a lawyer, you're working for somebody. Who is it?'

'Lord Cromwell,' I replied. 'My assistant has his seal.'

Bathsheba's brother and the big man at the door exchanged a look. 'Oh, George,' Bathsheba groaned, 'what have we done?'

The brother grabbed my arm and slammed me against the far wall, the knifepoint pressed against my throat. 'Why? God's death, how is he involved in this?'

'George,' Bathsheba cried out then, wringing her hands, 'we have to tell them everything, we have to throw ourselves on their mercy—'

George turned to her angrily. 'Mercy? Cromwell? No, we'll kill the crookback and his mate and dump their bodies in the Thames, there'll be nothing to show they were ever here—'

There was a yell from the madam standing outside, then a loud crash. The man with the club staggered across the room as the door was flung open. He landed on the bed and Bathsheba screamed. Barak lunged in; he had unsheathed his sword and now he brought it down on George Green's knife arm as he turned. Green yelled, dropping the dagger.

'You all right?' Barak asked me.

I gasped. 'Yes—'

'I heard these fellows in the hallway, though they tried to muffle the noise they made.' He turned to George, who was gripping his arm, blood running through his fingers. 'You'll be all right, matey, I just cut you. I could've had your arm off, but I didn't. In return you can do some talking—'

'Look out!' I shouted. The big man had jumped up from the bed and raised his club, ready to smash it down on Barak's head. I threw myself at him and managed to throw him off balance. He staggered against the wall. Barak turned and in that moment George grabbed his shocked-looking sister by the hand, threw open the shutters and jumped from the window, Bathsheba screaming as she followed. The big man steadied himself, dropped his club and fled through the open doorway.

Barak ran to the window. 'Stay here!' he shouted as he jumped after Bathsheba and her brother, whom I could just see disappearing round a corner. I sat on the bed, trying to gather my wits. After a few moments I realized the house was totally silent. Had everyone fled? I wondered. I lifted myself from the greasy bed and, picking up George's dagger, walked back to the dining chamber. The girls and their customers had gone. The madam sat alone at the table, her head in her hands. Her shock of red hair, evidently a wig, lay among overturned tankards. Her own hair was thin and grey.

'Well, lady?' I said.

She looked up at me, her expression despairing. 'Is this the end of my house?'

I sat down. 'Not necessarily. I want to know about Bathsheba's doings with Michael Gristwood, and the attack on her. Was that attack the reason you were worried when we came asking after her?'

She nodded, then looked at me fearfully. 'I heard you mention Lord Cromwell's name,' she whispered.

'Ay. I work for him. But he doesn't care what trugging houses there are in Southwark so long as the owners don't cross him.'

She shook her head. 'The girls shouldn't get involved with the customers. It happens sometimes when a girl isn't pretty or getting past her prime, and Bathsheba's past twenty-five. Sometimes they fancy themselves in love. Not that I'd anything against Michael Gristwood, he'd a merry way with him for a man of law. Some afternoons we all sat round this table together laughing. But when he was alone with Bathsheba he'd start crying and bewailing his woes.' Her mouth twisted bitterly. 'He should have my troubles, have a mark like this.' She pointed to her cheek. The 'W' stood out clearly in the dim light; ashes would have been rubbed into the burn to ensure the mark never faded.

'So you discouraged Bathsheba.'

'When I saw she was getting in too deep. These things always end in trouble.' She looked at me with hard blue eyes. 'There were things Gristwood told Bathsheba that worried her, I knew that. He was in trouble of some sort.'

'Did you learn what trouble?'

'No, Bathsheba turned close as an oyster. Then Michael stopped coming. Bathsheba thought he'd left her. She went across to Queen-hithe to make enquiries and came back here crying and wailing that he was dead. I told her she should get away, go back to Hertford where she came from. But she didn't want to leave her brother. He's a wherryman on the river.'

'They're close?'

'Close as can be. Then three men came to the house. They weren't cunning like you, they just barged in with drawn swords, told the girls to get out and demanded Bathsheba.'

'And one of them was a tall man with the marks of smallpox.'

'Ay. Face as scored as a butcher's block, and another ugly ruffian with him.'

'Do you know who sent them?'

'No.' She crossed herself. 'The devil perhaps, they had killing looks on them. The girls ran. I sent the boy for George, same as I did today. He came back with a dozen of his mates. By the time they arrived they had Bathsheba in her room and the pock-faced one was beating her. But the wherrymen were too many for them and they ran.'

'Did they get any information from Bathsheba?'

She shrugged. 'I don't know. I ordered her out of the house. If this place gets a reputation for fighting it'll be the end of it. Some of the girls have already left. Bathsheba came back this morning, asking me to take her on again.' She shrugged. 'I'm short of girls, so I let her. More fool me.'

The door opened and Barak came in, breathless. 'They've got away,' he said. 'Run to some rat hole!' He glared at Madam Neller. 'What's the old troll got to say?'

'I'll tell you outside.' I got to my feet. I took out my purse and laid a gold half angel on the table. 'There's two more if you let me know if Bathsheba returns, or if you find where she is. I mean her no harm, mind.'

The beldame grabbed up the coins. 'And there'll be no trouble from Lord Cromwell?'

'Not if you do as I ask. You will find me at Chancery Lane.'

She pocketed the coins. 'Very well,' she said and nodded briefly.

Barak and I left the place and walked rapidly back to the river stairs, watchful for danger though all was quiet. The Thames was still thronged and there were no boats waiting. Barak sat down on the top step and I followed, removing my satchel, which was making my shoulder ache. I told him what the madam had said. 'By the way,' I added, 'thank you for saving my life back there.'

Barak smiled ruefully. 'And to you for saving mine. That knave would have had my brains out. What about that well? D'you want to go there tonight?'

'No, I have to go to Lincoln's Inn to prepare for tomorrow's case. And I want to find some books on Greek Fire too.'

He looked over the river. The sun was getting low, turning the water silver. 'Tomorrow's the first of June. Nine days left then.' He smiled wryly. 'You do need me, you see?'

I sighed heavily and met his gaze. 'Ay.'

Barak laughed.

'There's something you could do for me tonight,' I said. 'Ask round the taverns at Lothbury, see if anyone knows anything about the Wentworth family, any tales. Would you do that?'

'All right. Never say no to an evening's drinking. I can go to the sailors' taverns too; make some enquiries about that Polish drink.'

I looked across at the palace. Liveried servants were scurrying to and fro outside, and a great red carpet was being unrolled. 'It looks like Bishop Gardiner is having visitors. Look, here's a wherry, let's get away.'

# Chapter Eighteen

B ARAK AND I SUPPED EARLY at Chancery Lane. We talked little, exhausted by our adventure, but ate in a feeling of better fellowship. Barak left the table early to walk back to the City and spend his evening making enquiries round the taverns. With London as brimful of taverns as churches, I guessed that he had probably trawled them before for information on Cromwell's behalf. It could be a dangerous occupation, I thought. Meanwhile I had the Bealknap case to prepare and some books to look for in the library at Lincoln's Inn. I rose reluctantly and donned my robe once more.

Outside the sun was setting, one of those brilliant red sunsets that can follow a hot summer's day. I shaded my eyes as I turned into the road, looking round for any sign of strangers. Chancery Lane was empty as I walked quickly to the Inn, glad to pass under the safety of the gate.

I saw a long blue-painted coach was pulled up in the courtyard, the horses eating placidly from their nosebags while the driver dozed on his seat. A visitor of rank – I hoped it was not Norfolk come again.

There was a soft glow of candlelight from many windows, barristers working late now the law term had started. A hot dusty smell, not unpleasant, rose from the cobblestones and the setting sun gave the brick walls of Gatehouse Court a warm red glow. A group of laughing students passed on their way to some revel in the City, young lusty-gallants in bright slashed doublets.

As I turned towards my chambers, I saw two people sitting on a bench outside the hall and to my surprise recognized Marchamount and Lady Honor. Marchamount was half-leaning over her, speaking in a low, urgent voice. I could not see Lady Honor's face, but her demeanour looked tense. I sidled behind one of the pillars of the undercroft and watched. After a moment Marchamount rose, bowed and walked rapidly off. His face was set coldly. I hesitated, then walked across to Lady Honor, removed my cap and bowed deeply. She wore a silk gown with wide puffed sleeves and flowers embroidered on the bodice; I felt conscious of the sweaty stubble that covered my face, for I had still not had time to visit the barber. But maybe she would think I was being fashionable and growing a beard.

'My lady, you are visiting the Inn again.'

She looked up at me, brushing a wisp of hair under the stylish French hood she wore. 'Yes. Another consultation with good Serjeant Marchamount.' She smiled softly. 'Sit beside me a moment. You are coming to my banquet tomorrow?'

I took Marchamount's place on the bench, catching the faint tang of some exotic scent she wore. 'I am looking forward to it, Lady Honor.'

She looked around the courtyard. 'This is a peaceful place,' she said. 'My grandfather studied here – oh – seventy years ago. Lord Vaughan of Hartham. He fell at Bosworth.' There was a burst of raucous laughter as another pair of students crossed the yard. Lady Honor smiled. 'I fear he must have been like these young fellows, he came to the Inns to gain some law to help in running his estates, but he was probably more interested in the revels of the City.'

I smiled. 'Some things never change, even in the topsy-turvy world we have now.'

'Oh, they do,' she said with sudden emphasis. 'Nowadays these students will be of mere gentry birth; they will have their fun, but then they will settle down to the business of trying to make a fortune, which is all men care for nowadays.' She frowned suddenly, making sad dimples at the corners of her mouth. 'Even those one has time for may turn out not to be the gentlemen one thought.'

'That is sad.' I realized she probably meant Marchamount. She had not noticed I had seen them together. I felt guilty for my spying.

'Yes, it is.' She smiled again. 'But you, I think, are more than a mere money grubber. You have a look of inner care that does not go with such preoccupations.'

I laughed. 'Perhaps. You see much, Lady Honor.'

'Not always as much as I should.' She was silent a moment. 'I hear a friend of yours gave the Duke of Norfolk some hard words yesterday. He must be very brave or very foolish.'

'How did you hear that?'

She smiled. 'I have my sources.' Probably Marchamount, I thought. She liked to be mysterious, it seemed.

'Perhaps both brave *and* foolish.'

She laughed. 'Can one be both?'

'I think so. Godfrey is a strong evangelical.'

'And you? If you are Lord Cromwell's man you must be a reformer.'

I looked out over the darkening courtyard. 'When I was young I was in thrall to the writings of Erasmus. I loved his picture of a peaceful commonwealth where men worshipped in good fellowship, the abuses of the old Church gone.'

'I too was much taken with Erasmus once,' she said. 'Yet it did not turn out as he hoped, did it? Martin Luther began his violent attacks on the Church and Germany was flooded with anarchy.'

I nodded. 'Erasmus would never comment on Luther, for or against him. That always puzzled me.'

'I think he was too shocked at what was happening. Poor Erasmus.' She laughed sadly. 'He was much given to quoting St John chapter six, was he not? "The Spirit gives life, but the flesh is of no use." But men are ruled by their passions and always will be. And will take any chance to overthrow authority. Thus those who think humankind can be perfected by mere reason are always disappointed.'

'That is a bleak message,' I replied sombrely.

She turned to me. 'I am sorry, I am in a melancholy humour tonight. You must excuse me. You have probably come in to work, like those fellows I see hunched over their candles through the windows. I distract you.'

'A welcome distraction.' She inclined her head and smiled at the compliment. I hesitated, then went on. 'Lady Honor, there is some/thing I must ask you—'

She raised a hand. 'I know. I have been waiting for you to raise the matter. But please, not tonight. I am tired and out of sorts, and due back home.' She looked at me seriously. 'I hear he is dead. Michael Gristwood. And his brother. Gabriel told me, he said you would be coming.'

'Both murdered.'

She raised a hand. 'I know. But I cannot deal with that tonight.'

'That is your coach by the gate?'

'It is.' She looked at me seriously. 'Tomorrow, Master Shardlake, we shall talk. I promise.'

I should have pressed her, but only got up and bowed as she rose and walked gracefully to the gate, her wide dress brushing the cobbles. I turned and made for my chambers, where I saw a light burned in Godfrey's window.

My friend sat at his desk, frowning over the papers in one of my cases. Moths fluttered around the candle on his desk, burning their wings as the poor silly creatures always do. Godfrey's fair hair was sticking up where he had run his hands through it and he wore little round reading glasses that gave him an aged, scholarly look.

I smiled. 'Godfrey, are you labouring this late on my account?'

'Ay, but of my own will. I welcome the distraction.' He sighed. 'I learned today I am to go before the treasurer himself to account for my conduct. I expect a heavy fine.' He smiled sadly. 'So this extra work of yours will be useful. I do wish Skelly could put papers in proper order, though. He tries, poor fellow, but somehow he can get nothing right.'

'It was dangerous to bait the Duke of Norfolk,' I told him seriously.

His glasses flashed in the candlelight as he shook his head. 'I did not bait him. I spoke up for God's Word. Is that a crime?'

'It depends on how you do it. Some who do it wrongly have ended in the fire.'

His face set. 'What is half an hour of agony against eternal bliss?'

'Easy to say.'

He sighed, his shoulders slumping. 'I know. Another evangelical preacher was arrested yesterday. I wonder if I would have the stomach for the fire. I went to John Lambert's burning, do you remember?'

'Ay.' I remembered Barak talking of Lambert's proud martyr's demeanour.

'I went to fortify myself by watching his courage. And he was as brave as a man could be. Yet it was an awful thing.'

'It is always awful.'

'I remember a breeze got up, blew terrible greasy smuts at the crowd. Lambert was dead by then. Yet some deserve it,' he said with a sudden flash of anger. 'I watched Friar Forest burn too, the papist renegade.' He clenched his fists. 'The blood sweated from his body till his soul fell down to hell. Sometimes it is necessary. The papists will *not* triumph.' His face took on that steely fanatical look again and I shivered that a man could turn thus from gentleness to brutality in a moment.

'I must go, Godfrey,' I said quietly. 'I have to prepare the Common Council's case against Bealknap.' I looked at his set face. 'But if the fine is heavy and places you in difficulty, you can always come to me.'

His face softened again. 'Thank you, Matthew.' He shook his head. 'It is a sad thing the profits of the dissolution go to base men of spoil like Bealknap. They should be used to fund hospitals and true Christian schools for the commonwealth.'

'Yes, they should.' But I recalled Lady Honor's words about the making of fortunes being all men cared for now.

✝

I worked on the case for two hours, revising case notes and sketching out my arguments. Then I gathered my papers into my satchel, slung it over my shoulder and went across to the library. I wanted to follow up what one of the papers Gristwood had gathered from St Bartholomew's had said about something like Greek Fire being known to the Romans hundreds of years before the Byzantines. What was the substance the Romans had used, yet been unable to develop in the way the Byzantines had? That was strange, given the legendary efficiency of Rome's armed forces.

Most windows were dark now but there was a yellow glow from the library window. I went in. The huge bookshelves loomed over me in the semi-darkness. The only light came from the librarian's desk, where Master Rowley was working surrounded by a little ring of candles. The librarian was a scholarly old fellow who loved nothing better than to pore over legal works, and he was deep in a volume of Bracton. He had never been near a court, yet had an encyclopaedic knowledge of case law and was often discreetly consulted by the serjeants. He got up and bowed as I approached.

'May I take a candle, Rowley? I have some books to find.'

He smiled eagerly. 'Anything I can help you find? Property law, aren't you, Master Shardlake?'

'Not tonight, thank you.' I lifted a candle from the rack and lit it from one of those on Rowley's desk. Then I crossed to the shelf where works on Roman law and history were kept. I had a list of works the papers had referred to: Livy, Plutarch, Lucullus, the great chroniclers.

Every single book I needed was gone. The row was gap-toothed, half empty. I frowned. Had Michael Gristwood been here before me? Yet books were lent rarely and only to senior barristers; Gristwood had been a mere attorney. Rowley's desk was strategically placed, no one could have walked out with half a dozen books without him seeing them. I walked back to his desk. He looked up with an enquiring smile.

'All the books I need have been taken out, Rowley. Every one on this list.' I handed it to him. 'I'm surprised at so many being allowed out. Can you tell me who has them?'

He frowned at the list. 'These books haven't been borrowed, sir. Are you sure they haven't been misfiled?' He looked up at me and in the uneasiness of his smile I knew the old fellow was lying.

'There are big gaps in the shelf. Come, you must have a list of books that are lent out?'

He licked his lips uneasily at my severe tone. 'I'll see, sir,' he said. He made a pretence of consulting a paper, then took a deep breath and looked up at me again.

'No, sir. These have not been taken out. The clerk must have misfiled them, I'll have a search done tomorrow.'

I felt a pang of sorrow that he could lie to me thus. Yet I saw too that he was frightened.

'This is a serious business, Master Rowley. I need those books and they are valuable. I must raise this with the keeper of the library.'

'If you must, sir,' he said, swallowing.

'I shall see Keeper Heath.' But whoever Rowley was scared of, he was more frightened of them than of the keeper. He only repeated, 'If you must.'

I turned and left him. Outside I clenched my fists and swore. Every turn I took someone else had been there first. But I had learned something; what was in those books had a bearing on the Greek Fire story. I had other sources; I would go to the Guildhall library.

I walked to the gate, noticing that the weather had changed; there was a close, sticky feel to the air. The watchman called, 'Good night.' As I turned down Chancery Lane I saw a flicker of movement by the gatehouse. I turned quickly and saw a burly young man with a round, dull-looking face and a warty nose standing just by the gatehouse, his face momentarily illumined by the light from the window. My hand went to the dagger at my belt. The man's eyes followed my movement, then turned away and I heard footsteps disappearing up the lane.

I stepped back under the gatehouse arch, breathing heavily. A man with wens on his nose, George Green had said. I looked around to see if the pock-faced man was here too, peering into the shadows of the walls of the Domus opposite, but could see nobody. The big man no doubt had followed me to the Inn unnoticed and waited to see if he could jump me when I emerged. I shivered.

I waited a little longer, then walked carefully up the dark lane, my ears on the alert. It was a relief at last to turn into my gate, but I cursed as I realized it would be foolish to go out alone at night again.

# Chapter Nineteen

Next morning I rose to find a bank of heavy clouds louring over the City. The air coming through my open bedroom window was heavy, oppressive. It was the first of June; nine days till Elizabeth returned to the Old Bailey courthouse and to the demonstration of Greek Fire before the king.

Over breakfast I told Barak about the missing books and the man in the shadows by Lincoln's Inn. In return he related what he had discovered during his evening touring the taverns. He had heard that the strange Baltic drink had been offered for sale at a riverside tavern in Billingsgate, the Blue Boar. He had also visited the taverns round Walbrook but found none of the Wentworths' servants; they were known as a sober, churchy lot.

'I got to speak to the servant from the house next door, but he said only that the Wentworths kept themselves to themselves. He bent my ear for an hour about how his old dog had gone missing.'

'You had a busy night.' Despite the beer he must have quaffed last night, Barak looked quite fresh.

'I did some more asking after pock-face and the man with the wens on his face too. Nothing. They must be out-of-town men. I was starting to wonder if they'd been called off, but it seems not from what you say.'

Joan entered with a note. I tore open the seal.

'From Goodwife Gristwood. She'll meet us at Lothbury at twelve. If the case is heard on time we can make it by then.'

'I'll come to Westminster with you first, if you like.'

There was nothing else he could usefully do that morning. 'Thank you. I will feel safer. Have you something in sober black?'

'Ay, I can look respectable when I need. Lady Honor's tonight.'
He winked. 'Bet you're looking forward to that.'

I grunted. I had not mentioned meeting her at Lincoln's Inn;
Barak would have upbraided me for not questioning her there and
then. And he would have been right, I thought.

As we walked down to catch a boat at Temple Stairs I noticed
people casting looks at the louring sky. I was already sweating in the
heavy, putrid air. With luck there would be a thunderstorm soon.
Early as it was, a little crowd had gathered along Fleet Street. I
wondered what they were waiting for, then heard the grate of iron
wheels on cobbles and a cry of 'Courage, brothers!' It was hanging
day. I watched as a big cart, drawn by four horses, passed by, a group
of guards in red and white City livery walking alongside. It was on
its way to Tyburn, going via Fleet Street so more of the populace
might see – and be warned where crime led.

We halted to let the cart pass. There were a dozen prisoners
within, hands bound behind them and ropes around their necks. I
reflected Elizabeth might have been in there, might still be the
following week. The end of the felons' last journey would be the big
multiple gallows at Tyburn, where the cart would halt while the ropes
were secured to hooks on the gallows. Then the cart's tail would be
let down, the horses led on, and the prisoners be left hanging by their
necks, to strangle slowly unless friends pulled on their heels to break
their necks. I shuddered.

Most of the condemned were making their last journey with heads
bowed, but one or two smiled and nodded at the crowd with terrible
forced jollity. I saw the old woman and her son, who had been
convicted of horse stealing – the young man was staring ahead, his
face twitching, while his mother leaned against him, her grey head
resting on his chest. The cart passed creaking by.

'We'd better get on,' Barak said, shouldering his way through the
crowd. 'I've never liked that sight,' he said quietly. 'I've pulled the
legs of an old friend at Tyburn before now, ended his last dance.' He
gave me a serious look. 'When d'you want me to go down that well?'

'I'd say tonight, but there's the banquet. Tomorrow, without fail.'

As we rode a wherry downriver I felt guilty. Each day's delay was another day in the Hole for Elizabeth, another day of desperate anxiety for Joseph. The bulk of Westminster Hall loomed into view and I forced my mind to the Bealknap case. One thing at a time, I thought, or I must go mad. Barak looked at me curiously and I realized I had whispered the words aloud.

✝

As always during the law term, Westminster Palace Yard was thronged with people. We shoved through them into the hall, where under the cavernous roof lawyers and clients, booksellers and sightseers, trod the ancient flagstones. I stretched to see over the heads of the spectators crowded at the King's Bench partition. Inside, a row of barristers stood waiting at the wooden bar, beyond which lay the great table where the court officials sat with their mounds of papers. Under the tapestry of the royal arms the judge sat on his high chair, listening to a barrister with a bored expression. I was disconcerted to see the judge was Heslop, a lazy-minded fellow who I knew had bought a number of monastic properties. He was unlikely to favour a case against a fellow man of spoil. I clenched my fists, reflecting that today I had drawn a low card in the gamble of the law. Nonetheless, after the previous evening's labour I was ready to present what should have been conclusive arguments, all else being equal.

'Master Shardlake.' I gave a start and turned to find Vervey, one of the Common Council attorneys, at my elbow. He was a clerkly, serious man of my own age, a stalwart reformer. I bowed. Evidently he had been sent to keep an eye on the case; it was important to the council.

'Heslop is fair racing through the cases,' he said. 'We shall soon be on, Master Shardlake. Bealknap is here.' He nodded to where my adversary stood leaning on the bar with the other advocates, sleek in his robes.

I forced a smile and lifted my satchel from my shoulders. 'I am ready. Wait here, Barak.'

Barak stared at the attorney. 'Nice day for a bit of devilment,' he said cheerily.

I went through the partition, bowed to the bench and took a place at the bar. Bealknap turned round and I bowed briefly. A few minutes later the current case ended and the parties, one smiling and the other scowling, passed through the bar. 'Common Council of London and Bealknap,' an usher called.

I opened by saying the cesspit in dispute had been badly built and the sewage leaking into the tenement next door was making life miserable for the inhabitants. I spoke of the ill construction of Bealknap's conversion. 'The turning of the old monasteries into such mean and dangerous habitations is against the common weal as well as the City ordinances,' I concluded.

Heslop, who was sitting back comfortably in his chair, gave me a bored look. 'This is not the Court of Chancery, Brother. What are the *legal* issues at stake?'

I saw Bealknap nod complacently, but I was ready. 'That was by way of introduction, your honour. I have here half a dozen cases confirming the sovereignty of the Common Council over monastic properties in cases of nuisance.' I handed up copies and summarized their arguments. As I spoke I saw a glazed look had come over Heslop's face and my heart sank. When a judge looks thus it means he has already made up his mind. I pressed on manfully, however. When I finished, Heslop grunted and nodded to my opponent.

'Brother Bealknap, what do you say?'

He bowed and rose. With his lean features newly shaved and a confident smile on his face, he looked every inch the respectable lawyer. He nodded and smiled as though to say, I am an honest fellow who will give you the truth of this.

'Your honour,' he began, 'we live in a time of great changes for our city. The going down of the monasteries has brought a glut of land to the market, rents are low and men of enterprise must make the best shift we can to turn our investments to a profit. Otherwise more monastic sites will go to ruin and become the haunt of vagabonds.'

Heslop nodded. 'Ay, and then the City will have the trouble of dealing with them.'

'I have a case that I think will settle the matter to your honour's satisfaction.' Bealknap passed a paper up to the judge. '*Friars Preachers* v. *the Prior of Okeham*,' your honour. A case of nuisance brought against the prior, remitted to the king's council as the monastery was under his jurisdiction. As all monastic houses are now. I submit therefore that when a question relating to the original charter arises, it must be submitted to the king.'

Heslop read slowly, nodding as he did so. I looked out over the crowd. Then I froze as I saw a richly dressed man, a retainer on either side, standing near the bar. The rest of the crowd had moved a few paces away from him, as if afraid of approaching too close. Sir Richard Rich, in a fur-lined gown, staring at me with those grey eyes, cold as an icy sea.

Heslop looked up. 'Yes, Brother Bealknap, I agree with you. I think this case settles the matter.'

I rose. 'Your honour, if I may answer. The cases I passed to you are both more numerous and later in time—'

Heslop shook his head. 'I have the right to choose which precedent best expresses the common law and Brother Bealknap's case is the only one that deals directly with the issue of royal authority—'

'But Brother Bealknap *bought* this house, your honour, a contract intervenes—'

'I have a full list today, Brother. Judgement for the plaintiff, with costs.'

We left the court, Bealknap smiling. I glanced over to where Rich had stood, but he had disappeared. It was no surprise to see him at Westminster Hall, his own Office of Augmentations was nearby, but why had he stood staring at me like that? I walked over to where Vervey and Barak stood together. I reddened at the thought that Barak had now seen me lose two cases, Elizabeth's and Bealknap's. 'You bring me bad luck when you come to watch me,' I told him grumpily to cover my embarrassment.

'That was a monstrous decision,' Vervey said indignantly. 'It made a nonsense of the law.'

'Yes, it did. Sir, I am afraid my advice must be to take this matter to Chancery, expensive as that will be. Otherwise that judgement gives carte blanche to all purchasers of monastic properties in London to flout the City regulations—'

I broke off as Barak nudged me. Bealknap was at my elbow. I frowned; it was a breach of etiquette to approach a fellow lawyer in conference with a client. Bealknap too was frowning, his composure ruffled.

'You would take this to Chancery, Brother?' he asked. 'But you would merely lose again. To put the Common Council to such expense—'

'I was having a private conversation, Bealknap, but that will be my advice. That was a biased judgement and the Court of Equity will overturn it.'

He laughed with a show of incredulity. 'When it comes on. Have you any idea how long cases are waiting in Chancery these days?'

'We will wait as long as we must.' I looked at him: as ever his eyes evaded mine. 'A word, Brother.' I led him away from the others and leaned close to him. 'How did the case come to be on Heslop's list, hey? Did a little gold pass between you and him?'

'Such an accusation—' he blustered.

'I would put nothing past you, Bealknap, where your pocket is concerned. But we shall have a fair contest in Chancery. And do not think I have forgotten that other matter. I have been investigating your links with French merchants. They would pay much for that formula.'

His eyes widened at that. 'I wouldn't—'

'I hope not, for your sake. If you have been involved in anything treasonable, Bealknap, you will find you have been playing with fire in more ways than one.'

For the first time he looked afraid. 'I haven't, I swear. It was all as I told you.'

'Was it? It had better be.' I stood away from him. He brushed himself down, recovering himself, and gave me a look of pure venom.

'I will have my costs for this case, Brother,' he said, a momentary tremble in his voice. 'I will send the Common Council a fee note—'

'Ay, do that.' I turned my back on him and rejoined Barak and an uncomfortable-looking Vervey. Bealknap slunk away.

'He promises us a fee note,' I said, forcing a smile. 'Master Vervey, I will let the council have my recommendations. Once again, I am sorry for this outcome. I suspect the judge may have been bribed.'

'It would not surprise me,' Vervey replied. 'I know of Bealknap. Will you write to us with your views as soon as may be? I know the Common Council will be worried by the implications.'

'Ay.'

Vervey bowed and disappeared into the throng. 'What did you say to Bealknap?' Barak asked. 'I thought you were going to rough him up.'

'I warned him I still had my eye on him. Told him I'd been looking into his connections with the French.'

'Bealknap was definitely the arsehole who came to my – my stepfather.' He spoke the word bitterly.

I set my lips. 'Do you think you could find more about his running fake compurgators? Find an adult who could give evidence. It would be something to threaten him with—'

I was interrupted. There was a stir in the crowd around us, and I turned to see Rich bearing down on me, a smile on his face but his eyes holding me with the same cold stare as they had in court.

'Brother Shardlake again and his ruffled-headed assistant.' He smiled at Barak. 'You should have a care to comb your hair, sir, before coming to court.'

Barak returned his stare evenly.

Rich smiled and turned to me. 'That's an impertinent fellow you keep, Brother Shardlake. You need to teach him manners. And perhaps learn some yourself.'

Rich's stare was unnerving, but I held my ground. 'I am sorry, Sir Richard, I do not know what you mean.'

'You involve yourself in matters beyond your station. You should stick to helping country farmers with their land disputes.'

'What matters do you mean, Sir Richard?'

'You know,' he said. 'Don't play innocent with me. Take care or you'll suffer for it.' And with that he turned round and was gone. There was a moment's silence.

'He knows,' Barak said, his voice low and intense. 'He knows about Greek Fire.'

'How? How could he?'

'I don't know, but he does. What else could he have meant? Perhaps Gristwood did go to see him after all during those missing six months.'

I frowned. 'But – if he threatens me, he threatens Cromwell.'

'Perhaps he doesn't know the earl's involved.'

I looked after Rich thoughtfully. 'Bealknap scurries away and a second later Rich appears. And he was doing something that involved Rich that day at Augmentations.'

'Perhaps he has Rich's protection.' Barak set his lips. 'The earl must know of this.'

I nodded reluctantly. 'God's death, Rich involved too.' I exclaimed crossly as someone jostled me. 'Come, let's get out of here. We're due at Lothbury.'

# Chapter Twenty

THE RIVER WAS CROWDED again and we had to wait at the steps for a boat. Barak leaned on the parapet.

'Do you think Bealknap bribed that judge?' he asked.

'I wouldn't be surprised. Heslop has a poor reputation for honesty.'

'Will you win if you take the case to Chancery?'

'We should do. They'll look at the merits of the matter. But God knows when we'll get on. Bealknap's right about their delays – I named my horse for their slow ways.' I looked at Barak seriously. 'Find one of these compurgators. We can offer a reward and perhaps immunity from prosecution if Cromwell will agree. We need a lever over Bealknap, especially if he's got Rich behind him.'

'Ay, I'll do it.' He turned to face me. 'I'll not go to my stepfather, though, even if I knew where he and my mother lived. Not even for the earl.'

'No? I thought there were no limits to your loyalty.'

His eyes flashed. 'I loved my father, for all he smelt of shit. My mother would have nothing to do with him; he took up his trade after I was born or I'd not be here at all. I was twelve when he died.' I nodded, interested. For the first time my difficult companion was showing me something of himself.

'We'd had this cheating attorney as a lodger for years, Kenney his name was. He had the best part of the house while we had two rooms. He was good with words and my mother liked him, he was – ' Barak almost bit off the words – 'a step up the social chain. She married him a week after father died: the poor old arsehole wasn't even cold in the ground. D'you know what she said to me? Same as you did coming from that house in Wolf's Lane. "A poor widow must look after herself."'

'So she must, I suppose.'

'After that, I went mad for a while.' He gave a bark of laughter. 'Sometimes I think I'm still a bit mad. I ran away from home, left school, though I'd been doing well. I got in with the gangs. A poor child must look after himself too, you know.' He stared out over the water. 'Ended by getting caught stealing a ham. I was put in prison and would have faced the rope; it was a big ham, worth over a shilling. But the warden was a Putney man and recognized my father's name. Coming from the same part of the world as Lord Cromwell he had contacts with him; I ended up going before him and he put me to work, running errands at first and then other things.' Barak turned to me. 'So I owe the earl everything. My very life.'

'I see.'

He stood up, taking a deep breath. 'There was a pub by the Tower where my stepfather met Bealknap. I think it was a meeting place for Bealknap's stable of rogues. I'll go down there, try to find it.'

I looked at him. 'No wonder you have no good opinion of lawyers.'

'You're more honest than most,' he grunted.

'You never see your mother or stepfather?'

'I've seen them once or twice about the City, but I always turn away. I'm dead for all they know or care.'

✠

WE TOOK A WHERRY as far as Three Cranes Stairs, then walked north to Lothbury. I had to hurry to keep up with Barak's loping pace. By the Grocers' Hall a couple of young gentlemen in fine doublets were mocking a beggar who sat in the doorway, displaying a face caked with weeping sores to stir the public's pity.

'Come, fellow, you should go for a soldier!' one was saying. 'Everyone is needed at muster now, to fight the pope and the king's enemies.' He took a sword from a leather scabbard and waved it. The beggar, who looked hardly fit to rise let alone take up arms, scrabbled back in panic, making the hoarse grunts of a dumb man.

'He can't speak the king's English,' said the other fellow. 'Maybe he's a foreigner.'

Barak walked over, hand on his own sword, and looked the young gallant in the eye. 'Leave him,' he said. 'Unless you'd like to try your luck with me?'

The fellow's eyes narrowed, but he sheathed his sword and turned away. Barak took a coin from his pocket and laid it by the beggar. 'Come on,' he said curtly.

'That was a brave gesture,' I said. The words of the motto on the barrel of Greek Fire came back to me. *Lupus est homo homini*: man is wolf to man.

Barak snorted. 'Those arseholes are only fit to bait those who can't fight back.' He spat on the ground. 'Gentlemen.'

We reached Lothbury Street. Ahead of us stood St Margaret's church, beside which narrow lanes led off into a warren of little buildings from where a metallic clangour could be heard. Because of the endless noise virtually no one save the founders lived in Lothbury.

'Goodwife Gristwood will meet us at her son's foundry,' I said. 'We go up here, Nag's Lane.'

We turned into a narrow passageway between two-storey houses. Cinders and fragments of charcoal were mixed with the alley dust and there was a harsh smell of hot iron. Nearly all the houses had workshops attached; their doors were open and I could see men moving within. Spades scraped on stone floors as coal was loaded into furnaces from which a bright red, concentrated glow was visible.

At length I halted in front of a small house. The workshop door was closed; Barak knocked twice. It opened and a wiry young man wearing a heavy apron over an old smock pitted with burn holes looked at us suspiciously. He had Goodwife Gristwood's thin, sharp features.

'Master Harper?' I asked.

'Ay.'

'I am Master Shardlake.'

'Come in,' the founder replied in a less than friendly tone. 'Mother's here.'

I followed him into his little foundry. An unlit furnace dominated the room, a pile of charcoal beside it. A collection of pots was stacked by the door. On a stool in one corner Goodwife Gristwood sat. She gave me a surly nod.

'Well, master lawyer,' she said. 'Here he is.'

Harper nodded at Barak. 'Who's that?'

'My assistant.'

'We founders stick together,' he said warningly. 'I've only to call out for half Lothbury to be here.'

'We mean you no harm — it is only information I want. Your mother has told you we seek information about Michael and Sepultus's experiments?'

'Ay.' He sat down beside his mother and looked at me. 'They told me they wanted to build something, an arrangement of pumps and tanks. That's beyond my capacity, but I do a lot of casting for a man who works for the City repairing the conduits.'

'Peter Leighton.'

'Ay. I helped Master Leighton cast the iron for the pipes and the tank.' He looked at me keenly. 'Mother says there could be danger for those who know about this.'

'Perhaps. We may be able to help there.' I paused. 'The liquid that was to be put in the tank? Did you see anything of that?'

Harper shook his head. 'Michael said it was a secret, it was better I didn't know. They did some tests in Master Leighton's yard. They leased the whole yard from him and wouldn't let him near. It has a high wall; he keeps lead pipes there for work on the conduits.'

I wondered what Harper's relationship had been with Gristwood, who was, after all, his stepfather. I guessed it had not been one of affection, but that the nature of his employment made him useful.

'What was this apparatus like?' I asked.

He shrugged. 'Complicated. A big watertight tank with a pump attached and a pipe leading off. It took weeks to make, then Master Leighton said I'd have to have another try – the pipe was too broad.'

'When did the brothers first employ you?'

'November. It took till January to get the apparatus right.'

Two months before they went to Cromwell. 'Are you sure?'

'Yes.'

'And where was it kept? In Master Leighton's yard?'

'I believe so. They paid him well for its use.'

Goodwife Gristwood laughed mirthlessly. 'Did Master Leighton get his money?'

'Ay, Mother, he did. He insisted on payment in advance.'

She frowned. 'Then where did Michael get the money? Neither he nor Sepultus had any.'

'Perhaps someone else paid,' I suggested.

'They'd have had to,' the goodwife answered bitterly. 'I spent fifteen years dealing with Michael's mad schemes. Sometimes I had hardly any bread for the table. And it's all ended with him dead and David in danger.' She looked at her son with a tenderness that softened her face.

'I can make sure you are both kept safe,' I said. 'But I would like to speak to Master Leighton.' I looked at David Harper. 'Have you told him I was coming?'

'No, sir. We thought it better not.'

'Will he be at his foundry?'

'Ay, he has a new contract to repair the Fleet Street conduit. He said last Friday he'd have some casting for me. Pleased with himself, he was.'

'Can you take us there?'

'And will that be the end of this business?' Goodwife Gristwood asked.

'You need be involved no further, madam.'

She nodded at her son. He rose and led the way outside. His mother scuttled after him.

We walked up the lane, further into Lothbury. Through open doors we saw sweat-soaked founders, stripped to the waist, labouring over their fires. People looked out at us curiously as we passed by. At the bottom of a winding lane David stopped before a corner house, larger than most, with a workshop next to it and a high wall beside that.

'If there were sounds and signs of fire,' Barak muttered to me, 'they wouldn't attract attention here.'

'No. This was a clever place to choose.'

David knocked at the door of the house. It was shuttered, as were the windows of the workshop. Harper tried the workshop doors too, but they were locked.

'Master Leighton,' he called. 'Master Leighton, it's David.' He turned to us apologetically. 'Many founders grow deaf in their later years. But it's odd his furnace isn't lit.'

I had a sense of foreboding. 'When did you last see him?'

'Friday, sir, when he told me about his new contract.'

Barak looked at the lock. 'I could have that open.'

'No,' Harper said. 'I know who has a key. Everyone has a neighbour's key in case of fire. Wait here.' He went off down the lane. All around us the banging and clanging resounded in our ears. Goodwife Gristwood began twisting her hands together nervously.

Her son reappeared, a large key in his hands. He unlocked the door and we entered the yard. It was indeed a good place for Michael and Sepultus to have chosen; the high wall enclosed it on three sides and the windowless rear of the adjacent house occupied the fourth. There was a pile of pipes and valves, for Leighton's work on the conduits, no doubt. Blackened patches all over the walls caught my eye, like the ones I had seen in the Gristwoods' yard only larger.

Goodwife Gristwood and her son were standing nervously by the gate. I gave David Harper a reassuring smile – he looked as though he might run off any minute.

'Master Harper,' I said, 'tell me: does anything unusual strike you about this yard?'

He looked around. 'Only that it's been given a good clean recently.'

I nodded. 'That's what I thought. It's spotless.'

'Why would anyone want to keep a founder's yard spotless?' Barak asked.

'To hide all traces of what had been here.' I bent close to him and whispered, 'I think someone has removed the apparatus, and all traces of Greek Fire as well.'

'Leighton?'

'Possibly. Come, I think we should have a look in the house.'

I led the way out of the yard. We knocked again at the house door, but still there was no sign of life. I wiped a hand over my brow; it seemed hotter and stickier than ever up here among the foundries. All around us the clanging and scrating continued.

'We can get in via the workshop,' Harper said. 'It's the same key.' He hesitated, then opened the workshop door and stepped inside calling, 'Master Leighton?' Barak followed him.

'I'll stay outside,' Goodwife Gristwood said nervously. 'Take care, David.'

I followed Barak in. David opened the shutters and I saw a cluttered workshop, more pipes and valves and pans and an empty furnace. Harper picked up a coal from it. 'Stone cold,' he said.

Set in one wall was a door to the house. Harper hesitated, then inserted the key in the lock and opened it. Another darkened room. I caught a slight, familiar tang and grabbed Barak's arm. 'Wait,' I said.

Harper opened the shutters and turned round. Then his mouth fell open. We were in a parlour, surprisingly well appointed, but it was in chaos. The buffet cupboard had been overturned and lay on its side, silver plates scattered around.

David Harper had gone pale. He stood with his hand over his mouth. 'They got him too,' I whispered. 'They took the apparatus and killed him.'

'Then where's the body?' Barak asked.

'Somewhere in the house, maybe. I smell blood.' Instructing Harper to stay where he was, Barak and I searched the rest of the founder's home, Barak drawing his sword as we climbed the narrow stairs. Everything was in order, it was only the parlour that had been wrecked. We returned there to find David Harper had gone outside; through the window I saw him with his mother, looking at the house with a frightened expression. A man with a load of pans on his back passed by, giving them a puzzled look.

'They took the body with them,' I said, 'together with the apparatus. They didn't want a hue and cry about a murder in Lothbury.' I knelt and examined the floor. 'See, this part of the floor's been cleaned, there's no dust.' I saw a pair of flies buzzing around the overturned buffet, and took a deep breath. 'Here, Barak, help me move this.'

I wondered what horror we might find underneath the buffet, but there was only a patch of dried blood. Barak whistled.

'Where did they get the key?'

'From Leighton's body, perhaps.' I looked over to the front door. 'They didn't break the door in. I guess they knocked, and when Leighton answered they shoved him inside and then followed and killed him. Probably a quick blow with an axe again.'

'Risky. What if he called out and neighbours came? Harper's right, the founders are a close lot.'

'Perhaps Leighton knew them.' I bit my lip. 'Or knew someone who was with them. One of our potential conspirators, maybe.'

'We should ask the neighbours.'

'We can, but I'm willing to bet they came at night when no one was about. Come, there's no more we can do here.'

We rejoined Harper and Goodwife Gristwood in the street. Standing together, they were very alike, even to their looks of drawn anxiety.

'What's happened, sir?' Harper asked. 'Is Master Leighton—'

'He is not there. But I am afraid there are signs of violence—'

Goodwife Gristwood gave a little moan.

'I am concerned for the safety of you and your son, madam,' I said. 'Is the watchman still at your house?'

'Ay, he brought me here, then I sent him back.'

I turned to Harper. 'I think your mother should stay with you for now. I will try and find somewhere safer.'

The old woman gave me an appalled look. 'What did they do? For Jesu's sake, what did Michael and Sepultus *do* here?'

'Meddled with dangerous people.'

She shook her head, then looked at me again, her mouth tightening into its old hardness. 'That whore,' she asked abruptly, 'did you see her?'

'I tried to, but she ran away.' I turned to David. 'Is it possible someone could carry away that apparatus without being noticed? Perhaps on a cart?'

He nodded. 'People are always trundling carts through Lothbury with goods to take to customers and the shops. Day and night too when we're busy.'

I nodded. 'Ask around, would you, among the neighbours? Just say Leighton's missing. Would you do that?'

He nodded, then put his arm round his mother. 'Are we truly in danger, sir?'

'I think your mother may be. Who knows where she is?'

'No one save me and the watchman at Wolf's Lane.'

'Tell no one else. Can you read?'

'Ay.'

I scribbled my address on a piece of paper. 'If you have any news, or require anything, you can reach me here.'

He took it, nodding. His mother clung to his arm. I was glad they had each other; they had no one else now.

☩

I WAS WEARY, but insisted on stopping at a barber's for a shave in preparation for the banquet. Barak waited for me, then we caught a boat back to the Temple and walked home. I insisted on resting before getting myself ready. I dozed an hour and woke feeling unrefreshed. The sky was as leaden, the air as close, as ever. How I wished the weather would break. I got up, feeling stiff, and for the first time in days did some of Guy's back exercises. I was bending over, trying to touch my toes and getting nowhere near, when there was a knock at the door and Barak entered. His eyes widened in surprise.

'That's a strange way to pray,' he said.

'I'm not praying. I'm trying to find some relief for my sore back. And haven't you the manners to be asked to enter a room before barging in?'

'Sorry.' Barak sat down cheerfully on the bed. 'I came to tell you I'm going out. An old contact of mine has some information on the two we're after. Pock-face and his big mate. I'm going to meet him, then I'm going to see the earl.' His expression grew serious. 'Tell him about Rich. He may want to see you.'

I took a deep breath. 'Very well. You know where I'll be. And ask if he can find somewhere safe for the Gristwoods.'

Barak nodded, then gave me a warning look. 'So far we've had more requests for him than information.'

'I know, but we're doing all we can.'

'You'll have to ride to Lady Honor's house alone.'

'It is still light.'

'Afterwards I'll find that tavern where Bealknap met my stepfather. It'll keep me occupied while you're at the banquet.'

'Very well.'

'Are you sure you don't want to have a crack at that well later? After the banquet?'

I shook my head. 'I'll be too tired, I have to get some sleep. I have to pace myself, Barak,' I added irritably. 'I've more than ten years on you. Just how old are you, by the way?'

'Twenty-eight in August. Listen, I've been trying to puzzle something out. I can understand whoever organized the killing of the Gristwood brothers keeping the formula close, perhaps to sell abroad when things have quietened down. But why try to kill the founder Leighton? Why kill everyone associated with this?'

'They could have killed Leighton just as a way of getting to the apparatus. We know they've no care for life.'

'And they're keen to get you. They don't seem to like you being on the case.'

I frowned. 'But is that just because I might uncover who is behind this, the person who is paying these rogues? Or is it that they fear I might find something out about Greek Fire? Is that why those books have gone?'

Barak's eyes widened. 'You can't still think it may all be a fraud, surely? Not after what you've seen and heard?'

'There's something that's not right. I must go to the Guildhall, find copies of those books.' I clutched at my head. 'God's death, there's so much to do.'

'It beats me what you can hope to find from a lot of old books.' He sighed. 'Four possible suspects now. Bealknap and Rich. Marchamount. And Lady Honor. Make sure you question her tonight.'

'Of course I will,' I snapped.

Barak gave his sardonic smile. 'You're sweet on her, you're still a man of juice under all that learning.'

'You've a coarse tongue. Besides, as you pointed out yourself, she's out of my league.' I looked at him. He had mentioned seeing a girl on the first night he came to my house, but beyond that I knew nothing of what women there might have been in his life. Many, I guessed, for all the fears of the French pox these days.

He lay back on the bed.

'Bealknap and Rich,' he said again, 'Marchamount and Lady Honor. One or more of them a murdering rogue. So much for people of rank being honourable, not that I ever believed it.'

I shrugged. 'The idea of raising oneself up to gentle rank has always seemed a worthy thing to me. But perhaps that ideal will turn to dust, like Erasmus's hopes of a Christian commonwealth. In these whirling days, who knows?'

'Some things last,' he said. He smiled. 'I said I'd show you this, remember?'

'What?'

Barak sat up and unbuttoned his shirt. There was something gold on the end of a chain, glittering against his broad chest. It wasn't a cross, it looked more like a little cylinder. He lifted the chain over his head and proffered it. 'Take a look.'

I examined the cylinder. The surface had been engraved once but the gold was worn almost smooth with time. 'It's been passed down my father's family for generations,' he said. 'It's supposed to be to do with the Jewish religion. My father called it a mezzah.' He shrugged. 'I like to have it by me, to bring me luck.'

'The workmanship is fine. It looks very old.'

'The Jews were kicked out more than two hundred years ago, weren't they? One of them must have kept it when he converted and passed it down. A reminder of the past.'

I turned it over in my hands. Tiny as it was, the cylinder was hollow, with a slit down one side.

'Father said they used to put a tiny scroll of parchment in there and put the mezzah by the door.'

I handed it back. 'It's remarkable.'

Barak replaced it, buttoned up his shirt and got up. 'I must be gone,' he said briskly.

'And I should get ready. Good luck with the earl.'

As the door shut behind him, I turned to the window and looked out over my parched garden. The clouds were so heavy now that although only it was only late afternoon it was dim as dusk. I unlocked my chest and began reaching for my best clothes. Somewhere, away over the Thames, a distant rumble of thunder sounded.

# Chapter Twenty-one

LADY HONOR'S HOUSE WAS in Blue Lion Street off Bishopsgate. It was a big old four-storey courtyard house, the front giving directly onto the street. It had been sumptuously refurbished in the recent past. I could see why it was known as the House of Glass; new diamond-paned windows had been put in along the whole frontage, with the Vaughan family crest in some of the centre panes. I studied it: a rampant lion with sword and shield, the epitome of martial virtues. There was something feminine about the overall effect, however; I wondered if the work had been done since Lady Honor's husband died.

The front door was open, with liveried servants standing outside. Although I was dressed in my uncomfortable best, I worried that I would appear an unsophisticated fellow for I was unused to mixing in such high company. I pulled a little ruff of silk shirt above the collar of my doublet to display the needlework.

I had ridden Chancery to the banquet; the old horse appeared recovered from his recent exertions and trotted along happily enough. A lad took the reins as I dismounted and another servant bowed me through the front door. He led me through a richly decorated hall into a large inner courtyard. Here too all the rooms had large glass windows, and heraldic beasts had been carved on the walls as well as the Vaughan crest. There was a fountain in the middle of the courtyard, with just enough water emerging to make a merry, tinkling noise. Opposite, a large banqueting hall occupied the first floor. Candles flickered behind the open windows, casting ever-changing shadows on the people moving to and fro within, and there was a merry clatter of cutlery. It struck me that if Lady Honor had been involved in the Greek Fire business, it was certainly not because she needed money.

The steward led me up a broad flight of stairs to a room where bowls of hot water were set out on a table with a pile of towels. The bowls, I saw, were gold.

'You will wash your hands, sir?'

'Thank you.'

Three men were already standing washing; a young fellow with the Mercers' Company badge on his silk doublet and an older man in a white clerical robe. The third man, who looked up with a beaming smile on his broad face, was Gabriel Marchamount. 'Ah, Shardlake,' he said expansively, 'I hope you have a sweet tooth. Lady Honor's banquets positively drip with sugar.' Evidently he had decided to be affable tonight.

'Not too sweet, I must watch my teeth.'

'Like me you still have a full set.' Marchamount shook his head. 'I cannot abide this fashion for women to blacken their teeth deliberately so people will think they live off nothing but fine sugar.'

'I agree. It is not pretty.'

'I have heard them say the pains in their mouth are worth it, if people respect them more.' He laughed. 'Women of Lady Honor's class, though, women of real estate, would disdain such effect.' He dried his hands, replacing the showy emerald ring on his finger and patted his plump stomach. 'Come then, let us go in.' He took a napkin from a pile and flung it over his shoulder; I followed his example and we went out to the banqueting chamber.

The long room had an old hammerbeam ceiling. The walls were covered with bright tapestries showing the story of the Crusades, the papal tiara carefully stitched out where the Bishop of Rome was shown blessing the departing armies. Big tallow candles, set in silver candleholders, had been lit against the dark evening and filled the room with a yellow glow.

I glanced at the enormous table that dominated the room. The candlelight winked on gold and silver tableware and serving men scurried to and fro, placing dishes and glasses on the broad buffet against one wall. As was the custom, I had brought my own dining knife, a silver one my father had given me. It would look a poor thing among these riches.

The salt cellar, a foot high and particularly ornate, was set at the very top of the table, opposite a high chair thick with cushions. That meant nearly all the guests would be below the salt and therefore that a guest of the highest status was expected. I wondered if it might even be Cromwell.

Marchamount smiled and nodded round at the company. A dozen guests were standing talking, mostly older men, though there was a smattering of wives, some wearing heavy lead rouge to brighten their cheeks. Mayor Hollyes himself was there, resplendent in his red robes of office. The other men mostly wore Mercers' Company livery, though there were a couple of clerics. Everyone was perspiring in the oppressive heat despite the open windows; the women in their wide farthingales looked especially uncomfortable.

A boy of about sixteen with long black hair and a thin, pale face, badly disfigured with a rash of spots such as boys sometimes have, was standing by himself in a corner, looking nervous. 'That's Henry Vaughan,' Marchamount whispered. 'Lady Honor's nephew. Heir to the old Vaughan title and to their lands, such as they have left. She's brought him down from Lincolnshire to try and get him received at court.'

'He looks ill at ease.'

'Yes, he's a poor fellow; hardly cut out for the rumbustuous company the king likes.' He paused, then said with sudden feeling, 'I wish I had an heir.' I looked at him in surprise. He smiled sadly. 'My wife died in childbirth these five years past. We would have had a boy. When I began my petition to establish my family's right to a coat of arms, it was in hope my wife and I would have an heir.'

'I am sorry for your loss.' Somehow it never occurred to me to see Marchamount as a man who could be bereaved and vulnerable.

He nodded at the mourning ring in the shape of a skull I wore. 'You too have known loss,' he said.

'Yes. In the plague of 'thirty-four.' Yet I felt a fraud as I spoke, not just because Katy had announced her betrothal to another shortly before she died but because these last two years I had thought of her less and less. I thought with sudden irritation I should stop wearing it.

'Have you resolved that unpleasant matter we discussed earlier?' Marchamount's eyes were sharp, all sentiment gone.

'I make progress. A strange thing happened in the course of my investigations.' I told him of the books that had gone missing from the library.

'You should tell the keeper.'

'I may do.'

'Will your investigation be – ah – hindered, without the books?'

'Delayed a little only. There are other sources.' I watched his face closely, but he only nodded solemnly. A serving man took up a horn and sounded a long note. The company fell silent as Lady Honor entered the room. She wore a wide, high-bosomed farthingale in brightest green velvet and a red French hood with loops of pearls hanging from it. I was pleased to see she wore no leaden rouge; her clear complexion had no need of it. But it was not to her that all eyes in the room turned; they fixed on the man who followed her, wearing a light scarlet robe edged with fur despite the heat, and a thick gold chain. My heart sank – it was the Duke of Norfolk again. I bowed with everyone else as he strode to the head of the table and stood eyeing the company haughtily. I wondered with a sinking heart whether he would remember I had been sitting next to Godfrey on Sunday; the last thing I wanted was to attract the notice of Cromwell's greatest enemy.

Lady Honor smiled and clapped her hands. 'Ladies and gentle-men, please, take your places.' To my surprise I was placed near the head of the table next to a plump middle-aged woman wearing an old-fashioned box hood and a square-cut dress, a large ruby brooch glinting on her bosom. On her other side Marchamount sat just below the duke. Lady Honor guided the nervous-looking boy to a chair next to Norfolk, who stared at him enquiringly.

'Your grace,' Lady Honor said, 'may I present my cousin's son, Henry Vaughan. I told you he was coming from the country.'

The duke clapped him on the shoulder, his manner suddenly friendly. 'Welcome to London, boy,' he said in his harsh voice. 'It's good to see the nobility sending their pups to court, to take their rightful place. Your grandfather fought with my father at Bosworth, did you know that?'

The boy looked more nervous than ever. 'Yes, your grace.'

The duke looked him up and down. 'God's teeth, you're a skinny fellow, we'll have to build you up.'

'Thank you, your grace.'

Lady Honor guided Mayor Hollyes to a place next to the Vaughan boy, then sat herself almost opposite me. The boy's eyes followed her anxiously.

'Now,' Lady Honor said to the company, 'the wine and our first confection.' She clapped her hands and the servants, who had been waiting still as stocks, bustled into action. Wine was set before the guests, in delicate Venetian glasses finely engraved with coloured patterns. I turned mine over in my hands, admiring it, then the horn sounded again and a swan made of white sugar, nestling in a huge platter of sweet custard, was brought in. The assembly clapped and the duke barked with laughter. 'All the Thames swans belong to the king, Lady Honor! Had you permission to take this one?' Everyone laughed sycophantically and reached out with their knives to cut into the magnificent confection. Lady Honor sat composedly, yet her eyes followed everything that went on in the room. I admired her skills as a hostess, wondering when I would get the chance to question her.

'Are you a lawyer, like Serjeant Marchamount?' the woman next to me asked.

'I am. Master Matthew Shardlake, at your command.'

'I am Lady Mirfyn,' she replied grandly. 'My husband is treasurer of the Mercers' Guild this year.'

'I do some business with the Guildhall, though I have not had the honour of meeting Sir Michael.'

'They say at the guild, you have some other business now.' She eyed me severely with little blue eyes that stood out sharply in her painted face. 'The disgraceful business of the Wentworth girl.'

'I am defending her, yes.'

She went on staring at me. 'Sir Edwin is devastated by what happened to his son. He deplores that his wicked niece should be allowed to delay justice. My husband and I know him well,' she added, as though that were the last possible word on the matter.

'She is entitled to a defence.' I noticed the duke had turned to Marchamount and was talking to him earnestly, ignoring the Vaughan boy, who sat staring down the table, quite at sea. Thank God the duke had showed no sign of recognizing me.

'She's entitled to hang!' Lady Mirfyn would not let go. 'No wonder the City is crawling with impertinent masterless beggars when justice is seen to be evaded so! Edwin *doted* on that boy,' she added fiercely.

'I know it is hard on Sir Edwin and his daughters,' I said mildly, hoping the woman would not go on like this all evening.

'His daughters are good girls, but they cannot take the place of a son. He had laid all his hopes on the boy.'

'But he has taught his girls to read scripture, has he not?' I decided I might as well make the best of things: this opinionated woman knew the family, she might let something interesting drop.

Lady Mirfyn shrugged. 'Edwin has advanced ideas. I don't think it serves girls to teach them religion – their husbands won't like arguing ideas with them, will they?'

'Some might.'

She raised her eyebrows. 'I never even learned to write, and I'm glad to be able to leave such things to my husband. I'm sure that's what Sabine and Avice would prefer too, good well-mannered girls that they are. Poor Ralph was a mischievous child, but that is to be expected in boys.'

'Was he indeed?' I asked.

'They said his misbehaviour helped drive his mother to her early grave.' She gave me a sharp look, suddenly realizing she had said too much. 'That doesn't excuse his vile murder, though.'

'No, indeed. It does not.' I was going to add that I believed the real murderer could still be at large, but Lady Mirfyn took my words for agreement, nodded with satisfaction and looked at Lady Honor.

'Our hostess is a learned woman,' she said with a note of disapproval. 'But I suppose she has the status of a widow and may live independently if she chooses. It is not a fate I would wish for.'

I heard a loud whisper from Norfolk to Marchamount. 'I'll not take the boy up unless she agrees.' I lowered my head, trying to catch the serjeant's reply, but he spoke softly. 'Damn it,' the duke hissed, 'she'll do as I command.'

'I fear she won't.' I heard Marchamount this time.

'God's death, I'll not be defied by a woman. Tell her I'll do nothing for the boy unless I get what I want. She's skating on thin ice.' I saw the duke take a long swig from his glass, then stare at Lady Honor. He was red-faced now and I remembered it was said he was often drunk and could turn brutal then.

Lady Honor met his eyes. The duke smiled and raised his glass. She raised her glass in return, with a smile that looked nervous to me. A servant appeared by her side and whispered something. She nodded and, looking relieved, stood up. 'Ladies and gentlemen,' she said. 'Many of you have heard of the edible, yellow *things* from the New World that have been raising eyebrows since they arrived last month.' She paused, and there were guffaws of bawdy laughter from some of the men. 'Well, we have some tonight on beds of marzipan. Ladies and gentlemen, the sweetest fruit of the New World.'

She sat down and there was more laughter, and clapping, as the servants laid half a dozen silver trays on the table. There, on beds of marzipan, lay strange, pale yellow crescents. I understood the bawdy laughter, for the things were the size and almost the shape of a big erect cock.

'So this is what everyone is laughing about,' Lady Mirfyn said. 'Such naughtiness.' She giggled, turning innocently girlish as rich matrons will when confronted with bawdy humour.

I picked up one of the strange fruits and bit into it. It was unyielding, with a bitter taste. Then I saw people were peeling back the skins to reveal a pale yellow fruit within. I followed their example. It was floury, rather tasteless.

'What are these called?' I asked Lady Mirfyn, who had also taken one.

'They have no name I know of,' she said. She looked down the laughing table, shaking her head indulgently. 'Such naughtiness.'

I heard my name on Lady Honor's lips and turned to find her smiling at me. 'The mayor says you have a knotty case for the council, involving the suppressed monasteries,' she said.

'Ay, Lady Honor. I fear we lost the first round, but we shall gain the second. It is a matter of the City's rights to regulate these buildings for the good of all the citizens.'

Mayor Hollyes nodded seriously. 'I hope so, sir. People don't understand that the regulations on cleanliness need to be enforced to keep away the foul humours that bring plague. And so many houses are let out as poor tenements now.' He spoke animatedly, as one who has mounted a hobby horse. 'You heard about the house near the Joiners' Hall that collapsed last month? Killed fourteen tenants and four passers-by—'

'Let them all fall!' There was a shout from the head of the table and all eyes turned to the duke. He slurred his words and I saw that he was, indeed, drunk. His conversation with Marchamount seemed to have put him in a foul temper. 'The more houses fall on the diseased populace of this great cesspit the better. Perhaps that will scare some into going back to their parishes where they belong, to work on the land as they did in our fathers' time.'

A silence fell on the company, as deep as had fallen at the Lincoln's Inn dinner. The Vaughan boy looked as though he wished to crawl under the table.

'Well, we may all agree much needs amending,' Lady Honor said. She tried to make her voice light, but it had a strained quality. 'Did not Bishop Gardiner preach a sermon last week, saying all must labour according to their station to keep the realm in proper order?' As she quoted these anodyne words from the leading conservative bishop she looked round the table, hoping for someone to help defuse the topic. She did not wish for controversy tonight, it seemed.

'So we must, Lady Honor,' I said, stepping into the breach. She gave me a smile of gratitude as I stumbled on. 'We must all aim to work for the common good.'

The duke snorted. 'Your *work*. Pen-pushing. I remember you, lawyer, you were with that churl who spouted Lutheran sentiments at me last Sunday.' I confess I quailed under his cold, hard stare. 'Are you a Lutheran, too, lawyer?'

Every eye turned to me. To answer yes was to risk a charge of heresy. For a moment my voice caught, I was too frightened to answer. I saw one of the women rub a hand across her face, leaving a smear of rouge. There was another rumble of thunder, closer now.

'No, your grace,' I said. 'A follower of Erasmus only.'

'That Dutch pederast. I heard he lusted after another monk when he was a boy, and d'you know what his name was, eh?' He looked round the table, grinning now. 'Rogerus. Roger-us, hey?' He gave a sudden bark of laughter that broke the spell. The men up and down the table began laughing with him. I sank back in my chair, my heart thudding, as the duke turned to young Henry Vaughan and began telling tales of his soldiering days.

Lady Honor clapped her hands. 'Some music, now.' Two lute players appeared together with a gaudily dressed young man, who began singing popular songs, loud enough to hear but not too loud to stifle conversation. I looked down the table. The conversation had become desultory; between the heat, the drink and the sweet food most of the diners looked sticky and tired. Further sweetmeats followed, including a model of the House of Glass itself made of marzipan set with strawberries, but the guests only picked at it.

The young man was trilling a lament, 'Ah, Gentle Robyn,' and the diners stopped talking to listen. It caught the gloomy mood that seemed to have fallen on the company. Norfolk, alone, was talking to Marchamount again. Lady Honor caught my eye and leaned forward.

'Thank you for trying to help me earlier,' she said. 'I am sorry it turned out ill.'

'I was warned your table talk could be controversial.' I leaned across to her. 'Lady Honor, I must talk with you—'

Her face was suddenly wary. 'In the courtyard,' she said quietly, 'afterwards.'

Everyone jumped as a crack of thunder sounded from outside. A draught of cool air swept through the room. People murmured with relief and someone said, 'Is this the rain at last?'

Lady Honor took the words as her cue and stood up with an air of relief. 'It is a little early, but perhaps you should leave now, get on the road before the rain starts.'

People got up, brushing the backs of their robes and skirts where they had stuck to the benches. Everyone bowed as the duke rose to his feet, stumbling slightly. He bowed curtly to his hostess and strode unsteadily from the room.

As the guests went to take their farewell of Lady Honor I hung back. I saw Marchamount bend close to her and speak intently. As at Lincoln's Inn, her reply did not seem to satisfy him; he was frowning slightly as he turned away. As he passed me he paused and raised his eyebrows.

'Be careful, Shardlake,' he said. 'I could have had the duke as a friend for you, but you seem to court his disapproval. If the times change, that could have consequences.' He gave me a cold nod, then left the chamber.

Consequences, I thought: if Norfolk supplanted Cromwell there would be grim consequences for all but the papists. And if I could not find Greek Fire the king would be in a rage. Was that what whoever was behind this wanted, a papist victory? Or only profit?

I made my way downstairs and stood outside in the courtyard by the door. There was another rumble of thunder, closer now. The evening air seemed to sing with the tension of it. No one else came out that way; I guessed they were taking a direct route to the stables. I wondered what it was that Norfolk wanted so much to get from Lady Honor. Something Marchamount knew about.

There was a touch at my elbow. I jumped and turned round. Lady Honor stood beside me. Her strong, square face had a hectic look, as well it might after the evening's events.

'I am sorry, Master Shardlake, I startled you.'

I bowed. 'Not at all, Lady Honor.'

She sighed heavily. 'That was a *disaster*. I have never seen the duke in such bad humour, I am sorry for the trouble he caused you.' She shook her head. 'It was my fault.'

'Was it? Why?'

'I should have got the servants to watch his glass,' she said. She took a deep breath, then looked at me directly. 'Well, you have some questions for me. Serjeant Marchamount has told me what happened to the Gristwoods,' she added quietly.

'He is a friend, the serjeant?'

'A friend, ay,' she said quickly. 'I am afraid there is little I can tell you. Like Serjeant Marchamount I was only a messenger. I took a package to Lord Cromwell for the serjeant, passed a message that the contents would be of great interest to him. It was after one of my banquets, in circumstances rather like this.' She smiled wryly. 'That was all; further messages went via Lincoln's Inn. I never even met Gristwood.'

Something about her speech was too pat. And now I was close to her, I realized with a shock that the scent she wore was the same musky odour the Greek Fire papers had had about them.

'Did you know what the package was?' I asked.

'Papers relating to the old secret of Greek Fire. Serjeant Marcha-mount told me. I suppose he shouldn't have done but he does like impressing me.' She laughed nervously.

'How long did you have the papers?'

'A few days.'

'And you looked at them?'

She paused and took a deep breath, her bosom rising.

'I know you did,' I said gently. I did not want to hear her lie.

She gave me a startled look. 'How?'

'Because that alluring scent you wear was on them. A faint trace – I could not place it till just now.'

She bit her lip. 'I fear I have a woman's curiosity in full share, Master Shardlake. Yes, I read them. I resealed the package afterwards.'

'Did you understand them?'

'All except the alchemy books. I understood enough to make me wish I'd left them alone.' She looked at me directly then. 'It was wrong, I know. But as I told you I am as curious as a cat.' She shook her head. 'But I know, too, when something is better left alone.'

'This means that you are the only person who handled those papers to open them. Unless Marchamount did.'

'Gabriel is too careful to do that.'

But he knew this was about Greek Fire. Had he told Norfolk? Was Norfolk pressing Lady Honor to tell him more? I felt my guts tighten at the thought Norfolk himself might be involved. Was that why he had remembered me?

'Did you think the papers actually held the secret of Greek Fire?' I asked her.

She hesitated, then looked me in the eye. 'It seemed to me perhaps they did. The account of the old soldier was very clear. And those papers were old, they weren't some forgery.'

'One was torn.'

'I saw. I did not tear it.' For the first time I saw a look of fear in her eyes.

'I know. That was the formula. The Gristwoods kept it back.'

Somewhere over the river lightning flashed. Another crack of thunder sounded, making us both start. Lady Honor's mouth was tight with worry. She looked at me earnestly. 'Master Shardlake, will you have to tell Lord Cromwell I looked at the papers?' She swallowed.

'I must, Lady Honor. I am sorry.'

She swallowed. 'Will you ask him to deal with me kindly?'

'If you truly told no one, no harm has been done.'

'I didn't, I swear.'

'Then I will tell him you admitted frankly that you read the papers.' But I doubted she would have done so had I not told her I recognized her scent.

She let out a sigh of relief. 'Tell him I am sorry for what I did. I confess I have been worried I would be found out.'

'You must have been afraid when Serjeant Marchamount told you the Gristwoods were dead.'

'Yes, I was shocked when I heard they had been killed. I have been so foolish,' she added with sudden passion.

'Well,' I said, 'foolishness may be forgiven.' I hoped Cromwell would agree.

She looked at me curiously. 'You have a bloody trade, sir. Two murders to investigate.'

'Believe it or not, my specialism is property law.'

'Did that old shrew Lady Mirfyn tell you anything useful about the Wentworths? I saw you talking to her.'

Truly she missed little. 'Not much. All still depends on getting Elizabeth to talk. And I have been neglecting that matter.'

'You care about her.' She had recovered her composure quickly; her tone was light again.

'She is my client.'

She nodded, the pearls in her hood catching the light from the window. 'Perhaps you are a man of too gentle feeling to deal with blood and death.' She smiled softly.

'As I told you last week, I am a mere jobbing lawyer.'

She shook her head, smiling. 'No, you are more than that. I thought so when I first saw you.' She inclined her head, then said, 'I felt your whole being resound with sadness.'

I stared at her in astonishment; I felt tears prick suddenly at the corners of my eyes and blinked them away.

She shook her head. 'Forgive me. I say too much. If I were a common woman, I would be called malapert.'

'You are certainly out of the common run, Lady Honor.'

She looked over the courtyard. There was another rumble of thunder after a flash of lightning, which showed sadness in her face. 'I miss my husband still, though it has been three years. People say I married him for his money, but I loved him. And we were friends.'

'That is a fine thing in a marriage.'

She inclined her head and smiled. 'But he left me the memories of our time together and also a widow's status. I am an independent woman, Master Shardlake, I have much to be grateful for.'

'I am sure you are worthy of that status, my lady.'

'Not all men would agree.' She moved away a little and stood by the fountain, facing me in the gloom.

'Serjeant Marchamount admires you,' I ventured.

'Yes, he does.' She smiled. 'I was born a Vaughan, as you know. My early life was spent learning deportment, embroidery, just enough reading to make good conversation. The education of a woman of good birth is very dull. I wanted to scream with the boredom of it, though most girls seem happy enough.' She smiled. 'There, now you *will* think me a malapert. But I could never help nosing into men's affairs.'

'Not at all. I agree with you.' The Wentworth girls came into my mind. 'I too find conventionally accomplished girls dull.' As soon as I had said the words I wished I had not, for they could be taken as flirtatious. I found Lady Honor fascinating, but did not wish her to know that. She was, after all, still a suspect.

'Lady Honor,' I said, 'I have Lord Cromwell's commission. If – if anyone is putting pressure on you to give information about those papers, he will afford you his protection.'

She gave me a direct look. 'There are those who say he will soon have no protection to afford anyone. If he cannot resolve the king's marriage problems.'

'Those are rumours. The protection he can give now is real.'

I saw her hesitate, then she smiled, but tightly. 'Thank you for your care, but I have no need of protection.' She turned away a moment, then looked back at me, her smile warm again. 'Why are you unmarried, Master Shardlake? Is it because all these ordinary women bore you?'

'Perhaps. Though – I am not an attractive proposition.'

'In some dull eyes, perhaps. But some women prize intelligence and sensitivity. That is why I try to bring good company round my table.' She was looking at me keenly.

'Though sometimes the mixture turns explosive,' I said, turning the conversation into a jest.

'It is the price I pay for trying to bring men of different ideas together, in hope that by reasoned discussion over good food they may resolve their differences.'

I raised an eyebrow. 'And perhaps the arguments are entertaining to watch?'

She laughed and raised a finger. 'You have found me out. But usually it does no harm. The duke can be good company when he is sober.'

'You would like your nephew to regain your family's old fortunes? A place at court beside the king?' Norfolk could offer that, I thought – in return for information about Greek Fire? Was that why he had first welcomed the boy, then ignored him?

She inclined her head. 'I would like my family to regain what it lost. But perhaps Henry is not the one to do it, he is not the brightest boy, nor the most robust. I cannot see him at the king's side.'

'They say the king's manners can be rougher than the duke's.'

Lady Honor raised her eyebrows. 'You should be careful what you say.' She looked around quickly. 'But no, you are right. Have you heard the tale that the duke's wife once complained to him about his flaunting his mistress before her, and the duke ordered his servants to sit on her till she was silent? They kept her lying on the floor till blood flowed from her nose.' Her lip curled with disgust.

'Ay. You know, I have a workfellow just now whose origin could not be lower, and he and the duke have much the same manners.'

She laughed. 'And you stand between the highest and the lowest, a rose between the thorns?'

'A poor gentleman only.'

We both laughed; then our laughter was lost in a tremendous crash of thunder right above us. The heavens opened and a great torrent of rain fell down, soaking us in an instant. Lady Honor looked up.

'O God, at last!' she said.

I blinked the rain out of my eyes. The cold water was indeed marvellous after the broiling heat of the last days. I gasped with the relief of it.

'I must go in,' Lady Honor said. 'But we must talk more, Master Shardlake. We must meet again. Though I have no more to tell about Greek Fire.' And then she came close and quickly kissed my cheek, a sudden warmth amidst the cold rainwater. Without looking back, she ran though the door to the stairs and closed it. As the rain pelted down on me I stood there with my hand on my cheek, overcome with astonishment.

# Chapter Twenty-two

I RODE AWAY FROM THE House of Glass through sheets of rain that fell straight and hard, bouncing off my cap like a million tiny pebbles. But the storm was quickly over; by the time I reached Cheapside the last fading rumbles of thunder were sounding. The sewer channels had been turned into streams, fed with refuse from lanes that had been turned from dust to mud in half an hour. The last light of the long summer evening was fading and I jumped as Bow bells sounded loudly behind me, striking the curfew. The Ludgate would be closed and I would have to ask for passage through. Chancery was plodding on, his head down. 'Come on, old horse, we'll soon be home.' I patted his wet white flank and he gave a little grunting whicker.

The extraordinary conversation with Lady Honor went round and round in my head like a mouse in a jar. Her kiss, while chaste, was a daring thing from a woman of rank. But it was only after I had got her to admit she had read the papers that her tone became intimate. I shook my head sadly. I was attracted to her, all the more so after this evening, but I must be wary; this was no time to allow my mind to be cloyed by affection for a woman. Tomorrow would be the second of June, and only eight days left.

There was a stir about the Ludgate; men were going to and fro with torches to one side of the ancient gatehouse that held the debtors' prison. I wondered whether someone had escaped, but as I drew closer I saw a small part of the outer wall, where scaffolding had been erected, had collapsed. I pulled Chancery to a halt in front of a constable, who stood examining a pile of flagstones in the road with a lantern, watched by the gatekeeper and some passers-by.

'What has happened?' I enquired.

He looked up, doffing his cap when he saw I was a gentleman. 'Part of the wall's collapsed, sir. The old mortar was crumbling and the workmen dug it out today, then the storm soaked what was left and some of the wall fell down. It's ten feet thick, or the prisoners would be scrambling out like rats.' He squinted up at me. 'Pardon me, sir, but are you able to read old languages? Only there's something written on these stones, like pagan symbols.' There was a note of fear in the man's voice.

'I know Latin and Greek.' I dismounted, my thin pantofle shoes squelching on the wet cobbles. A dozen ancient flagstones lay in the road. The constable lowered his lamp to the inner surface of one of the blocks. There was some sort of writing carved there, a strange script of curved lines and half-circles.

'What do you think it is, sir?' the constable asked.

'It's from the time of the old druids,' someone said. 'Heathen spells. The stones should be broken up.'

I traced one of the marks with my finger. 'I know what this is, it's Hebrew. Why, this stone must have come from one of the Jews' synagogues after they were expelled near three hundred years ago. They must have been used on some previous repair – the gatehouse goes back to Norman times.'

The constable crossed himself. 'The Jews? That killed Our Lord?' He looked at the writing anxiously. 'Perhaps we should break them up after all.'

'No,' I said. 'These are of antiquarian interest. You should tell the alderman – the Common Council should know of this. There is a new interest in Hebrew studies these days.'

The man looked dubious.

'There may be a reward in it for you.'

He brightened. 'I will, sir. Thank you.'

With a last glance at the ancient writing I returned to Chancery, my shoes squelching unpleasantly in the mud. The keeper opened the gate and I rode over Fleet Bridge. I heard a great rush of water beneath me, and it made me think of all the generations who had lived in this City, dashing and scurrying through their lives, some to leave great monuments and dynasties of children, others rushing only to oblivion.

✟

WHEN I REACHED HOME Barak had not yet returned and Joan was abed. I had to rouse young Simon to take the horse to the stables; I felt a little guilty sending the boy stumbling off into the night, heavy-eyed with sleep as he was. I took a mug of beer and a candle and went up to my room. Looking through the open window, I saw the sky was clear, all the stars visible. The heat was gathering again already. Rainwater had come in, dripping on the floor and on my Bible, which stood on a table beside it. I wiped it, reflecting it was many days since I had last opened it. Only ten years ago the very idea of a Bible in English being allowed would have filled me with joy. I sighed and turned to the papers on the Bealknap case I had brought back from court, for I must prepare my recommendations for the council about an application to the Court of Chancery.

It was late when I heard Barak come in. I went to his room and found him in his shirt, in the process of hanging his doublet out of the window to dry.

'You were caught in the storm, then?'

'Ay, I've had a busy time going from place to place and the tempest caught me on my way to the tavern where the compurgators gather.' He gave me a serious look. 'I've seen the earl. He's not pleased. He wants progress, not a stream of refugees.'

I sat down on the bed. 'Did you tell him we've been going back and forth across London day after day?'

'He has to go to Hampton Court to see the king tomorrow, but he wants to see us the day after, and he wants some progress by then.'

'Was he angry?'

Barak shook his head. 'Anxious. He didn't like the idea Rich may be involved in this. I talked to Grey. He gave me disapproving

looks like he usually does but he said the earl's a worried man.' I saw
again the fear behind Barak's customary bravado, fear for his master
– and for himself if Cromwell fell. 'What happened at the banquet?'
he asked.

'The Duke of Norfolk was there, in a foul mood and drunk.' I
told him all that had passed. I even told him about Lady Honor's
kiss, impelled to frankness by the worry I had seen in his face. For
good or ill, Barak and I were in this together. I half-expected some
mocking remark, but he only looked thoughtful.

'You think she was making up to you because you found out
she'd read those papers?'

'Perhaps. There's more besides.' I told him of the conversation I
had overheard. 'Norfolk wants something from her, something that
Marchamount knows about.'

'Shit! Norfolk may be in the know too. That would be far worse
than Rich. Lord Cromwell will have to be told about that. Do you
think Norfolk's trying to get what was in those papers out of her?'

'Perhaps. There's not that much information in them, but he
doesn't know that. But if he's pressing her, why didn't she tell me?' I
looked at him seriously. 'I had the sense she thinks Cromwell may not
be able to offer protection to his friends much longer.'

Barak shrugged. 'That's the rumour.'

'I'm going to see her again tomorrow. I'll take the papers, say I'd
like to go through them with her, use that as an excuse to press her
further.'

Barak smiled wryly and shook his head. 'Caught by her rich
woman's scent, eh?'

'Yes. I knew the smell on those books was familiar.'

Barak ran his fingers through his hair. 'Perhaps they're all in
together. Bealknap, Lady Honor, Marchamount, Rich, Norfolk. That
would bake a fine pie.'

'No. That doesn't make sense. Whoever killed the Gristwoods
and Leighton – for I think he must be dead too – knows all about

Greek Fire. They have the formula, and they're trying to stop people's mouths. If I'm right, Norfolk may be trying to open Lady Honor's mouth. That means he *doesn't* know about Greek Fire. Not yet.'

'The earl should have had Bealknap and Marchamount and her ladyship in the Tower at the start, shown them the rack.'

I winced at the thought of Lady Honor in the Tower. Barak looked at me. 'Fine feelings won't help us in this,' he said impatiently.

'And if those people were taken to the Tower, how long would it have been before some gaoler or torturer started rumours that Greek Fire's been found and lost again?'

Barak grunted. 'That's why Lord Cromwell won't do it. Though there'll be plenty going to the Tower if he falls. Probably you and me with them, if the pope comes back.' He shrugged. 'At least I've made some progress on other matters. I've found who pock-face is.'

I sat up. 'Who?'

'He's called Bernard Toky. He's from out Deptford way, he started life as a novice monk apparently.'

'A monk?'

'Ay, he can pass for an educated man. But he was defrocked for something, spent the rest of his youth soldiering against the Turk and developed a taste for killing apparently. The other man, the big one, is called Wright. He's an old mate of Toky's. They've been involved in various bits of dirty business, though they've never been caught. Toky had a bad dose of smallpox a few years back, which accounts for his face, but it didn't change his habits.'

'Dirty business for whom?'

'Whoever will pay. Rich merchants with scores to settle mostly, who don't want to dirty their fine hands. He left London for somewhere in the country a few years ago, things were getting too hot for him. But now he's back. He's been seen, although he seems to be avoiding old friends. But I've got people looking for him.'

'Let's hope he doesn't get to us first.'

'And I found the tavern where the compurgators hang out.'

'You've had a busy time.'

'Ay. I told the tavern keeper I'd pay well for information about Bealknap. He'll be in touch. And I went to the tavern where the sailors hang out too. Offered money for information about that Polish cargo. The tavern keeper remembers someone trying to sell the stuff there, a man called Miller. He's at sea now, bringing coal down from Newcastle, but he should be back the day after tomorrow. If we go to the tavern then the innkeeper can introduce us.'

'Excellent. And if we can follow its trail from there to the Gristwoods' house . . . you've done well, worked hard.'

He looked at me seriously again. 'We've much more to do,' he said. 'Much more.'

I nodded. 'I sat next to a mercer's wife at the banquet, who said a strange thing about young Ralph Wentworth. Told me he drove his mother to an early grave. What can she have meant?'

'Was that all she said?'

'Ay, then she clammed up.'

We both jumped suddenly at a knock on the front door. Barak reached for his sword as we hurried down the stairs. Joan, roused from her bed, was already at the door, a startled look on her face. I motioned her back. 'Who is it?' I called.

'A message,' a childish voice called. 'Urgent, for Master Shard/lake.'

I opened the door. An urchin stood, holding a letter. I gave him a penny and took it.

'Is it from Grey?' Barak asked.

I studied the superscription. 'No. This is Joseph's writing.' I broke the seal and opened the letter. It was brief, and asked me to meet him first thing tomorrow at Newgate, where a terrible thing had happened.

# Chapter Twenty-three

NEXT MORNING WE RODE out early again. Any hope the storm might have heralded a change in the weather was gone; it was hotter than ever, not a cloud in the sky. The puddles were drying already and a malodorous steam rose from heaps of rubbish washed down from the alleyways.

I had thought there might be an argument with Barak over my plans for the morning; I intended to go to Newgate, then to the Guildhall to present my recommendations for transferring the Bealknap case; while there I planned to seek in the library the books that had been taken from Lincoln's Inn. I would be spending some hours away from the Greek Fire case. However, Barak raised no objection, saying he would visit the taverns again to see if there was more news of the compurgators or of Toky, and to my surprise he offered to come to Newgate with me and see Elizabeth. I promised I would visit Lady Honor again that afternoon to question her.

We rode up to Newgate again and left our horses at the nearby inn. I ignored the hands at the begging grate, and banged on the door.

The fat gaoler opened it. 'The lawyer again,' he said. 'Your client's given us a peck of trouble today.'

'Is Joseph Wentworth here? He asked me to meet him.'

'Ay.' He stood in the doorway, barring our entrance. 'He won't give me a sixpence he owes me.'

'What for *now*?'

'Shaving the witch's head when she went mad yesterday. After she started screaming and howling and throwing herself around the Hole. We've had to chain her and I got a barber to come and shave her head to cool her wild brain. That's what you're supposed to do with mad people, isn't it?'

Wordlessly, I passed him a sixpence. He nodded and stepped aside, letting us into the dark entrance hall. The heat had now penetrated even Newgate's thick stones and the interior was a warm, stinking fug. Water dripped somewhere. Barak wrinkled his nose. 'This place stinks like Lucifer's privy,' he muttered as we went to where Joseph sat on a bench. He looked crushed and barely brightened when he saw me.

'What's happened?' I asked. 'The gaoler said Elizabeth's run mad.'

'Thank you for coming, sir. I don't know what to do. She'd been the same since the trial, wouldn't utter a word. Then they took that old horse thief away yesterday.' He took out the handkerchief Elizabeth had given him and wiped his brow. 'As soon as the woman was taken out they say Lizzy went mad. Started screaming, throwing herself at the walls. Jesu knows why, the old woman was never kind to her. She had to be restrained, sir, they put her in chains.' He looked up at me in anguish. 'They cut off all her hair, her black curly hair that used to be so lovely, and tried to make me pay for the barber. I wouldn't – I hadn't asked for such a cruel thing.'

I sat beside him. 'Joseph, you know you have to pay them what they ask. If you don't they'll only treat her worse.' He bowed his head and nodded reluctantly. I guessed arguing with the gaolers over money was the only way poor Joseph could preserve a little dignity.

'How is she now?'

'Quiet again. But she's cut and bruised herself—'

'Let's go and see.'

Joseph looked enquiringly at Barak. 'A colleague,' I said, remem-bering Joseph had seen me ride off with him after the hearing with Forbizer. 'Do you mind if he comes too?'

He shrugged. 'No. Anyone who can help.'

'Come on then,' I said with a cheerfulness I did not feel. 'Let's see her.' It was only a few days since I had visited Elizabeth, but it felt like far longer.

Once again the fat turnkey led us past the cells where the men lay in their chains, down to the Hole. 'She's quiet this morning,' he said, 'but she was wild yesterday. Struggled like a demon when the barber came – lucky he didn't cut her head wide open. We had to hold her still while he used the razor.'

He opened the door and we passed through into a stink even more overpowering than before. My jaw dropped open when I saw Elizabeth, for she scarcely looked human now. She lay crouched in the straw, her face covered with grazes and streaks of blood, and her head had been shaved quite bald, the white dome making an obscene contrast to her dirty, bloodied face. I went over to her.

'Elizabeth,' I said calmly, 'what has happened to you?' I saw her lip was split, someone had hit her when they were restraining her yesterday. She stared back at me with those vivid dark green eyes. There was more life in them today, angry life. Her gaze flickered past me to Barak.

'That's Master Barak, a colleague,' I said. 'Did they hurt you?' I reached out a hand and she shrank back. There was a clanking, and I saw she was manacled to the wall by long chains, heavy gyves on her wrists and ankles.

'Was it when they took the old woman away?' I asked. 'Did that make you angry?'

She did not reply, only continued fixing me with that ferocious stare. Barak knelt close and whispered to me. 'May I ask her something?'

I looked at him dubiously. But what more harm could he do? I nodded.

He knelt before her. 'I don't know what your sorrow is, Mistress.' His tone was gentle. 'But if you won't talk, no one will ever know. You'll die and people will forget. In time they'll just give it up as a puzzle and forget it.'

She stared back at him for a long moment. Barak nodded. 'Was that why the old woman being taken made you angry? The thought you might be ripped out of the world unheard, like her?' Elizabeth moved an arm and Barak jumped back lest she was about to strike him, but she only scrabbled for something in the filthy straw. Her hand came up holding a wafer of charcoal. She leaned forward painfully, clearing a space in the straw at her feet. I moved to help her but Barak lifted a hand to restrain me. Elizabeth brushed a smear of dried shit from the exposed flagstones and began to write. We looked on in silence as she traced out some letters, then sat back. I leaned forward, wrinkling my eyes to make out the words in the gloom. It was Latin: *damnata iam luce ferox*.

'What is that?' Joseph asked.

'*Damnata*,' Barak said. 'That means damned, condemned.'

'It's from Lucan,' I said. 'She had a volume of his in her room. 'Furious by daylight, having been condemned.' It refers to some Roman warriors who knew they were about to lose a battle and killed themselves rather than be condemned to defeat.'

Elizabeth sat back against the wall. The effort of writing seemed to have tired her, but her eyes darted between the three of us.

'What does it mean?' Joseph asked.

'I think she means she would rather die by the press than be humiliated by going through a trial she would inevitably lose.'

Barak nodded. 'That's why she won't speak. But that's silly, girl. You'll lose the chance to tell your story, maybe get off.'

'So if you *were* to plead, Elizabeth,' I said slowly, 'you would plead not guilty.'

'I knew it,' Joseph said. He wrung his hands. 'Then tell us what happened, Lizzy. Don't torment us with riddles, it's cruel!' It was the first time he had lost patience with her. I could not blame him. For answer Elizabeth only looked down at the words she had written. She shook her head very slightly.

I thought a moment, then bent closer to her, wincing as my knees cracked. 'I have been to your uncle Edwin's house, Elizabeth. I have spoken to your uncle and your grandmother, your cousins and the steward.' I was watching to see if her look changed at the mention of any of those names, but she just continued staring angrily. 'They all say you must be guilty.' At that a bitter smile played round the corner of her mouth, the movement causing blood to seep from her cut lip. Then I leaned in close, so only she would hear, and said, 'I think there is something down the well in the garden, where Ralph fell, that they are trying to hide.'

She shrank back, her eyes full of horror.

'I propose to investigate it,' I said softly. 'And I have been told Ralph was a great worry to his mother. I will find the truth, Elizabeth.'

Then she spoke for the first time, her voice cracked from disuse. 'If you go there, you will do naught but destroy your faith in Christ Jesus,' she whispered. The words were followed by a fit of coughing; she doubled over, racked with it. Joseph brought a mug to her lips. She grasped it and swallowed, then sat forward, burying her head in her knees.

'Lizzy!' Joseph's voice was trembling. 'What did you mean? Tell us, please!' But she would not lift her head.

I stood up. 'I don't think she'll say any more. Come, let's leave her for now.' I looked round the Hole. There was a round depression in the filthy straw by the far wall where the old woman had lain.

'She'll be ill if she stays down here much longer,' Barak observed. 'After what she's been used to no wonder her wits are affected.'

'Lizzy, please tell us more!' Joseph shouted, his control gone. 'You are cruel, cruel! Unchristian!'

Barak gave him an exasperated look, and I put a hand on the farmer's trembling shoulder. 'Come, Joseph, come.' I knocked at the door and the gaoler led us away, back to the main door. This time it was even more of a relief to be outside again.

Joseph was still agitated. 'We can't just leave her there, now she's started to talk. We've only got eight days, Master Shardlake!'

I raised my hands. 'I have an idea, Joseph. I can't tell you what it is now, but I hope to find the key to this riddle soon.'

'*She* has the key to the riddle, sir, Lizzy!' He was shouting now.

'She won't give it to us. That's why I'm following other chan⁄nels!'

'Other channels. Legal language. Oh, God, what did you say to her in there?' He shook his head.

I did not want to tell him; it was better Joseph did not know I planned to break into his brother's garden. I made my voice calm. 'Joseph, give me till tomorrow. Trust me. And if you visit Elizabeth again, please, in Jesu's name, do not harangue her. That will only make things worse.'

'He's right, you know.' Barak said.

Joseph looked between us. 'I haven't any choice but to do as you say, have I? Though it's driving me mad, sir, mad.'

We walked to the inn where we had left the horses. The way was narrow and Joseph walked a little way behind Barak and me, his shoulders slumped.

'He's near the end of his tether.' I sighed. 'But so am I.'

Barak raised his eyebrows. 'Don't *you* start playing the martyr. It's bad enough with him and her.'

I looked at him curiously. 'You had the measure of her in there. It was you got her to write that sentence.'

He shrugged. 'I've had some experience of her way of thinking. When I ran away from home I felt all the world had turned against me. It took being arrested to bring me out of it.'

'It hasn't done that for her.'

He shook his head. 'Something bad must have happened to drive her to those depths. Something the girl thinks will never be believed.' He lowered his voice. 'We'll see what's in that well tonight.'

# Chapter Twenty-four

I SAID FAREWELL TO JOSEPH, promising I should have news for him tomorrow. As I rode down Cheapside to the Guildhall I wondered again what might be down that well. I had to ride carefully to avoid the small boys playing in the puddles, squelching joyously with their bare feet in the ooze even as the puddles shrank around them. I thought of the sun's fire turning the water to vapour, drawing it upwards from the earth through the hot air. Earth, air, fire, water: the four elements that, combined in a million ways, made up everything under the moon. But what was the combination that produced Greek Fire?

Arriving at the Guildhall, I left Chancery in the stables and went to find Vervey in his shaded office. He was studying a contract with leisurely carefulness, and I found myself envying his peaceful routine. He welcomed me warmly and I gave him the opinion I had written out the previous evening. He read it, nodding occasionally, then looked up at me.

'You are hopeful, then, of a victory in Chancery?'

'Ay, though it may be a year before we get there.'

He looked at me meaningfully. 'We may need to take more than the usual fee to the Six Clerks' Office up at the Domus.'

'That may help get the matter listed more quickly. I am going to look at Bealknap's property this morning, by the way. The Chancery judge will want to know all the circumstances of the nuisance.'

'Good, good. The council places the highest priority on this. Some of these tenements in the old monastic properties are shocking. Hovels of cheap wood, unsanitary and a fire risk too, with everywhere as dry as tinder.' He looked out of his window at the clear blue sky. 'If a fire breaks out people may not be able to get enough water from the conduits to quench it. Then the Common Council will be blamed. We're trying to stop leaks in the pipes, but some of them run miles from the streams.'

'I know of a man who is working on repairing the conduits. Master Leighton.'

'Yes. I have a note to chase him, he was supposed to bring our contractors some new pipes but he hasn't appeared. Do you know him?'

'Only by repute. I hear he is a skilled man.'

Vervey smiled. 'Ay, he's one of the few founders who knows that type of work. A skilled fellow.'

Probably a dead fellow, but I could not tell him. I changed the subject. 'I wonder if I might have a look at your library while I am here. Perhaps borrow one or two books if you have them?'

He laughed. 'I can't see that we would have anything Lincoln's Inn does not.'

'It's not legal works I'm after. Some Roman history. Livy and Plutarch, Pliny.'

'I will prepare a note for the librarian. I heard about your friend Godfrey Wheelwright and the Duke of Norfolk.'

It was safe to speak, for Vervey was known as a reformist. 'Godfrey should be more careful.'

'Ay, the times grow dangerous again.' Although we were alone, he lowered his voice. 'There's a pair of Anabaptists booked for burning at Smithfield next weekend unless they repent. The council has been asked to help with the arrangements, ensure all the apprentices attend.'

'I hadn't heard.'

He shook his head sadly. 'I fear for the future. But come, let me do this note.'

I had a niggling fear the books might be gone from the Guildhall library too, but they were all there, on the shelf. I grasped them eagerly.

The librarian was one of those fellows who believes books should be kept on shelves, not read, but with the aid of Vervey's note I was able to get past him. He watched sourly as I put the volumes in my satchel. As I walked down the Guildhall steps I felt a little pleased with myself, for the first time in days. Then I almost walked straight into Sir Edwin Wentworth.

Elizabeth's other uncle seemed to have aged even in the few days since I had seen him, his face lined and drawn with suffering. He was still dressed in black. Beside him walked his elder daughter Sabine, while the steward Needler followed behind, some large account books under one arm.

Sir Edwin pulled up short at the sight of me. For a second he looked as though he had been struck. I touched my cap and made to pass, but he stepped into my path. Needler passed his books to Sabine and stood protectively beside his master.

'What are you doing here?' Sir Edwin's face reddened and his voice trembled with anger. 'Making enquiries about my family?'

'No,' I said mildly. 'I have a case on with the Common Council.'

'Oh, yes, you lawyers have your long fingers in every pie, don't you? You crookbacked churl. How much is Joseph paying you for keeping that murderess alive?'

'We have not discussed a fee,' I said, ignoring the insult. 'I believe your niece to be innocent,' I added. 'Sir Edwin, does it not occur to you that if she *is* innocent, you will kill an innocent person while a guilty one goes free?'

'Know better than the coroner, do you?' Needler said boldly.

At his insolent manner, more than Sir Edwin's insult, something snapped inside me. 'Do you let your steward speak for you, sir?' I asked Sir Edwin.

'David speaks true. He knows as well as I that you will drag matters out as long as you get paid for it.'

'Have you any idea what death by the press means?' I asked him. A couple of aldermen walking up the steps stared round at my raised voice, but I took no heed. 'It means lying for days under heavy stones, in an agony of thirst and hunger, struggling to breathe as you wait for your back to break!'

Sabine began to cry. Sir Edwin looked round at her, then turned back to me. 'How dare you speak of such things in front of my poor daughter!' he shouted. 'She aches for her lost brother as I ache for my son! Black-robed, stinking, bent lawyer! You can tell *you* have no children!'

His face was contorted, spittle gathering at the corners of his mouth. People going up and down the steps had stopped to watch; someone laughed at his tirade of insults. To stop the spectacle making Elizabeth's name a talking point again, I stepped past Sir Edwin. Needler sidestepped too, blocking my path, but I stared at him fiercely and he gave way. Followed by a host of stares, I walked down the steps and away to the stables.

When I reached Chancery's stall I found I was trembling. I stroked his head and he nuzzled my hand, hoping for food. Sir Edwin's fury had been unnerving; there seemed something almost unbalanced in his hatred of Elizabeth. But he had lost his only son and he was right – I had no children, I could only imagine how he must feel. I slung my bag of books over my shoulder, mounted and rode out. Sir Edwin and his party had disappeared.

I rode north towards the City wall, where the former Franciscan priory of St Michael's lay. It was situated in a street where good houses were mixed in with poor tenements. The street was empty, quiet and shady, St Michael's halfway along. It was a small place, the church no bigger than a large parish church. The wide doors stood open and, curious, I dismounted and looked in.

I blinked with surprise at the interior. Both sides of the nave had been blocked off with tall, flimsy-looking wooden partitions. There was a series of doors at ground-floor level and rickety steps led up to more doors, making a dozen apartments in all. The centre of the nave had become a narrow passage, the old flagstones strewn with dirt. The passage was dark, for the partitions blocked off the side windows and the only light came from the window at the top of the quire.

Beside the door a couple of iron rings had been hammered into an ancient font. From the piles of dung on the floor I could see this was where horses were tethered. I slung Chancery's reins round a ring and walked down the central passage. So this was Bealknap's conversion. It was so rickety it looked as though the construction could come down at any moment.

One of the doors on the upper floor opened. I glimpsed a poorly furnished room, where cheap furniture was lit by rich multi-coloured light from the stained-glass window that now formed the apartment's outside wall. A thin old woman stepped out and stood at the head of the staircase; it wobbled slightly under her weight. She gave my robe a hostile look.

'Have you come from the landlord, lawyer?' she asked in a sharp northern accent.

I doffed my cap. 'No, madam, I represent the City council. I have come to look at the cesspit; there have been complaints.'

The old woman folded her arms. 'That pit's a disgrace. Thirty of us share it, those who live here and the others round the cloister. The vapours off it would stun a bull. I'm sorry for them living next door to the church, but what can we do? We have to go some-where!'

'No one blames you, madam. I am sorry for your trouble. I hope we may get an order for a proper cesspit to be built, but the landlord is resisting.'

She spat fiercely. 'That pig Bealknap.' She nodded at her apart-ment. 'We've refused to pay him rent till he takes these great windows out and boards them up. We bake with the sun coming through them, the wretched papist things.'

She leaned on the rail, warming to her theme. 'I'm here with my son and his family, five of us in this one room, and we're charged a shilling a week! Half the floorboards fell out of one of the tenements last week – nearly killed the poor creatures living there.'

'Your conditions are clearly bad,' I agreed. I wondered whether

her family was one of the thousands being forced off their land in the north to make way for sheep.

'You're a lawyer,' she said. 'Can he throw us out if we don't pay our rent?'

'He could, but I guess if you withhold your rent Bealknap will negotiate.' I smiled wryly. 'He hates losing money above all.' Speaking thus about another lawyer was professional disloyalty, but where Bealknap was concerned I did not care. The old woman nodded.

'How do I get to the cesspit?' I asked.

She pointed up the passage. 'There's a little door by where the altar was. The pit's in the cloisters. Hold your nose, though.' She paused. 'Try and help us, sir. This is a hellish place to live!'

'I'll do what I can.' I bowed and walked to the door she had indicated, which hung drunkenly from loose hinges. I felt sorry for the old woman; there was little I could do in the short term with the case going up to Chancery. But if Vervey bribed the Six Clerks' Office, that might help.

The former cloister yard had been converted too, the roofed walkway filled with more wooden partitions between the pillars to make a quadrangle of tiny ramshackle dwellings. Rags hung at the windows in place of curtains; these were hovels for the poorest of the poor. I blinked in the sunlight reflected from the white quadrangle stones where once the friars had paced.

The smallest of the little dwellings had an open door, from which a horrible stink issued. Holding my nose, I looked inside. A hole had been dug in the earth, with a plank set on bricks thrown across. It was a 'whistle and thud' cesspit, and should have been twenty feet deep so the flies could not reach the top, but from the cloud of them buzzing round the planks I guessed it was no more than ten feet deep. I held my nose as I looked down the dark, evil-smelling pit. It had not even been lined with wood, let alone the mandatory stone: no wonder it leaked. I remembered what Barak had said about his father falling down one of these pits and shuddered.

I stepped outside with relief. I must visit the house next door, the one the council owned, then get back to Chancery Lane. The morning was wearing on, the hot sun near its zenith. I paused and rubbed my sleeve across my brow, easing the uncomfortable weight of my satchel.

Then I saw them. They stood one on each side of the door to the church, so still that I had not immediately noticed them. A tall thin man with a pale face as pitted with pox marks as though the devil had scraped his claws across it, and on the other side an enormous, hulking fellow who kept small frowning eyes fixed on me as he hefted a chopping axe, the shaft cut short to make a fearsome weapon, in his big hand. Toky, and his mate Wright. I swallowed, feeling my legs begin to tremble. Other than the door to the church there was no way out of the cloister yard. I glanced along the rows of doors but all were shut, the inhabitants no doubt out at work or begging in the streets. I felt for my dagger.

Toky smiled, a broad smile that showed a perfect set of white teeth, as he lifted his own dagger. 'Didn't see us following you, did you?' he asked cheerfully in a sharp voice with a country burr. 'You've been getting careless without Master Barak at your side.' He nodded at the cesspit. 'Fancy going down there? They wouldn't find you till they cleaned it out, wouldn't notice the smell with what's down there already.' He grinned at Wright. The big man nodded briefly, never taking his gaze off me. His eyes were focused and still, like a dog stalking its prey; Toky's glittered with the bright cruel intensity of a cat's. He smiled with pleasure.

'Whatever you are being paid,' I said, trying to keep my voice steady, 'Lord Cromwell will double it in return for the name of your employer, I promise.'

Toky laughed, then spat on the ground. 'That for the tavern keeper's son.'

'Who is paying you?' I asked. 'Bealknap? Marchamount? Rich? Norfolk? Lady Honor Bryanston?' I watched their faces for any sign of recognition, but they were both too professional for that. Toky spread his arms and began moving towards me while the big man stepped to the side, raising his axe. Toky was trying to nudge me towards his confederate, so he could make the killing blow, guiding me to the slaughter like a sheep. 'Help!' I called out, but if anyone was within the wooden hovels they were not going to intervene. None of the window curtains stirred. My heart thudded in my breast and despite the heat I felt cold, paralysed. I was done for this time. I almost gave in. Then in my mind's eye I saw Sepultus Gristwood's shattered face and I resolved, if I was to end like that, at least I would go down fighting.

Their eyes were concentrated on my dagger arm. I let my shoulder drop so the strap of my satchel slid down my other arm, then I grabbed it and swung at Wright with all my strength. The heavy books caught him on the side of the head and he stumbled with a cry.

I ran for the doorway, thanking God for the broken door. I heard Toky close behind me and winced in anticipation of a blade thrust into my back. I grabbed at the door. It came right off the hinges. I turned and thrust it at Toky; he stumbled against it with a cry, giving me time to run into the nave. The old woman was still on her staircase, talking to a younger woman who had emerged from the next-door hovel. Their mouths fell open in amazement as I ran down the passage. I passed them and turned. Toky was standing in the doorway, blood running from his nose. To my surprise, he laughed.

'We'll put you down the pit *alive* for this, matey,' he said. He stepped aside as Wright charged through the door and headed straight for me, axe raised high.

Then he stopped with a howl as a flood of liquid landed on him from above, followed by an earthenware pot that banged on his shoulder. I stared upwards. The old woman had thrown a full pisspot at him. Her neighbour ran from her door, carrying another. She hurled it too at the big man. This time it caught him on the forehead and he stumbled against the wall with another cry, dropping his axe.

'Run!' the old woman yelled. Toky was running down the aisle, fury in his eyes now. I sped for the main door, jerking Chancery's reins free. He was wide-eyed and trembling with anxiety, but allowed me to haul him outside. Riding away was my only chance – on foot they would get me in the street. I leaped clumsily into the saddle and grasped the reins. Then they were seized from below, jerking Chancery's head aside. I looked down. To my horror I saw Toky directly underneath me, staring up at me with a snarling smile, the sunlight flashing off his dagger. I fumbled frantically for my own, which I had slipped up my sleeve as I mounted, but I was too late. Toky thrust upwards at my groin.

Chancery saved me. As Toky stabbed he reared up, neighing in terror and kicking out. Toky jumped back. I saw with a thrill of horror that his dagger was bloody; I glanced down at my waist, clutching the slippery neck of the rearing horse, but it was Chancery's blood that stained it, welling from a great gash in his side. Toky dodged the flying hooves and struck at me again but Chancery, screaming now, shied away, almost unseating me. Toky looked quickly round; along the street shutters were banging open; a group of men had appeared in the doorway of an inn at the top of the street. I pulled at the reins and Chancery stumbled towards them, his blood dripping on the road. I looked over my shoulder. Wright had joined Toky now but half the street lay between us. The sunlight glinted on Wright's axe.

'Hey, what's going on?' someone called. 'Constable!' The men from the inn spilled into the road; doors were being opened along the street, people looking fearfully out. Toky glanced at them, gave me a savage look, then turned and ran off up the street, Wright running after him. The men from the inn came over to where Chancery stood trembling from head to foot.

The innkeeper approached me. 'You all right, lawyer?'

'Yes. Thank you, yes.'

'God's death, what happened? Your horse is hurt.'

'I must get him home.' But at that moment Chancery shuddered and slipped forward to his knees. I had barely time to jump off before he fell on his side. I looked at the blood still welling on to the dusty cobbles, and thought how easily it could have been mine. I looked at his eyes and but already they were glazing over; my old horse was dead.

# Chapter Twenty-five

SOME HOURS LATER, as the heat of the day began to fade, I sat under the shade of a trellis in my garden. I had told the crowd in the street that I had been the victim of a robbery, bringing forth mutterings about the type of people living at the old friary. The innkeeper had insisted a cart be sent for to remove the horse, which was blocking the narrow street, and that I pay for it. When the cart arrived I had a ridiculous urge to ask the driver to take Chancery's corpse to my house; but what would I do with it there? As they loaded him on the cart, to take him to the Shambles, I walked down to the river to catch a boat. I blinked back tears. There was no point in going to Lady Honor's now, I was too dusty to present myself at the House of Glass, and my legs were trembling as I walked.

I closed my eyes at the memory of the sudden stillness in Chancery's eyes. He had died of shock as much as loss of blood and I blamed myself; for days I had ridden him beyond endurance through London in the heat. The poor old horse, with his quiet gentle ways. Young Simon wept when I told him Chancery was dead. I had not realized the boy was so fond of him; he had seemed more taken with Barak's mare.

I remembered the day I bought Chancery. I had been eighteen, not long in London, and he was the first horse I had bought for myself. I remembered how proud I had been as I led the pretty white creature with the broad hooves from the stables, how gentle he had been from the start. I had promised myself I would put him out to grass, but now he would never enjoy those last years in the orchard behind my garden. Tears formed at the corners of my eyes again. I wiped them away.

There was a cough at my elbow and I turned to find Barak, looking hot and dusty.

'What's happened? The boy tells me your horse has died.'

I told Barak of the attack. He frowned as he sat beside me. 'Shit, that's more bad news for the earl tomorrow. How did they know you were going there?' He thought a moment. 'It was Bealknap's property. That points to him.'

I shook my head. 'Bealknap had no idea I was going there today. No, I think Toky was following me again. I wasn't looking round me as I should, I was careless. I had an – an – encounter with Sir Edwin Wentworth at the Guildhall. They knew who you are,' I added. 'They know you have been looking for them.'

'Word's got around.' He shook his head. 'What did Lady Honor have to say?'

'I didn't go to see her. I was covered in dust and blood and sore shaken.'

'We've only eight days.' He eyed my face. 'Have you been weeping?'

'For Chancery,' I said, my voice gruff with embarrassment.

'God's death, it was only a horse. Well, I've been working while you've been sitting here. I've found a man Bealknap used as a compurgator, vouching for the good character of people he'd never heard of.'

I sat up. 'Where is he?'

Barak jerked his head towards the house. 'In there. He keeps a clothing stall in Cheapside, works for Bealknap on the side. I've put him in the kitchen. Want to talk to him?'

I followed Barak to the kitchen, trying to pull myself together. A middle-aged man sat at the table. He was plump and respectable looking, which no doubt was why Bealknap had chosen him. He rose to his feet and gave a deep bow. 'Master Shardlake, sir, a pleasure to meet you. Adam Leman, sir.'

DARK FIRE

I sat down opposite him, while Barak stood looking on.

'Well, Master Leman, I hear my brother in the law, Stephen Bealknap, has employed you as a compurgator.'

Leman nodded. 'I have assisted him.'

'To swear to the good character of men held in the bishop's gaol under benefit of clergy.'

He hesitated. I noticed his eyes were watery, and his nose a mess of broken red veins. A drunk, probably unable to run his stall properly and in need of extra cash for strong beer.

'Master Bealknap is kind enough to pay me a retainer,' he said cautiously. 'Perhaps I do not know all the gentlemen whose character I swear to as well as I might, but I feel I am doing a Christian service, sir. The conditions in the bishop's gaol—'

I cut through his nonsense. 'You pretend to know people you have never heard of and pervert the course of justice for money. We both know that. Now, have a beer.' I nodded at Barak, who fetched a jug from the cold cupboard. Leman coughed, then sat up in his chair.

'Bealknap hasn't paid me, sir. I said I'd do no more work for him till he did. He's the meanest man alive, he'd skin a flea for its hide and tallow. Makes a point of never paying anyone if he can get out of it.' He nodded self-righteously. 'Well, now it's caught up with the bastard. I've told your man I'll help you nail him and I shall. Thank you.' He took a cup from Barak and gulped noisily. 'That's good in this hot weather.' He looked at me sharply. 'You can give me immunity?'

I ever preferred a rogue who would come to the point. I nodded. 'In exchange for an affidavit to go before the disciplinary authorities of Lincoln's Inn. But once we've completed the affidavit I want you to come with me and tell Bealknap to his face what damage you can do him. Will you do that?'

He hesitated. 'How much?'

'A pound for the affidavit, another for coming to see Bealknap.'

'Then it'll be a job I'll be happy to do, sir.' His looked at me curiously. 'You got some grudge against him yourself?'

'You mind your business,' Barak said.

I rose. 'Come then, Master Leman, let us go to my study and prepare this affidavit.'

I spent an hour with the rogue. He signed the document with a scrawled flourish and I sent him on his way with five shillings on account for his fee. As I rubbed sand over the florid signature to dry it Barak laughed.

'I've never seen an affidavit taken before. The way you kept him to the point.'

'It's an art you learn. Now I am hungry. I'll get Joan to make us an early supper.'

'And then – the well?' Barak looked at me. 'We may not get another chance.'

For myself, now the business with Leman was done, the horror of the day's earlier events was crowding back into my mind and the expedition to Sir Edwin's house in the dark was the last thing I wished for. But it had to be done.

'Yes, the well. We'll have to wait till it's dark.' I glanced at the satchel, which I had retrieved from the cloister of St Michael's before returning home, and slung in a corner. 'I'll take the chance to look at those books.'

☦

I RETURNED TO MY STUDY after a quick supper. I read for hours, lighting candles as the summer sun dropped to the horizon and the moon came up with the thick, hot darkness. As ever, reading soothed my mind and took me far away from my troubles. I read about Roman experiments with fire weaponry that seemed to come to naught. The name Medea came up again and again; the name of the ancient Greek sorceress who presented her enemy with a shirt that burst into all‑consuming fire when it was put on. Placing 'the Shirt of Medea' on victims in the arena was a sport in Nero's time, mentioned in Plutarch and Lucullus. But what was it that made the shirt burn, and why had the Romans not developed this 'infernal fire' for military use?

I read on, finding references to military experiments with a mysterious substance called 'naphtha' that was found in Mesopotamia, on the
eastern frontier of the empire. Pliny said it bubbled to the surface from
underground and could be set on fire even if it spilled into a river. So
God had seeded something in the earth there, as he seeded gold or iron
in different places. I knew alchemists were able to locate deposits of
some desired substance, such as iron or coal, by studying the nature
of the ground, though they had never found deposits of the fabled
'philosopher's stone' that could turn base metals into gold, however
often they might gull poor fools into believing they had.

I laid down my book and rubbed my eyes. I must see Guy, I
thought. Barak would not like me telling Guy more, so I would have
to keep the visit from him. This world of the discovery and transform-
ation of matter was alien to me, yet there was something in these
books, some clue, I was sure. Or why had the Lincoln's Inn copies
been stolen? Who had stolen those books? Who was it the old librarian
was afraid of? I sighed. Every step I took seemed only to throw up
more puzzles.

I jumped at a knock on the door. Barak stood there, dressed in
black doublet and hose, suppressed excitement in his eyes. 'Ready?' he
asked. 'It's time to go to Sir Edwin's.'

✠

WE WALKED DOWN TO Temple Stairs to catch a boat. Barak
carried a heavy knapsack that he told me contained tools to break the
locks on the well cap, candles and a rope ladder to climb down. It
felt strange to be out on illicit business at night; if a constable asked
to see the contents of that knapsack we would be in trouble. Barak,
though, seemed quite unconcerned, nodding and smiling at the occasional watchman who lifted his lamp as we passed.

We took the path through Temple Inn, silent and dark save for
the occasional flicker of candles at a window. We passed the great
round bulk of Temple church, where the crusading Knights Templar
had worshipped.

'Those were the fellows, eh?' Barak said. 'The Christian powers were on the march in those days, not forever being beaten by the heathen Turks like now.'

'Christendom was united then.'

'Maybe it will be again if we get Greek Fire. Under us. King Henry's navies burning the French and Spanish navies off the seas. We could cross the Atlantic and take the Spanish colonies.'

'Don't get carried away.' I gave him a cold look. The way he talked of burning navies repelled me. Had he not seen the burnings at Smithfield? Seen what fire did to men? 'Perhaps it would be better if it never came to pass.'

He inclined his head, but did not reply. A moment later he bent down and picked up some of the pebbles that separated the rose-filled flower beds from the path, putting them in his pocket.

'What are you doing?'

'These might come in useful,' he said ambiguously.

The Thames came into view, broad and shining in the moonlight, the lamps on the boats pinpricks on the water. 'We're in luck,' I said. 'There's a wherry at the stairs.'

✞

THE MOONLIT RIVER was quiet, only a few boats carrying officials between the City and Westminster. I sat looking at the faint lights on the Southwark shore, thinking of Chancery again. Well, he was gone, gone to nothing for animals have no souls, but that was better than hell, where most men must have their end, perhaps me too for all I knew. I realized that when I was attacked I had thought only of survival, my mind sharpened by danger, I had not thought to pray or of what might happen after if I was killed. Was that sinful? I shook my head; I was exhausted, but I had to stay awake and sharp.

The wherry bumped into Dowgate steps with a soft thud. Barak stepped out, offering me a hand, and we set off to Walbrook.

✞

When we reached Sir Edwin's house it was dark, the shutters closed on the ground floor, though the upper windows were open to let in some air. Barak turned into Budge Row and I followed him down a narrow alley, stinking of piss.

'There's an orchard on the other side of that wall,' he whispered, 'and beyond that is Wentworth's garden. I had a look around earlier.' He stopped beside a flimsy wooden door in the wall, then stepped back and put his shoulder to it. It fell open with a crack. He darted inside. I followed, finding myself in a medlar orchard. The white scentless blossoms of that strange fruit, which must be left to hang on the tree till it decays before it may be eaten, showed luminous in the moonlight. A couple of pale shapes rose up in the long grass, making me jump before I realized they were rooting pigs. They ran off grunting between the trees. I looked back at the door: there had been a bolt on the inner side that Barak's shove had ripped from the wood.

'That was someone's property,' I said.

'Hush,' he hissed angrily. 'D'you want any passer-by to hear?' He closed the door carefully, then gestured at the ten-foot-high wall. 'Perhaps you'd've preferred to climb over there,' he whispered. 'Now, come on.'

I followed him through the orchard, jumping again as a clutch of hens fled clucking from under our feet. Barak made for the far wall; this wall was lower, perhaps seven feet high. He gestured to me to stand beside him. His face was alert; he looked as though he was enjoying himself.

'The garden's on the far side. If I help you up, can you drop down?'

I looked up dubiously. 'I think so.'

'Good. Come on, then.' He squatted, making a stirrup of his hands. I reached up, grasped the top of the wall and placed a foot in his cupped hands. He took a firm grip and hoisted me into the air. I scrabbled at the wall and a moment later was lying spreadeagled on top, looking down into Sir Edwin's garden. The effort had brought me out in a sweat. I blinked water from my eyes, looking rapidly around. Beyond the lawn and the trellised flower beds the rear of the house was as dark as the front, all the windows closed. The round structure of the well was only fifteen feet away.

'Everything quiet?' Barak whispered from below.

'Seems to be. All the lights are out.'

'No dogs?'

'I can't see any.' I had not thought of that, but it was quite likely a wealthy house like this would be guarded by dogs at night.

'Throw a couple of pebbles before you go over. Here.' I felt some small stones being pressed into my hand. So that was why he had wanted them. I managed to sit upright on the wall and threw one into the garden. It bounced off the well cap with a clunk that would have brought any dog running and barking, but everything remained quiet and still.

'It's all right,' I whispered.

'Get down, then, and I'll follow.'

I put the other stones back in my pocket, took a deep breath and jumped onto the lawn, jarring my spine uncomfortably. I leaned against the wall, conscious that I was trapped there now. If something happened I doubted I could climb up again on my own. There was a scrabbling sound and Barak dropped down beside me. He stood looking round, watchful as a cat.

'You keep watch,' he breathed. 'I'll get that well open.'

He loped quickly across the grass. He dropped his knapsack to the ground and there was a faint clink as he pulled out a couple of tools. I made for the cover of the big oak and sat on the bench underneath, trying to calm my rapidly beating heart, watching the still dark house. Barak seemed to know what he was doing, frowning a little as he inserted a narrow metal rod like a jeweller's tool into a padlock. I wondered how many locks he had picked before on Cromwell's orders. The padlock came free. He tossed it to the ground and started on the other. I glanced at the silent house again, thought of the old woman asleep, the two girls, Sir Edwin, the steward Needler. What had happened in the garden that day? This was the bench where

Sabine and Avice said Elizabeth had been sitting when they came out after hearing Ralph yell. Elizabeth had told me that if I went to the well, what I saw would shake my faith. I shivered.

Barak grunted as the other padlock came off, and gestured me over. 'You'll have to help me with this. It's heavy.'

'All right.' I felt strangely reluctant to grasp the wooden cap, remembering the dreadful stink I had smelt before, but I helped him slide it off. We propped it against the side of the well and looked down. A few rows of bricks were visible and, below that, darkness. I felt a draught of cold air and caught again the miasma of decay.

'Still smells, then,' Barak whispered beside me.

'It seems less strong than before.'

He leaned over and dropped a pebble down the well. I waited to hear it splash into water or clatter on stone, but there was no sound at all. Barak looked at me. 'Seems to have landed on something soft.' He took a deep breath. 'I'd hoped to get some idea how deep it was. Well, just have to hope the ladder's long enough.' He pulled the rope ladder from his knapsack and quickly secured it to a metal rod in the brickwork where the well bucket must once have hung. He let the ladder go and it unfurled into the darkness. Barak took a deep breath, squared his shoulders and looked at me seriously. I realized he was daunted by the prospect of that descent.

'Give me a shout if anyone stirs. I wouldn't want to be caught down there.'

'I will.'

'I've candles and a tinderbox for when I get to the bottom,' he said. 'Wish me luck.'

'Good luck. And thank you.'

He lifted a hand to his shirt and, loosening a button, put his hand inside to finger his little Jewish symbol. Then he clambered over the side of the well. He found the ladder with his feet and began climbing down. The top of his head vanished into darkness, giving me the strange feeling the well had swallowed him up.

I leaned over. 'Are you all right?' I asked in a loud whisper.

His voice came back, hollow and echoing. 'Ay. That smell's stronger.'

I glanced at the house again. All was still silent.

'I've touched bottom.' Barak's voice echoed with a ringing hollowness. I guessed the well must be deep, perhaps thirty feet. 'I'm on something soft.' He called. 'Cloth. And something else, like fur. Ugh. I'm going to light the candle.'

I heard a scrape, caught a tiny spark far below in the darkness and then another. 'The arsehole won't catch! Wait, there it is – oh, hell!' I jumped back as a startled yell echoed from the pit. At the same moment a sudden flicker of light appeared at a first-floor window in the house.

I grasped the side of the well and leaned in, regardless of the stench. Barak's candle had gone out again. 'There's a light in the house!' I called out. 'Get up, now!'

There was a frantic scrabbling as he hauled himself up. I glanced at the house again. The light had moved to the next window. Someone was walking around with a candle. Had they seen or heard us, or was it just someone going to the privy? The end of the rope ladder trembled as Barak climbed rapidly. I reached in and thrust a hand into the darkness. 'Here!'

A hard hand grasped my own. My back screamed in pain as I helped Barak up. He scrambled out as though the devil were behind him and stood panting beside me, looking over at the house. His eyes were wide and there was a rotten, meaty smell on him. The candlelight was still there, but no longer moving, flickering at one of the windows. Was someone looking out? We were a good distance from the house and partly shaded by the tree, but the moonlight was bright.

'Here, come!' Barak whispered urgently. He had grasped the well cap. 'They may not have seen us. If someone comes out, run!'

We slid the cap back into place and Barak scrabbled for the padlocks he had laid on the lawn. He put them back in place, moving with smooth, practised speed.

'The light's gone out!' I whispered.

'Right, nearly done.' He shut the second padlock with a click and stepped away. Just then I heard the creak of a door opening, and a voice I recognized as Needler's called out, 'Hey! Who's that!'

Barak turned and ran for the wall. I followed; he had already bent and made a stirrup of his hands. I glanced back: it was hard to make anything out across the lawn and flower beds but there seemed to be dark shapes in the open doorway. Then I heard an angry bark.

'Dogs,' I hissed.

'Get up, for Jesu's sake!'

I grasped the wall, put my feet in Barak's hands, and again he hauled me up. I almost overbalanced but managed to sit astride the wall. I looked back fearfully to see two large black dogs loping across the flower beds, not barking now but running towards Barak in deadly, intent silence.

'Hurry!'

He grabbed the top of the wall and, setting his feet against the bricks, began hauling himself up. The dogs were almost on him. Behind them I heard footsteps. Needler was following. Then Barak cried out. One of the dogs, a big mongrel, had his shoe and was holding on, growling evilly. The other dog leaped up at me. I almost overbalanced but managed to hold on. Fortunately the wall was too high and the creature fell back. It stood, paws against the wall, barking angrily up at me.

'Help me, for Christ's sake!' Barak hissed. For a second I could not think what to do, then remembered the pebbles in my pocket. I pulled out the largest and threw it straight at the eyes of the dog that held his foot.

It yelped and jumped back, startled. It only lost its grip for a second but that was enough for Barak to haul his leg up and we both half-dropped, half-fell into the long grass of the orchard, just as Needler's voice shouted again from the other side of the wall. 'Who's that? Stop!'

We lurched back into the cover of the trees, half-expecting the steward's face to appear over the wall, but he remained on the other side, where the dogs were barking frantically. No doubt he was afraid to pursue us on his own. I heard a voice that sounded like Sir Edwin's calling from the lawn. Barak grasped my arm and led the way through the orchard at a fast limp. We went back through the broken door into the lane, back into Budge Row and down Dowgate. Only then did he stop, leaning against a wall and lifting his foot to examine it.

'Are you hurt?' I asked anxiously.

'Just a graze. Thank Christ I had my pattens on, look.' He showed me where the dog's teeth had gouged bite marks in the wooden soles, then looked at me keenly. 'Would that steward have recognized you?'

'He didn't get close enough to see.'

'Just as well he's a coward and didn't come after us, or you'd have had some explaining to do.'

I looked nervously around the deserted street. 'Sir Edwin will rouse the constable.'

'Ay, just give me a minute.'

'What – what made you cry out in the well?' I asked. 'What did you see?'

He looked at me grimly. 'I'm not sure. There are clothes down there, cloth and fur. And I seemed – I thought I saw eyes down there.'

'Eyes?'

He swallowed again. 'Dead eyes, glinting in the candlelight.'

'Whose eyes? For God's sake, whose?'

'I don't know, do I? Small eyes. Two pairs at least. It gave me a shock.'

'There's a body down there? More than one?'

'God's death, I'd hardly a second to look before you called to me to get out!' Barak shook his head. 'I don't know. I felt bones crunch, though, little bones. I'm sure that's what it was.' He lifted his hand to his shirt again and touched the talisman inside, then stepped away from the wall.

'Let's get out of here.' Still limping, he led the way back to the river.

# Chapter Twenty-six

T HAT NIGHT I SLEPT DEEPLY, exhausted. I woke with a leaden feeling of tiredness and the realization that I should have to face Cromwell that afternoon. The third of June. In exactly a week's time the demonstration would be due. My back ached horribly from pulling Barak out of the well. I lay there, wondering how much longer I could keep up this pace, cope with the constant danger.

I did Guy's exercises carefully, in case I did more harm than good, then went and looked out over my garden, the flowers wilting in their beds under a sun whose heat was powerful already. I thought of Joseph's farm, his crops shrivelling in the fields. I would have no news for him this morning after all; we still did not know what was down that well. Barak had manfully offered to try again: but not tonight, for they would certainly be on watch. I wondered if they had guessed at our purpose. Barak had left no sign the well had been disturbed; most likely they thought they had surprised a pair of burglars. I scribbled a hasty note to Joseph, saying it would be another day or two before I got back to him and asking him to keep faith with me.

Barak was already at breakfast when I went downstairs. Joan was serving and kept giving us worried glances; these last few days she had noticed how tense I seemed. I had told her that Chancery had simply collapsed and died of heatstroke, but I suspected she did not believe me.

'Well, what now?' Barak asked after she had left.

'I'll go to Lady Honor's first, question her again. If I go early I'm most likely to catch her in.'

He was as ebullient as ever. 'What's it they say? A ship could be rigged in the time it takes a lady of fashion to get ready. I see you've put a new doublet and robe on for her.'

'Might as well look my best.'

He took a deep breath and made a grimace. 'We've to see the earl at one. He wants us at Whitehall. I hope you find out something new from Lady Honor. Shall I come with you?'

'No. I thought perhaps you might visit Madam Neller again; see if there is any news of the girl Bathsheba. I'll come back here and meet you at twelve. And I'll send Simon to Leman, asking him to come here at two. Then we can go to Lincoln's Inn and confront Bealknap.' I did not want Barak to know that after seeing Lady Honor I planned to visit Guy and tell him more about Greek Fire. I felt obscurely that the fact the Romans knew of it or something similar, but had been unable to develop it, went to the heart of the matter.

I saw Barak was giving me one of his keen looks and wondered if he had noticed something unusual in my manner. He was sharp enough for anything. I remembered anew that his loyalty was to Cromwell, not to me.

'We have that inn to visit tonight,' I said, 'where they tried to sell that Polish stuff.'

'Yes. I suppose it'd do no harm to see old Neller, remind her we haven't forgotten her. I'd rather not hang about here thinking about our meeting with the earl. But are you sure you'll be safe on your own?'

'Ay. I'll be going by public ways, and I'll be keeping a careful eye out.'

We were interrupted by a knock at the door. Joan stood there, a look of surprise on her face. 'There's a messenger, sir, from Lord Cromwell's office. He has a new horse for you, sir.'

Barak got up, nodding. 'I sent a message to Grey yesterday afternoon, saying your horse was killed and asking for a new one to be sent. You've no time to go to the market.'

'Oh.'

'You need a horse, we can't go everywhere by water. I asked for a younger horse, better able to keep up with Sukey.'

'Oh,' I said again. I was suddenly filled with anger. Did Barak think Chancery's loss could be repaired so casually? Yet from a practical point of view he was right. I went outside. Simon had brought both horses round. Barak's sleek mare was accompanied by a big brown gelding. I patted it. It seemed placid enough. Yet it felt almost a betrayal to see this animal in Chancery's place.

'What's his name?' I asked Simon.

'Genesis, sir. Though as he's a gelding he won't be able to generate a foal, will he?' Simon smiled shyly, pleased at his own cleverness.

I looked at the pattens on his feet. 'How are you managing with those?'

'Very well, thank you, sir. They are easy on the feet after a while.'

'The effort was worth it, you see.' I gave him two notes. 'Take this to Master Wentworth's lodging house, please, and the other to the stall of a Master Leman, at Cheapside.'

I heaved myself into the saddle. Barak had come to the door, that speculative look still on his face. I gave him a brief wave and rode off.

I decided to go to Lady Honor's house by the quieter route, via Smithfield and entering the City through the Cripplegate. It would give Genesis a chance to get used to me. I rode on steadily, half an eye always open for danger. I had brought the Greek Fire papers with me and they bumped against my side in the knapsack I had used yesterday to hit Wright. I shuddered again at the thought of his axe.

My thoughts turned to the Wentworths. What in God's name was going on in that family? I could not see any of the family engaged in what now seemed likely to be more than one murder. The old woman was harsh and ruthless, but her interest was only in her family and her blindness prevented her taking an active role in any devilry. The two girls too surely had no horizons beyond their family and a good marriage; if Sabine was engaged in some girlish fancy for the steward that was surely not so unusual. Both were classic Little Lady Favours, well-brought-up, well-mannered girls as content with their lot as cows in a field.

I turned my thoughts to Sir Edwin. He was a man consumed by

fury and sorrow and it was hard to guess what he was like in normal circumstances. From all I had heard he seemed to be a typical rich merchant, concerned above all to build up his and his family's status. Needler, the steward, was a nasty piece of work but his main interest seemed to be keeping well in with the family. All normal, really. In fact the only members of the Wentworth household whose behaviour was abnormal were Elizabeth, whom I believed innocent, and Ralph himself.

We had reached Smithfield. I looked around the open space, St Bartholomew's Friary and the hospital still empty and guarded. By the market I saw men in City livery stacking temporary seats in tiers. Others were hammering bolts with chains attached into a long wooden pole. I remembered Vervey telling me there was another burning planned for the next week, a pair of Anabaptists who denied the sacraments and would hold all goods in common. I shuddered, praying they might repent and be spared this horror, and turned the horse towards the priory and Long Lane, where my route lay.

I noticed a little group of retainers in the red and gold Howard livery standing quietly holding their horses by the gatehouse. Then I saw the Duke of Norfolk himself was by the doorway, his scarlet robe a bright slash of colour against the grey stone. He was talking to another man, who stood in the gatehouse doorway with arms folded in a proprietorial gesture. To my surprise I recognized Sir Richard Rich.

They had already seen me and were staring across at me. The duke raised an arm. 'Hey, master lawyer! Over here!'

Hell, I thought, what now? I turned Genesis's head towards the group, praying the horse would continue to behave. I noticed there was a new doorman on the gate, and wondered what had happened to the fat fellow Barak had kicked out of the library. As I pulled up, Rich gave me a cold, angry look, though Norfolk for once looked amiable enough. I guessed Rich had been in the act of welcoming Norfolk to the priory when I turned up and I had a feeling they were not pleased at having been seen together. So febrile was the atmosphere lately that whenever two councillors were seen talking together away from Whitehall, rumours of plots were sparked. And indeed they were an unusual pair to be meeting out here, Cromwell's protégé and his greatest enemy. I dismounted and bowed to them.

'Master Shardlake.' Norfolk's lined face cracked into a thin smile. 'Lord Rich, this is a clever lawyer I met at a banquet of Lady Honor's the other night. Not one of your Augmentations brood, I think.'

'No, he's a Lincoln's Inn deviller, isn't that so, Brother Shardlake? Though he devils in some strange places – I found him wandering about in my garden a few days ago. You haven't come to steal my washing, have you?'

I laughed uneasily at the jest. 'I was passing only, on my way to Bishopsgate. I have a new horse, I wanted to avoid taking him through the City crowds.'

Norfolk turned to Rich. 'A colleague of Master Shardlake's was impertinent to me at Lincoln's Inn a few days ago, read me a lesson on the new religion.' His cold eyes glittered at me. 'But you tell me you're not a Bible puncher, don't you?'

'I follow the rules our king has laid down, your grace.'

Norfolk grunted. He turned to Genesis, looking the horse over with a professional eye. 'That's an ordinary-looking nag. But you can't take a horse of spirit to the City. And I suppose you might have difficulty with a hard ride,' he added brutally, with a glance at my back. He stretched his arms. 'God's wounds, Richard, I'll be glad when parliament rises and I can return to the country. Though you're another City urchin, aren't you?'

'I am a Londoner, your grace,' Rich said stiffly. He turned to me. 'The duke has come to discuss the transfer of some monastic lands.' There was no need to tell me anything at all; he was providing me with an explanation for the meeting in case I spread rumours of conspiracy. What he said might be true: it was well known that Norfolk, for all his religious conservatism, had taken his full share of the monastic spoils.

'Ay,' Norfolk said. 'And you've transferred Barty's to yourself in all but name, eh Richard?' He laughed. 'Sir Richard has granted houses round Bartholomew Close to so many of his officials you might as well call this the Smithfield office of the Court of Augmentations. And poor Prior Fuller not yet dead. It's not true you're poisoning him, is it, Richard?'

Rich smiled thinly. 'The prior has a wasting sickness, your grace.'

I guessed the duke's mockery was intended as further evidence for me that they were not friends. Rich turned aside as a servant appeared at the gate, holding a heavy sack, and murmured something to him. 'Put them in my study,' Rich said sharply, 'I'll go through them later.'

Norfolk looked curiously at the sack as the servant went back inside. 'What's in there?'

'We are digging up the monks' graveyard in the cloister, to make a garden. It seems there is an old custom here that when a man died some personal possession was buried with him. We have found some interesting items.'

I remembered the boys scrabbling in the coffins when I came here to see Kytchyn, the little golden trinket the watchman had appropriated.

'Valuable, eh?'

'Some, yes. Things of antiquarian interest too. Old rings, plague charms, even dried herbs buried with an infirmarian. I have an interest in such things, your grace. My mind does not run on profit all the time,' he added sharply and I realized that for all his ruthlessness and brutality Rich did not enjoy his reputation for venality.

'A strange custom.'

'Yes. I don't know where it came from. But everyone buried here, whether monk or hospital patient, had something personal buried with him, something that was most characteristic of his life, I believe. We'll be finished with the monks in a couple of days, then we'll start on the hospital graveyard. I might have some houses built there.'

I drew a sharp breath as I realized what might have been buried with the old soldier St John. Someone was going to great lengths to conceal all signs of Greek Fire, but what if some was still here at Barty's, buried under the ground?

I became aware Rich was looking at me. 'Something piqued your interest, Shardlake?'

'Just that I too have antiquarian interests, my lord. I found some old stones at the Ludgate, from an ancient synagogue——'

'We had best get to business, my lord,' Norfolk interrupted rudely. 'It's too hot to be out in the sun all day.'

'Yes, your grace. Well, good morning, Brother Shardlake.' He looked at me, the grey eyes narrowing. 'Don't devil too far into others' business; remember, you might get your fingers burned.' And with that they turned and walked away to the gatehouse. The duke's retainers looked at me curiously as I turned Genesis round and rode away. I found I was sweating, and not just from the heat. What had Norfolk and Rich met to discuss? Sales of monastic property, or plots against Cromwell? Or Greek Fire? Rich's warning, mentioning fire, sounded like a reference to that. But was it?

It was with relief that I turned into Long Lane and rode away to Lady Honor's, my mind running now on opened graves.

# Chapter Twenty-seven

THE HOUSE OF GLASS lay quiet and still in the morning heat. A servant in the Vaughan livery answered the door. I asked if I might see Lady Honor on an urgent matter of business and he admitted me, asking me to wait in the hall. Looking through a window into the inner courtyard, I saw the banqueting hall was shuttered against the heat. One of the panes had a family motto under the coat of arms. I bent to look closer. *Esse quam videri.* To be rather than to seem. To be a truly powerful noble family at the heart of the king's court, as the Howards were and the Vaughans had once been – I wondered what price would Lady Honor pay to achieve that end. In a few hours I would see Cromwell; I had to find out.

The servant reappeared and said Lady Honor would see me. He led me up to a first-floor parlour. Like the rest of the house it was richly decorated, with tapestries on the walls and an abundance of big embroidered cushions on the floors. There was a fine portrait on one wall, an elderly man in Mercers' Company livery. The face above the short white beard had a kindly look despite the formal pose.

Lady Honor sat in a cushioned armchair, dressed in a light blue dress with a square bodice and a square hood, for once free of attendants. She was reading a book that I saw was Tyndale's *Obedience of a Christian Man*: the book Anne Boleyn had used to help persuade the king to assume the headship of the Church.

Lady Honor stood. 'Ah, Master Shardlake. You will have read Master Tyndale, no doubt.'

I bowed deeply. 'Indeed, my lady. In the days when he was frowned upon.'

Although her tone was friendly, Lady Honor's forehead was drawn in a slight frown even as she smiled. I wondered if she was embarrassed by that sudden kiss two nights before, and afraid I might remind her of it. I felt suddenly conscious of my bent back.

'How do you like Master Tyndale?' I asked.

She shrugged. 'He makes his case well. His interpretation of the biblical passages has some force. Have you read the exchanges between Tyndale and Thomas More? Two great book writers descending to vulgar abuse in refuting each other's views of God.' She shook her head.

'Yes. More would have had Tyndale burned had he not been safe abroad.'

'The Germans burned him in the end. And Tyndale would have burned More if he could. I wonder what God thinks of them all, if he thinks anything.' An angry weariness entered her tone as she placed the book on the table. 'But of course God watches us all, does he not?'

Her slight undertone of sarcasm made me wonder for a moment if Lady Honor might be one of those whose heresy was the most dangerous of all, one that people scarcely dared speak of: those who doubted God's very existence. It was a thought that clawed at the minds of many confronted with the violent religious conflicts of these days; once or twice it had clawed at mine, leaving me feeling as though suspended over a dark chasm.

'Will you sit down?' Lady Honor asked, gesturing to some cushions on the floor. I lowered myself to them gratefully. 'Some wine?'

'Thank you, no, it is rather early.'

She watched as I unhitched my satchel. 'Well,' she said softly, 'what have you brought for me today?'

I hesitated. 'The papers about Greek Fire, my lady. I know nobody else who has seen them, you see. I would welcome your opinion on one or two matters—'

Anger flashed in her eyes, though her tone remained even. 'So you would find out how much I read, how much I understood. I told you two nights ago, enough to make me wish I had kept my curiosity under control and no more.'

'Enough to make you think Greek Fire might be real?'

'Enough to make me fear it might be, given what it could do. Master Shardlake, I have nothing to add. I told you the simple truth.'

I studied her carefully. Two nights ago she had tried to charm me into believing her, today she was hostile and angry at my questions. Was that because she had truly told me all?

'Lady Honor,' I said, choosing my words carefully, 'I have to make a report to Lord Cromwell this afternoon. I have not got as far as I would like in my enquiries, not least because the founder who aided the Gristwoods in their work has disappeared and has probably been killed. Attempts have also been made on my life.'

She took a deep breath. 'Then all who were involved in the matter are in danger?'

'Those who helped the Gristwoods in their work.'

'Am I in danger?' She tried to keep her composure, but a nerve flickered under her eye.

'I do not believe so. So long as you have truly told nobody but me that you looked in those papers.'

'Nobody.' She took a deep breath. 'And the earl? If you tell him I looked in those papers, he may seek to try my testimony with rougher methods than yours.'

'That is partly why I came this morning so I can make the fullest report to him. Lady Honor, the night I came upon you at that bench at Lincoln's Inn I saw you talking to Serjeant Marchamount. You both looked as though you were discussing something serious.'

'Are you spying on me, then?' she asked angrily.

'I came on you accidentally but yes, I paused and hid to find out what I could hear. I confess it. I caught no words though, I only saw your faces. You both looked worried. As you did when you talked together after the banquet. And the serjeant too had custody of those papers.'

I braced myself for anger, but she only sighed and lowered her head, screening it with an upraised hand. 'Jesu,' she said quietly, 'where have I brought myself with my foolish curiosity?'

'Only tell me everything,' I said. 'I would help you with the earl if I could.'

She looked up then, and smiled sadly. 'Yes, I believe so, for all that you are sent after me like a hunter. I see it in your face. You do not like this work, do you?'

'What I like is neither here nor there, Lady Honor. I must ask what you and the serjeant were talking about.'

She got up and went to the buffet, where a fine gold cup was prominent. 'Gabriel Marchamount gave me this, it is a gift. He advises the Mercers' Company, you know; he used to advise my husband and now he is gone Gabriel advises me on the many legal matters I have to deal with.' She took another deep breath. 'He has been, shall we say, attentive.'

'Ah.' I felt myself redden.

'He has indicated more than once that he would like to take my husband's place.'

'I see. He loves you.'

She surprised me with a sudden mocking laugh. 'Loves me? Master Shardlake, surely you have heard of Gabriel's attempts to persuade the College of Heralds to provide him with a coat of arms, though his father was a fishmonger? He can bring no proof of noble birth and is not sufficiently elevated to get the king to intervene with them. His attempts have failed. But he wants more than anything to have a son who one day can say he is of noble birth. He lusts after nobility as a pig lusts after truffles. So now he is looking for another way to get it. He would like to marry into a noble family.'

'I see.'

Her face was red now too, with embarrassment and anger. I felt ashamed.

'But truly, Master Shardlake, there are some who are not fit to rise above their station and Marchamount is one.' Her voice trembled. 'He is an ambitious boor under all his smoothness. I have refused him, but he will not give up his designs. Oh, he is full of plans.' She lowered her head a moment, then returned her gaze to me, her eyes bright. 'But I have never mentioned looking at the Greek Fire papers to him. I would not be such a fool. And he has never mentioned them to me.' The nerve in her face trembled again and she turned to the window, looking across the courtyard to the banqueting hall. I half-rose, then sat down again. I was ashamed of humiliating her, but there remained another question I must ask.

'I overheard something else at the banquet, Lady Honor. The Duke of Norfolk muttered to Marchamount that there was something he would have you do, but that you would not.'

She did not turn round. 'The Duke of Norfolk covets land, Master Shardlake. He would be the greatest landowner in the realm. My family still has some left and the duke would have part of it in return for advancing my cousin at court. But I have advised Henry's father not to give away what little we have left, whatever advance Norfolk might seem to promise. Henry is not cut out for the role of saviour of our family.'

I stared at her rigid back. 'I am truly sorry to expose these private sorrows,' I said.

She turned round then and to my relief she was smiling, if ironically, making those engaging dimples at the corners of her mouth that showed her age and yet were somehow charming.

'Yes, I believe you are. You have done your work well, Master Shardlake. Some charged with the task you have been given might have come here bullying and blustering, and perhaps I would not have told them all I have told you.' She thought a moment, then crossed to the little table and picked up a bible. 'Here, take this.'

Puzzled, I rose and took the heavy book. She laid her hand on it, the long fingers pressed flat against the leather cover, and looked me in the face. Close to, I saw she had the lightest of down on her upper lip, making a momentary flash of gold as it caught the light.

'I swear by Almighty God,' she said, 'that I have never discussed the contents of the papers relating to Greek Fire with any living soul other than you.'

'And the duke has made no request to you to do so?'

She met my eyes firmly. 'I swear he has not.' She took a deep breath. 'Will you tell the earl that I made this oath freely and of my own will?'

'I will,' I said.

'And though you must tell him everything, I ask you to keep these – these difficulties with Gabriel and the duke secret.'

'I will, my lady. I know the reputation lawyers have as gossips, but I promise to tell no one but the earl.'

She smiled, her old warm smile. 'Then we may be friends again?'

'I would like nothing better, my lady.'

'Good. You caught me in an ill humour earlier.' She nodded at the gold cup. 'That arrived, together with an invitation to the bear-baiting tomorrow. Gabriel is making a party of it and I feel obliged to go.' She paused. 'Would you care to come as well? He said to bring whoever I chose.'

I inclined my head. 'Would you really wish me to come? After my interrogation of you?'

'Yes. To prove there is no ill feeling?' Her look had something flirtatious in it again.

'I will come, Lady Honor, with pleasure.'

'Good. We meet at noon, at Three Cranes—'

Lady Honor broke off as the door opened and her young nephew came in. His face was red and angry. He was dressed for company, a purple slashed doublet and a wide cap with a peacock feather. He took off his cap and threw it on the cabinet.

'Cousin Honor,' he said petulantly, 'please do not send me to such people again.' He broke off as he saw me sitting on the cushion. 'I am sorry, sir, I did not mean to intrude.'

Lady Honor took the boy by the arm. 'Master Shardlake has called for a brief visit, Henry. Now come, settle yourself. Have some wine.'

The youth plumped down on a cushion opposite me as Lady Honor fetched him wine. She gestured me to sit again. 'Henry has been visiting Mayor Hollyes's family,' she told me. 'I thought it would be useful for him to meet his children.' She gave him a goblet of wine and returned to her chair, smiling at him encouragingly. 'Well then, Henry, what has happened?'

'Those children are common rogues.' The boy took a long draught of wine. 'By God they are.'

'The mayor's daughters? What on earth do you mean?'

'I had looked forward to meeting the girls, I heard they were pretty. There are three of them. Mayor Hollyes's wife was there and the conversation was pleasant enough at first – they asked about life in Lincolnshire, the hunting. But then Madam Hollyes was called away and I was left with the girls. Then they—'

'What, Henry? Come.'

He looked down at the floor, running a hand over the pustules on his face. 'The moment the old woman left the girls became cruel. They – they began to mock my – my spots, asking if I had the pox. One said even a pocky whore would not have me.' His voice shook. 'Cousin Honor, I hate it in London. I want to go back to Lincolnshire.' He hung his head again, greasy hair falling over his face.

'Henry,' Lady Honor said with a touch of impatience, 'these things happen. You must be more robust—'

'They should not happen!' he burst out. 'I am a Vaughan, I am entitled to some respect.'

'It is a cruel thing to be mocked,' I said.

Lady Honor sighed. 'Go upstairs to your room, Henry. I will come and talk to you in a moment.'

Without a word the boy got up and, without looking at me, went out and slammed the door behind him. Lady Honor leaned back in her chair and smiled sadly.

'You can see now why I fear Henry does not have the robustness to make his way in London. It was a mistake to bring him here. But he is the Vaughan heir. We had to try.' She sighed. 'Poor boy.'

'Some boys feel slights greatly at that age. I did.'

'Young girls can be cruel.' She smiled ironically. 'I could, myself.'

'You, madam? I find that hard to be believe.'

'You know how girl children are told how to behave down to the last detail? How to walk, how to sit, when to smile.' She smiled sadly. 'I wonder how many scream with frustration inside, as I did. And how many turn to cruel thoughts beneath sweet rosy faces?'

'It takes a woman to understand such things.'

'I shall send Henry back. There is another Vaughan cousin. He is young, but perhaps in a few years—'

I rose, conscious time was passing. 'I fear I must go.' I was reluctant to leave her, glad my questioning had not broken the beginning of friendship, but I wanted to get Guy's opinion on those books before I saw Cromwell.

'And I must try to console Henry. I will see you out.' Lady Honor led me downstairs.

In the hall I turned to her. 'I am sorry for your troubles,' I said again. 'And for raking them up.'

She laid a hand lightly on my arm. 'You were doing your duty even though it was uncomfortable. I admire that.' She studied me. 'But you look tired. You are meant for finer, gentler things than work like this. You demean yourself, Matthew.'

'I have no choice.'

'For now, perhaps.' She took my hand. 'Until tomorrow. Remember, Three Cranes Wharf at noon.'

As I walked to the stables to fetch Genesis, I felt warmed and soothed by her care. Yet still my sceptical brain worried away at the thought she might only want to keep me on her side in my dealings with Cromwell. She had sworn on the Bible, but the dark thought that she might be an atheist returned to me. To such a person, a Bible oath would mean nothing.

# Chapter Twenty-eight

IT WAS A SHORT RIDE to Guy's shop, but when I arrived I saw the shutters were drawn. On the door was a note, in Guy's spiky hand, saying the shop would be closed until the morrow. I stood looking at it, filled with frustration. I remembered that once a month or so he went out to a fair in Hertfordshire, where herbs and physic were sold, to replenish his stock. I left a message with a neighbour asking him to contact me as soon as he returned, then turned the placid horse for home.

✝

BARAK WAS WAITING for me in Chancery Lane, a gloomy look on his face.

'Any news?' I asked.

'I went and reminded that old troll Madam Neller you'd promised her money if the girl turns up again. And told her what to expect from Lord Cromwell if Bathsheba turns up and she doesn't tell us. But she knows nothing. No one knows anything except the dead, and they won't tell. I found where Toky and Wright have been staying, too, a cheap lodging house by the river. They left yesterday, though.'

'Perhaps they were afraid the hue and cry would be out for them.'

'They'd only been at the lodging house three days. I suspect they're moving from place to place so we can't find their trail. What did Lady Honor have to say?'

'She told me Marchamount is after her hand and she has refused him; that was what they have been talking about. And the Duke of Norfolk is trying to get some lands from her in exchange for

286

introducing her nephew at court. She says she's told no one else she opened those papers.'

'Do you believe her?'

'She swore it on the Great Bible.' I sighed. 'She's invited me to the bear-baiting tomorrow. I thought I'd go. Marchamount will be there as well. It will be a chance to check her story.'

'Looks like that lead's closed off. You'll be glad to see her in the clear, eh?'

'I admit I like her, but I would not let liking for a woman cloud my judgement.'

'Never knew it not to.'

I gave him a look; he was worried by the coming interview, I could tell, and diverting himself at my expense.

'I found something else too.' I told him about my encounter with Norfolk and Rich, the possibility something might have been buried with the old soldier.

'It's a long shot,' he said.

'I know. But what could be more characteristic of that old soldier than Greek Fire? And the monks weren't to know a day would come when hallowed monastic ground would be casually dug up. I think I'll have another word with Kytchyn. The earl will know where he is.'

'All right. Don't say anything about desecrating monastic ground, though.'

'I know better than that.' I got up. 'Well, we had better go. We'll take the wherry.'

'How's the new horse?'

'Quiet enough,' I said, then added, 'he's no personality.'

Barak laughed. 'I'm sorry, I should have asked at the royal stables if they'd a horse that could talk.'

'When you are in a bad humour you become oafish,' I said sternly. 'But we'll do no good sniping at each other and I am too tired for it. Come on.'

We said little on the journey. I felt a growing nervousness as the wherry drew in at Westminster Stairs. We disembarked and walked past Westminster Hall, heading for Whitehall Palace just beyond. As we approached the huge Holbein Gate, colourful with its coats of arms and terracotta roundels of Roman emperors, Barak turned to me.

'Perhaps we should have taken Leman to confront Bealknap this morning.'

'It was just as important to see Lady Honor.'

He gave me one of his keen looks. 'You'll threaten to expose Bealknap, won't you, unless he gives us full answers? No lawyers sticking together?'

'Yes. Though if Bealknap is hauled up before the secretary, my name will stink in Lincoln's Inn. Lawyers aren't supposed to report each other. But yes, I'll do it.' I gave him a steady look. 'What have you said about me, by the way, in your reports to the earl? Come, you must have said something?'

'That's private,' he said uneasily.

'I want to know what to expect.'

'I've done nothing but report what we've done,' Barak replied matter of factly. 'I've given no bad opinion of you, if you must know. But that will cut no ice – what he needs is progress.'

He walked ahead under the great gate, which gave us a few moments of welcome shadow. Building was going on everywhere, half-built tennis courts and accommodation blocks rising from the earth, scaffolding and dust everywhere. They said the king meant Whitehall Palace to be the finest in Europe. We turned into the new Privy Gallery building, where Lord Cromwell had offices; Barak exchanged a word with the guard and we passed inside.

A long hall stretched away from us, richly decorated with tapestries, large windows giving onto an enormous garden. I knew the king often received visitors here. I caught my breath as I saw, guarded by a halberdier, Holbein's great mural of the Tudor dynasty. The giant painting was as magnificent as I had heard. The king's dead parents, Henry VII, whom Lady Honor's family had fought against at Bosworth, and his wife, Elizabeth of York, stood on either side of a stone bier. Below them stood Jane Seymour, the only one of Henry's wives he cared to remember, unexpectedly plain. Opposite her, the king stood with his hands on his hips. He was painted wearing a richly decorated gown with enormous shoulders, a shirt encrusted with jewels and a prominent codpiece. He stared, it seemed, directly at me. His expression was one of cold authority mixed with something else. Weariness? Anger? I shuddered at the thought that behind Cromwell, if Greek Fire was not found, lay the fury of the king himself.

'The earl is waiting,' Barak whispered urgently at my elbow.

'Of course, I'm sorry.'

Barak seemed to know his way through the echoing corridors. Courtiers and black-robed officials walked past quietly and sedately lest the king might be in residence. I looked out at the magnificent garden, which was dominated by a fountain that, despite the drought, still pumped a good head of water. Barak stopped outside a door guarded by another halberdier, and we were admitted to an outer office where Grey, ubiquitous as ever, sat behind a desk. He rose and greeted us. As on the previous occasion there was a nervous look on his round scholarly face.

'Master Shardlake, is there any more news? I have seen Barak's messages. There is so little time left—'

'Our news is for the earl,' Barak told him sharply.

Grey looked at him and inclined his head. 'All right, Barak, but I just wanted to warn you he's in no good frame of mind. And he has the Duke of Norfolk with him – he's been there two hours.'

'Really?' I said. 'I saw the duke earlier, at Smithfield. He was with Richard Rich then.'

Grey shook his head sorrowfully. 'All the earl's old friends are plotting against him. It is cruel.' He shook his head, stared nervously at the inner door, then bent his head towards me. 'I heard shouting a little while ago.' He bit his lip anxiously, reminding me for a moment of Joseph.

'Should we wait?' Barak asked.

'Yes, yes. He wants to see you. '

Grey broke off as the inner door burst open. The duke strode out. He flung the door casually shut behind him, a breach of manners I could scarcely believe, then turned to us with a wolfish smile on his long face. I bowed deeply.

Norfolk laughed harshly. 'You again! You seem determined to impress yourself on my mind.' His penetrating eyes were full of malice, the politeness he had shown when I met him with Rich gone. He nodded. 'The friend of the heretic. Don't worry, Master Shardlake, I have you well marked.' He turned to Barak. 'You as well, my young friend with the Jewish name. Did you know that some Spanish traders have been exposed as secret Jews here in the City? The Spanish ambassador wants them back to burn. God's death, there are heretics everywhere.' He turned to Grey. 'You too, I have you all marked.' He gave us a triumphant nod then walked out, slamming the office door behind him.

Barak blew out his cheeks. 'Shit.'

Grey swallowed. 'He's crowing, crowing like he's cock of the roost already.' He stared at the closed inner door a moment, then got up, knocked nervously and went in. A few moments later he reappeared.

'Lord Cromwell will see you.' We walked to the door, my heart sinking with dread at the thought of the mood he would be in now.

Cromwell sat in a large office whose walls were lined with shelves and drawers, behind a desk covered with a clutter of papers. I saw he had a magnificent globe, showing the New World with its indented coastlines and empty interior where monsters roamed. He sat very still, his square heavy face strangely expressionless, eyes fixed thoughtfully on us as we bowed low.

'Well, Matthew,' he said quietly. 'Jack.'

'My lord.'

He wore a plain brown robe today, his gold chain of office the only colour in his costume. He fiddled with the chain a moment, then reached for a quill, a pretty green peacock's feather with swirling colours that made the shape of an eye. He toyed with it, looking at the eye, seemingly lost in thought. Then he smiled bleakly and nodded at the door.

'Grey says the duke made an exhibition of himself out there.'

I could not think how to reply. Cromwell went on in the same reasonable, quiet voice. 'He came to demand I release Bishop Sampson from the Tower. I shall have to, he couldn't be got to confess to any plots even when they showed him the rack.' He looked again at the eye in the feather, then began pulling it to pieces. 'The papists are craftier than the most cunning fox, they keep their conspiracies so close I've nothing for the king that would turn him against Norfolk's party. Not even murmurings.' He shook his head, then said mildly, 'Jack here tells me you have been busy on a case against the Bealknap man. You were visiting a property of his when you were attacked.'

'Yes, my lord.'

His tone stayed quiet, but when he spoke again his eyes were full of anger. 'You waste time on trifles while the one thing I have to keep me in the king's favour, Greek Fire, remains lost and the thieves slaughter all those who know of it under your very nose.'

'We managed to get to Goodwife Gristwood and her son, and the ex-monk—' I said.

'And little they had to tell.'

'We've been working hard, my lord,' Barak ventured.

Cromwell ignored him. He leaned forward, pointing the mutilated quill at me. 'One week only until that demonstration is due. The king's insisting on a divorce from Queen Anne now and I'm the one who must find the way. Then he'll marry that little whore Catherine Howard and Norfolk will never be out of his presence, telling him he should have my head for tying him to that German drab. Greek Fire's the only leverage I have now – if I can give him that he'll keep me in his service. Perhaps then I can turn the tide before the Howards have us back under Rome.' He laid down the remains of the quill and leaned back. 'Perhaps, then, I will be allowed to *live*.' His heavy frame seemed to quiver slightly as he uttered the last word. 'The king does know gratitude,' he muttered softly, as though to himself. 'He does.'

I realized with a sinking heart that he was almost at the end of his resources. He blinked, then stared at me again.

'Well? Is there any more news? Have you achieved anything apart from landing me with that menagerie of scared fools?'

'I needed to discover what they knew, my lord.'

'You didn't believe in Greek Fire, did you?' he asked bluntly.

I shifted my feet nervously. 'I needed to trace the matter back to its source—'

'Do you believe in it now?'

I hesitated. 'Yes.'

'So what of the suspects, the people who matter?'

'They all say they know nothing. Lady Honor I have questioned closely.' I repeated all she had had told me.

He grunted. 'She's a fine woman. Pretty.' His hard eyes bored into mine. I wondered if Barak had told him I liked her. I remembered Cromwell was a widower now; his only son Gregory was said to be, like Henry Vaughan, a poor sort of fellow.

'I intend to check her story with Marchamount.'

'Another one who still maintains he knows nothing. Bealknap makes a third.'

'Bealknap has questions to answer. I have found a way of bringing pressure on him, by threatening to expose some of his ill dealings. I shall see him this afternoon.'

'Expose him? To the Inn authorities?'

'Yes.'

He nodded approvingly. 'You do mean business then.'

'I will question him on his involvement with Richard Rich.'

Cromwell's face clouded at that name. 'Yes, you have added him to our list of possible suspects, Barak tells me. Him and Norfolk.' He gave a sudden furious glance at the closed. I shuddered at the thought of what he would do to the duke if he had him in his power.

'Bealknap and Marchamount are under their respective patronage.' I hesitated. 'I saw them together this morning, at Barty's. I wondered whether they might be plotting something together.'

'Everyone is plotting. All my protégés are falling away, becoming spies and enemies, making shift to protect their places on the council if the tide turns against me.' He looked at me again. 'If Bealknap told Rich about Greek Fire, Rich could have told Norfolk.'

'It is all guesswork, my lord.'

'Yes, it is.' He nodded grimly.

'I learned they are digging up the graves of the monks at Barty's,' I said, 'and planning to start on the graves from the hospital. It struck me that the old soldier might have had Greek Fire buried with him. It would be a way for us to get hold of some. I thought I might speak with Kytchyn.'

He nodded. 'It's worth a try, I suppose. If I had *some*, at least I could tell the king we might be able to make more. Do it, but don't let Rich know what you're about. Ask Grey for the address of the house where I've put Kytchyn and Mother Gristwood. Grey's the only one who knows it. Almost the only one who's safe now. And see Bealknap soon. Solve this, Matthew,' he said with sudden passion. 'Solve this.'

'We will, my lord,' Barak said.

Cromwell was thoughtful a moment. 'Did you see the Holbein mural on your way in?' he asked me.

I nodded.

'I thought that would catch your eye. Realistic, is it not? The figures seem as though they could walk out into the hall.' He picked up the quill and tore at the remaining vanes. 'The king magnificent, calves thick and strong as a carthorse. You should see him now, his ulcerated leg so bad that sometimes they have to wheel him round the palace in a little cart.'

'My lord,' Barak said quickly, 'it is dangerous to speak thus—'

Cromwell waved a hand. 'It relieves me to talk, so you'll listen. It's my belief there'll be no more little princes – he's so ill I don't think he's capable. I think that's why he was so shocked when he saw Anne of Cleves – he realized he couldn't raise his member for her. He hopes he may with pretty little Catherine, I'm sure, but I wonder.'

He pulled the last of the vanes from the quill and threw down the bare stalk. 'And if he can't, then in a year or less the fault will be Catherine's as now it is Queen Anne's. And then Norfolk may find himself out of favour once more. I want to survive till then.'

I felt cold, despite the warmth of the room, at the coldly calculating way he spoke of the king. And to say the king was incapable of fathering more children was bordering on treason. Cromwell looked up, his face grim.

'There, that's unsettled you, hasn't it?' He looked from one to the other of us. 'If you fail and that demonstration doesn't take place you can expect harsh desserts. So don't fail.' He sighed deeply. 'Now leave me.'

I opened my mouth, but Barak touched my arm and shook his head quickly. Bowing again, we left. Barak closed the door behind us very gently.

Grey looked at us anxiously. 'Are there any instructions?' he asked.

'No.' I paused. 'Only to give me the address where Master Kytchyn is kept.'

'I have it here.' He delved in a drawer, wrote it down and handed it to me. 'He and the Gristwoods make strange housemates,' he said with an attempt at a smile.

'Thank you. Take care, Master Grey,' I added softly.

# Chapter Twenty-nine

BARAK AND I SAT IN a corner of the Barbary Turk. The tavern where Barak had arranged to meet the sailor from the Baltic was a gloomy, cavernous place, smelling equally of stale beer and salt water, for it was right on the river front. Through the small window I could see Vintry Wharf, crowded with warehouses. I was reminded that the warehouse whose conveyancing I had lost was nearby, at Salt Wharf.

It was early evening and there were few other customers as yet. In the middle of the room a huge thigh bone, thrice the size of a man's, hung in chains from the high rafters. When we had arrived, Barak went to fetch some beer and I looked at the plaque fixed to it: *The leg of a giant of old times, dug from the Thames silt, anno 1518.* The year I came to London. I touched the thing lightly, causing it to swing gently in the embrace of its chains. It felt cold, like stone. I wondered whether it could indeed be from some gigantic man. Certainly humankind took some troubling forms. I thought of my own bent back and the king's diseased leg, which perhaps was the cause of all his marital troubles. A touch at my arm made me jump, as though someone had divined my dangerous thoughts. But it was only Barak pointing me to the gloomy corner.

✝

WE HAD HAD AN unsuccessful afternoon, all the more frustrating after Cromwell's demand for urgency. We had taken a wherry back to Temple Stairs, then walked up to Chancery Lane.

Leman was waiting there, a little the worse for drink, I saw, and we walked him up to Lincoln's Inn. Once through the gates he looked round nervously at the imposing buildings and the black-robed barristers walking by, but perhaps the thought of the money to come gave the red-faced stallholder a measure of courage, for he allowed us to lead him to Bealknap's chambers.

We climbed the narrow steps to Bealknap's door only to find it closed, a heavy padlock through the handle. Enquiry of the barrister who occupied the chambers below brought the curt response that Brother Bealknap had gone out early that morning and that he preferred not to enquire after his doings.

Frustrated, we went across to my own chambers. Godfrey was in the outer office, going over some papers with Skelly. He looked up in surprise as I came in with Barak and Leman in tow. I left them in the office and went with Godfrey to his room.

'No problems with your work,' he told me, 'but I'm afraid you've another case gone. The house conveyance down by Coldharbour.'

'God's death, as if I haven't enough to worry about.' I ran my hands through my hair. 'These are all new matters that are going too, new clients.'

Godfrey looked at me seriously. 'You ought to look into this, Matthew. It seems that someone is putting out bad words about you.'

'You're right, but I haven't time now. I won't have before next Thursday.'

'You'll be free then?'

I smiled wryly. 'Oh, yes. One way or another.' I noticed that Godfrey looked tired and felt a twinge of conscience. 'Are my matters taking up much time?'

'No, but I had some news this morning. I'm to be fined ten pounds for my insolence to the duke.'

'That is a heavy load. I'm sorry, Godfrey.'

He looked at me seriously. 'I may have to take up your offer to loan me money. Though it will do you no good if it gets out you are supporting me.'

I raised a hand. 'That is the least of my worries at the moment. You shall have it.'

He leaned forward and grasped my hand. 'Thank you.'

'Let me know what you need.'

He looked relieved. 'I must work out how much I can raise myself. So far as I am concerned it is all money spent on God's work,' he added piously.

'Yes.'

'How goes it with the Wentworth case?'

'Slowly. Everything goes slowly. Listen, Godfrey, I need to speak to Bealknap, but he's out. Can you watch for him, tell him I wish to speak to him urgently? Tell him it is the business we discussed before and I want him to contact me at once.'

'Ay, all right.' He looked at me curiously. 'Is this the other matter you are working on?'

'It is.'

He nodded at the door. 'You have acquired some odd work fellows.'

'Yes, I'd better get back to them. Pox on Bealknap, he's probably drumming up shady business in the City. That bottled spider has such a reputation his neighbour downstairs won't even take messages for him.'

'He is a worshipper of money, a slave to Mammon.'

'Him and half of London.'

I went back to the outer office. Leman sat at the window, looking idly at the lawyers' comings and goings. Barak was standing at Skelly's desk, listening with interest as the clerk explained how copying was done.

'Come, gentlemen,' I said, 'Godfrey will let us know when Bealknap arrives.'

'I should be at my stall,' Leman said. I agreed to let him go, for I could hardly keep him all day and the Cheapside stalls were near enough to send Simon to fetch him. Barak and I walked back to my house.

'You work poor Skelly hard,' Barak said. 'He told me he's been there copying since seven.'

'It takes him two hours to do what most scribes could do in one,' I snapped. 'You don't know what it's like employing people. It's not easy.'

'No easy life for Skelly, either.'

I did not reply.

'There's something I've been thinking about,' he said. 'If a man steals a sack of apples, and they're worth more than a shilling, he's hanged at Tyburn.'

'That is the law.'

'Yet often enough people don't pay their debts, do they? That arsehole Bealknap for one from what you say. Your fellow Skelly was copying out a writ for debt, which said the debtor was "scheming fraudulently and craftily to defraud him".'

'Those are the standard words on the writ.'

'Yet even if the debtor is found guilty, shown to be a liar who has taken a man's money, he will have to pay the money back, but nothing else will happen to him, will it?'

I laughed. 'God's death, Barak, is that all you have to worry about?'

'Turning things over keeps my mind from my worries.'

'The difference is that in a matter of debt the parties are arguing over a contract, whereas a thief simply takes what is not his. And in a civil court you don't require the strong evidence you need to hang a criminal.'

Barak shook his head cynically. 'We saw what criminal trials are like that day at Newgate. I think the point is more that thieves are poor men while those who make contracts are rich.'

'A poor man may make a contract and be cheated as much as a rich one.'

'And if a poor man is cheated by a rich one, what's he to do? He can't afford to go to court.'

'He can go to Poor Man's Pleas,' I said. 'I agree the poor are disadvantaged in the law. But the law can still bring justice. That is its purpose.'

Barak looked at me askance. 'You're a simpler man than I thought if you believe that. But then you'd see things from the viewpoint of a man of means, one who can tilt his cap at a fine lady of title.'

I sighed. Why was this converse, like every other I had with him, turning into an argument? We had reached my garden, and I stepped through the doorway without another word. Inside I found a note from Joseph, bemoaning the fact I had no news for him. He reminded me, as though I needed telling, that Elizabeth would be back in front of Forbizer in just a week. I crumpled the note angrily. I considered asking Barak if he thought it safe to go back down the well tomorrow night, but thought it better to leave that request till later. Pox on the fellow and his moods.

I told Joan to bring us an early supper. Afterwards I walked back up the road to Lincoln's Inn, but although all the places of business were long shut the padlock was still on Bealknap's door. I returned home and told Barak we might as well ride down to the tavern; there was no point in waiting any longer for Bealknap.

✟

THE GIANT'S BONE I had set swinging still turned to and fro in the dim light, creaking ominously in its chains. A man sitting alone at a table eyed it with drunken, puzzled intentness. Barak reappeared and set two mugs of beer before us.

'The landlord says Master Miller and his friends don't usually come in before eight.' He took a long draught of beer, wiping his hand on his sleeve. 'I've been a bit of an arsehole this afternoon, haven't I?' he added unexpectedly.

'You could say that.'

He shook his head. 'It was the earl,' he said, lowering his voice. 'God's wounds, I've never seen him in such a parlous state. We mustn't repeat a word he said about the king. Saying he could have no more children – Jesu.' He looked nervously around, though no one was near.

'Why in God's name did he tell us?'

'To scare us. Make us privy to his own dangerous words.'

I shook my head sadly. 'I remember the earl when I first knew him ten years ago. He was only Wolsey's secretary then, but you could sense the power in him. The confidence, the force. Today he seemed – desperate.'

'I think he is desperate.'

I leaned close, lowering my voice to a whisper. 'But Cromwell can't fall. Half the king's council are tied to him and London's a reformist city—'

He shook his head sadly. 'Londoners are fickle as seed. I should know, I've lived here all my life. No one will help the earl if the Howards turn the king against him. Christ alive, who would dare defy the king?' He blew out his cheeks, then shook his head. 'Did you hear Norfolk referring to my Jewish name? He must have a list of the earl's people.' He laughed hollowly. 'Maybe he'll put me in the Domus to be converted. They still put the odd shipwrecked Jew in there, I know.'

'But your family converted hundreds of years ago. You're as much a member of the Church of England as I am.'

He smiled sardonically. 'When I was a boy I remember at Easter the priest always gave a sermon about how the Jews crucified Our Lord, how wicked they were. Once I let out an almighty fart; I'd been holding it in specially and it was a ripper. The priest looked up and all the boys sniggered. My mother gave me a real beating when we got home. She didn't like my father talking about how he was descended from Jews.' His voice took on the bitter note it had whenever he spoke of her. 'I want another drink.'

'We may be here some time before these sailors arrive. We should stay sober.'

'My head can take some more. I need it. God, I'm supposed to see my girl later, but I don't feel like it. I've no taste for women tonight.'

'She'll think you've tired of her,' I said. I wondered if Barak was one of those who, finding the conquest of women easy, treat it as a light business and never form a lasting relationship. It was of a piece with his restless, roving nature.

He shrugged. 'Perhaps I am.' He changed the subject. 'You'll be seeing your friend Lady Honor again tomorrow.'

'Yes. At the bear-baiting.'

'I haven't been to a baiting for an age. Last time I went to the bull-baiting a great bull tossed one dog so high people in the street saw it above the top of the stadium. It made a real mess when it landed again.'

'I was wondering whether we might try Sir Edwin's well once more tomorrow night,' I said hesitantly.

He nodded. He looked at the giant's bone, still swinging slightly. 'All right. God's death, that gave me a scare last night. I'd swear it was eyes glinting up at me.' He got up and crossed to the hatch where the beer was served. I watched him, frowning. I wondered if it might have been jewellery Barak had seen down the well, the glint of precious stones in the candlelight. But I feared it was not.

The door opened again and half a dozen big heavy fellows tramped in, sunburnt and tired looking. Their hands and smocks were black with coal dust. I wondered if this was Miller and his friends. The landlord signalled to them and Barak joined them at the hatch. The men looked suspicious as they crowded round Barak, who was talking fast. I wondered whether to go over, but nods from the men indicated the conversation had come to a satisfactory conclusion. Barak walked back to me, laying two more mugs of beer on the table.

'That's Hal Miller and his mates. They arrived in London at lunchtime and they've been unloading coal all afternoon, as you can see from their looks. They didn't want to talk to me at first.'

'They looked quite ugly for a moment.'

'Ay, but I promised them money and showed them the earl's seal for good measure. Let them get their beer before we join them.'

The men took their drinks across to a large table in the centre of the room. They looked over at us. Not friendly looks – they seemed worried. But why, if they had wonders to tell, for sailors like nothing better than tale-telling? I was watchful as I followed Barak over to them. He introduced me as one of Lord Cromwell's officials and we sat down. The gritty smell of coal dust made me want to sneeze.

'Been working hard, bullies?' Barak asked.

'All day,' one said. 'Coal for the king's bakeries.' He had a strange, singsong accent and I realized that like many of the collier men he came from the wild northern counties.

'Hard work in this heat,' I ventured.

'Ay, and not well rewarded,' another said, with a meaningful look at Barak, who nodded and slapped the purse at his belt, making the coins jingle.

'Which one of you is Hal Miller?' I asked, deciding to bring matters to the point.

'I'm Hal.' A burly man in his forties, with a bald head and big gnarled hands, spoke up. Keen blue eyes stared at me from his red, dirt-streaked face.

'I wanted to talk to you about a new drink that was brought from the Baltic shores some months ago. I understand you had a part in trying to sell it.'

'I might have done,' he said. 'Why is Lord Cromwell interested?'

'Mere curiosity,' I said. 'He is interested in how it was made.'

'There were others who were interested. Others who threatened me.'

'Who?' I asked sharply.

'A man who called himself Toky.' Miller spat on the floor. 'Bold as a savage for all his poxy looks.'

'The earl can offer you his protection,' Barak said.

'What was his interest in this stuff?' I asked.

'He wanted to buy it from us.'

'Did he now?'

'Ay.' Miller sat silent a moment, then leaned forward, resting his big arms on the table. 'Last autumn I was offered a place on a ship one of the Merchant Adventurers was running up to the Baltic Sea. You know they're trying to open trade up there, break the Hanseatic

League's monopoly?' I nodded. 'My mates told me to stay on the colliers and I wish I had. We were three weeks crossing the North Sea and sailing up the Baltic and once we were there we daren't stop at the German ports in case the Hanse merchants had us arrested. We were hungry and damned cold by the time we'd sailed up to the wild parts where the Teutonic Knights rule. By Christ, it's dismal up there. Nothing but pine forests right down to the shore. The whole sea freezes over in winter—'

'You made landfall?' I asked.

'Ay, at a place called Libau. The Polacks there were keen to trade with us. We took on a cargo of furs mainly, and some other curiosities Captain Fenchurch had never seen, like a strange doll that you open up to find other dolls inside. And a barrel of this stuff called wodky the Poles drink. We crewmen tried a little, but the stuff burned like fire. Just a cupful made us sick as dogs. Captain Fenchurch brought half a barrel back with him, though.'

As the soldier St John once brought another barrel back from Constantinople, I thought. 'What happened to it?'

'Captain Fenchurch paid us off in London. With the costs of the voyage he'd made little profit even with the furs, and he'd no plans then for another. So I went back to the colliers. But he gave me a bottle of the Polish stuff as a keepsake and I brought it here. Remember that night, Robin?'

'I'll not forget it in a hurry.' One of the others, a young fair-haired fellow, took up the tale. 'Hal came in and told us all about the Poles, their long beards and pointy fur hats and the dark forests, then he brought out this bottle of pale stuff and passed it round, saying it was what the Poles drank. You warned us it was strong stuff though, Hal, told us only to take a sip.'

'You knew better, though, Robin,' one of the others said, laughing.

'I thought I did,' the fair-haired fellow replied. 'I took a long swig at the bottle and, by Our Lady, I thought my head was going to burst. I spat the stuff straight out, right across the table. It was winter and dark, there were candles on all the tables. The stuff hit the candle and knocked it over and then – by Jesu—'

'What?'

'The whole table caught light. The stuff should have put the candle out, but the whole top of the table burst into a strange blue flame. You can imagine the effect it had. Everyone jumped up – all over the tavern people were shouting out and crossing themselves. Then the fire died as quickly as it started, leaving hardly a mark on the table. It was this very one.' He laid a hand on the scuffed table, top, which was indeed unmarked.

'It was like witchcraft,' Hal Miller said. 'After that I threw the stuff away.'

I frowned. 'You said this was in the winter.'

'Ay, January. I remember we weren't looking forward to the long voyage up the coast in the storms.'

'When did the man Toky approach you?'

Miller's eyes were watchful again. 'Later that month, when we got back from Newcastle. The story had got around, see, about a foreign drink that could catch fire. He came here one night with another, a big man. Strutted in as though he owned the place and came right up to us. His big mate was carrying an axe – half the tavern emptied at the sight of it. He said he'd been asked to get some of this stuff, said his master would pay.'

'Did he say who his master was?'

'No, and we didn't ask. He said he'd pay good money, though. He didn't believe me at first when I said I'd chucked the bottle off Queenhithe dock. Started to get threatening, but he went away when I gave him Captain Fenchurch's address. I was sorry I did, but I was afraid. I enquired after Fenchurch later, from one of his servants. Fenchurch had told the servant he'd managed to sell the barrel on and made a handsome profit.'

'Who to?'

'The servant knew no more. The pock-faced man, I assumed.'

'Marchamount? Bealknap? Bryanston? Do any of those names ring any bells with you?' I did not add Rich or Norfolk's names, for everyone in London knew those.

'No, sir, I'm sorry.'

'Where does Captain Fenchurch live?'

'On the Bishopsgate Road, but he's abroad again. He's taken a ship to Sweden. He asked me to join him, but I've had enough of these devilish places. He won't be back till the autumn.'

Then at least he had not been killed too. 'Thank you, anyway.' I nodded to Barak, who took out his purse and passed some coins to Miller. 'If you think of anything more,' he said, 'you can reach me by way of the landlord.'

I led the way outside, halting a little way from the inn. The Vintry crane stood outlined against the starlit sky like the neck of a huge swan. I looked out over the dark river.

'Stumped again,' Barak said. 'If only that arsehole captain hadn't gone abroad.'

I raised a hand. 'Think of the dates, Barak,' I said excitedly. 'Master Miller causes a great stir in the tavern in January. That's three months after the Greek Fire was found at Barty's, but two months *before* the Gristwoods contacted Bealknap as the first step in getting to Cromwell. What were they doing in those months?'

'Building and testing the apparatus?'

'Yes.'

'And trying to produce more Greek Fire, using the formula? The Polish stuff must be part of it.' Barak looked excited.

'Or perhaps they heard the story of the fiery liquid, and sent Toky down here to try and get some to see if it could be of use.'

'But they must have known what they needed and what materials. They had the formula.'

'You'd think so, wouldn't you? So Toky's paymaster, whoever it was, was involved at a very early stage. Working *with* the Gristwoods. Months before the approach to Cromwell.'

'That doesn't make sense. If he was working with the Grist-woods, why have Toky kill them?' He stared at me. 'Perhaps the

Gristwoods went to Cromwell behind their first sponsor's back, perhaps they were looking for a better offer.'

'Then why wait until two months after the approach to Cromwell to kill them? And if the person behind the killings is one of our suspects, the Gristwoods wouldn't use any of them as an intermediary to Cromwell.' I raised my eyebrows. 'I must talk to Bealknap, Barak. We need to lay hold of him.'

He gave me a serious look. 'What if Toky's got to him already? Shit, they got to the founder just before we did – what if Bealknap's dead too?'

'I'd rather not think of that. Come on, we can check at Lincoln's Inn before we go home.' I cast a glance back at the gloomy tavern. It was a strange place. It struck me that it was only at night that London showed its true, sinister face.

At Lincoln's Inn there was only a note from Godfrey to say Bealknap had not returned. His door was padlocked and next morning, when I went in again, it was still locked. His locks and the guards at the gatehouse protected his chest of gold, but of Bealknap himself there was still no sign. And six days left now.

# Chapter Thirty

IT WAS TURNING INTO a frustrating morning. After going to
Lincoln's Inn to find no trace of Bealknap again, I had ridden over
to Guy's, but my note was still on his door. Why could people not
stay in one place, I thought as I rode to my next port of call, the house
where Cromwell had sent the Gristwoods and Kytchyn, to keep them
out of sight.

The house was in a poor street near the river, with flaking paint
on the doors and shutters, which were closed despite the heat of the
morning. I tied up Genesis and knocked at the door. A large man in
a dun-coloured smock opened it. He stood in the doorway, eyeing me
suspiciously.

'Yes?'

'My name is Matthew Shardlake. I had the address from Lord
Cromwell.'

He relaxed. 'Ay, sir, I had word you would be coming. Come
in.'

'How are our guests?'

He made a grimace. 'The old monk's not too bad, but that
woman's a termagant and her son's crazy to get out. Any idea how
long they're to be kept here?'

'It shouldn't be more than a few days.'

A door opened and Goodwife Gristwood emerged. 'Who is it,
Carney?' she asked nervously. She looked relieved when she saw it
was only me. 'Master lawyer.'

'Ay. How are you, madam?'

'Well enough. You can go, Carney,' she said in a peremptory

tone. The big man made a face and walked away. 'He's an impertinent fellow,' Madam Gristwood said. 'Come into our parlour, sir.'

She led me into a hot shuttered room, where her son sat at a table. He stood when I entered. 'Good day, sir. Have you come to tell us we may go? I want to be back at my work—'

'I am afraid there is still danger, Master Harper. A few days more.'

'It's for our safety, David,' his mother said reprovingly. Goodwife Gristwood had got over her shock, it appeared, and recovered her natural character as one who would rule any roost she landed in if she could. I smiled.

'I would like to get back to my house, though,' she said. 'It has been decided David is to live with me there. He earns enough at the foundry to keep us both. Then when the market improves we shall sell the place. We shall have money then, eh, David?'

'Yes, Mother,' he said obediently. I wondered how long it would be before, like Michael, he kicked against the traces.

'Where is Master Kytchyn?' I asked. 'I need to see him.'

Goodwife Gristwood snorted. 'That creeping old monk? In his room, I should think. Upstairs.'

I bowed to her. 'Then I shall go up. I am glad you and your son are safe.'

'Yes.' Her face softened again for a moment. 'Thank you, sir. You have kept faith with us.'

I mounted the stairs, oddly touched by Goodwife Gristwood's unexpected thanks. She had not asked about Bathsheba Green, perhaps she did not care any more now she had her son. I saw that only one door on the upper floor was closed and knocked quietly. There was silence for a moment, then Kytchyn's voice called hesitantly, 'Come in.'

He had been praying, I saw, for he was still rising slowly to his knees. I saw the bulge of a bandage on one arm through the thin stuff of his white cassock. His thin face was pale, drawn with pain.

'Master Shardlake,' he said anxiously.

'Master Kytchyn. How is your arm?'

He shook his head sadly. 'I do not have the use of my fingers as I did. But at least the arm has not gone bad, I must be thankful for that.' He sat on the bed with a sigh.

'How do you find it here?'

He frowned. 'I do not like that woman. She tries to rule the place. Women should not do that,' he said definitely. I realized he had probably had few dealings with women over the years, so Goodwife Gristwood must terrify him. How at sea in the world he was.

'It should not be for much longer, sir.' I smiled encouragingly. 'There is something I would ask you.'

The scared look returned to his face. 'About Greek Fire, sir?'

'Yes. A question only.'

His shoulders slumped and he sighed heavily. 'Very well.'

'They are clearing out the graves at Barty's now.'

'I know. I saw that the day we met there. It is a desecration.'

'I am told there was an old custom there that people buried in the precincts would have something personal buried with them, something that related to their lives on earth. The friars, and the patients in the hospital too.'

'That is true. Many times I have been at vigil for a dead brother. Before they laid him in his coffin they laid a symbol of his life on the body, carefully, reverently.' Tears appeared in the corners of his eyes.

'I wondered if the old soldier, St John, might have had some of the Greek Fire buried with him.'

Kytchyn stood up, looking interested now. 'It is possible. Yes, I suppose if the monks knew of anything that defined his life it would be that. And they would not know Richard Rich would come and desecrate the graves,' he added bitterly.

I nodded. 'Then I think I should find it before Rich goes digging there. I hope there is time. He has ordered the things they find in the graves be brought to him.'

Kytchyn looked at me. 'Ah yes. Some will be gold or silver.'

'Yes.' I returned his gaze. 'Master Kytchyn, something has troubled me. The monks hid that barrel, and the formula. They knew what Greek Fire could do.'

Kytchyn nodded seriously. 'Ay, they did. That motto.'

'"*Lupus est homo homini.*" Man is wolf to man. But, if they knew that, why did they keep the damned stuff? Why not destroy it? If they had, none of this trouble would have come on any of us.'

A sad flicker of a smile crossed Kytchyn's face. 'Struggles between Church and State did not begin with the king's lust for the Bullen whore, sir. There have often been – differences.'

'That is true.'

'St John was at Barty's in the days of the wars between York and Lancaster. Unstable, warlike times. I imagine the monks kept Greek Fire in case they should find themselves under threat and could use it as a bargaining tool. We had to be politicians, sir. Monks always were. Then, when the Tudors restored stability to the land, Greek Fire was forgotten. Perhaps deliberately.'

'Because the Tudors made England safe.' I smiled sadly. 'There's an irony.'

✝

I FELT ENCOURAGED as I rode down to the river bank to meet Lady Honor. Here was some possible progress at last: I would go to Barty's again tomorrow. I would have to invent some story for being there. I turned possibilities over in my mind as I left Genesis at an inn stables and walked down a crowded lane to Three Cranes Wharf. The big cranes which gave the place its name came into view over the rooftops, outlined against a sky where white clouds were scudding along. They gave no promise of rain, but provided welcome moments of shade as they passed beneath the sun. Flower sellers were doing a brisk trade at the bottom of Three Cranes Lane, where Marchamount's party was to meet. I had left off my robe for the occasion, donning a bright green doublet that I seldom wore and my best hose.

The Thames was alive with wherries and barges. Innumerable tilt boats passed up and down, some of the passengers playing lutes and pipes under the canopies, a merry sound across the water. All London seemed to have come to the river to savour the breeze. A raucous crowd was waiting at the wharf for boats to take them across to the bear-baiting, and I saw Lady Honor standing with Marchamount at the centre of a group by the river steps. Today she wore a black hood and a wide yellow farthingale. She smiled at some remark of Marchamount's, making those engaging dimples round her mouth. How well she can disguise her feelings when she needs to, I thought: one would think him her best friend.

I recognized some of the other guests as mercers who had attended the banquet; a couple had brought their wives. Lady Honor's two attendant ladies and a pair of servants stood beside her, together with young Henry, who was looking nervously around at the crowds. Armed men kept the throng waiting to cross to the bear ring at a distance, watchful for cutpurses.

Lady Honor saw me and called out, 'Master Shardlake! Quick! The boat is here!'

I hurried across and bowed. 'I am sorry, I hope I have not kept you waiting.'

'Only a few minutes.' Her smile was warm.

Marchamount bowed briefly to me, then began ushering people officiously towards the river steps. 'Come along, everyone, before the tide turns.'

A large tilt boat with four oarsmen was waiting, its bright blue sail flapping gently in the breeze. The party was in good spirits, all chattering merrily as they stepped aboard. 'Tired of your robe, Shardlake?' Marchamount asked as I settled myself opposite him. He was wearing his serjeant's robe, and sweating mightily.

'A concession to the heat.'

'I've never seen you dressed so brightly.' He smiled. 'It looks quite extraordinary.'

I turned to Lady Honor's cousin, who was sitting beside me. 'Are you enjoying London better, Master Henry?'

The boy reddened. 'It is hard to get used to after Lincolnshire. So many people crowded together, they give me a headache.' His face brightened. 'But I have been to dine with the Duke of Norfolk. His house is very splendid. I hear Mistress Howard is often there, that they say may be queen soon.'

I coughed. 'I'd be careful what you say about that in public.'

Marchamount laughed. 'Come, Shardlake, it's as certain as can be. Cromwell's days are numbered.'

'I hear Lord Cromwell is a great rogue, of no breeding,' Henry said.

'You really *should* be careful where you say that,' I warned him.

He gave me an uncertain look. Lady Honor was right, this boy had not the wit to make a path for his family at court. I glanced at the head of the boat, where Lady Honor sat looking out over the river, her face thoughtful. Ahead, on the Southwark side, the high circular arena of the bear-baiting ring loomed up. I sighed inwardly, for I had ever disliked watching the huge, terrified animals torn apart to the roars of the crowd.

I felt a touch on my arm. Marchamount beckoned me to lean down so he could whisper to me. I felt his hot breath in my ear.

'Are you any closer to finding those missing papers?' he asked.

'My investigations continue—'

'I hope you will not be troubling Lady Honor further about them. She is a woman of great delicacy. I like to think she looks on me as a counsellor now that her poor husband is dead.'

I leaned back and stared at him. He nodded complacently. Remembering what Lady Honor had told me, I had to resist an urge to laugh in his face. I glanced at Henry Vaughan and saw he was staring over the water, lost in his own gloomy thoughts. I leaned in to Marchamount's large, hairy ear.

'I have had my eye on you, Serjeant, by the authority of Lord Cromwell. I know you have had certain conversations with Lady Honor, involving matters of interest to yourself and to the Duke of Norfolk.' At that his head jerked aside and he gave me a startled look.

'You have no right—' he blustered, but I gave him a set look and crooked a finger so that, reluctantly, he bent his head again.

'I have every right, Serjeant, as well you know, so don't piss me about pretending an authority you do not have in this matter.' I was surprised at my own crudity; I was picking up Barak's ways.

'That's a private matter,' he whispered. 'Nothing to do with – with the missing papers. I swear.'

'Your interest is of a romantic nature, I believe.'

His face reddened. 'Please say nothing about that. Please. For her sake as well as mine. It is – it is embarrassing.' His look was suddenly pleading.

'She did not tell me willingly, Marchamount, if that is any consolation. But, be assured, I will say nothing. Nor about the duke being after her lands.'

His eyes widened briefly for a moment in surprise. 'Ah, yes, the lands,' he said a little too quickly. 'A privy matter.'

I had to lean back then because the boat hit the Bankside steps, making us all jerk slightly. The ladies laughed. The boatman began helping them out. Looking at Marchamount's broad back as he clambered ahead of me, I thought, he was surprised when I spoke of the duke being after Lady Honor's lands. Was it something different that Norfolk really wanted of her? I remembered her hand on the Bible as she swore the duke had never asked her to discuss Greek Fire, and my doubts about her faith.

The bank was crowded with people, mostly of the common sort, heading for the baiting. A man in a jerkin brushed against Lady Honor's broad skirts. One of her attendants gave a yelp and a servant shoved him away. Lady Honor sighed.

'Really, one wonders if coming here is worth it with all this crush and noise.' I saw there was a sheen of perspiration on her lip.

'It will be, Lady Honor,' Marchamount said. 'There is a fine bear from Germany called Magnus being baited today. He's over six feet tall, killed five dogs yesterday and ended the day alive. I've a shilling on him going down today, though, he was much bloodied.'

C. J. SANSOM

Lady Honor looked over at the high wooden amphitheatre. A great crowd was waiting by the gates, and shouting and cheering could already be heard from within: the old blind bears were already in the ring, the dogs loosed on them. She sighed again.

'When is the great Magnus to be brought on?'

Marchamount did not appear to notice the ironic emphasis in her voice. 'Not for an hour or so.'

'I will join you then, I think. I don't think I can stand that dreadful kerlie-merlie of noise right now. If you will forgive me, I will take a walk along the bank with my ladies.'

Marchamount looked crestfallen. 'As you wish, Lady Honor—'

'I will join you by and by. Would any of the other ladies care to join me?' She looked around. One of the mercers' wives looked as though she would have, but when she glanced at her husband he shook his head.

'I'll join you, Lady Honor,' I said.

She smiled. 'Excellent. Company would be pleasant.'

Marchamount shook his head. 'Surely you don't prefer the companies of ladies over manly sport, Brother Shardlake?'

'When has the company of ladies not been preferable to that of bears and dogs?'

Lady Honor laughed. 'Well said! Lettice, Dorothy, come along.' She turned and began walking upriver along the Bankside path. I stepped to her side. Her two women walked a few paces behind, with the pair of sword-carrying servants.

Lady Honor's wide skirt brushed against my legs and I felt the wickerwork frame underneath, which held the farthingale out from her legs. I thought of the legs underneath the frame and blushed momentarily.

She made a moue of distaste as another loud roar came from the stadium. 'A manly sport indeed. It'll be manly when they set a man on the bear instead of dogs.' She turned to me with a wicked smile. 'Gabriel Marchamount perhaps, how d'you think he'd fare?'

314

I laughed. 'Not well. I do not like bear-baiting either. The taking of pleasure in another creature's suffering.'

'Oh, it's the noise I can't stand. You sound like one of those extreme reformers, sir, that would ban all pleasures.'

'No, I have always felt thus.'

We walked slowly on. 'They're naught but dumb brutes.' Lady Honor sighed. 'But no, you do not see humanity at its most edifying at the baiting. To be honest I was afraid I might faint, it would be so hot in there today, and smelling of blood. Ah, this is better. Goodwife Quaill looked as though she'd have liked to join us, but she wouldn't speak unless her husband allowed her.'

'The advantages of a widow's independence,' I said.

She smiled broadly, showing her white teeth. 'You remember our conversation. Yes indeed. I am widening my business interests, you know. I have bought a workshop for the sewing of silk garments down by St Paul's. Gabriel helped me, he's good at that sort of thing.' She smiled again. 'But I dare say you are too.'

'I could do with some new clients,' I said ruefully. 'Mine are abandoning me.'

'More fool them. Why is that?'

'I do not know.' I changed the subject. 'You hire women to do the sewing?'

'Yes. Silk is such a difficult material; many ladies prefer to have their clothes made up for them now. I have six seamstresses working there, all ex-nuns.'

'Really?'

'Yes. From St Clare's, St Helen's, Clerkenwell nunnery. Some of the nuns were happy enough to leave the cloister, I've heard one or two of them have ended up down there – ' she nodded back at the Southwark stews – 'but my women are older. Pitiful creatures, afraid to walk in the streets. They're happy enough to work at sewing.'

'It must be hard for them,' I said.

'The poor old things like working together again. I feel it is important the ex-religious are found places where they feel secure. Everyone should have their settled place in society. If proper attention was given to that, we should not have all these masterless men roaming the streets.' She shook her head. 'It must be a troubling thing to have no place. One must feel very insecure.' For the first time it struck me that for all Lady Honor's sophistication there were whole areas of the world, indeed of the very city in which she lived, of which she could have no conception.

'It is better that people should have the chance to rise if they have the merit.' I said.

'But so few have, Matthew, so few.' Her use of my Christian name gave me an unexpected frisson. 'I think you do, but you are not ordinary.'

'You compliment me, Lady Honor,' I said, bowing hastily to cover my confusion.

'There is such a thing as natural nobility.'

I blushed, and thought suddenly: I must not let my feelings get the better of me. I must not. 'The king's government is full of new men,' I said hastily. 'Cromwell. Richard Rich.' I dropped that name to see how she would react, but she only laughed.

'Rich. A cruel brute in a velvet doublet. Did you know, his wife is a mere grocer's daughter?'

'She is mistress of Barty's now.'

By now we had walked some distance up the bank, as far as the Paris garden, the houses starting to give way to open countryside. Lady Honor stopped and looked across the river at the bulk of Bridewell Palace. Her ladies and servants halted at the same moment, ten paces behind. A cloud passed across the sun, softening the light and easing the heat.

She looked at me seriously. 'Matthew, I do hope I am not in trouble with Lord Cromwell. It preys on my mind. Did you talk with him?'

'I repeated what you said. He spoke of you admiringly.'

She looked relieved. 'Yes, they all like coming to my banquets,

Lord Cromwell and the duke and all the courtiers. But in these times
– well, I know each side wonders if my sympathies lie with the other.
When in truth – ' she gave a little laugh – 'I am with neither. I know
if the duke learned I was helping Lord Cromwell in connection with
secret enquiries, he would not be pleased.' She smiled sadly. 'You see
how I am trapped. Yet I only ever wanted good conversation round
my table.'

I grimaced. 'In these times it is hard to avoid getting caught in the
tangles of the great. Often I think I would like to retire to the country.'

'I am thinking of escaping to Lincolnshire, to my family estates.
Though I love London, unlike my nephew. But I suppose the earl
would want me to stay while this business is on.'

'Yes. I think he would, my lady.' I hesitated. 'I spoke with
Serjeant Marchamount in the boat coming over.'

'I saw your heads together.' Her eyes were suddenly watchful.
'Were you checking what I had told you?'

'Yes, I had to. You must understand that.'

Her face reddened. 'And I thought we might relax today, have a
pleasant day out.'

'Come, Lady Honor, you know better than that.'

Her lips set. 'Do I? Is it so strange I should hope for a little
converse with a congenial companion, having answered all his
enquiries?'

I was not to be distracted. 'Marchamount appeared surprised when
I said the Duke of Norfolk was after your lands.' I hesitated. 'My
impression was that that was not the subject the two of them were
discussing at the banquet, when he spoke of getting Marchamount to
press you.'

'Am I to have no peace?' she asked softly. She closed her eyes a
moment, then met mine again, fiercely. 'Matthew, I swore on the Bible
that Norfolk has asked me no questions about Greek Fire and I swore
truly. And it is true that he is after my lands. That is how it started.'

'How what started?'

'Something that became more complicated. A family matter that is none of your business. It has no connection with your wretched papers and formulae.'

'Can you be sure of that?'

'Yes.' She sighed wearily. 'I am going to say no more, Matthew.' She raised a hand. 'If you want you can tell Cromwell and he can have me brought before him. He will get the same answer. Some matters are private.'

'The days of private matters among aristocratic families are gone, my lady. Such matters led to the wars of Lancaster and York.'

She turned a face to me that was utterly weary. 'Yes, all power is with the House of Tudor now. Yet is it not hard to take seriously, the king as head of the Church deciding how his people should relate to God, when his policy is ruled by his fickle passions?'

She spoke softly, but nonetheless I glanced back nervously at her servants. She smiled ruefully. 'I have been accompanied everywhere by servants since I was a baby. I know how to pitch my voice so they cannot hear.'

'That is still dangerous talk, Lady Honor.'

'It's the talk of the streets. But you are right, these days we have to be careful what we say.'

We walked on for a little in silence. 'It is not easy always having servants around one,' she said suddenly. 'Often I wish them far away. I remember once when I was a little girl my mother took me to the roof of our house. She showed me all the fields and woods, stretching away in every direction. She said, "They are ours, Honor, as far as you can see, and once our family owned the country all the way to Nottingham." It was a windy spring day, she held my hand as we stood on the flat leads. Her ladies and my governess were there with their dresses billowing in the wind and all at once I wished I could fly away over those woods and fields, alone, like a bird.' She shook her head sadly. 'But we are bound to the earth, are we not? We are not birds. We have responsibilities. Mine is my family.'

'I am sorry I pressed you again, but—'

'No more, Matthew, I am weary.'

'Perhaps we should return to the baiting—'

She shook her head. 'No, I cannot face it. Would you walk with me a little further, to the next river stairs? I will send a servant back to say I have been taken faint.' She screwed up her eyes as the cloud passed and the hot sun appeared again, bringing sparkling waves of silver to the brown Thames water.

We walked on slowly. I felt a boor for constantly pressing her thus. But I had to; my feelings, and hers, were unimportant. A large barge, full of building materials, passed us on the way to Whitehall and for a moment I imagined it ablaze from end to end, the water around it on fire.

'Perhaps you think my devotion to family foolish,' she said, interrupting my grim thoughts.

'Not foolish. Single-minded, perhaps.'

'Were not things better when the aristocracy owned the lands rather than it being turned over to these new men who put it to pasture and throw the peasantry on the road? Sheep eat men, they say.'

'Ay, and it is a great abuse. But I would not have learning and the chance to rise denied the common people.'

She shook her head though she smiled. 'I think you consider me innocent in some ways.' Jesu, I thought, how sharp she is. 'But I venture to say you are the innocent one. For every man who comes to town and manages to rise from the common herd there are a hundred, a thousand, who starve in the gutters.'

'Then measures should be taken for their welfare.'

'That will never happen. The lawyers and merchants in parliament will never allow it. Is that no so? They have put down all the reforms Cromwell had brought before them.'

I hesitated. 'Yes.'

'So much for your new man.'

I shook my head. 'Lady Honor, I think you are the cleverest woman I have met for a long time.'

'You are not used to bright converse from women, that is all.' She smiled at me. 'I think, Matthew, we disagree about the right ordering of society. Well, that is good, disagreement adds flavour to discourse. And I am glad you have known other women who were not content to drop their eyes and talk of cooking and embroidery.'

'I knew one.' I paused, fingering my mourning ring. 'I wished to marry her, but she died.'

'I am sorry,' she said. 'I know what it is like to lose a loved one. Is that ring for her?'

'Katy was engaged to another by then.' How Lady Honor could make me speak from the heart, of things I told few others.

'That is doubly sad. Did you not press your suit then?' Again, her directness was hardly good manners, but I did not mind.

'I did not. I was afraid she would not have me.'

'Because of your – your condition?' Even Lady Honor struggled for a moment to find the appropriate word.

'Ay.' I looked away, across the river.

'You are a fool to worry about that. You will waste your opportunities.'

'Perhaps.' I stepped aside to let a young couple pass, their pet dog gambolling at their heels. Even as her words warmed me I told myself: be careful.

'Perhaps you think all women seek in a man is a tall carriage and a fine calf,' she said.

'Those do not harm a man's prospects.'

'They are no help if he has coarse features or a poor wit. My husband was near twenty years older than me when we married. Yet we were happy. Happy.'

'Perhaps I should leave off this ring,' I said. 'I confess I think of Katy seldom now.'

'Mourning can become a fetter.' She gave me a direct look. 'When Harcourt died I decided I would not let it bind me. He would not have wanted that.'

I saw we had reached Barge House Stairs. A wherry stood there, waiting for business. 'Shall we cross here?' I asked. 'My horse is down by Three Cranes Wharf, we could return there.'

'Very well. A moment – I must send Paul back with a message or Gabriel Marchamount will think I have been robbed.' She walked over to where her servants and ladies stood, and spoke to the men.

Then I turned and saw Sabine and Avice Wentworth standing on the path in their bright summer dresses, their blue eyes startlingly wide, no doubt from nightshade potion. Their grandmother stood between them, her arms linked with theirs, still in her black mourning dress. The girls stood stock-still, looking at me. Their quality of wary, watchful stillness was unnerving.

'What is it, girls?' the old woman asked sharply. Her face was white and papery in the daylight, more like a skull than ever with those withered eye sockets.

'It is Master Shardlake, Grandam,' Sabine said soothingly.

I bowed quickly. The old woman stood still a moment longer, as though sniffing the air. Then her face set. 'I had hoped to hear your enquiries were done, sir. I still wear mourning for my grandson, as you see. I will not come out of it until justice is done to his murderer.' She spoke calmly, looking straight ahead. Lady Honor returned to my side and looked at the Wentworths enquiringly. One of her servants was trotting back to the bear pit.

'You must excuse me, Goodwife Wentworth,' I said. 'I have a lady present.'

'A lady? You? The crookback lawyer?'

'You are hardly one to mock the deformities of others, woman.' Lady Honor spoke sharply.

Goodwife Wentworth turned her head towards the strange voice. 'My deformities came with age,' she snapped back, 'as they will come to you in time. The lawyer's deformity is one he was born with and such things speak of an evil nature.'

'She should be put in the river for speaking so,' Lady Honor said hotly.

The old beldame smiled. 'On, Sabine,' she said. The girls led her on, heads down, but I caught a smile on the older girl's face. I stood looking after them, breathing heavily.

'Who was that beldame?' Lady Honor asked. 'She has a face from a nightmare.'

'Sir Edwin Wentworth's mother.'

'Ah. And the girls would be his daughters.'

'Yes. Thank you for defending me, but there was no need. People say such things.'

'Because they discern it is the way to hurt you.' She looked genuinely annoyed. Frowning, she picked up her skirts and began descending the steps.

In the boat the attendant ladies, one on either side of Lady Honor, cast curious glances at me from under lowered eyelids. They had seen everything. I avoided their gaze. The tide was going out and there was an unpleasant smell now from the rubbish-strewn mud at the river's edge.

Lady Honor turned to one of her ladies, who was trailing a hand in the water. 'Mind out, Lettice, there's a great turd there.' The girl pulled out her hand with a squeal. Lady Honor shook her head slightly at her foolishness. For all she had said she would like to be free of servants it struck me that to be attended everywhere, all your life, by retainers and servants, must make one feel a sort of earthly divinity. No wonder she had such family pride.

The boat bumped into the mud at Three Cranes Wharf. Lady Honor raised her eyebrows and smiled wryly. 'Well, here we are. I think I shall take the boat on to Queenhithe, then go home.' She paused. 'Visit me again soon. Give me news of how the converse with Lord Cromwell goes.'

'I will, Lady Honor.' She knew I could not leave the mystery that lay between her and the duke, but clearly she was determined to say no more. I stood up awkwardly and bowed. Planks had been set across the mud. I stepped onto them gingerly and crossed to the steps. By the time I grasped the rail at the stairs and could turn safely, the boat was sculling down the river. I shouldered my way through the crowds to the stables.

I felt as though caught in the middle of some dreadful dance between Lady Honor and Cromwell, used by them both. Yet her indignation at the way the Wentworth hag had spoken to me had been genuine. If I could once get out of the toils of secrets and half-truths, I knew there was no one whose company I would rather have. I rode home with a mind sorely unsettled.

✝

AT LAST I REACHED Chancery Lane. As I let myself into my hall, Barak was walking downstairs.

'You're back early,' he said. 'Thank God. I wasn't sure I could keep her much longer.'

'Who?'

He did not answer, but walked back into my parlour. I followed him. There, sitting uneasily on a hard chair, the brand prominent on her square pale cheek, was Madam Neller.

'She's back,' Barak said. 'Bathsheba Green.'

I looked at Madam Neller. She nodded. 'Came back last night with her brother, looking for shelter. Pock-face almost got them two days ago and they had to run from the friends they were with. I've let them stay, they're at Southwark now.' She looked at me fixedly. 'You promised me two more half angels if I brought you the news.'

'You shall have them,' I said.

She fixed me with her hard stare. 'I've persuaded them to talk to you. Convinced them it's the only course. But not at my house. I'm not having you coming down there and making more trouble. I've lost enough business as it is. More than two half-angel's worth,' she added, giving me a meaningful look.

I reached for my purse, but Barak put a hand on my arm.

'Not so fast. Where will Bathsheba meet us then?'

She smiled, that mirthless slash I had seen at the brothel. 'She and her brother will meet you at the house of Michael Gristwood at Wolf's Lane at Queenhithe. It's empty with his wife gone.'

'How do you know that?'

'Bathsheba told me. George Green broke in there a few days ago.

Bathsheba kept pestering him to try and get inside the house. There's something in there she believes Michael was killed for.'

'What was it?' I hesitated. 'A piece of paper?'

She shrugged. 'I don't know and don't care. George got into the house through a window, twice, and it was deserted. I don't think he found what he was after.'

I turned to Barak. 'So much for the watchman. He's still there?'

'Ay, Lord Cromwell wanted an eye kept on the place. He will make the man's arse smart for this. Listen, *if* Green was looking for a piece of paper, that would mean Michael had told Bathsheba about the formula.'

'Yes, it would.'

Madam Neller straightened her red wig. 'They'll meet you there tonight, after dark. They'll be in the house watching. If they see anyone other than you two, they'll be off.'

Barak grunted. 'They're an insolent pair.'

Madam Neller shrugged and looked at me again. I passed her two half angels. She bit the coins and slipped them into her dress.

'Tell them we'll be there,' I said.

She nodded, heaved her stocky form out of the chair and left the room without another word. She left the door to the hall open and I watched as she went to the front door. Joan, who was putting down fresh rushes, gave the brothel keeper a scandalized look as the woman let herself out.

Barak smiled. 'Poor Joan. She doesn't know what to make of all these goings on. You'll lose her if this continues much longer.'

'I'll lose more than her,' I said sourly. 'We both will.'

# Chapter Thirty-one

BARAK AND I SAT IN an alehouse on the corner of Wolf's Lane, almost opposite the Gristwood house. It was a dingy place, where men of the poorer sort sat at battered tables playing cards or talking. A slatternly girl passed wooden tankards of beer through a hatch in the wall. Opposite me, Barak was looking through the open door at the darkening streets.

'Should we not go now?' I asked.

'It's too early. She said they'd not be there till after dark. We don't want to startle them.'

I sat back. Despite my tiredness and aching back, I found myself seized with a new excitement. It was clear Bathsheba knew more than she had indicated at the whorehouse. Now, perhaps, we could find out how much. I took another drink of the watery beer as Barak studied a group of four men playing dice by the opposite wall. He leaned across to me.

'Those dice are loaded. See the gloomy-looking young fellow in the dull clothes? He's new to town, those others have invited him here to cheat him.'

'The City knows countless ways to cheat people. It's nothing to be proud of. The country has more honest ways.'

'Does it?' He looked at me with frank curiosity. 'I've never been there. All the country folk I meet seem dozy clowns.'

'My father has a farm near Lichfield. Country folk aren't stupid. Innocent in some ways, perhaps.'

'Look, he's having to get his purse out now, silly arsehole.' Barak shook his head, then leaned closer. 'Will you see Marchamount again tomorrow? Try to find out what's going on with Lady Honor?'

'Yes, I will. I'll go to Lincoln's Inn first thing.' I had told him reluctantly of the new mystery my conversation on the river had raised, but I realized that where Lady Honor was concerned I needed to sound the opinion of someone whose mind was unclouded by feeling. He had said I must ask Marchamount for the whole story of what was going on between him, Lady Honor and the Duke of Norfolk. I agreed, though with a sinking heart, for I hated the idea of picking her affairs apart with Marchamount again. 'Maybe there'll be some news of Bealknap, too, at last,' I added, for there was still no word of him. At least on my return from the river I had found a note from Guy, saying he was back and I could call on him on the morrow.

At the far table I saw the young man had been persuaded to start another game. I caught a country accent, he was from Essex like Joseph. I thought of Elizabeth languishing in the Hole, a distracted Joseph wondering what I was doing. 'We must go down that well again,' I whispered.

'I know, but it's risky with the dogs.' He frowned. 'I'll put my mind to how it might be done.'

'Thank you, I am grateful.'

'I see those Anabaptists have repented. It's the talk of the streets.'

'Are people disappointed that there won't be a big burning?'

'Some are, but it's a thing many prefer not to see.'

'I have always feared it,' I said. 'When I was first in London as a student it was fashionable to support reform in the Church. Even Thomas More supported it. But then forbidden Lutheran books started to appear and when More was made chancellor the burnings started in earnest. He was a great believer in burning as a purge for sin and to create fear. And it did. The time came when there were few who hadn't been to a burning, if only because it might be noticed if they didn't go.'

'I don't remember much about the days before Lutheranism, I was just a child.' Barak laughed sadly. 'Only the smell of shit my dad brought everywhere with him, making me escape to my schoolwork in the attic. Poor old arsehole, he only wanted to stroke my head.'

'Homework for St Paul's school?'

'Ay. The old monks were all right, but by God they lived well.'

'I know. I went to a monks' school too.'

He shook his head. 'I saw one of my old teachers begging in the gutter a couple of years ago. He looked half-crazed, one of those who couldn't cope with being put out in the world. It was a terrible thing to see.' He looked at me interrogatively. 'And where's it all going now, can you tell me that?'

'No. I fear the endless changes of the last ten years can only have undermined the faith of many.' I was thinking of Lady Honor.

'I never had too much faith.'

'I did once. But it grows less certain every day.'

'Lord Cromwell has faith. And he'd like to help the poor. But all his schemes – ' Barak shrugged his broad shoulders – 'between what the king wants and what parliament wants, they never seem to happen.'

'Strange. Lady Honor said something similar this morning.' I looked at him. Again he was showing a different side – reflective and, like many in King Henry's England, puzzled and insecure.

He nodded at the door. 'I think we can go now.' He rose, adjusting the sword at his waist. I followed him out into the night.

✟

IT WAS AFTER CURFEW and the streets were quiet. The air was hot and still, without a breeze. Candlelight shone from a few windows here and there, but the Gristwood house was dark, sinister-looking in the moonlight. Barak signed me to halt opposite the broken front door. 'Let them have a few minutes to see we're alone.'

I looked up at the shuttered windows. The thought of Bathsheba and her brother peering through the slats at us made me uneasy.

'Where's the watchman?' I asked.

'I don't know. I've been looking out for him. He's off somewhere, like they are when there's nobody to keep an eye on them. Arsehole.'

'What if this is a trap? They could have a whole gang of George Green's wherrymen in there, ready to spring on us.'

'What would they gain? Bathsheba and her brother have run out of places to hide. They've no alternative but to throw themselves on our mercy.' As ever when there was danger, his expression was alert, excited. 'All right, let's go.'

Barak crossed the road swiftly. He knocked gently at the front door, then jumped back in surprise as the door swung open. I saw the new lock, a flimsy thing, had been smashed in. Barak whistled. 'Insolent arseholes, they've broken it. Did that watchman see nothing?'

I looked uneasily at the strip of deep blackness beyond the half-open door. 'Madam Neller said George Green got in through a window.'

'You're right,' Barak said. He bit his lip, then kicked the door wide open. 'Hello,' he called in a loud whisper. 'Hello!' There was no reply.

'I don't like this,' he said. 'Something feels wrong.'

Barak stepped cautiously over the threshold, sword raised. I followed him into the Gristwoods' hall. Two closed doors and the staircase could just be made out ahead of us. Water dripped somewhere. Barak took out a tinderbox and handed me a pair of candles.

'Here, let's get these alight.' He struggled to strike a spark as I looked into the shadows. The dripping sound continued.

The tinder caught and I lit the candles. A dim yellow light illuminated the hall, flickering over the crooked walls and stairs, the dusty old tapestry and the dry rushes in the corners. 'Let's try the kitchen,' Barak said. He opened the door and I followed him inside. The table was dotted with mouse droppings. 'Look there,' Barak whispered. I lowered my candle and saw the dusty floor was marked by footprints, several pairs.

'There's at least three sets there,' I whispered. 'I told you, it's a trap.' I looked back at the door, putting my hand on my dagger and wishing I had brought a sword myself.

'Here!' Barak called, a sharp urgency in his tone. He had drawn the shutters back and was looking out at the unkempt yard. The gate was wide open and something was lying against the wall beside it, a heap of deeper blackness.

'It's a man,' I said.

'It's the watchman! Come on!'

The door to the yard, like the front door, had been broken open. It was a relief to be outside, to have a way of escape open to the lane behind the house. I looked up briefly at the shuttered windows, then joined Barak as he held his candle over the slumped figure by the gate.

For a moment I hoped that the man was asleep in some drunken stupor, but then I saw the great wound in his head, the pale shimmer of brains. Barak stood up, fingering the talisman inside his shirt. For the first time since I had known him he looked afraid.

'You were right,' he breathed. 'It's a trap. Let's get out of here.'

Then we heard the sound. I hope never to hear anything like it again. It came from inside the house, starting as a moan and rising to a keening wail, filled with sorrow and pain.

'That's a woman,' I said.

Barak nodded. His eyes roved around the yard. 'What shall we do?'

I was torn between the desire to run and the thought there was a woman in dreadful pain inside. 'Is it Bathsheba? It must be.'

Barak squinted up at the shutters. 'She might be pretending to be hurt to draw us in.'

'That sound is no pretence,' I said. 'We have to go to her.'

He took a deep breath, then raised his sword once more.

☦

I FOLLOWED HIM BACK through the kitchen, into the hall. The broken-down old house was silent again except for that slow drip-drip from somewhere.

'The sound came from upstairs,' I whispered. 'God's death, what's that?' I jumped back in alarm as four black shapes scurried along the side of the wall, then shot out of the door.

'Rats.' Barak gave a bark of nervous laughter.

'Why should they be running away?'

The awful moaning began again, a keening wail that broke into choking sobs. I looked up the dark staircase. 'That came from Sepultus's workshop.'

Barak set his jaw and, sword held ready, began mounting the stairs. I followed slowly. Barak held the candle high. It cast our shadows into monstrous forms on the wall.

The workshop door was open. Barak banged it wide, lest anyone was hiding behind it. But the room was silent, although the slow drip-drip was louder. He stepped inside. I followed him, nearly gagging at the awful stench. 'Oh, Jesus,' Barak whispered. 'Oh, our Saviour.'

The room was still bare except for Sepultus's large table. Young George Green was lying sprawled across it. His eyes, wide and still in death, glimmered in the candlelight. His throat had been cut horribly; the table was covered with dark blood that still dripped slowly, one thick drop at a time, to the floor. Sprawled over him, weeping, her arms flung round his body, was Bathsheba, her dress torn and cut and soaked with blood.

Barak was the first to move. He crossed to Bathsheba, who gave a little cry and flinched. He leant over her. 'It's all right,' he said. 'We won't harm you. Who did this?'

I stood beside him as Bathsheba tried to speak. To my horror, when she opened her mouth a foamy trickle of blood spilled out; she too was badly hurt. She tried to speak, but managed only to moan again. I laid a hand on her shoulder, trying not to shudder at the sticky wetness. I tried to see where she was injured, but it was too dark and she would not let go of her brother's body.

'It's all right,' I whispered. 'Don't speak. We'll help you.'

She lifted wild eyes to me, pale and frantic in her bloody face.

'Get—' she tried to speak, blood-soaked spittle running down her chin. 'Get – out – while you can—'

Barak turned swiftly to the doorway, but there was nothing there. The house was utterly silent. We looked at each other. Bathsheba's voice had sunk to that keening moan again. Then we heard a door open downstairs, the parlour, I was sure. A sudden harsh smell stung my nostrils, making me cough. Barak caught it too. His eyes widened. 'Shit,' he shouted. 'No—'

An extraordinary noise came from downstairs, a loud 'whump'. It was followed by a crash as someone threw shutters open. Barak and I dashed to the window. I made out the shapes of two men, running down the street. Toky and Wright. Toky paused and looked back at us and I caught an evil grin on his pale face. He looked at me and drew a finger across his throat. Then he turned again and ran after his confederate.

'Oh, Jesu. Shit.' I turned at Barak's voice. He was standing in the doorway, looking out. I could see the staircase was brightly lit with a red dancing light. There was a blast of heat, a crackling noise.

I ran to the door and stood beside him, hardly able to believe what I saw. The door to the parlour was wide open and the room was alive with fire, brighter than a thousand candles, the entire floor and walls covered in red flames that were already roaring through the open door and licking at the hall. The old tapestry outside caught fire immediately. A heavy, evil-smelling black smoke began rolling across the hall.

'Jesu,' Barak breathed. 'It's Greek Fire. They mean to kill us with Greek Fire. Come on!' He turned to Bathsheba. 'We've got to get out of here. Help me with her!'

I helped him lift Bathsheba from her brother's body. Desperately weak as she was, she tried to resist, she looked at me and I caught a throaty bubbling, 'No.'

'Your brother is dead,' I said gently. 'You can't help him.'

Barak and I heaved her up. As we lifted her I saw fresh blood run down her dress from a great wound in her stomach. The poor creature had been stabbed.

'Hold her,' Barak said. He ran back to the door. The fire was spreading with preternatural speed, the walls of the hallway had caught now and the flames were almost at the bottom of the staircase. The roaring, cracking noise was much louder. I caught a whiff of the thick black smoke and gagged. Barak paused a second, then unbuckled his sword and threw it to the floor. He grasped the workshop door and, with a tremendous heave, pulled it free of its remaining hinge.

'Follow me! Quick, before the staircase goes!'

'We can't get down there!' I shouted, trying to keep Bathsheba's slippery body from falling. She was very light or I could not have held her. She seemed insensible now.

'We can't get her out of the window, and we'd likely break our necks on the cobbles if we jumped! Come on!'

Holding the door in front of him like a shield, Barak stepped quickly across to the staircase and began descending. All the ground-floor walls were blazing now, the flames licking at the banisters, smoke curling upwards, ever thicker. This was it, the thing I had always feared had come to pass. Death by fire, red flames burning the skin from my body, sweating the blood out of me, my eyes melting. The words of a pamphlet reporting a burning returned to me. *The kiss of fire so light and agonizing.* I stood, paralysed.

Barak turned round and screamed at me. 'Come on, you arsehole! We've only seconds! See, there's the front door!'

His words brought me to my senses. Across the burning hallway I could see the half-open door to the street, a black shape in a red house of fire. The sight spurred me to follow him, dragging the girl with me. I made myself count the steps as I descended. One – two – three. From somewhere outside I heard a cry of 'Fire! Dear God, fire!'

The smoke made my eyes sting and I had to keep blinking, trying desperately to breathe, the air so hot it felt as though it too was burning. Barak and I were both coughing now. I had a terror the staircase would collapse and bury us in burning wood.

Then suddenly I was at the foot of the steps, red flames all around me. I heard Barak scream, 'Run.' I thought I was about to fall, but then a flame licked at my arm, I heard my doublet sizzle and from somewhere I found the energy to leap forward. Then in a moment I was outside, in the street, the searing heat and the smoke gone. Someone grasped me and I fell into their arms. Someone else took Bathsheba's weight and she slid away from me. I was lowered to the street and lay, gasping desperately for air, fearful I would suffocate, every intake of air burning my throat. There was a crackling of flames from the house and all around terrified yells of 'Fire!'

At length my breath returned. I sat up groggily. Ahead of me the Gristwoods' house was ablaze from end to end, flames roaring through every window. The roof had caught too and the fire had already spread to the neighbouring house. People had spilled from the alehouse and from all the houses in the street. They were running to and fro with terrified faces, calling for water, desperate to save their homes from this sudden, terrible outburst. I thought: thank God there's no wind. I saw Barak was sitting beside me, retching and coughing. Next to him lay Bathsheba, still as death. Barak turned to me, his face black and all the hair on one side of his head gone.

'You all right?' he gasped.

'I think so.'

A man in a watchman's jerkin, carrying a staff, bustled over to us. His face was alive with fury. 'What have you done to set the house on fire like that?' he shouted. 'Wizards!'

'We didn't do it,' Barak croaked. 'Fetch a physician – there's a woman hurt here.'

The man looked at Bathsheba, his eyes widening as he saw the blood covering her. I shook my head, the tumult of shouts and running feet seemed to have taken on a strangely distant, echoing sound.

'What have you done?' the watchman breathed again.

'It was Dark Fire,' I said. 'The rats knew.'

Then the noise of the fire and the shouting faded away, and I blacked out.

# Chapter Thirty-two

I REGAINED CONSCIOUSNESS slowly, as though swimming up from a dark lake. When I opened my eyes I thought for an awful moment I was blind. Then my eyes accustomed themselves to the darkness and I realized I was in an unlit room, at night. There was an open window to one side of the truckle bed I lay on, just visible as a slightly lighter square through which a hot breeze sighed.

I could not remember what had happened or where I was. I tried to sit up to see more of my surroundings but my body was seized with pain and I lay down again with a groan. My back was agony and I had a smarting pain in my left forearm. I realized I was thirsty, a terrible dry thirst; when I swallowed it was like gulping down thorns.

I became aware of a smell. Burning. Fire, I thought, and everything that had happened at Wolf's Lane flew back into my mind. I tried to sit up again and shout, but the effort was too much and I nearly passed out. For a few seconds I lay there in terror. Had the fire spread to wherever it was I had been taken? Then I lifted my right arm to my nose. The smell of smoke was coming from my shirt. I lay back, breathing heavily and painfully. I must gather my strength, then try to call out for water, find out where I was. The thought came that I had been arrested for starting the fire, put in prison. Where were Barak and poor Bathsheba? That awful tableau of the girl leaning over her dead brother, the pair of them boltered in blood, returned and I let out a harsh dry sob.

There was an unexpected sound from the window, a soft chirruping. Other birds joined in and as I lay there the sky began to lighten, turning from dark blue to greyish white. I made out the steep outlines of roofs and realized I was on the upper floor of a house somewhere. The sun appeared, at first a little dark-red orb but very soon, as the mist burned away, a fierce yellow ball.

As the light grew I studied the room I was in. It was sparsely furnished: just the bed I was lying on, a chest and on the wall a big cross, Christ hanging with agonized face and gaping wounds. I stared at it in puzzlement for a moment, then I remembered; it was Guy's old Spanish cross, I was at Guy's.

I lay back with a sense of relief. I must have slept again, for when next I stirred and looked around the sun was high, the room hot. My thirst was unbearable now. I tried to call out but could manage only a croak. I leaned over, wincing at a sharp pain from my left arm, and banged on the floor.

To my relief I heard movement downstairs, then footsteps. Guy came in, carrying a large flagon and a cup. His face was drawn with anxiety and lack of sleep.

'Wa – water,' I croaked.

He sat on the bed and lifted my head to the cup. 'Do not gulp it,' he said. 'You will want to, but you must take small sips or you will be sick.' I nodded, letting him trickle water slowly into my mouth. My throat seemed to sing with relief as it passed down. He sat with me thus for several minutes, letting me drink slowly. At length I lay back, noticing that my arm was bandaged.

'What happened?' I whispered.

'You were brought here insensible last night, on a cart with that man Barak and the girl Bathsheba. You are suffering from the effects of smoke and you have a burn on your arm.' He looked at me seriously. 'The fire has caused much damage. Two streets at Queen-hithe were quite burned down. Thank the Lord they were so close to the river – they were able to draw water from there.'

'Is anyone hurt?'

'I do not know. Your friend Barak has gone to rouse Lord Cromwell, he says he will need to deal with this. Barak was affected by the smoke too. I told him he should not go out but he insisted.'

'Bathsheba,' I said. 'The girl, how is she?'

Guy's face darkened. 'She has been stabbed in the stomach, there is little I can do. I have given her some drugs to ease her pain and she is sleeping. But it is only a matter of time. Who did that to her, Matthew?'

'The same villain who set fire to the house and left me and Barak to burn to death. There were two more bodies there, the girl's brother and the watchman.'

'Dear Christ.' Guy crossed himself.

'Barak is right: Cromwell's intervention will be needed here or there will be a great hue and cry.' I closed my eyes. 'Dear God, is this to be Scarnsea again, a host of innocent people torn from the world in blood and violence?'

Guy continued to look at me, sternly but also doubtfully, in a way he never had before.

'What is it?' I asked.

'I went out to buy some things I needed while you were sleeping. There are rumours abroad that the fire was started by supernatural means, that there is magic involved. Apparently it was not a normal fire, it roared up suddenly and consumed the ground floor of the house in a moment.'

'It did,' I said. 'I was there. But there is no magic, Guy, I promise you. Did you think I could ever become involved in the dark arts?'

'No, but—'

'No forbidden knowledge, I swear. An ancient way of making fire rediscovered, that is all. It is what I have been working on for Cromwell. I could not tell you.'

He continued to look at me questioningly. 'I see. Your friend distrusts me. Perhaps you did too, if this matter affects Cromwell whom, yes, I see as an enemy. I wondered why you would not tell me more.'

'I don't distrust you, Guy. God's wounds, I think you're the only one left I do trust.'

Guy looked at the cross. 'There is the only one you need to trust and follow.'

I shook my head sadly. 'Where was Christ when that poor girl and her brother were being cut to pieces last night?'

'Watching, in the sorrow you see there in his face, as men used the free will God gave them to do terrible evil.' He sighed. 'Here, take this flagon. Keep taking water but remember, drink slowly.'

✝

WHEN BARAK RETURNED an hour later, Guy brought him to my room and left us together. Barak's eyes were red and smarting and his voice was a strangled croak. His shirt was smoke-stained and the hair on the right side of his head was quite singed away, leaving only stubble. The contrast with the untidy brown locks on the other side was so bizarre I could not help letting out a bark of nervous laughter. He grunted.

'You should see your own face, it's black as soot. And Lord Cromwell's not laughing. He's going to have to put pressure on the mayor and coroner to keep this quiet. The people down at Queenhithe found what was left of George Green's body and the watchman's, little more than charred sticks, and they're talking about magic. You know there's two streets gone? It's lucky there was no wind or the fire could have spread across the City.'

'Was anyone else hurt?'

'A few have burns and plenty more are homeless. The Gristwoods' house is a pile of ashes. Goodwife Gristwood will have no home to come back to.'

'No. Poor old creature.' I paused. 'Well, now I've seen it. That was Greek Fire, wasn't it?'

'Yes, I recognized the smell as the fire started. Those bastards must have been waiting in the parlour till we were trapped upstairs. They must have coated the walls with the stuff, set light to it, then got out the window.' He sat down on the bed. 'Jesu, the terror when I saw it.

It was just like at the wharf, the whole place alive with red fire in a second. The same thick black smoke.' He frowned. 'Why try to kill us in that way? They could have surprised us and struck us down as they did Bathsheba and her brother.'

'To show Lord Cromwell they had Greek Fire.'

'That they could make and use it at will.'

'Yes. That was what they wanted him to think.' I looked at him again. 'Thank you, Barak. I would not have got out of that house without you. For a moment there I could not move from fear.'

'I know.' He grinned. 'I thought I might have to kick your arse downstairs.'

'How did you get us here?'

'I grabbed a horse and cart that had been used to bring water and got you and the girl on it, God knows how. I was afraid we'd be arrested or slain on the spot. I couldn't think where to go, then I remembered your apothecary lived nearby. It was only a few minutes' drive.'

I nodded. His quick thinking had saved us from arrest. He stood smiling, pleased with his success.

'How is the girl?' he asked.

'Like to die, Guy said. Are you all right?'

He fingered his talisman, then winced suddenly. 'I got burned on the shoulder as I went through the front door.'

There was a knock and Guy entered. He looked between us. 'The girl is awake,' he said quietly. 'She wants to speak to you.' He took a deep breath. 'I don't think she can last long.'

'Can you get up?' Barak asked me. I nodded and rose painfully from the bed, coughing again. Every muscle seemed to howl in protest.

Guy led us into a little room where Bathsheba lay on a bed, her eyes closed. Her breathing was shallow and she was deathly pale, the colour leached from her face. The whiteness of her skin contrasted with the vivid red spots on the bandage swathing her lower body. Guy had washed her face but her hair was still matted with blood. For a moment I felt giddy.

'I've given her something to ease the pain,' Guy said. 'She is very sleepy.' He touched Bathsheba gently on the shoulder and her eyes flickered open.

'Mistress Green, I have brought them as you asked.'

Bathsheba stared at us. She said something, her voice so faint I could not hear. I took a stool and sat beside her. She turned painfully and looked at me.

'They would have killed you too,' she whispered.

'Yes, they would.'

'I was going to tell you everything and throw myself on Lord Cromwell's mercy. But they were waiting for us, poor George and me. They rushed in at us, lashing with their swords. That man with the scarred face, he struck me in the stomach.' She shuddered. 'They left us for dead, said they would give the hunchback lawyer a spectacular death when he arrived.' She leaned back, exhausted with the effort of speaking.

'How did they know you were there?' I asked gently.

'It must have been Madam Neller, she must have told them. She'd do anything for gold.'

'She will pay for that.'

She winced with pain, then turned again to me and spoke rapidly. 'I want to tell you what Michael said to me. If it will help you find them.'

I tried to smile. 'Go on. You are safe now.'

'Those last weeks before he was killed Michael was afraid, terrified. He said he was involved in a scheme, something he and his brother thought could make them rich. It involved some papers he had at his house. He said he was afraid for their safety.'

'Madam Neller said your brother had been searching there.'

'Yes.' She winced with pain. 'He thought if he could find them, perhaps Lord Cromwell would help us. But they'll all be burned to cinders now.'

'I already have the papers, Bathsheba. Except for one that is missing. A formula. Did Michael say anything about that?'

'No. Only that he feared the people they were working with. He feared they would be killed. They were working to bring down Lord Cromwell.'

'But – but I thought he was working *with* Cromwell. He had something the earl wanted badly.'

'No. No, the scheme was *against* the earl.'

I stared at her. It made no sense. She coughed again, and a little watery fluid dribbled down her chin. She winced, then looked at me again. 'We were going to have a child. Michael talked of us escaping the country with his brother, going to Scotland or France and starting afresh. But then he was killed. That man last night, he killed my baby when he stabbed me.'

I reached out and took her hand. It was as light and thin as a bird's foot. 'I am sorry.'

'What do our lives matter?' she asked bitterly. 'What are any of us but pawns in the schemes of the great?' She shook her head in despair, then coughed again and closed her eyes. Guy stepped forward and took her other hand gently.

'Bathsheba,' he said quietly. 'I fear you are like to die. I am an ordained priest. Will you repent of your sins, acknowledge Christ as your Saviour?'

She did not reply. Guy pressed her hand harder. 'Bathsheba. You are about to face your Maker. Will you acknowledge Him?'

Barak leaned forward, put a finger to the pulse in the girl's neck. 'She's gone,' he said quietly.

Guy knelt by the bed and began praying softly in Latin.

'What good's that going to do?' Barak asked harshly. I rose and took his arm, leading him from the room. We returned to my chamber and I sat back on the bed, exhausted.

'Poor bitch,' Barak said. 'I'm sorry, I didn't mean any disrespect to the Moor.' He ran a hand through what was left of his hair. 'What in heaven's name did she mean, Michael was involved in a plot *against* Lord Cromwell?'

'I don't know. All this time we've assumed the person who took the formula stole it for reasons of profit, perhaps to sell to a foreign power.'

'Ay. But you've doubted whether there was a formula at all.'

'Yes. I wondered if the whole thing could have been a fraud on Cromwell, but that something went wrong and the rogues fell out.'

'But we know Greek Fire is real.'

I clenched my fists. 'There are still things that don't add up. Toky's involvement from the beginning, investigating that Polish stuff months before the Gristwoods went to Cromwell. Why the delay? And there are other things—'

I broke off as Guy entered, carrying a bowl of water and some cloths. There was an awkward silence for a moment. 'I must dress your arm, Matthew,' he said. 'You should rest here at least a day before you go abroad again.'

I remembered Marchamount and Bealknap. 'I can't.' We had lost half a day, there were only five days left now. 'I must go to Lincoln's Inn.'

He shook his head. 'You will make yourself ill.'

I sat up painfully. 'Will you dress my arm? Then I must go.'

'I've a burn on my shoulder,' Barak said. 'It stings horribly. Could you look at that too?'

Guy nodded. Barak took off his shirt, revealing a muscular torso boasting a number of scars from old knife thrusts. One shoulder was red and raw, the skin peeling. As Guy examined it he noticed the golden symbol hanging from its chain.

'What's that?' he asked.

'It's called a mezzah. An old Jewish symbol. You were right before when you said my name was Jewish.'

Guy nodded. 'Mezuzah is the full name. The Jews used to fix them on their doors with a scroll from the Torah inside. To welcome visitors. I remember them from my boyhood in Granada.'

Barak looked impressed. 'All these years I've wondered what it was for. You are a knowledgeable man, apothecary. Ah, that stings!'

Guy dressed his burn, coating it with a harsh-smelling oil, then sent him back to his room while he dressed my arm. I winced as he lifted my sleeve to expose the livid red mark, the puckered skin. He applied some of his oil and I felt the smarting ease a little.

'What is that stuff?'

'Oil of lavender. It has cold and wet properties, it draws the dry heat from the fire that has stung your flesh.'

'I remember you using it on the young founder who burned himself.' I looked at him seriously. 'There is a fire I think no amount of lavender could quench. Guy, I was going to talk to you anyway, ask you some questions about the matter that has caused all this death and ruin. It involves alchemy, as I told you, and there are aspects that have me sore puzzled. I would tell you all, if you will listen.'

'Is it safe for me to know?'

'If you keep it close, there should be no danger from those that pursue us. But I will not tell you if you would rather not know.'

'Cromwell would not be pleased, I think. I note you have waited till friend Barak was gone.'

'I'll take the risk if you will.'

'Very well.'

As he bound my arm with a strip of cloth, I told him all I knew of Greek Fire, from Cromwell's first summons to the fire last night. As he listened his face grew more troubled.

'Your aim is to catch these killers?' he asked.

'Yes. They have killed five people now. The Gristwood brothers, Bathsheba and her brother, and the watchman. A founder called Leighton is probably dead too.'

'I remember you were asking about founders.'

'Yes. I think we were too late to save him. And there are three more people kept in hiding for fear of these monstrous rogues. I want to catch them, stop them cutting this swathe through London.'

'And to recover the formula for Greek Fire for Cromwell?'

I hesitated. 'Yes.'

'Have you considered the havoc such a weapon may wreak? It

could burn whole navies. It could be used to fire a city, as we saw last night.'

'I know,' I said quietly. 'The image of great ships on fire forever comes unbidden to my head. But, Guy, if Cromwell does not get it, others will, foreign powers who would use it against England.'

'And take her back to Rome?' He raised his eyebrows, and I remembered he was neither English nor Protestant. He considered for a moment. 'What did you wish to ask me?'

'Do not answer if you feel you cannot. But I know now that there was a barrel of Greek Fire kept at Barty's for a hundred years. And that there was a formula. My belief is the Gristwoods used the period between their discovery last October and their approach to Cromwell in March to build their apparatus – there is evidence of that – but also to try and make some more, using the formula.'

'A barrel would not last for ever.'

'Exactly. And with two ships destroyed, most of the barrel is probably used up. That they could set that fire last night may indicate they have made more. But *how*, Guy? How does an alchemist create material from a formula?'

'By finding the correct mixture of the four elements. Earth, air, fire and water.'

'That all things are composed of. Yes, but that is no easy task.'

'To be sure. It is easy enough to make iron, using the minerals God has seeded in the earth, but hard to make gold or we would all be eating from gold plates and the stuff would be worthless.'

'And to make Greek Fire, how easy might that be?'

'Without the formula, it is impossible to tell.'

I sat up. 'You spoke of iron and gold just then. There are some things that are common, easy to find, like iron, and others like gold which are very rare.'

'Of course. That is obvious.'

'I have been reading about the history of fire weapons in the east. We know the Byzantines had no problem in finding the elements needed to create the liquid that is set on fire. Equally, similar substances are mentioned by the Romans, but they were not developed as weapons. I think that perhaps a crucial element needed to manufacture Greek Fire is hard to get. I think the Gristwoods may have been looking for a substitute for this missing element. This could have led them to the Polish drink that burned the table at the inn.'

He stroked his chin. 'So they used that to make Greek Fire?'

'I don't know. Perhaps.'

'And, from what you say, they were already working with the rogues who were to become their killers in a plot *against* Cromwell?'

'Yes. I don't know how that came about. But, Guy, if I was able to find some of the original Greek Fire in the Barty's churchyard I told you of—'

His face wrinkled in distaste. 'Desecrating graves—'

'Yes, yes, I agree. But it is to be done anyway. If I found some and brought it to you, could you analyse it for me, distil its essence or whatever it is you do?'

'I am an apothecary, not an alchemist.'

'You know as much of their arts as most of them do.'

He took a deep breath and folded his arms. 'To what end, Matthew?' he asked.

'To help me find out what has happened—'

He broke in sharply. 'Matthew, you forget what you are asking me. To analyse Greek Fire so that Thomas Cromwell may have the secret.' He paced the room, his dark face more serious than I had ever seen it. At length he turned to me.

'If you can find this cursed stuff and bring it to me I will look at it. But then I will destroy it. I will give you no clue to its manufacture that may help Cromwell. If my researches throw up anything that will aid you to catch these murderers without doing that, I will tell you. I am sorry, Matthew, but that is all I am prepared to do.'

'Very well. I agree.' I extended my hand and he took it. He still looked serious. 'St Gregory of Nyssa once said all the arts and sciences have their roots in the struggle against death. And so they should have. This thing of ruin and destruction is a perversion, a monstrosity. If you find that formula, you should destroy it and all the world will be safer.'

I sighed. 'I am bound to Cromwell. And to help my country.'

'And how do you think Cromwell, and King Henry, would use Greek Fire, ruthless men of blood that they are? For murder and mayhem, that is how.' He was angry. 'This is far worse than Scarnsea, Matthew. Cromwell has used you again not just to hunt a murderer, but to aid him in a brutal, cruel blasphemy.'

I bit my lip.

'And Barak,' he continued, 'how does he see things?'

'He is utterly loyal to his master.' I looked at Guy. 'I will tell him nothing of this conversation.' I leaned back on the bed with a sigh. 'You do well to upbraid me,' I said quietly. 'I have worried about what Greek Fire may do, but – yes, I have been driven on by a passion to catch these murderers, recover what was stolen. And to save Elizabeth Wentworth. At any cost.'

'That cost may be too high. You must decide when the time comes, Matthew. It will be between you and God.'

# Chapter Thirty-three

I T WAS LATE MORNING by the time we arrived home. I opened the front door quietly, hoping we might get upstairs without Joan seeing our sorry condition, but paused at the sight of a note in Godfrey's large round hand on the table. I broke the seal.

'Bealknap's back!' I said. 'He's in his chambers. Thank God, I feared he might be——' I did not finish the sentence.

'Let's get a message to Leman then,' Barak said, 'and go to Lincoln's Inn.'

Just then Joan appeared from the kitchen, alerted by our voices. Her eyes widened at the state we were in.

'Sir, what's happened now?' There was a slight quaver in her voice. 'When you didn't come back last night I was worried.'

'There's been a bad fire over at Queenhithe,' I said gently. 'We were caught up in it, but we're all right. I'm sorry, Joan, there have been many turmoils this week.'

'You look worn out, sir. What happened to your hair, Master Barak?'

'It got singed. I look monstrous, hey?' He gave her his most charming smile. 'What I need is someone to cut the other side, so I don't frighten the children.'

'I could have a try.'

'You are a pearl among women, Mistress Woode.'

While Joan fetched some scissors and took Barak up to his room, I scribbled a note to Leman and gave it to a wide-eyed Simon to take to Cheapside. Then I went up. I shut my bedroom door and leaned on it wearily. Guy's words about the nature of my mission returned to me. I had been too tired, too frightened for myself and the others involved, to think much further than uncovering the conspirators. But what if I were to succeed? What if the time came when the Greek Fire formula was in *my* hands? What would I do then? I remembered poor Bathsheba's words. A plot *against* Lord Cromwell. Just what had Michael and his brother planned that had been interrupted by their deaths? I shook my head. For now there was nothing to do but go on, beard Bealknap in his den now I had the chance. It was the fifth of June, I realized, only five days left.

☦

AT LINCOLN'S INN I left Barak and Leman in my rooms, then crossed the courtyard to Marchamount's chambers to enquire after him. Distasteful though the prospect was, I had to talk to him about Lady Honor once I had seen Bealknap. His clerk, though, said he was out at Hertford, appearing in a case before the circuit judge, and would not be back until the morrow. I cursed inwardly. At least on my mission for Cromwell three years before I had had all the parties secure in a monastery enclosure. I told the clerk I would return on the morrow also, and went back to where Leman and Barak waited, watching Skelly laboriously copying out the application for the Chancery writ for Bealknap's case. Leman, who seemed more confi-dent today, asked if Bealknap was in his rooms.

'So the message said. I shall just check with my colleague,' I replied.

Leman smiled, a grim smile that anticipated revenge.

I knocked at Godfrey's door and went in. He was standing looking from the window, a troubled expression on his thin face. He gave me a watery smile.

'Come to see Brother Bealknap, Matthew? I saw him go to his chambers earlier.'

'Good. Are you all right, Godfrey?'

He fingered the hem of his robe. 'I have had a letter from the secretary. It seems the Duke of Norfolk is not satisfied with my fine. He wants a public apology in hall.'

I sighed. 'Well, Godfrey, you did break all the rules of courtesy—'

'You know it is not about that!' he snapped out, his eyes flashing. 'However it is worded, it will be taken as an apology for my religious beliefs.'

'Godfrey,' I said seriously, 'for Jesu's sake, make your apology and live to fight another day. If you refuse you'll be debarred, and a marked man.'

'Perhaps it would be worth it,' he said quietly. 'It could become a legal cause célèbre, like the Hunne case.'

'Hunne was murdered for defying the Church by thugs employed by the papists.'

'It was a noble way to die.' A strange smile played round the corners of Godfrey's mouth. 'Is there any better way?'

I shuddered involuntarily. There it was again, that strange urge some had to be martyred, to exult in the righteousness of their suffering. I stared at him. He gave a little laugh.

'That's a strange look, Matthew.'

On the spur of the moment, I said, 'Godfrey, may I put a case to you?'

'Of course.'

'What if that God gave you a miraculous power, a thunderbolt that could fell all your enemies at once, whole armies. All you needed to do was raise your hand.'

He laughed. 'That is a far-fetched case, Matthew. There have been no such miracles since Our Lord's time on earth.'

'But just say you were given such a gift.'

He shook his head piously. 'I would not be worthy.'

'But say you had it,' I persisted. 'Something that, if used, would inevitably kill thousands, many of them innocent. Would you use it?'

'Yes, I would. I would place it at the service of King Henry to confound his enemies at home and abroad. Does not the Old Testament tell us that often many must die if God's cause is to be served? Remember Sodom and Gomorrah.'

'They were destroyed in fire and thunder.' I closed my eyes a moment, then looked at him. 'You won't apologize, will you?'

He smiled gently, that fierce holy light in his eyes again. 'No, Matthew, I will not.'

✝

We mounted the narrow stairs to Bealknap's rooms. The padlock had been taken away. I gave a peremptory knock on the door. Bealknap himself opened it. He had left off his robe and his doublet too in the hot weather, and was wearing only his white linen shirt. Coarse yellow hairs protruded above the collar. With his lawyer's regalia off, he looked more like the rogue he was.

'Brother,' I said, 'I have been trying to find you. Where have you been?'

He frowned. 'On business.' He eyed Barak's shorn head in surprise. 'Who's this?' Then he caught sight of Leman and his eyes widened. The stallholder gave him an evil grin. Bealknap tried to slam the door in our faces, but Barak was too quick for him, jamming his foot in the door and putting his shoulder to it. Bealknap staggered back, while Barak winced and rubbed his arm. 'God's death, I'd forgotten the burn.'

We stepped in. Bealknap's chamber was as untidy as ever, the chest prominent in its corner. The door to his living quarters was open. Bealknap stood in the middle of the room, his face red with outrage.

'How dare you!' he shouted. 'How dare you burst in here?' He pointed a long finger at Leman. 'Why have you brought that rogue, Shardlake? He has a grudge against me, he will tell any lies—'

Barak spoke up. 'You won't remember me, master, I was just a boy, but my stepfather used to be one of your witnesses in the bishop's court. Edward Stevens. Strange people, witnesses. Sometimes they'll appear out of the blue and swear to the honesty of a man they couldn't possibly have met.'

In all the time I had known this pestilential lawyer I had never seen him lose his composure, but now he stood with clenched fists, taking deep breaths. 'This is all lies,' he blustered angrily. 'I don't know what game you're playing, Shardlake—'

'No game.'

Bealknap's lips parted, showing long yellow teeth. 'If you're trying to pressure me into giving way on my properties, it won't work. I'll have you disbarred.'

'It's not that,' I said contemptuously.

'Your clutch-fistedness has caught up with you, Master Bealknap,' Leman said with pleasure. 'Only a tiny piece of gold from yonder chest to pay me what you owed would have saved you this.'

'Master Leman has prepared a statement,' I said. I took a copy from my robe and held it out to Bealknap. He clutched it and read, frowning. Yet as I watched him I sensed that something was wrong. He should have been terrified, facing the ruin of his career, yet he seemed only enraged. He lowered the statement.

'Hunting down a brother barrister,' he said in a savage whisper, 'getting Cheapside stallholders to swear false statements – what is this about? What do you want?'

'You remember I have a commission from Lord Cromwell?'

'I told you all I knew about that matter. Which was next to nothing.' He waved a hand angrily. If he was lying he did it well.

'I want to know the nature of your connection with Sir Richard Rich, Bealknap.'

'That is none of your damned business,' he said stoutly. 'Yes, I have a commission from Sir Richard, I work for him. It is his business I have been on these last few days.' He raised a hand. 'And I will not be questioned about that. God's death, I'll go to Sir Richard now, I'll tell him of your pestering—'

'Brother Bealknap, if you do not answer my questions, I shall go to Lord Cromwell.'

'Then he can speak to Sir Richard.' Bealknap nodded grimly. 'There, you did not expect that, did you?' He reached for his robe. 'I shall go to him now. You are out of your depth, sir; you have been dabbling in matters that are beyond you.' He laughed in my face. 'Have you not realized that yet? Now, out of my chambers.' He threw open the door. Barak clenched his fists.

'Lord Cromwell can have you on the rack, you great bony arsehole.'

Bealknap laughed. 'I think not, though he might make your arses smart after my master and he have spoken. Now leave!' He waved at the door.

There was nothing left but to go. As soon as we were outside, the door was slammed in our faces.

We stood on the landing. Barak gave me a puzzled look. 'I thought he'd be terrified.'

'So did I.'

'Lord Cromwell, Richard Rich.' Leman gave me a sidelong look. 'I don't want any more to do with this, sir, I'm going back to my stall.' And with that he turned and hastened downstairs, without even asking for the rest of the money I had promised him.

Barak and I were left looking at each other. 'Well, that went well,' Barak said sarcastically.

'What can Rich have to say to Cromwell that will turn his anger on to us?' I shook my head. 'Cromwell is the chief secretary, Rich is a big fish but nowhere near that big.'

'And what does he know about Greek Fire?' Barak took a deep breath. 'I'm going to have to get word to the earl about this.' He began descending the stairs.

I followed him. 'Do you know where Cromwell is today?'

'Whitehall again. I'll ride there now. You go home and rest. You look like you need it. Do nothing till I return.'

I wondered if he and Cromwell might have things to say he did not want me to hear. But if he did, there was nothing I could do about that.

# Chapter Thirty-four

I T WAS MORE THAN two hours before Barak returned. I waited for him in my parlour, looking out over the garden as the afternoon shadows began to lengthen. I was still exhausted after my terrifying experience of the night before, but though my eyes smarted with tiredness I could not rest. Thoughts chased each other round my head. What had Bealknap meant? What was it I should have realized? And what was I to do if my planned trip to St Bartholomew's proved successful and we actually found some traces of Greek Fire? My conversation with Guy nagged at me; I could not keep the broader implications of what I was doing from my mind. It would be better, surely, if nobody had Greek Fire. But Toky's master, whoever that was, had it already.

At length, tired of prowling round the room, I decided to go to the stables. As I stepped outside, I winced at the heat – it was hotter than ever – and became conscious that everything ached, my burned arm, my back, my eyes, my head.

Barak had collected Sukey, but Genesis stood quietly in his stall. He gave a whicker of recognition when he saw me. Young Simon was mucking out the stables.

'How is Genesis settling in?' I asked.

'Well enough, sir, he's a good horse. Though I miss old Chancery.'

'So do I. Genesis seems a placid beast.'

'He wasn't at first, sir. He was anxious in his stall, couldn't settle. I feared he might kick me.'

'Really?' I was surprised. 'He was no trouble to ride.'

'He's probably been well trained in Lord Cromwell's stables, sir, but I think he was used to larger quarters there.' Simon flushed as he mentioned the earl's name; it was a source of wonder to the boy that I was associated with so great a man.

'Maybe.'

'Master Barak told me he had his hair burned off last night in a fire.' The boy's eyes were wide with curiosity. 'Is he a soldier, sir? I sometimes think he looks like one.'

'No. Just a minor servant of the earl, like me.'

'I would like to be a soldier one day.'

'Would you, Simon?'

'When I'm older I shall train for the muster. Fight the king's enemies, who would invade our realm.'

From his words I guessed someone had been reading an official proclamation to him. I smiled sadly as I stroked Genesis's neck. 'Soldiering is a bloody trade.'

'But one has to fight the papists, sir. Oh, yes, I'd like to be a soldier or a sailor one day.'

I prepared to argue, but turned at the sound of hooves. Barak, looking tired and dusty, had come to a halt outside the stable. Simon ran out and took the reins.

'What news?' I asked.

'Let's go inside.'

I followed him back to the parlour. He ran a hand over his stubbly head, wrinkling the skin on his pate, then blew out his cheeks. 'The earl was fierce with me,' he said bluntly. 'Told me he'd had to waste half the morning persuading the coroner to keep the bodies they found at Queenhithe quiet for a few days. He was furious to hear your efforts to make Bealknap talk had sent him off to Rich.'

'I wasn't to know Rich could be a shield against Cromwell.'

'He can't. The earl was outraged at the very idea. He thinks Rich has been exaggerating his powers to Bealknap and Bealknap believed him. He's sending men out now to find Rich, find out what Bealknap meant. He says if Rich knows about Greek Fire he'll sweat it out of him one way or another. I don't envy friend Bealknap afterwards.'

I frowned. 'That doesn't sound right. Bealknap's every sort of rogue, but he's no fool where his own interests are concerned. He wouldn't have said what he did unless he knew he was safe. There's something we're not seeing.'

'Another thing the earl said: he knows how you like to find all the facts and lay them flat on the table before coming to a conclusion. He says there isn't time for that, you'll have to cut corners.'

I laughed bitterly. 'In dealing with an enemy as clever as ours and in a matter as complex and secret as this? Does he think I'm a miracle worker?'

'Maybe you'd like to ask him that. He was prowling around his office at Whitehall like a bear in the pit, ready to lash out. And he's scared. He says to go to Barty's now, today. It's a good time, with Rich taken in to be questioned. He wants that coffin opened.' Barak slumped down on the cushions. His face had a grey tinge under his tan; the events of last night were catching up with even his powerful constitution.

'How is your shoulder?' I asked.

'Sore. But better than it was. What about your arm?'

'The same. Bearable.' I pondered a moment. If I was to go to St Bartholomew's I wanted to go alone; if there *was* Greek Fire buried with the soldier, I would take it to Guy. Barak, I knew, would take it straight to Cromwell.

'I'll go over to Barty's on my own,' I said, my heart suddenly pounding fast. 'You're tired, you stay here.'

He looked at me in surprise. 'You look worse than I do.'

'I've had a chance to rest upstairs,' I lied, 'while you've been facing the earl in a bad temper. Let me go alone.'

'What if Toky's about?'

'I'll be all right.'

He hesitated, but to my relief relaxed deeper into the cushions. 'All right. Jesu, I don't think I've ever been so tired. The earl says Madam Neller will suffer for her betrayal once this matter is over.'

'Good. I'll get Simon to bring you in some beer. I'll be back before dark.'

'All right.' He laughed. 'I think the boy believes I'm a soldier of fortune. He's always asking me what I do for Lord Cromwell, whether he sends me to battles.'

'He's sent us both to one this time. Don't let Simon bother you.'

'He's no trouble.' He looked at me. 'Good luck.'

I left the room and stood in the corridor. I felt relieved at Barak's ready acquiescence, but also guilty. Evidently he trusted me now; I doubted he would have let me go alone on such a mission a week before. I shuddered at the thought that in deceiving Barak, I was deceiving Cromwell too.

☩

THE STREETS WERE quiet in the late afternoon heat as I rode up to Smithfield. As I turned into the open area a cart passed, driven by an old man with a rag covering his face. I saw that it was full of ancient bones, ribcages and sharp pelvises and limb bones piled together in an unholy jumble, skulls peering out with their mocking grins. Rotten scraps of ancient winding sheets trailed through the bones and as the cart passed I caught the damp, sickly smell of the tomb. I knew many skeletons from the monastic graveyards were driven out to the Lambeth marshes and quietly dumped; these must be from Barty's. I hoped that I would be in time; Rich had said it would be a few days before they got to the hospital graveyard. As I spurred Genesis on across Smithfield, feeling a welcome breeze in my face, I noticed that though the Anabaptists might have recanted the stake stood already planted in the ground, the iron fetters hanging from it a grim reminder of its purpose.

A new watchman from Augmentations stood by the priory gatehouse, a keen young fellow who demanded to know my business. I cursed when I remembered Barak had Cromwell's seal, but my lawyer's robe and mention of the earl's name were enough to gain me entrance. I enquired after progress in excavating the graveyards. Looking surprised, the man said the work on the hospital graveyard had just begun. He called to another watchman, a lantern-jawed old fellow with a limp, to escort me there.

The old man led me through a maze of buildings, some destroyed and others awaiting conversion to residences, across Little Britain Street to the grounds behind the priory hospital. The high crenellated City wall loomed in the distance.

'Is the work far advanced?' I asked.

'They started yesterday,' he grunted. 'There's hundreds of graves to dig up. Filthy business – it's a known fact corpse odours can bring plague.'

'I saw a cart full of bones on my way.'

'The labourers have no respect for the dead. Reminds me of my time fighting in France, corpses everywhere given no proper burial.' He crossed himself.

I smiled sadly. 'My stable boy wants to be a soldier.'

'More fool him.' The old man lowered his voice as we turned a corner. 'It's round here. Watch these men, sir. They're a rough lot.'

The spectacle that met our eyes was like something from an old painting of the Last Judgement. A wide graveyard, sewn thickly with tombstones, was being dug up. The sun was starting to set behind the hospital, casting a fiery ochre light over the scene. The work was organized methodically: as each coffin was dug up two men carried it to a trestle table, where an Augmentations official in a long robe sat with a clerk. I watched as a coffin was opened under the clerk's eye; he rose and delved inside, then nodded. The workmen began removing the bones and piling them onto a waiting cart; the clerk took a small object and laid it before the official.

A little way off a meal break was in progress; a group of labourers were playing football with a skull, kicking it to and fro. As we watched a long kick sent it crashing against a gravestone, where it shattered into a hundred pieces. The labourers laughed. The old man shook his head and led me across to the official, who looked me over with a cold glance. He was a small, plump fellow with a pursed mouth and small sharp eyes, the very embodiment of an Augmentations man.

'Can I assist you, master lawyer?' he asked.

'I am on Lord Cromwell's business, sir. Have you charge of these proceedings?'

He hesitated. 'Yes, I am Paul Hoskyn of Augmentations.' He nodded at the old man. 'That will do, Hogge.'

'Matthew Shardlake, of Lincoln's Inn,' I said as the old man hobbled away, leaving me feeling strangely exposed. 'I am looking for a grave which I have reason to believe may contain something of interest to my master.'

Hoskyn's eyes narrowed. 'Everything of value is kept for Sir Richard to examine.'

'Yes, I know.' I bent to look at the items on the table. Gold rings and badges, little daggers and silver boxes, giving off that sickly whiff of death. 'It is not an item of value. Of interest only.'

He eyed me shrewdly. 'It must be important, for the earl to send you here. Does Sir Richard know?'

'No. The earl has sent for him on another matter. He is probably there now. In truth, it is only of antiquarian interest.'

'I never heard the earl had any interest in such things.'

'He does. And I am an antiquarian,' I added, adopting an earnest manner. I had thought this story up on the way. 'I recently found some stones set in the Ludgate that had Hebrew markings. They came from an old synagogue, you know. All ancient things interest me.'

The official grunted, his face still full of suspicion.

'We think this man buried here may have been a foreign Jew,' I went on eagerly, 'and had Jewish artefacts buried with him. Hebrew studies are of interest now the Old Testament is so widely read.'

'Have you any authority from the earl you can show me?'

'Only his name,' I replied, looking the fellow in the eye. He pursed his little mouth, then rose and led me across the brown grass of the graveyard. I looked at the gravestones; they were small, of cheap sandstone, the older ones indecipherable.

'I am looking for a gravestone from the middle of the last century. The name is St John.'

'That would be over by the wall. I don't want to go digging over there yet,' he added pettishly. 'It'll throw my work plan out of joint.'

'The earl wishes it.'

He looked among the gravestones, then stopped and pointed. 'Is that it?'

My heart thumped with excitement as I read the simple inscription. '*Alan St John, Soldier against the Turk, 1423–54.*' Only thirty-one when he died. I had not realized he had been so young.

'This is it,' I said quietly. 'Can I have two of your men?'

Hoskyn frowned. 'A Jew would not have been buried in consecrated ground. Nor have a Christian's name.'

'He would if he was a convert. There are records that this man was in the Domus.'

He shook his head, then crossed to the men who had been playing football. They gave me unfriendly looks. I knew those who laboured for Augmentations had an easy time of it, they would not like outsiders barging in with extra duties. Two of the men returned with Hoskyn, carrying shovels. He pointed at St John's grave.

'He wants that one opened up. Call me as soon as it's uncovered.' With that, Hoskyn went back to his table, where three more coffins were laid out.

The two labourers, large young fellows in stained smocks, began digging at the hard dry earth. 'What're we digging for?' one asked. 'A box of gold?'

'Nothing of value.'

'We're supposed to stop work at dusk.' He glanced at the blood-red sky. 'That's our contract.'

'Just the one grave,' I said, mollifying him. He grunted and bent to his task.

✝

ST JOHN HAD BEEN buried deep, the light was failing and redder than ever before the shovel struck wood. The men dug out the earth around the coffin, then stood beside it. It was a cheap thing of some dark wood. I was aware several other labourers had come over and were standing watching.

'Come, Samuel,' one said. 'It's past time to go. It's nearly dark.'

'There's no need to take the coffin out,' I said. 'Just open it there, if you'll help me down.'

The other labourer helped me into the grave, then clambered out himself and called to Hoskyn that they were done. I watched as the man Samuel worked at the coffin lid with his spade. It came open with a crack. He slid it off, then stepped back with a gasp. 'God's wounds, what's that stink?'

I felt the hairs rise on the back of my neck. It was the same harsh smell that had wafted up the stairs of Madam Gristwood's house the night before.

I bent slowly and looked into the coffin. In the red light of sunset St John's remains looked strangely peaceful. His skeleton lay on its back, arms crossed. His skull was turned to one side, as though sleeping, the jaws closed rather than grinning open, a few brown hairs still clinging to it. The winding sheet had rotted away, there were only a few mouldy scraps of cloth in the bottom of the coffin. And among them, a little pewter jar, the size of a man's hand. There was a crack at the top, but when I bent and lifted it gently I could feel it was almost full. I was right, I thought. I have found it.

'What's that?' Samuel asked. He sounded disappointed, no doubt he had been hoping for the glint of gold after all. 'Here,' he called to his fellows. 'Bring a torch. We can hardly see here!'

I turned to see a man brandishing a flaming torch at the edge of the grave, about to hand it down. 'No!' I shouted. 'No fire, whatever you do!'

'Why not?' Samuel asked, frowning.

'It's witchcraft,' someone else said. 'That's some Christ-killing Jew down there.' Samuel crossed himself and there was a murmur among the crowd. I clambered back out, holding the jar carefully. No one leant over to help me and I had to balance on the coffin and heave myself up with one hand. I stood on the edge of the grave, breathing heavily. I looked for Hoskyn, but he had left his table and was nowhere to be seen. About ten labourers stood around me, their faces hostile and frightened, a couple carrying torches. 'Damned hunch-back,' someone muttered.

Then everyone turned at the sound of footsteps, and the men bowed and fell back like wheat before a gale as the frowning figure of Sir Richard Rich, in feathered cap and a yellow silk robe, stepped into the centre of the group, Hoskyn at his elbow.

'You men,' he called sharply, 'leave now. All of you.' The labourers melted away like smoke, Samuel clambering rapidly out of the grave and following them. Left alone with Rich and Hoskyn, I slid the hand with the little jar behind my back. Rich looked into the grave. His cold eyes passed over St John's remains, then he turned back to me.

'Jesu, what a stink. Christ's blood, Master Shardlake, it seems you cannot stay away from Barty's. First you're in my garden among the washing and now you're digging up graves looking for trinkets.'

I took a deep breath. 'I am here on Lord Cromwell's authority—'

He waved a hand dismissively. 'Hoskyn told me. Sounds like a cock-and-bull story to me. The earl doesn't collect monastic relics, he burns them.'

'It was not a relic I was seeking, sir. I – I thought Lord Cromwell had asked you to attend him—'

'I've heard nothing of it, I've been out on audit all day.' Rich frowned. 'You are a hard man to get rid of, Shardlake.' He nodded at the grave. 'If I find this is some frolic of your own, I'll put you in there to add to the smell.' He turned, frowning, as a servant ran up to him. Rich looked at him irritably.

'Sir Richard,' the man gasped, 'an urgent message. From Lord Cromwell. His man has been trying to find you all day. He wishes to see you at once at Whitehall.'

Rich gave me a startled look. He set his lips, then nodded to the steward. 'Make my horse ready.' He turned back to me. 'You are becoming a nuisance, Shardlake,' he said. His voice was low, but furious. 'A serious nuisance. I do not tolerate nuisances. Be warned.' With that he turned and stalked away, Hoskyn waddling after him. I clutched the jar hard. Then, my legs shaking like jelly, I walked quickly out of the graveyard.

# Chapter Thirty-five

I SAT IN MY BEDROOM, staring down at the jar of Greek Fire on my table. I had brought a plate from the kitchen and poured a little onto it; the brownish-black viscous liquid lay there, glistening like a toad's skin. I pulled the table over to the open window to dispel the acrid tang of the stuff. I left the candle on the other side of the room for safety, though that meant there was insufficient light to examine it further. In truth, I was afraid of it. Tomorrow, I had decided, I would take it to Guy.

A knock at the door made me jump. Wincing at a spasm from my back, I hastily covered the jar and plate with a cloth, calling, 'Wait a moment!'

'It's me,' Barak replied through the door. 'Can I come in?'

'I – I'm getting dressed. Wait in your room, I'll come to you.'

To my relief I heard retreating footsteps. I sniffed the air, but the smell was faint and could not have reached him through the door. Leaving the window open, I slipped out of the room, locking it behind me.

Barak had been asleep when I had returned from St Bartholomew's half an hour before and I had left him. As I knocked at his door I recalled that in the conflicts that had raged around reformers over which of apparently conflicting biblical passages one should follow, I had ever preferred, 'Obey God rather than man,' over 'Let every man be subject to the governing authorities.' I knew I would have to lie to Barak now, and did not relish it, but I felt in my heart that taking the Greek Fire to Guy was the right course. I shuddered at the thought that if the servant had not arrived when he did, Rich might have had it. Although he might have plenty already, for all I knew.

Barak was sitting on the bed in his shirt, mournfully examining a pair of dusty netherstocks. He put his finger through a hole. 'Hard riding's done for these,' he said.

'I'm sure Lord Cromwell will pay for more.' The room was a mess, dirty clothes and greasy plates strewn over the floor and the table. I remembered my former assistant Mark, who had once had this room, how tidy he had kept it.

Barak crumpled the torn stocks into a ball and threw them into a corner.

'Any luck at Barty's?'

'No. We dug up the grave but there was nothing in it, only St John's skeleton. Rich was there. He came up and demanded to know my business.'

'Shit. What did you tell the arsehole?'

'I thought there might be trouble, but the summons from Cromwell arrived just then and he went off in a hurry.'

Barak sighed. 'Another trail gone cold. We must see what the earl gets out of Rich. He'll send a message once he's talked to him.'

'And Marchamount is back tomorrow. I'll go into chambers and see him.'

Barak nodded, then looked up at me. 'Are you up to trying the well again tonight? There won't be a message from the earl for hours, perhaps not till tomorrow morning. My shoulder's much better.'

I was far from up to it, I ached with tiredness from head to toe and my arm hurt. But I had promised, and after all it was for Elizabeth that I had agreed to do everything else in the first place. I nodded wearily. 'Let me just get some food, then we will go.'

'Good idea. I'm hungry too.' Barak, evidently restored by his rest, leaped from the bed and led the way downstairs. I followed, guilt at my deception of him gnawing at me.

Joan had prepared a pottage for us, which she brought to the parlour.

Barak scratched at his near-bald pate. 'Shit, this itches, damn it.

I'll have to wear a cap when I go out from now on, I hate the way people stare at me, my head bald as a bird's arse like some old dotard—'

He was interrupted by a loud knock at the front door. 'That'll be the message,' he said, rising. 'That was quick.'

But it was Joseph Wentworth that Joan showed into the parlour a moment later. He looked exhausted, his clothes were dusty and his hair glinted with sweat. Haggard eyes stared from a dirty face.

'Joseph,' I said. 'What has happened?'

'I've come from Newgate,' he said. 'She's dying, sir. Elizabeth is dying.' And then the big man burst into tears, covering his face with his hands.

I made him sit down and tried to calm him. He wiped his face with a dirty rag of handkerchief, the same one he had brought the day he first came to the house, which Elizabeth had embroidered. He looked up at me, helpless and distraught, his earlier anger at my lack of progress apparently forgotten.

'What has happened?' I asked again gently.

'These last two days Elizabeth has had another cellmate. A child, a mad beggar girl who has been running round the wards accusing all she meets of abducting her little brother. She made trouble at a baker's shop in Cheapside—'

'We saw her the other day—'

'The baker complained. She was picked up by the constable and taken to the Hole. Elizabeth wouldn't talk to her, any more than she would to the old woman who was hanged—' He paused.

'She went wild when the old woman was taken out, though. Has that happened again?'

Joseph shook his head wearily. 'No. When I went to visit Lizzy this morning the turnkey told me the child had been examined by a doctor and removed to the Bedlam. He reckoned her mad. But he said when he went to take them food last night, he heard Lizzy and the girl talking. He couldn't hear what they were saying but he remarked it; it was the first time he had heard Elizabeth speak, and the girl had been sullen and quiet too since she was put in the Hole.'

'What was her name?'

'Sarah, I believe. She and her brother were orphans, kicked out of St Helen's foundling hospital when the nunnery closed.' He sighed. 'This morning Elizabeth just sat, hollow-eyed, would not even look at me or at the food I had brought, though her last meal was lying there untouched. Then when I went this evening—' He broke off and put his head in his hands again.

'Joseph,' I said, 'I was hoping to have some news for you tomorrow. I know you feared I had forgotten you—'

He looked up at me. 'You're all I have, Master Shardlake. You were my only hope. But now I fear it's too late. This evening Lizzy was lying insensible on the straw, her face burning hot to the touch. She has gaol fever, sir.'

Barak and I exchanged glances. Outbreaks of fever were common in gaols, blamed on the foul humours released by the stinking straw. Whole prisons had sometimes died of it, and it had been known to penetrate the Old Bailey, felling witnesses and even judges. If Elizabeth had it, her chances were slim.

'The turnkeys won't go near her,' Joseph said. 'I said I'd pay to have her put somewhere better, get a physician. Though God knows how, I hear my crops are ruined by the heat.' A note of hysteria entered his voice.

I rose wearily. 'Then I shall have to take a hand. I have assumed a responsibility for Elizabeth and it is time I met it. I'll come to the gaol. I know they have good rooms for those who can pay. And I know an apothecary who can cure her if anyone can.'

'She needs a physician.'

'This man is a physician, though as a foreigner he is not allowed to practise here.'

'But the cost—'

'I'll deal with that – you can repay me later. God knows,' I muttered, 'at least this is something clean and clear to do.'

'I'll come if you like,' Barak said.

'You will?' Joseph looked at him, staring a little as he noticed his shaven head for the first time.

'Thank you, Barak. Then come, I will get Simon to run to Guy with a note, ask him to come to Newgate.' I stood up. From somewhere, God knew where, I had found a last reserve of energy. Joseph might have thought me self-sacrificing, but I felt that if Elizabeth died now before our time was up, after all my decision to act for her had led me into, the irony would be so dark as to be beyond bearing.

✝

THE GAOL LOOKED DARK and sinister at night, its towers a grim outline against the starry sky. The gaoler was sleepy, angry at being woken until I pressed a shilling into his hand. He summoned the fat turnkey. The man's face fell when the gaoler told him to take us to the Hole and he led us below ground without his usual brutal badinage. Quickly unlocking the door, he retreated fast and stood against the opposite wall.

The stink of urine and bad food that hit us in the hot cell was appalling: it stung the throat and brought tears to the eyes. We held our sleeves to our noses as we went in. Elizabeth lay insensible on the straw, her limbs askew. Even unconscious her face was troubled, the eyes working beneath the closed lids in some fevered dream. Her colour was high, her obscenely bald head shining bright pink. I put my hand to her brow. Joseph was right – she was burning. I motioned the others to go back outside and went over to the turnkey. 'Listen,' I said, 'I know you have comfortable rooms upstairs.'

'Only for those that can pay.'

'We'll pay,' I said. 'Take me back to the gaoler.'

The turnkey locked the door again and, motioning the others to remain behind, I followed him back up to the gaoler's room, a comfortable chamber with a feather bed and a wall hanging. The gaoler was sitting at his table, a worried look on his hard features.

'Is she dead yet, Williams?' he asked.

'No, master.'

'Listen,' I said. 'We want to get her out of these foul airs. I'll pay for a good room.'

The gaoler shook his head. 'Moving her will only spread the humours of her fever round the gaol. And the judge's order was she was to stay in the Hole.'

'I'll answer to Forbizer. I have an apothecary who may be able to help her. He might be able to cure her fever. Then it won't spread, eh?'

He still looked doubtful. 'Who's to carry her up there? I'm not going near, and nor are my men.'

I hesitated a moment, then said, 'We will. There must be some back stairs we could use.'

He pursed his lips. 'Two shillings a night's the price. I'll show you where to take her.' Even in his terror of gaol fever the man's greed glinted in his sharp eyes.

'Agreed,' I said, though the price was outrageous. I reached for my purse and held up a gold half angel. 'For five nights. That'll cover her till she goes before Forbizer.'

That seemed to decide the wretch. He nodded, holding out his hand for the coin.

✝

IT WAS A NIGHTMARE climb, up four floors from the Hole to the tower room my half angel had bought. The gaoler walked well ahead with a candle while Barak and Joseph carried the unconscious Elizabeth between them. I clambered up behind as they half-dragged, half-carried the poor girl up the stone steps, the outlines of Elizabeth's and Barak's two shaven heads making weird shadows on the walls. A vile smell came from poor Elizabeth's unwashed, feverish body. As I climbed painfully upwards, I realized my strength was ebbing again – I could not possibly make it to the well that night.

We were shown into a light, airy room with a good bed with a blanket, a ewer of water on a table and a large window which though barred was at least open; a gentleman prisoner's room. Joseph and Barak laid Elizabeth on the bed. She seemed unaware of her removal, only stirring slightly and moaning, Then she muttered a name. 'Sarah,' she muttered. 'Oh, Sarah.'

Joseph bit his lip. 'The girl who went to Bedlam,' he whispered.

I nodded. 'Maybe if she recovers she will speak at last, tell us why the girl upset her so. Tell us everything she has chosen to keep to herself while we are distracted with worry,' I added with sudden bitterness.

Joseph looked at me, then said softly, 'I become angered with her too.'

I sighed. 'My apothecary should be here soon.'

'You are generous, sir,' Joseph said. 'How much—'

I raised a hand. 'No, Joseph, we can discuss that later. Barak, you look exhausted. You should go home.'

'I can stay,' he said. 'I'd like to see whether the Old Moor can help her.'

It was strange, even touching, to see how absorbed he had become in Elizabeth's fate. Yet I did not want him here when Guy came; I had secreted the pewter jar of Greek Fire in a pocket of my robe. 'No, go,' I said sharply. 'I don't want you risking gaol fever, I need you fit.'

He nodded reluctantly and went out. I clutched at the jar of Greek Fire as Joseph and I stood in silence, listening to Elizabeth's fevered breathing.

✝

GUY ARRIVED an hour later. The gaoler himself fetched him up, goggling at his brown face till I bade him sharply to be gone. I introduced Guy to Joseph, who likewise stared at him in surprise, although Guy affected not to notice.

'So this is the poor girl whose travails have worried you so,' he said to me.

'Yes.' I told him of the onset of her fever. He looked at her for a long moment.

'I don't think it's gaol fever,' he said at length. 'The fever would be higher. I'm not sure what it is. It would help to see her urine. Does she have a pisspot?'

'She was left to piss on the straw in the Hole.'

He shook his head. 'Then I will give her something to try and stop her burning up, and it would be good if she were to be washed and that filthy dress taken off her.'

Joseph blushed. 'Sir, it would hardly be proper for me to see her unclothed—'

'I will do it, if you like. In my trade a naked body is hardly a new sight. Could you buy her a shift tomorrow and bring it here?'

'Yes. Yes, I will.'

As we watched Elizabeth stirred and made a little moan, then lay back again. Guy shook his head. 'What pain and anger there are in that face, even while her mind sleeps.'

'Is there any hope, sir?' Joseph asked.

'I do not know,' Guy said frankly. 'This may be one of those cases where much depends on the sufferer's will to live.'

'Then she will surely die,' he said.

'Come, we do not know that.' Guy smiled gently. 'And now, if you will leave me, I will wash her.'

Joseph and I waited outside while Guy carried out his task. 'I cannot help being angered, sir,' he said. 'But I love her; for all she has put me through I still love her.'

I touched his shoulder. 'That is very plain, Joseph.'

At length Guy called us back. He had laid Elizabeth under the blanket and lit some sort of oil in a lamp, which made a sweet smell in the room. A cloth, black with dirt, floated in the ewer. Elizabeth's face was clean, the first time I had seen it so.

'She is pretty,' I said. 'How sad she should come to this.'

'Sad whether she is pretty or ugly,' Guy said.

'What is that smell?' Joseph asked.

'An infusion of lemons.' Guy smiled. 'Sometimes when a soul is in pain a foul or cruel environment can drive it deeper into darkness. Thus light and cleanliness and soft airs may help lift her spirit, perhaps even reach it while she lies unconscious.' He shrugged self-deprecatingly. 'So I think, at least.' He looked at us. 'You both look exhausted. You should sleep. I will stay with her till morning if you wish.'

'I could not ask that—' Joseph protested.

'Please, I would be happy to.'

'I would stay a little too,' I said. 'I have something else I wish to discuss with you.'

Joseph left, with fulsome thanks, his weary footsteps clattering down the stairs.

'Thank you for this, Guy.' I said.

'It is all right. I confess I am intrigued. This is a strange condition.'

'I have something even more intriguing,' I said. I reached into my pocket and took out the cloth with the pewter jar in it. 'This, I believe, is Greek Fire. No one else knows I have it.' I unwrapped the jar and laid it on the table, first putting the oil lamp on the floor. 'Don't bring the candle near, Guy. I fear it may take light.'

He examined the stuff as best he could in the weak light, rubbing the dark liquid between his fingers, sniffing it with a look of distaste. 'So this is it,' he said. 'Dark Fire.' I had never seen his face more serious.

'Ay. I wondered how fire could be dark; I see now they meant the liquid was black.'

'Perhaps they also meant the darkness it could bring to men's lives.'

'Perhaps. They called it the devil's tears as well in the old books.' I told him how I had found it at Smithfield, how narrowly it had escaped Rich's clutches. 'Take it. Will you examine it tomorrow?'

'On the terms I gave you. I will do nothing to help Cromwell use it.'

'Agreed.'

He shook his head. 'You would be in serious trouble, Matthew, if he were to find you had given this to me instead of to him.'

I smiled nervously. 'Then we must be sure he does not find out.' I shook my head. 'Yet I cannot help thinking – ' I hesitated – 'Crom-well has done many evil things. But at least he has a vision of a Christian commonwealth, while Norfolk would take England back to superstition and darkness.'

'A Christian commonwealth? Is such a thing even possible in this fallen world? Surely the annals of the last thousand years show it is not. That is why many like me chose to escape to the cloister before that was forbidden.'

'Yes, the old Church always believed the sinful world was heading towards a final cataclysm; nothing man did could make any difference. And that excused much oppression.'

'You would need fierce measures to make a perfect commonwealth. If you were to end poverty and beggary you'd need to squeeze their wealth from the rich, for example.'

'Sometimes I think that would be a good thing.'

'Now you sound like an Anabaptist.'

I laughed. 'No, just a puzzled old lawyer.'

He looked at me seriously. 'But ending social injustice is not Cromwell's first priority, you know that. What matters to him is the Protestant faith and he would use Greek Fire to cut a terrible swathe to achieve that if he could.'

I nodded sadly. 'Yes, you are right. He cannot be trusted with it. No one can.'

Guy looked relieved. 'Thank Christ you see that.' He looked at the pewter pot, then carefully put it in his pocket. 'I will let you know as soon as I have something to tell you.'

'Thank you. Tomorrow if you can – there are only five days now till the demonstration before the king.' I sighed. 'On the day Elizabeth goes back to court.'

As though in response to her name Elizabeth stirred, her legs moving beneath the blanket. We turned to her. 'Sarah,' she muttered again, then, 'that evil boy. The evil boy.' And then her eyes fluttered open and she looked at us uncomprehendingly.

Guy leant over her. 'Miss Wentworth, you are in a clean room in the prison. You have a fever. I am Guy Malton, an apothecary. Your good uncle and Master Shardlake had you brought here.'

I leant over her. Her eyes were heavy with fever but she seemed fully conscious. Knowing this was a chance that might never come again, I said slowly, 'We are still trying to find the truth, Elizabeth. We are trying to save you. I know there is something in the well at your uncle's house—'

She seemed to shrink back. 'The death of God,' she whispered. 'The death of God.'

'What?' I asked, but her eyes closed again. I made to shake her but Guy held my arm.

'Do not distress her further.'

'But – what did she mean? The death of God? God's death is a common curse, but—'

He looked at me seriously. 'The death of God is despair. When I was a monk sometimes one of my brethren would lose his faith, succumb to despair. Usually they came back to faith, but until they did – ' he shook his head – 'it felt as though God was dead.'

'The well,' Elizabeth muttered. 'The well.' And then she fell back to her pillows, sinking once more into unconsciousness.

# Chapter Thirty-six

I LEFT SOON AFTER. I was so exhausted that the short ride home through the darkness felt as though it lasted for ever, and once I had to pinch myself to stop myself from falling asleep in the saddle. I wondered whether Guy would be able to fathom how Greek Fire was made up. So many had died to keep that secret.

When I arrived home it was past two in the morning and Barak had already gone to his room. I hauled myself upstairs and fell fully clothed onto the bed. I fell asleep at once, but found myself troubled by a nightmare. I dreamed I was back in Forbizer's court, sitting watching as the judge coldly sentenced a succession of prisoners to death. Yet their faces were those of people already dead: Sepultus and Michael Gristwood, Bathsheba and her brother, the watchman and a strange man in a leather apron whom I knew must be the founder. All their faces were sad, yet whole, not shattered and bloodied as I had seen them. In my dream I took the pewter jar of Greek Fire from my robe, lifted it and let it fall on the floor. At once a roaring tide of flame shot from it, engulfing everyone: prisoners, spectators, judge. I saw Forbizer raise his arms with a scream as his beard flared and crackled. I sat in the centre of the flames, untouched for a moment, but then the fire seemed to gather itself and rushed at me, engulfing me. I felt its searing heat on my face and screamed, then jolted awake to the bright light of morning, the sun hot on my face and the bells of London's hundred churches clamouring in the distance, calling the City to prayer. It was Sunday, the sixth of June.

I was stiff and aching, and as I dressed slowly I told myself that when this matter was done I would leave London. It seemed my clients had had enough of me, and I had just enough money for a quiet life in the countryside if I was careful. Still frightened by my dream, I stumbled downstairs to find Barak sitting at the parlour table, staring gloomily at a letter.

'From Cromwell?' I asked, taking a seat.

'Ay. It's from Hampton Court, he must be there on some business for the king. You might as well see it.' He tossed the sheet of paper over to me. It was in Cromwell's own hand.

*I have spoken to Rich. You have both been worrying at the wrong hare, his schemes with that churl Bealknap have nothing to do with Greek Fire. Continue your investigations, for what they are worth, and I will see you at Whitehall tomorrow, when I return to London.*

I laid the letter on the table. 'He's not pleased with us.'

'No. What in God's name were Bealknap and Rich up to?'

'Jesu knows. We will find out tomorrow. Today there is Marchamount to deal with.'

'We'd better get on. I left you to sleep, or I thought you'd be fit for nothing, but half the morning's gone. We've only four days left.'

'D'you think I've forgotten that?' I snapped, then raised a hand. 'We do no good sniping at each other, I've told you before.'

'No.' He scratched his stubbly head. 'The tone of that letter worries me, that's all.'

I ate a hasty breakfast and then we walked along the dusty lane to the Inn. Looking at the cloudless sky, I thought of Joseph and his ruined crops. Wheat would be scarce and there would be hunger by autumn.

'Elizabeth had a moment of consciousness last night,' I said. 'I mentioned the well again and she said, "Death of God". Guy said it means she's in despair. And she said something about the girl and "that evil boy".'

'Her young cousin or the mad girl's brother?'

'I don't know.' I looked at him. 'But we must go to the well again tonight. We must delay no more.'

He nodded. 'I want to see the truth of this too. That poor creature reminds me of when I was in the gutter, consumed with fury at my mother for marrying that confederate of Bealknap's.' He laughed bitterly. 'I may end up back in the gutter if I lose the earl's favour.'

'There's still time,' I said.

I hoped Marchamount would be in. I hoped desperately that, whatever secret Lady Honor was still keeping, it was not incriminating. As we entered the courtyard I saw the service had ended in the chapel and the lawyers were filing out. I saw Marchamount among the throng, walking back to his chambers, his robe billowing around his portly form.

'All right if I come with you?' Barak asked.

I hesitated. What if Marchamount told me something that led the way to the Gristwoods' stock of Greek Fire? But I could not exclude Barak again. I nodded, wondering whether Guy was even now examining that dreadful stuff.

We caught up with Marchamount at the door to his chambers. He looked round in surprise.

'Brother Shardlake, this is an unexpected meeting.' He smiled, that little flash of white teeth. 'What happened to you on Friday? Had you no stomach for the bear-baiting?'

'Lady Honor did not feel like attending,' I said briskly. 'I went for a walk with her.'

He stared at Barak. 'Who is this?'

'An agent of Lord Cromwell's. He is helping me on the Greek Fire matter.'

Barak took off his cap and made a little bow. Marchamount's eyes widened at his bald head, then he frowned in exasperation. 'I have told you all I know. How many times—'

'As many times as I see fit, Serjeant.' I had decided bluntness was the best way. 'May we come in?'

He set his lips but permitted us to follow him to his private room. There he sat in his thronelike chair and gave us a haughty stare. I leaned forward.

375

'In the boat going to Southwark, Serjeant, we spoke of a certain pressure his grace the Duke of Norfolk was putting on you, to obtain something from Lady Honor. You confirmed he wanted to obtain some of the Vaughan lands in return for furthering young Henry Vaughan to a place at the king's court.'

Marchamount sat very still. I knew at once I had struck a nerve.

'I thought you seemed evasive in the boat, so I asked Lady Honor about the matter on our walk—'

'Sir, you had no right. For a gentleman to ask—'

'Lady Honor told me the matter began with pressure from the duke over the land, but then it developed into something else. She refused to say more, but I need to know what it was.'

He smiled shrewdly. 'So you come to me, as an alternative to Cromwell putting pressure on her?'

'Never mind why. I want the whole story, Marchamount. No bluster, no evasions, just the story.'

He sat back in his chair. 'It is nothing to do with Greek Fire.'

'Then why it is so secret?'

'Because it is shameful.' He frowned, reddening. 'I had an interest in Lady Honor, a romantic interest. You know that.' He took a deep breath. 'She would not have me and I would not press a lady who rejected me.' He fingered his emerald ring, then looked me in the eye. 'But the duke would.'

'The *duke*?'

He frowned. 'He does not just want her family lands in return for helping that boy. He wants Lady Honor as his mistress.'

'But, dear God, he's in his sixties.'

Marchamount shrugged. 'In some men the sap still runs into old age. The duke is one, though you would not think it to look at him. He would not approach her directly' – he laughed bitterly – 'he's too proud for that. He made me act as intermediary.'

'Poor Lady Honor.'

Marchamount shifted uncomfortably. 'It was a job I disliked, sir, but I could not gainsay the Duke of Norfolk. He said the

Vaughan boy's a fool and a weakling, which is true enough, and he'd have to exert a mighty effort to get him accepted at court. He wanted a high price in return. Lady Honor knows his reputation for cruel ways with women; she's refused him time and again. But he's one of those that is only excited further by refusal.' He shifted uneasily again. 'I have had to try and persuade her. I told you, the duke is not one to be gainsaid.'

'What has Norfolk promised you in return? Help towards a knighthood perhaps?'

Marchamount set his lips. 'I want something for my family's future too. To advance one's family, that is no dishonourable thing.'

'Thirty pieces of silver would be the right reward for what you have done,' I said. Barak laughed harshly and Marchamount gave him a furious look. He glared at me, his face reddening further.

'How dare you talk to me like that! And you – you are no impartial witness. You lust after her yourself.'

'Come, Serjeant, you are losing control of yourself. So that is the whole story, is it?' I asked. 'No connection at all to Greek Fire? That is what I need to know, Marchamount.'

'I have told you before, I know nothing of that. Nothing.'

'Are you quite sure?'

The merest hesitation. 'Of course.' He ran a hand through his red hair, then began to bluster. 'You have troubled me enough with this. No gentleman—'

I stood. 'Come, Barak. I think I have an apology to make to Lady Honor.' Barak got up and made another bow to Marchamount, a mocking, exaggerated one.

The serjeant glared at me. 'You have embarrassed me, Shardlake, in front of this churl,' he said. 'I will not forget it.'

✞

OUTSIDE IN THE courtyard, I turned to Barak. 'He's still keeping something back – I'd swear he is. But what? I'll have to talk to Lady Honor.'

'She won't be pleased you know this story. Nor at being questioned further.'

'There's no help for it. She knows my position. I'll go there now.'

'I suppose there's nothing else we can we do today. But—'

'What?' I asked impatiently.

'You should have squeezed what else he's hiding out of him. You shy at every fence,' he said in sudden irritation.

I glared at him. 'I do not shy. If I feel someone will say no more, and I've no evidence to use as a lever, I go and find the evidence. That's what I've always done and it's what I'm going to do now with Lady Honor.'

He grunted.

'What else could I do?' I raised my voice in exasperation. 'I pushed him as far as he'd go, how could I make him tell me more? How? Eh?'

'Threaten him with the earl, as you did with Bealknap.'

'And look where that led. No, I will leave him to stew in his own juice, see if Lady Honor can tell me more, then come back later. Unless you've a better idea.'

He shrugged. 'No. I haven't.'

'I'm going into chambers for a minute.'

I entered the office to find Skelly working by the light of a candle he hardly needed in the full daylight. 'Here again on Sunday, John?' I asked, hiding my irritation.

He gave me a shifty look. 'I'm behind, sir.'

I could not face looking over his scribbles. I turned to Godfrey's door. 'Master Wheelwright in?'

'Yes, sir.'

Godfrey was working quietly at his desk. 'Here on the Sabbath?' I asked. He looked at me seriously.

'God will forgive me. I want to get my cases in order. Word is I am to be disbarred if I don't apologize to the duke.' He smiled wryly. 'That will create a mighty furore. Perhaps it will make our brothers consider who it is we lawyers serve, God and the commonwealth or the Duke of Norfolk.'

'Many will ease their consciences by saying it was a matter of discourtesy, Godfrey, not religion.'

'Then they deceive themselves.'

'What will you do if you leave chambers?'

'Become a preacher.' He smiled. 'I believe that is what God is calling me to do.'

'Dangerous times may be coming.' If Cromwell falls, I thought. If I fail. If he doesn't get Greek Fire. The hideous tangle of loyalties I was caught in made me feel faint for a moment and I clutched at the edge of a chair.

'Are you all right, Matthew?'

I nodded. 'I have been working hard.'

'At least no more of your cases have gone,' he said.

'Good.' I decided to make one last attempt to make him see reason. 'Godfrey, would it not be a dreadful thing to throw over your position, the talent you have used these many years?' And yet, I thought even as I spoke the words, was that not what I too had been thinking of doing?

'Sometimes God calls us to a new life.'

'And to great tribulations.' I gave up. 'I may not be in for a few days now.'

I stepped back into the office, where Barak was talking to Skelly in a low voice. Getting gossip about me, I supposed. 'I'm going to Lady Honor's,' I said.

'I'll ride with you,' he said. 'Then I can call in at the Old Barge.'

We walked back down Chancery Lane in silence. I cursed inwardly. I had hoped Barak would leave me to go to Lady Honor's alone, for afterwards I planned to go to Guy's. But he seemed to be sticking to me today.

# Chapter Thirty-seven

WE FETCHED THE HORSES and rode down to the City. Barak was still morose, saying little. As we rode under the Ludgate I noticed a patch of lighter colour in the wall where the repairs had been completed.

'The stones from the old synagogue came from there,' I said to make conversation.

Barak grunted. 'I bet the watchman had some ripe comments about Christ killers ready when you said they came from a synagogue.'

'I don't remember,' I said, though I well recalled that he had.

We rode on past St Paul's, the huge spire casting a welcome patch of shade. As we came into the sun again, Barak pulled his horse in close. 'Look round slowly,' he said. 'Don't stop the horse. By the bookstalls near St Paul's Cross.'

I turned and saw Toky leaning against a rail, ignoring the crowds and scanning the passers-by with that pale ravaged face of his.

'I thought he'd disappeared,' I said. 'Could we not try to apprehend him? Or call the constable?'

'If Toky's there, Wright's nearby and they'll be armed. I don't fancy a tussle with the two of them, and some old constable wouldn't last long.'

'They know a great deal. Their capture could solve many of our problems.'

'That's why Lord Cromwell's men are looking for them all over town. The yard's a good place to see who's coming in and out of the City. I wonder who he's looking out for.'

'Us probably.'

'Well, he missed us. I know who's dealing with it for the earl — I'll send word to them.' He shook his head, half-admiringly. 'They're as smart a pair of rogues as I've ever seen, the way they dodge about the City.'

'They swim in its filthy waters, hidden by its blackness.'

'You sounded like your evangelist friend Godfrey, then.' He rode on into the crowds of Cheapside and I followed, keeping a wary eye out even though Toky was far behind us.

✝

WE PARTED COMPANY at the Walbrook. Barak went off to send a message to Cromwell, saying to my dismay that he would call to collect me in an hour at Lady Honor's. We should stay together, he said, if Toky was about. I could think of no objection, though that meant I could not go to Guy's. Barak rode off and I went on to Blue Lion Street.

At the House of Glass a couple of servants were washing the windows with vinegar. Informed that Lady Honor was at home, I passed Genesis to a stable boy and was ushered through the house to the inner courtyard. A servant was watering the plants set in pots round the walls. Lady Honor sat on a bench watching him. She wore a blue dress and her blonde hair was uncovered today, tied in a bun with a silk ribbon. She smiled in welcome.

'Matthew. This is an unexpected visit.'

I bowed. 'I apologize for coming unannounced. But—'

'Official business?'

'I fear so.'

She took a deep breath. 'Come then, sit with me. Edward, that will do for now. Finish the watering this evening.' The man bowed and left us. Lady Honor looked over her courtyard. 'I fear my little bushes are dying in the heat. See there, I have been trying to grow pomegranates, but my foolish servants know nothing about the care of plants, they water them at the wrong times, too much or too little.'

'Everything is dying in this fierce weather. The crops will be bad.'

'Will they?' she asked indifferently. 'But you have not come to talk of planting, I think.'

'No. Lady Honor, I have a confession.' I cursed my awkwardness. I should not be apologizing for questioning her, it was my duty. 'I know about the Duke of Norfolk's pursuit of you,' I said bluntly. 'I needed to follow up the question you left me with on the river bank. I spoke to Marchamount.'

I half-expected anger but she only turned away and stared ahead for a moment. When she turned back to me her face wore a tired smile. 'After we spoke on the river I feared you would report me to Cromwell and I should be in trouble. Did you ask Marchamount first to save me from the earl's rough ways?'

'Perhaps.'

'You are gentle with me, more than I deserve. I felt that if the duke's insulting demands were forced out of me by Cromwell, my honour would be less besmirched. A foolish notion, perhaps.'

'I am sorry I could not save you from my knowing.'

'At least you will not gossip like most would.' She looked at me seriously. 'Will you? It is a tasty morsel, I realize.'

'You know I think too much of you for that, Lady Honor.'

She laid a hand on mine for a second, then lifted it, although I had the odd sensation it was still there. 'You are a natural gentleman.' She sighed. 'I have sent Henry back to the country. He could never make his way at court. So I have been able to reject the crude advances of that old brute with a clear conscience.'

'I did not realize you disliked the duke so.'

'He is unfit for the position he occupies. He may be the senior peer of the realm, but his lineage is not old, you know.' She smiled. 'Unlike the Vaughans.'

I took a deep breath. 'Lady Honor, I must ask – for the last time, I promise – is there anything you have not told me that could be of any possible relevance, however remote, to my search for the Grist-woods' murderers?'

She looked at me impatiently. 'Matthew, I swore that already on the Bible. If you recall, I made oath the duke had put no pressure on me about Greek Fire. And I swore true. He has never mentioned it to me and Marchamount did so only to warn me against you. As I have said, I wish my foolish curiosity had never led me to look at those papers.'

I looked into her eyes. 'I felt when Marchamount spoke about the duke and you this morning he was still keeping something back.'

She smiled again. 'If he did, it is nothing to do with me, I swear. Shall I fetch the Bible again?'

I shook my head. 'No. That is not necessary. Forgive me.'

She looked at me indulgently. 'By Our Lady, you are a courteous inquisitor.'

'Marchamount would not agree.'

'That puffed-up creature.' She looked over her wilting plants again. 'He is a rogue despite his smoothness and he would do anything to advance himself.' She gave a shudder. 'I told you I am thinking of escaping to the country, to my Lincolnshire estates. I have had enough of the City, of Marchamount and the duke and everyone.' She smiled quickly. 'Almost everyone.'

'I would miss you. Though I have also been thinking of taking a quiet house in the country.'

She looked at me in surprise. 'Would not the country bore you?'

'I come from Lichfield – my father has the freehold of a farm there. Though he is old now, even his steward is not getting any younger. The farm is hard for them to manage.' I smiled sadly. 'But I have never been fitted to be a farmer, nor wanted to be one.'

'But he would like to have his son by him in his old age?'

'I don't know.' I shrugged. 'I always felt he was ashamed of me. Yet he seems pleased to see me when I visit, which I do not do enough.'

She was silent a moment, then asked quietly, 'The Wentworth girl comes back before the judge this week, does she not?'

'On Thursday the tenth. She is very ill and may not last till then.'

'Poor Matthew. How you take the sufferings of others on yourself.' She laid her hand on mine again and this time did not move it. I turned to her and she inclined her head towards me. Then she jerked away as footsteps sounded in the yard. I turned to see Barak standing with the steward, cap in hand. The steward's face was impassive but Barak was grinning broadly.

'Come at a bad time, have I?' he asked.

Lady Honor stood, her face dark with anger. 'Matthew, do you know this fellow?'

I rose too. 'This is Jack Barak,' I said hastily. 'He is assisting me. He works for Lord Cromwell.'

'Then the earl should teach him some manners.' She rounded on him. 'How dare you burst in on us like this? Do you not know how to comport yourself in a lady's house?'

Barak reddened too, his eyes angry. 'I have a message for Master Shardlake from Lord Cromwell.'

'Have you never been told to bow to a lady? And what is the matter with your head? Do you have nits? You had better not spread them in my house.' She spoke with a harshness I had never heard from her, but Barak had been extremely discourteous.

'I am sorry, Lady Honor,' I said quickly. 'Perhaps we should withdraw.' I took a step away, then gasped as my head swam. My legs seemed suddenly heavy and I half-fell, half-sat on the bench again. Lady Honor's face was at once full of concern.

'Matthew, what is it?'

I struggled up, though my head still swam. 'I am sorry – the heat—'

'Come inside,' she said. 'You,' she snapped at Barak, 'help your master. This is your fault.'

Barak gave her a hard look but put my arm round his shoulder and helped me into the parlour, then sat me on a pile of cushions. Lady Honor waved him away. He gave her another look, but left the room.

'I am sorry. A moment's weakness—' I struggled to get up. What a fool I must look. Damn Barak, if he had not come then—

Lady Honor stepped to a cabinet. I heard her pour some liquid into a glass. She crossed and knelt beside me, smiling gently. 'I have some aqua vitae here, my apothecary prescribes it for faintness.'

'Aqua vitae?' I laughed as I took the delicate little glass she gave me.

'You have heard of it?'

'Oh, yes.' I took a cautious sip of the colourless liquid. It burned, but far less than the Polish stuff. It seemed to reawaken me. 'Thank you,' I said.

She looked at me thoughtfully. 'I think you have had much to try you, it has brought you low. Who is that creature?'

'Lord Cromwell has set him to work with me on the Greek Fire matter. He lacks grace, I fear.' I stood up, ashamed at my weakness. 'Lady Honor, I must go. If Barak has a message from the earl I must attend to it.'

'Come again soon,' she said, 'to dinner. Just the two of us. No Marchamount, no duke, no Barak.' She smiled.

'I should like that, Lady Honor.'

'Honor will do.'

We stood facing each other a moment. I was tempted to lean forward and kiss her, but I merely bowed and left the room. Outside I cursed myself for my cowardice.

Barak was standing glowering in the hall. I led the way out and we stood waiting while the horses were brought round.

'What was the message?' I asked curtly.

'He's brought the meeting forward, to eleven o'clock.'

'Was that all? It could have waited.'

'A message from the earl could have waited? I think not. What did Lady Honor tell you, by the way?'

'She confirmed the Duke of Norfolk has sought her for his mistress; she didn't want to talk about it, felt it would have been less dishonourable to her if the information was forced from her by Cromwell.'

He grunted. 'It wasted our time.'

'It was fealty to her family.'

'You are sure she knows no more?'

'She knows nothing more than what she has told me before. I am convinced of that now.'

'Rude woman,' he said.

God's death,' I snapped, 'you *are* a churl. You enjoy mocking your betters, don't you? Refinement seems a crime in your eyes.'

'She's got haughty ways and a vile tongue,' Barak said, 'like all her class. People like her grow rich on the sweat of those who toil on their lands. Put her out to fend for herself and she wouldn't last a week.' He smiled bitterly. 'They use honeyed words when it suits them, but see how they address their inferiors and you divine their true natures.'

'Oh, you are a bitter man, Jack Barak,' I said. 'Your time in the gutter has soured you like an old apple. She has more care for the people around her than you do.'

'And you?' he asked unexpectedly. 'Do you have a care for your servants?'

I laughed. 'You are hardly a servant. If you were I should have put you out long ago.'

'I did not mean me. I mean your clerk John Skelly. Has it never occurred to you why his copying is so bad, why he works with a candle?'

'What on earth do you mean?'

'The man is half blind.'

'What?'

'He can hardly see. I noticed it the first time I saw him. He's afraid to say anything lest you put him on the street. But you didn't notice, did you? Neither you nor your holy friend, Brother Wheelwright.'

I stared at him, realizing that if Skelly could not see properly that would explain all his inefficiencies. 'I – I did not think—'

'No. He was beneath notice,' Barak replied bitterly. He jammed his cap back on his head as a boy appeared, leading the horses. 'Well, where to now?' he said. 'Did the fine lady tell you anything new?'

'No. Whatever Marchamount is hiding, I think perhaps it is now time to leave the earl to pressure him.'

Barak grunted. 'You're seeing sense at last.'

# Chapter Thirty-eight

WHEN WE REACHED HOME I felt faint again as I dismounted. I almost fell down in the yard. I leaned against the horse, taking deep breaths. Barak looked at me.

'You all right?'

'Yes,' I replied curtly. 'But I think I'll lie down for a while.'

'What about Marchamount? Shall I send word to the earl, get him brought in for questioning?'

'Yes. But to Cromwell's house, not the Tower. Being ordered there should be enough to make him talk and it will keep the matter privy.'

He nodded. 'I'll ride on to Whitehall, then. I'll be back later. Don't go out till I return, it may not be safe.'

I nodded and went indoors to ask Joan to get me some bread and cheese and a jug of beer. I took them up to my room. Sitting on the edge of the bed, I put my hand on my brow and was relieved to find no sign of fever. My faintness must have been due to the strain of the last two weeks, coupled with constant chasing across London in this endless, burning heat. I would not let infirmity make a victim of me. Four more days and everything would be settled one way or another. And then – then I would see Lady Honor again, and next time I would not play the coward. All the questions surrounding her had been answered, yet still she wanted to know me. I had felt it, more strongly than ever on the bench; she cared for me as I did for her. Curse Barak for his interruption.

My burnt arm was stinging. I removed the bandage and applied some of Guy's oil to the red, puckered skin, shuddering as I remembered the flame licking at it. *The kiss of fire so light and agonizing.* I bound my arm up again and lay back on the bed.

I fell asleep at once and again slept for several hours, this time without dreams. I woke to find the air mercifully cooler, long shadows stealing across the garden. My head felt clearer and I lay thinking about what Barak had said about John Skelly, how it made sense. I had been angry with Skelly because I thought him careless, unworthy of the kindness I had shown him, while all the time − I thought of his tired red eyes looking up at me, and shook my head.

It occurred to me that perhaps his problem could be solved with spectacles. More and more people wore them, the king himself it was said. I could buy him a pair. I nodded happily at the thought of telling Barak that. Then I frowned. Why should I tell him anything? What did his good opinion matter to me? With luck our association would soon be over and I should have no more of his brutal crudity or incon‚ stant moods. I smiled at the memory of how Lady Honor had spoken to him: few people could have put Barak in his place, yet she had.

His place. My conscience assailed me again as I remembered saying that if he worked for me I would have sacked him. Yet then I should have lost a man of brains and courage, for all his impudence, a man who had saved my life. And whom I needed to go down the Wentworths' well tonight.

I heaved myself up and descended the stairs. I found Barak in the kitchen, washing the chain that held his mezuzah with vinegar. The little gold tablet itself lay on the kitchen table. He gave me a sharp look; he was still angry with me.

'Where's Joan?' I asked.

'Having a rest before preparing supper. Even servants need a rest,' he added pointedly.

I sat opposite him. 'I have been thinking about Skelly. I shall take him to Guy, see if there may be spectacles he can prescribe that may help his sight.'

Barak stared at me with his sharp eyes. 'Skelly wouldn't be able to afford spectacles.'

'I shall pay.'

He grunted. 'And if spectacles won't help him? Will you put him out?'

'I shall have to. God's death, Barak, I have to turn a profit. I'd see if there are any charitable foundations that could help him. Come, let's not quarrel.'

He grunted. 'Yes, you want me to go down that well tonight, don't you?'

'If you will.'

'I said I would.' He replaced the mezuzah round his neck.

'Did you get the message to Cromwell?'

'I left it with Grey. He made a tart comment about how I kept asking the earl to do things when it ought to be the other way round.'

I smiled. 'He's a sober old fellow. You probably rub him up the wrong way.'

'Like Lady Honor.' He gave me a direct look. 'But are you sure the lady is all she seems? Can you see her clearly?'

'I try to.' I frowned. 'Yes, I believe so. I think we can clear both her and the duke from our calculations: that was another wrong trail.' I studied him. 'Why do you dislike her, Barak?'

He shrugged. 'People with that much pride in rank bring bad luck to those around them. I've seen how these fine families spit and scratch at each other around the court. It is dangerous to get caught in her wake. But never mind that. So she is no longer a suspect. Nor, it seems, are Bealknap and Rich.'

'Not necessarily. We should wait and see what Cromwell says about them. I hope he can make Marchamount talk.'

'He can make anyone talk. He'll show him the rack if he won't cooperate.'

'Marchamount has courage under his pomposity. He's come far from nothing.'

Barak shrugged. 'If he's defiant he'll pay the consequences.'

We stopped talking as footsteps sounded on the stairs. Joan

appeared and we went through to the parlour while she prepared supper. It was starting to get dark.

'Are you fit to go to the well after we have eaten?'

'Ay,' I said. 'I don't know what came over me earlier. Heat maybe, the strain of it all.' I looked at him. 'But I shall hold fast. Let us go tonight, then perhaps at least we shall have one thing solved.'

✝

ONCE AGAIN WE WALKED UP Budge Row and down the dark little alley. A new lock had been put on the door to the orchard, but Barak broke it open as casually as before. We slipped through the trees to the Wentworths' wall. Again Barak made a stirrup of his hands and I climbed up, grasping the top of the wall, to take a look. I set my teeth as my back protested.

There was someone in the garden. I could see two dim figures walking there, one holding a lamp. There was a faint murmur of voices. It was Needler and Joseph's mother. I thought an old woman walking with a stick could easily slip in the gloom, then remembered that light or dark made no difference to her. I signed to Barak not to move and stood there uncomfortably, my foot in his hands and my arms on the wall. I lowered my head so that my pale face would be concealed and waited as the pair came closer. My dark hair, I was sure, would be invisible.

'She was screaming at me like the devil,' I caught Needler saying. 'I can't manage her any more. She's terrified under that pert exterior and so's Avice.'

The old woman sighed. 'I must tighten the girls' reins.' They were very close now, but I took the risk of raising my head and peeping at their faces. Needler's heavy features looked worried. The old woman's face, like a demon from a painting of hell in the flickering lamplight, wore a frown.

'We must help them, David—' she said, then stopped suddenly.

She seemed to cock her head. I remembered the blind often have remarkable hearing.

'What is it?' Needler asked sharply.

'Nothing. A fox perhaps.' To my relief they turned and walked back to the house. I heard no more of what they said. A door shut in the distance and shortly afterwards lights were extinguished all over the house. I stumbled down again. Barak stood rubbing his hands.

'God's death,' he whispered, 'you've near dislocated my wrists.'

'I'm sorry, but I couldn't move. The old beldame heard something as it was.'

'What in God's name was she doing in the garden in the dark?'

'She was with the steward. They wanted to talk alone, I think. I only caught a snatch of what they said. Something to do with the two girls being frightened.'

We waited for a while. An owl swooped down from a tree in the orchard, a white ghostly shape, and some small creature in the long grass screamed as it was carried off. At length I climbed the wall again. The lights were out, the garden silent, the well a dim shape in the moonlight.

'There's no sign of the dogs,' I said.

Barak hauled himself up beside me. 'That's strange. Surely if you'd had people trying to break in you'd loose the dogs at night?'

'I agree, but it seems they haven't.'

Barak sat astride the wall and pulled a couple of greasy pieces of meat wrapped in paper from his satchel. He threw them on the lawn, then tossed a stone he had found somewhere at the tree. It bounced off with a clack.

'The Moor said if a dog ate that it'd be asleep in minutes,' he whispered.

'You got that from Guy?'

'Ay. I told him the story yesterday while you were asleep. I thought he'd know of something.' He grinned. 'I found I got on well with the Moor on better acquaintance.'

I looked out over the silent lawn. 'Still no dogs.'

He scratched his chin. 'What say we risk it?'

I looked at the blank windows of the house. 'So long as we keep an eye out.'

He looked at me. 'You all right?'

'Yes, yes!'

'Right then, down we go.'

Barak leapt easily onto the lawn and I followed, wincing at the jarring my spine took as I landed. I watched the house as Barak fetched his hunks of meat and replaced them in his knapsack.

'Best not to leave these, or they'll know someone's been here.'

He removed the padlocks from the well, then I helped him off with the lid. The smell was fainter now, but the sight of that black opening still made my stomach clench. Barak unfurled his rope ladder and climbed quickly down. I kept glancing over at the house. For a moment I thought I saw a movement, a deeper blackness, at one of the upper windows, but when I looked again I saw nothing.

This time Barak managed to light his candle the first time. I turned from the house as a faint white glow lit the well and leaned carefully over the side. It was shallower than I had expected, no more than twenty feet. It was weird to see Barak standing at the bottom of that long circular hollow. He was crouching, looking at a huddle of dark shapes. He explored them with his hands. This time he was quite silent. I could not see his face.

'What is it?' I whispered.

He looked up at me, shadows from the candle making eerie shapes on his face. 'Animals. There's a cat here, a couple of dogs.' He bent down again. 'Shit, there's horrible things been done to them – the cat's had its eyes put out. This is where that neighbour's retriever went – Jesu, it's been hanged.' He half-turned and examined a larger shape. This time he did cry out, an abrupt shout that echoed off the bricks.

'What? What is it?'

'I'm coming up,' he said abruptly. 'For God's sake, keep watch on the house.'

He snuffed out the candle and clambered up again. I peered at the house, my heart beating so fast it made my vision judder. All remained dark and silent. Barak clambered over the top of the well. His eyes were wide.

'Help me get the well cap back on,' he breathed. 'We have to get out of here.'

We slid the cap back and Barak replaced the locks. With a last look at the silent house we ran back to the wall and clambered over. Back in the orchard, Barak leaned against a tree. He stared at me, then gulped.

'Someone in that house has been torturing animals. But not just animals. There's a little boy down there, a ragged boy of about seven. He's been – ' he broke off ' – you don't want to know, but he's dead and he didn't die quick.'

'The mad girl's brother,' I breathed. 'The girl that was put in Elizabeth's cell.'

'Perhaps. Whoever took him probably thought a beggar boy wouldn't be missed, didn't matter.' He blew out his cheeks. 'It scared me, I'll admit. I thought, if whoever did that came I would be helpless down there. I had to get out.' His voice trembled.

'I don't blame you.'

He stared at me aghast as a thought struck him. 'Could it have been Elizabeth Wentworth who killed the boy? Was that why she lost the will to live after the girl was put in with her? If that's the girl's brother down there—'

I thought a moment. 'No. Joseph said Elizabeth had a cat she was devoted to. Needler said it ran away, but I think it's her cat down there. No, it wasn't her. I think young Ralph did this. First the animals, then the child.'

'But then— Don't you see? This gives Elizabeth a motive to put the boy down the well! You could say it was apt justice for the wretch. Perhaps she found out what he was doing—'

'But why, when Needler pulled Ralph from the well, did he say nothing about the animals or the dead child?' I shook my head. 'He must have seen what was down there. I have to see Elizabeth again – I have to get her to talk.'

'If she's still alive.'

'I'll go first thing tomorrow. Thank you for what you did,' I added awkwardly.

Barak gave me a sombre look. 'You think me hard, but I'd never hurt a defenceless creature.'

'I believe you,' I said. 'Come, let's get back to Chancery Lane.'

He nodded. 'All right. Jesu, I'll be having nightmares tonight.'

# Chapter Thirty-nine

NEITHER BARAK NOR I slept well that night. There had been a message from Guy when we returned, saying Elizabeth was a little better, her fever lower. He also asked me to call on him to discuss 'the other matter'. Barak had ridden out again to Joseph's lodging house, with a message for him to meet us at the gaol at nine.

As I dressed on that seventh of June I thought how much I had to do that day; visit Elizabeth, see Guy, then answer Cromwell's summons. My heart sank at the thought of that last. There were only three days left. But by now, hopefully, Cromwell would have questioned Marchamount. If Lady Honor knew nothing, and Rich and Bealknap were out of the picture, that left only him. I hoped he would lead the way to the Gristwoods' killers; but what if, under pressure, he gave Cromwell the Greek Fire formula? Well, I thought as I dressed, if he did, that was out of my hands.

Barak wanted to come with me to Newgate. He could not find his riding shoes and asked me to wait for him. I stood outside the house. The morning was hot again but a wind had risen, a hot breeze that sent little white clouds racing across the sky. Simon appeared, leading the horses.

'Out again early, sir?' he asked.

'Ay. To Newgate gaol.'

The boy squinted at me from under his blond mop, his narrow face full of interest. 'Has Master Barak been fighting robbers, sir? Is that how he lost his hair?'

I laughed. 'No, Simon. Do not be so nosy.' I looked at the sturdy little shoes he wore. 'Are you used to these now?'

'Yes, thank you, sir. I can run faster, which is well with all the messages I have run lately.' He smiled at me hopefully.

'I suppose it is. Here's sixpence then, towards new shoes when those wear out.'

I smiled as the boy ran back into the house. It struck me I knew nothing of the poor lad's background, only that he had come to the door and Joan, liking his looks, had given him a job. Another of London's innumerable orphans, no doubt.

Barak appeared and we set off. As we rode down Fleet Street I told Barak my burn was giving me pain and I intended to consult Guy after we had seen Cromwell. I was worried he might want to come too, but he only nodded. His face was still marked with the shock of what he had found down the well; I was surprised how deeply it had affected him. But then, of course, he too had once been a beggar boy.

Joseph was waiting outside the gaol. He looked tired and unshaven, his cheeks sunken. He could not go on like this much longer. I told him I had had word Elizabeth was a little better, and that seemed to cheer him.

The gaoler answered our knock. 'William!' he called out. The fat turnkey appeared.

'We would see Mistress Wentworth,' I said.

'How is she this morning?' Joseph asked at the same moment.

'I don't know,' the turnkey answered. 'No one's been up there – we don't want her fever. Apart from that black apothecary; he came again yesterday, but maybe gaol fever doesn't affect such as him.'

'Will you take us to her?'

The turnkey grunted, but led us away to the stairs. It was a relief not to have to see the Hole again. I turned to Joseph as he followed me up the winding stair. 'I have some news,' I said. 'Some fresh evidence at last. I want to try again to get Elizabeth to speak.'

A desperate hope lit Joseph's features. I looked at him seriously. 'I must tax her with some hard things, sir. Things that will not be good to hear. About Sir Edwin's family.'

He took a deep breath, then nodded. 'Very well.'

The turnkey let us into Elizabeth's room. The breeze blew through the barred windows, stirring the cloth on the little table. Elizabeth was lying on her back, very still, but at least she was not twitching and muttering now. Her face was pale. I took a stool and sat down, bending forward so my face was close to hers. Joseph and Barak stood behind me, looking on. I saw the cut on her lip was unhealed, there was a nasty black scab all round it.

She must have been awake for as I leaned close she opened her eyes. They were dull and heavy. I took a deep breath.

'Elizabeth,' I said, 'Jack Barak here has been down your uncle Edwin's well.' Her eyes widened slightly, but she did not speak. 'We broke in last night, and took off the cap that had been put over it. Barak climbed down and saw what was there.'

Joseph's mouth fell open. 'You broke in!'

'It was the only way, Joseph.' I turned back to the silent girl. 'We placed ourselves in danger, Elizabeth, to find the truth. For your sake.' I paused. 'We saw them. All the poor animals. Your cat. And the boy.'

'What boy?' Joseph's voice was sharp with fear.

'There is the corpse of a little boy down the well.'

'Oh, Jesu.' Joseph sat down heavily on the bed. I saw tears well up in Elizabeth's eyes.

'I am sure you did not do those terrible things, Elizabeth—'

'Never,' Joseph said hotly. 'Never!'

'Was it Ralph?'

She coughed, and then finally spoke, in a low, sighing voice. 'Yes. Yes, it was.'

Joseph brought his hands up to his mouth, his expression horri-fied. I could see the thought had come to him, as it had to Barak, that here was a clear motive for Elizabeth to kill her cousin. I continued quickly. 'When I visited your uncle Edwin I noticed a bad odour coming from that well, and remembered Joseph telling me Ralph's body had a terrible smell on it when it was laid out at the coroner's. Elizabeth, when the steward Needler went to fetch up your cousin's body he must have seen what was down there, yet he said nothing and the family sealed off the well.' I paused, but though tears trickled down Elizabeth's cheeks her stare remained dull and hopeless. I went on.

'That must have been because the discovery of the boy down there would have resulted in a separate investigation. Needler said nothing in order to protect someone else. Who was it, Elizabeth?'

'Speak, girl, for Jesu's sake.' Barak said with sudden anger. 'You are putting your uncle through the torments of the damned.'

'You return to Judge Forbizer in three days.' I said quietly. 'If he cannot be satisfied, if you still do not speak, you will be crushed.'

She looked at me, her eyes empty. 'Let the crushing come. You cannot help me, sir. No one can. You must not try, it is no use. I am damned.' She continued, with a dreadful calmness. 'Once I believed in God, God who took care of all his creatures and showed man how he should live well and be saved by study of the Bible. The Bible the king gave to the people. I believed God helped us through the fallen world.'

'So should we all, Elizabeth,' Joseph said, clutching his hands together. 'So must we all.' She gave him a look I realized was pity, wincing as salt tears flowed onto her cut lip.

'What about the justice of this world?' Barak asked. 'What about punishment for murderers?'

She only glanced at him; his words did not stir her this time. 'I told you what was down there would shake your faith,' she told me. She paused, then let out a long, groaning breath. 'First Mother died, so painfully, from the great lump in her chest that wasted her to nothing. Then Father died too.' She coughed again. I offered her a bowl of water but she waved it away, looking at me fixedly.

'I sought consolation in books of prayer, sir. I entreated God to help me understand, but I seemed to be praying into a great dark silence. Then I was told our house was lost, our house where I grew up and was happy. I thought I would go to Uncle Joseph's in the country, but he said I must go to Uncle Edwin's.'

'It was for your good, Elizabeth,' Joseph said desperately. 'We thought it best for your prospects.'

'Grandam and Uncle Edwin did not want me, I knew that. They thought with my rough ways I might spoil their turning their three children into gentlefolk. But they did not know how cruel they were. They did not know how Ralph would torture any animal he could lay hands on, exploring all the different ways to inflict pain. Sabine and Avice brought him my poor Grizzy.'

'*Sabine and Avice!*' Joseph's voice was incredulous.

'Ralph got them to bring him animals – they thought what he did amusing, though they didn't like getting blood or fur on their clean clothes. They were glad to have me to tease and torment, to relieve their boredom. They always used to say how bored with their lives they were.'

'What about your uncle Edwin?' I asked. 'Your grandmother? You could have appealed to them.'

'Grandam knew, but she turned her blind eyes from it. She kept everything from Uncle Edwin, what his children really were. He cared only that they should make the best show they could as young gentlefolk.'

I passed a hand across my brow. 'It sounds like madness, a madness the three of them infected each other with. Then you came—'

'I did not know about Ralph at first. I thought he was different from his sisters; he was not fine manners one minute and cruelty the next, in the beginning he was friendly in a rough boy's way. I look like him, you know. Maybe God has chosen me to suffer for all their sins – do you think so?'

'No,' I said. 'It is you that are choosing to suffer now.'

She shook her head. 'Ralph took me for a walk and showed me a fox he had caught in a trap and left until it was weakened. He had come with a needle to put its eyes out. I freed it and told him it was a wicked thing he did. That turned him against me. After that he joined with his sisters in finding ways to torment me.'

'You should have told Edwin,' Joseph said.

Elizabeth smiled then, a smile so despairing it chilled me. 'He would have believed nothing against Ralph or the girls. And Gran' dam cares only to see the girls well married. Sabine has a fancy for the steward Needler and Grandam used that, used him to try and keep the girls under control. She needs them to behave well on the surface until they have found rich young men.' She looked away. 'Pity any such gentleman, not to know what he has married until it is too late.'

'What about the other servants? How much do they know? There must have been – been terrible cries from the animals.' All at once I felt sick, black bile curdling in my stomach.

'Ralph did his vile deeds down the well. He had a little ladder. It was his torture cell as well as his hiding place. I think the servants heard things, but they said nothing – they wanted to keep their positions. Uncle Edwin pays well even if he makes them all go to church twice on Sundays.' Elizabeth had stopped crying now, her eyes had taken on a more focused look. 'I remember Ralph had talked of finding some beggar child to toy with, but the girls said he must be careful not to be caught. There was a little crippled boy and his sister who begged around our street.'

'And the girl was Sarah?'

'Yes. When poor Sarah was put in the Hole I remembered her. Ralph must have enticed her brother away.'

'Dear Jesu,' Joseph said. 'The coroner will have to be told.'

'Yes,' I agreed. 'But the family may try to turn the beggar boy's death against Elizabeth. Perhaps get Needler to say he did not see the beggar boy.'

'That won't be believed, surely.'

'Public feeling has been stirred against Elizabeth. Remember that pamphlet? Forbizer will not want to let her go. And who did kill Ralph? Or was it an accident, Elizabeth? Did he fall?'

She turned her face away. I wondered, for an awful moment, had she done it after all? But then why had Needler said nothing when he saw the well?

'Ralph must have been possessed,' Joseph said. 'Possessed by some demon.'

'Yes.' Elizabeth spoke to her uncle directly for the first time. 'By the devil, or perhaps by God, who is one and the same.'

He looked aghast. 'Elizabeth. That is blasphemy!'

She lifted herself on her elbows, coughing painfully. 'Don't you see? That's what I've come to understand. I know now that God is cruel and evil. He favours the wicked, as anyone who looks around the world can see. I have read the Book of Job, read the torments God inflicted on his faithful servant, I have asked God to tell me how he can do such evil, but he does not reply. Does not Luther say God chooses who will be damned and who saved, before one is even born? He has chosen me to be damned and for my damnation to start in this life!'

'Rubbish!' I turned with surprise to Barak. He glared at her. 'You should listen to your self-pity.'

Then she lost control. 'Who else has pitied me? My faith is gone, I wait for my death so I may spit in God's face for his cruelty!' She glared at Barak, then leaned back, exhausted.

The words rang round the room. Joseph waved his hands anxiously, as though he could bat them away. 'Lizzy, that is blasphemy! Do you want to be burned as a witch?' He put his hands together and began praying aloud. 'O merciful Jesu, help your daughter, strike the beam from her eye, turn her to obedience—'

'That'll do no good!' Barak shouldered past Joseph and leaned over Elizabeth. 'Listen, girl. I've seen that little boy. His death should be avenged. Ralph may be gone, but there are others who covered up his killing that beggar child as though it was a thing that mattered not at all. And his sister, Sarah, maybe they'll release her from Bedlam when they find her brother *was* taken and killed?'

'Release her to what?' Elizabeth asked despairingly. 'To beg again, or go for a whore?'

I put my head in my hands, full of the horror of it all; a cheerful innocent girl, visited with calamity after calamity and then the appalling, relentless cruelty of Sir Edwin's monstrous family, finally turning her fury on the God who had seemed to desert her. She had been pious once, no doubt, but the terrible blows she had suffered had turned her faith inside out. And was there not an awful logic in her belief that God had deserted her? Surely he had? I thought of the thousands of children who lay abandoned, begging in the streets.

Joseph was in a terrible state, wringing his hands. 'She could be charged with blasphemy,' he moaned. 'Atheism—' I glanced at the door, wondering whether the turnkey had been listening, for if he had Elizabeth's words were indeed enough to put her under a new charge. But undoubtedly the man would stay clear of the sick chamber.

'Calm down, Joseph, for mercy's sake,' I said. I looked at Elizabeth. She was sobbing now, a low miserable keening. 'Is it a wonder she has been driven to think as she does?'

Joseph looked at me aghast. 'You are not excusing—'

'Elizabeth.' She looked up at me again. The outburst had brought some colour to her white cheeks. 'Elizabeth, whatever you think God has done, surely Barak is right? It is your uncle Edwin's family you should be blaming, for it was they that did the evil. And if one of them killed Ralph, you should tell. They should be brought to justice.'

'They will not be. I am damned, I tell you.' Her voice rose again. 'Let God have his way, let me be killed. Let his work be done!' She lay back, exhausted.

'Very well,' I said. 'Then I shall have to confront the family myself.'

She did not reply. She closed her eyes. She seemed to have retreated back into that dark place where she lived now.

After a few moments I rose from the stool and turned to the others. 'Come,' I said. I opened the door and called for the turnkey, who had retreated to the bottom of the steps. We left the cell, Joseph stumbling and almost falling.

Outside the gaol he shivered, despite the heat. 'I thought it could get no worse,' he said quietly.

'It was enough to freeze the blood, I know. But I beg you, Joseph, remember Elizabeth's mind is distracted, remember what she has been through.'

He looked at me and I saw stark terror in his face. 'So you believe her,' he whispered. 'My brother has spawned a family of devils.'

'I will find who did this,' I said.

He shook his head, his mind in utter turmoil. We took him to a tavern and sat with him half an hour while he calmed himself. By then it was time to go to Cromwell.

'Come, Joseph, we will ride with you as far as your lodgings,' I said. 'Then we must catch a boat. We have business at Whitehall. Perhaps we may leave our horses at your lodgings?'

He looked up with a flaint flicker of interest. 'This other matter you are engaged on, it is a matter of state?'

'Yes, it is. But I will have an answer from your family, Joseph, I promise.'

'He will,' Barak added encouragingly.

Joseph looked at me.

'Do you want me to come with you?'

'No. I will go alone, or with Barak here.'

'For God's sake,' he said, his eyes full of fear, 'be careful.'

# Chapter Forty

T HE THAMES WAS BUSY and we had difficulty finding a wherry at the river stairs. Barak cursed roundly, fearing we would be late. At length a boat arrived and we sailed upriver, a strong southerly wind plucking at my robe and driving the craft briskly through the water. I thought of Elizabeth, how terrible her state of mind must be, her whole being dominated by her hatred of the savage God before whom she meant to martyr herself. I shuddered at the darkness that overlay her mind, even as, I felt, I understood it. I glanced at Barak: he sat hunched and gloomy in the stern of the boat. I thought perhaps he understood too. But we but dared not talk of such things before the boatman.

At last the wherry bumped into Westminster steps. Barak jumped out and we scrambled up the stairs, half-running across to the Privy Gallery. We stopped a moment to catch our breath under the mural, the king frowning down on us, then walked through to Cromwell's office.

Grey was at his desk, working on a bill to be presented to parliament, running a rule down the long sheet of parchment. He looked up sharply. 'Master Shardlake, I was beginning to fear you would be late. The earl is — is not in a patient mood today.'

'I am sorry, the river was busy—'

'I'll take you in.' He got up with a sigh. 'My master is sending so many bills to this parliament that his work lacks its usual level of care.' He shook his head. 'He is very preoccupied.' He knocked on Cromwell's door, and ushered us inside.

The earl was standing by the window, looking out at Whitehall.

He turned a dark, frowning face towards us. He was dressed magnificently today in a robe of red silk such as the rules allowed only barons to wear, edged with sable fur. The star of the Order of the Garter hung from a colourful ribbon round his neck.

'Well,' he said grimly, 'you've come.' He strode to his desk, which was heaped high with papers. He must recently have thrown down his quill in anger, for it lay in the middle in a pool of ink. He sat down heavily in his chair and stared at us, his face set hard.

'Well, Matthew, it seems you have sent me on a fool's errand.'

'My lord?'

'Sir Richard Rich,' he snapped. 'I called him in here on Saturday night.' He linked his hands together and banged them down on the table. 'The reason Rich has been making threatening remarks to you and the reason Bealknap thought he was safe from me have nothing to do with Greek Fire.'

'Then what?'

'You have been acting for the Common Council, have you not, on a case involving whether a monastic property may be exempt from the City statutes?'

'Indeed. It is going up to Chancery.'

'No,' he said heavily. 'It is not.' He took a long breath. 'Many influential people have bought monastic properties in London, Matthew. The City was full of the pestilential places before we dissolved them. Unfortunately, there are so many on the market now that the value of land has fallen. I have had complaints from several people that they were induced to make bad investments. When the case over that damned cesspit of Bealknap's arose, Rich came to me and said it was important Bealknap won. Otherwise the council would use the case as a precedent and make life difficult for the new owners, some of whom can only turn a profit by converting their properties into housing of the cheapest type. Do you see now?' He raised his eyebrows. 'Many of these are men whose loyalty I am trying to keep, in these days when all are ready to turn against me.'

'Oh.'

'Rich did not tell me you were the lawyer acting for the council, or I would have guessed what all this was about long ago. I agreed to his bribing Judge Heslop to get the right judgement, which owners of monastic properties could then use as a precedent in any future cases. Rich tells me he put pressure on some men who are his clients to take cases they had with you to other lawyers as a warning. A Chancery judgement against Bealknap could upset the whole applecart – do you see?' He spoke coldly, distinctly, as though to a foolish man. 'That's what his threats were about and that's what Bealknap thought you were pressuring him about. And you didn't realize.'

I closed my eyes.

'It's a dog's breakfast, isn't it?' He gave a hollow laugh. 'Weren't you worried, Matthew, that cases were being taken from you? Didn't you investigate? You would soon have seen all the clients were Sir Richard's men.'

'I have been too busy, my lord,' I said. 'I have thought of nothing but Greek Fire and the Wentworth case. I have had to leave my work with my chambers fellow.'

He gave me a sharp look. 'Oh, yes, Master Wheelwright. His holiness will carry him into the fire one day.' He closed his jaw hard. Once Cromwell could have protected radical reformers, but no more. He stood up abruptly and walked over to the window, looking at the courtiers and clerks milling outside. Then he turned back to me.

'It seems clear to me, from their reactions, that neither Bealknap nor Rich is holding anything back about Greek Fire. Rich didn't even know about it. I managed to elicit that without alerting him to its existence. Just.'

'I see. I am sorry, my lord.' I felt a fool, a dolt.

'That leaves Lady Honor and Marchamount.' He began pacing the room, his head bent. 'So, next, what about Lady Honor? I gather you and she have been having a merry time together.'

I glanced at Barak, who gave a shrug.

'There was something she was holding back,' I said. 'Something between her and Marchamount and the Duke of Norfolk. It has taken some digging, but that too was nothing to do with Greek Fire.'

'What was it?' he asked sharply.

I hesitated a moment. I had promised to tell nobody. But when Cromwell raised his head and gave me a look of great fierceness, I told him.

He only grunted. 'Well, let Norfolk chase her all over London instead of plotting against me. So, there is no evidence to link her with Greek Fire either?'

'No, my lord. None.' My stomach was knotted with shame for betraying Lady Honor's confidence.

He turned and paced the other way. 'And Marchamount?'

'Just a feeling he was not telling all, my lord. Barak said you would summon him.'

'I did.' He stopped and looked at me. It surprised me to see his face was not angry, only filled with a desperate weariness now. 'Marchamount has disappeared.'

'He is not always easy to find. Last week I could not reach him – he was out of London on a case.'

Cromwell shook his head. 'I sent a couple of men to his chambers. They found his clerk in a state because he had not turned up for a case, had not been in his rooms all night.' He stared at me. 'Did you threaten him with my wrath?'

'Not directly.'

'But he may have guessed he was not out of the woods and fled. Or has he gone the way of the Gristwoods?'

I shivered. 'If he is not safe, Bealknap and Lady Honor may not be either.'

Cromwell sat down again, shaking his head. 'They've been one step ahead of you all the time, haven't they?' he said in the same quiet tone. 'Whoever is behind this is the most cunning, clever rogue I've ever encountered and I've met many.' A smile flickered across his granite face. 'In another context I could admire him. Or her.'

Then, to my relief, he shrugged his heavy shoulders. 'You've done your best. The game's almost done. There are only three days till the demonstration and we're no further forward in finding the formula, or the apparatus. Where in Jesu's name have they hidden that?' He turned to Barak. 'Jack, try once again to trace Toky and Wright. Tell your contacts I'll pay the pair anything if they'll come over to me.'

'I will, my lord. But even if I trace them, I doubt they'd risk changing sides at this stage.'

'Well, try again. I think I must tell the king tomorrow, Wednesday at the latest. Matthew, Barak reported the prostitute who died said the whole thing was a plot against me from the beginning.'

'Yes, my lord.'

'Well, there have been enough of those. Don't give up yet. Put your *mind* to it.' There was desperation in his voice. 'And go to Lincoln's Inn. They'll maybe tell you things they won't tell my men. Search Marchamount's rooms.'

'Give me until Wednesday, my lord. I will do what I can. Do not tell the king till then.'

'Have you some lead?' His eyes bored into mine. I swallowed.

'I – no. But I will think, as you ask.'

He looked at me hard for another long moment, then turned back to his desk. 'Go then,' he said. 'God's death, Grey will bury me in papers.'

His resigned, almost gentle manner so surprised me that I stood there a moment, fighting a sudden urge to tell him I had found some Greek Fire and given it to Guy. I realized that my old loyalty to him was not quite dead, after all. Barak motioned to the door and, to my surprise, I heard footsteps scurrying away as he opened it. We stepped out to see Grey sitting down at his desk, his face flustered.

Barak grinned. 'Been eavesdropping, master secretary?'

He did not reply, but reddened.

'Leave him, Barak,' I said. I thought: Grey is terrified of what may be about to happen. He is right to be. And I have found some

Greek Fire and hidden it from Cromwell. For a moment I felt faint again.

✟

BARAK AND I SAT on the steps of Westminster Hall, each deep in gloomy thought.

'I expected he'd be furious,' I said, 'but he seems – almost resigned.'

'He knows what will happen if he has to tell the king Greek Fire is lost,' he said quietly.

'What in God's name has happened to Marchamount? Is he villain or victim?'

Barak shrugged despairingly. 'Jesu knows. I'll try again for news of Toky and Wright, but I fear I'll find nothing. I think some of my contacts are being paid to keep their mouths shut.'

'Isn't it strange how, every time we approach the truth, the person we seek is killed? Almost as though someone was telling the enemy of our movements. And who took those books from Lincoln's Inn, and frightened the librarian?'

He frowned. 'I don't see that. It was Madam Neller that betrayed Bathsheba and her brother. The founder disappeared long before we got there. And Marchamount may have fled of his own accord.'

I nodded. 'That would mean he was the one behind it all. It starts to look that way.'

'It does. But we need more evidence.'

'We could go through his rooms.'

'I must look for Toky first. I'll come with you later.'

I stood up. 'Very well.' I looked at him. 'Be careful. It could be dangerous for you.'

'I can look after myself.' He stood and dusted himself down. 'It's letting my master down, that's what's hard.'

'There's still time,' I said. 'I'll meet you at home later.' I took a deep breath. 'My arm hurts.'

'My shoulder's better. He knows a few things, that old Moor.' He stood looking out over the river a moment. I followed his gaze. Something bright and fiery on the water made me start for a moment, then I saw it was only a ray of sunlight falling through the light cloud, flecking the little waves tossed up by the wind a flickering bright yellow.

✝

I COULD SEE NOBODY through the window of Guy's shop and feared he had gone out, but when I knocked footsteps sounded in the furthest reaches of the building and he appeared. He looked tired.

'You got my message, Matthew?'

'Yes.' I slipped inside and he closed the door.

'How is Elizabeth?' he asked. 'I am going to visit her later.'

'Better. In body at least.' Briefly, I told him what we had found down the well and of my conversation with her. He gave me a penetrating look.

'And you intend to confront the family?'

'Yes. And it must be very soon. Elizabeth is back before Forbizer on Thursday.'

'Be careful,' he said. 'There is something of pure evil in this story.'

'I know.' Suddenly I felt faint again and I sat down quickly in a chair.

'What is the matter?'

'A moment's faintness. The heat.'

He came and looked down at me. 'Have you had this before?'

'Yesterday.'

'You have taken on more than a man can reasonably bear.'

'Barak seems able to manage.'

Guy smiled. 'I talked with Master Barak when he brought you here after the fire. He improves somewhat on acquaintance.'

'Ay, he said you gave him something to put in the dogs' meat.'

'Yes. But do not compare yourself to him. He is a man of the streets, a lot younger than you. And he has an adventurer's disposition.'

'And a straight back.'

C. J. SANSOM

'That need not trouble you so much if you would do my exercises.
I suppose you will say you have had no time.'

'God's truth, I haven't.' I looked him in the eye. 'All my leads
have run into the ground. And one of our suspects has disappeared,
the lawyer Marchamount. We don't know yet if he's the man behind
it all or if he's been killed like the others. Guy, the one thing I have
left is that Greek Fire.'

He nodded. 'Come through to my workshop.'

I followed him to a back room. With its bottles and retorts full of
strange fluids, its bench and complex apparatus of oddly shaped
distilling glasses, it reminded me of Sepultus Gristwood's workshop.

'I did not know you had such a place here, Guy.'

'Experimenting with distillation interests me.' He smiled. 'I keep
it quiet in case the locals say I'm a magician.'

I saw the pewter jar of Greek Fire on the windowsill. Guy pointed
a finger at one wall and I saw that it was blackened as the Gristwoods'
yard had been. 'Some of the stuff caught fire yesterday while I was
trying to distil it. Filled the place with filthy black smoke. Luckily I
used only a very little.'

I stared at the jar, then turned to him. 'What is it, Guy?' I asked
passionately. 'What is it made of?'

He shook his head. 'I do not know, Matthew. In a way I am
glad, for I would not wish anyone to have this weapon.' He spread
his hands. 'I have distilled it, tried to see how it reacts with other
substances, tried to find some clue to what it is. But it has defeated
me.'

I felt my heart sink, though at the same time a part of me was also
relieved.

'I know some reputable alchemists,' he said. 'They might be able
to help, given time.'

I shook my head. 'We have no time. And I would not trust
anyone but you to keep this secret.'

He spread his hands. 'Then I am sorry.'

'You did your best.' I went and opened the jar, looking at the brown stuff inside. 'What are you?'I whispered.

'All I can say is it resembles no substance I have ever seen before. Certainly its composition is nothing like that Polish stuff.'

I thought a moment. 'If you cannot work it out, how could Sepultus? By all accounts he was a rogue and no true scholar.'

'He had months to experiment. Did you not say there were six months between the stuff's discovery and his approach to Cromwell?'

'Yes.'

'And the formula may say what the constituent elements are. At least tell him enough to give him more of a start than we have. It must all come down to earth and air, fire and water in the end.' He spread his hands. 'But in which of the millions of possible combinations?'

I nodded sadly. 'Thank you for trying. You know, you are the only man I feel I can always rely on to give me true answers, solve my problems. Perhaps I expect too much.'

'Perhaps you do,' Guy said. 'I am only frail human clay, for all people think I have strange powers to go with my strange looks.'

'Perhaps I should not have asked you to deal with something so devilish.'

He looked at me seriously. 'What will you do now?'

'I don't know what is left. Cromwell asked me to think.'

He nodded at the jar. 'What shall I do with that stuff? May I destroy it?'

I hesitated, then said, 'Yes. Destroy it now. Pour it in the river.'

He raised his eyebrows. 'Are you sure? We could both be accused of treason.'

'I am sure.'

His face flooded with relief. He gripped my hand fiercely. 'Thank you. You have done right, Matthew, you have done right.'

✟

I WALKED DOWN TO the river and stood on the bank watching the ships unload their cargo. Every week came some new wonder. I wondered whether, one day, a ship might bring something else as terrible and dangerous as Greek Fire here. I thought of St John landing a hundred years ago with his papers and the barrel. He had looked at peace in his grave. I knew now that I could never be at peace if I gave anyone in power the chance of making this thing, no matter what the consequences.

I looked across to the far bank, where I had walked with Lady Honor. The bear pit and bull ring rose high above the houses; I could hear a faint cheering from the bear pit – there must be a baiting on. I wondered if Marchamount had enjoyed his afternoon there. What had happened to him? Part of me felt, like Barak, that the game was played out. But the deadly puzzle still nagged at my mind.

A little way off I saw the tavern where we had met the sailors, the Barbary Turk. I went in. At this hour the place was empty and my footsteps echoed on the boards of the large, dusky drinking room. The giant's thigh bone still hung in its chains. I studied it for a moment, then went over to the serving hatch and ordered a mug of beer from the landlord. He was a burly fellow with the look of an ex-sailor about him. He looked curiously at my good stitched doublet.

'We don't often see gentlemen. You were in here a few nights ago, weren't you, talking to Hal Miller and his friends?'

'Ay. They told me of the time they set their table alight.'

He laughed, resting his arms on the edge of the hatch. 'That was a night. I wish they'd given me some of that stuff – I like novelties.'

'Like the giant's bone?' I nodded towards it.

'Ay, it was washed up just by the wharf here. Twenty years ago, in my father's time. Just appeared in the mud one ebb tide. People went hunting for the rest of the giant, but found no more of him. My father took the bone and hung it up here. Imagine what size the man must have been. But we are told of giants in the Bible, so that must be what it is. Better to have had the whole skeleton, but that one bone's enough to bring people here to look and that's good for trade.'

He would have talked on, but I wanted to be alone and took my beer over to the dark corner where I had sat with Barak that night.

His words, though, kept coming back to me. *That one bone's enough to bring people here to look and that's good for trade.* I thought of the Gristwoods, working with Toky and Wright and whoever their master was for six months before going to Cromwell, trying to make Greek Fire, hunting out the Polish drink. What a profit they must have anticipated. Profit from what had been, from the start, a plot against Cromwell.

And then, all at once, I saw what had happened. What and how, though not whom. My heart began to beat excitedly. I turned the theory over in my mind half a dozen times. It fitted the facts better than anything else. Abruptly I got up and left the inn, so preoccupied I stumbled into the giant's bone on the way out, setting it swinging once more in its chains.

✞

I WALKED RAPIDLY to Joseph's lodgings, to fetch Genesis from the stables. The horse was waiting in his stall, placid as ever. As I rode out I glanced back at the building; it was a poor enough place, but it would be costing Joseph far more than he could afford. Faithful, tenacious Joseph, how his enthusiastic godliness and fussiness irritated me sometimes. Yet he had been utterly steadfast in his loyalty to Elizabeth. I should have gone to the Wentworths' house today, but I realized I wanted Barak with me when I did. Guy was right: there was real evil in that house. And I saw that, if my theory was correct, we could still rescue Cromwell from his plight. There was no need for more secrets.

Barak was not at home when I returned. I waited impatiently for two hours as the sun slowly set. I remembered my warning to him earlier, and hoped he had not met with danger. It was a great relief when at last I heard him come in and throw off his boots. I called him into the parlour.

'Not more bad news?' he asked, looking at my flushed face.

'No.' I closed the door. 'Barak,' I said excitedly, 'I think I have worked out what happened. This afternoon I went back to that tavern, the one where we met the sailors. There was a giant's bone hanging from the ceiling, do you remember that?'

He raised a hand. 'Wait. You're going too fast for me. What's the giant's bone to do with anything?'

'It was something the landlord said. "Better to have had the whole skeleton, but that one bone's enough to bring people here to look and that's good for trade." That set me thinking – my mind has been too full for proper thought, that's why I didn't make the connection between the Bealknap case and Richard Rich. Listen, we've wondered all this while why the Gristwoods waited six months between finding Greek Fire and going to Cromwell. Especially when according to Bathsheba they were plotting against him from the start.'

'Ay.'

'The Gristwoods knew, when they first stumbled on Greek Fire at Barty's, that this was something very big. And very profitable. Michael Gristwood worked at Augmentations and he would have known the anti-Cromwell faction was growing.'

'Everyone knew that.'

'So I think they decided to offer it to someone within the anti-reformist faction as something *they* could take to the king and use to advance themselves. Again, everyone knows the king's interest in ships and weaponry. The Gristwoods probably thought it was safer to be in with the coming faction.'

'Then who?' Barak asked, excited himself now. 'Marchamount? He's a protégé of Norfolk's, the earl's biggest enemy.'

'Possibly. Though, being at Augmentations, Michael had a channel to Rich and Cromwell says Rich is plotting. This puts him and Bealknap back on the list.'

'Then we have to include Lady Honor too. She's no reformist.'

'All right, for the sake of argument. At all events, the Gristwoods went to someone. Call them Cromwell's enemy for now. They took the barrel and the formula, and promised to make more Greek Fire for them. Toky and Wright were set to work to help them and probably to keep an eye on them too.'

'Yes, that fits.'

'So for six months they try to make more Greek Fire. But the stuff is like nothing they've ever seen and the formula, perhaps, referred to the use of an element they didn't have. I wondered earlier why the Romans, who knew of something like Greek Fire, didn't develop it as a weapon. There were sources, pools of strange flammable liquid in the ground, which the Byzantines had access to but the Romans didn't. Far beyond Jerusalem. And we don't have access, either, to whatever it was.'

His eyes were wide with interest now. 'Something essential to make Greek Fire?'

I nodded. 'I see Michael and Sepultus following all sorts of trails, like the Polish drink, trying different experiments, increasingly desperate.'

'Because they couldn't make Greek Fire despite having the formula.'

'Exactly. And how frustrating that must have been for them, and their masters, to have this opportunity for such power and wealth just beyond their grasp. Remember that they had reconstructed the apparatus that was used to project Greek Fire with the aid of Leighton the founder, and practised in his yard using the stuff in the barrel. They knew it worked. How frustrated, and how angry, they must have become as the winter passed and Cromwell found himself in ever greater trouble over the Cleves marriage.'

'So the demonstrations, the one I saw and the other one, used up all the stuff from the barrel?'

'They must have. All, or nearly all.'

'Ay. There must have been nearly half a barrelful in that tank, even if it was only partly filled.'

'By March I think Cromwell's enemy was losing patience with the Gristwoods. Perhaps with a better alchemist they could have divined some alternative, perhaps not. But they dared not spread the word beyond a very small circle. So they devised another plan — they decided to try and turn the fact they only had a limited amount of Greek Fire to their advantage. Oh, they have been very clever.'

'So —' Barak raised a hand, frowning — 'they went to the earl and said they *had* got Greek Fire, said they *had* made some, and he told the king.'

'Exactly. And they used a chain of contacts to reach him — Bealknap, Marchamount, Lady Honor — that would make the story sound more plausible.'

'Then none of those three need have been involved.'

'None, or some, or all.'

Barak whistled. 'And then they staged the demonstrations, using what was in the barrel. To trick the earl into making a promise to the king that he could never keep.'

'Yes. Perhaps the Gristwoods were told they'd be paid off and could flee England before Cromwell found out that there was no more Greek Fire. They weren't told about the final part of the plan — to kill them and make it appear as though the formula had been stolen and might be given to a foreign power. *After* Cromwell had got the king excited, and promised him a demonstration.'

'On Thursday.'

'Yes. The unfortunate founder was killed because he knew too much, I'd guess. Also the throwing device was probably in his yard and Cromwell's enemy needed to take it away.'

Barak nodded. 'You were right to go back to the beginning after all.' He frowned. 'If you're right.'

'It's the only reconstruction of events that makes everything fit.'

He stood a few moments, nibbling thoughtfully at his knuckles. I watched him anxiously, frightened he might see some hole in my theory that I had missed. But he only nodded. 'And poor Bathsheba was killed lest Michael Gristwood might have told her something between the sheets. As he had.'

'I suspect they fired Goodwife Gristwood's house with what little of the stuff they had left to show Cromwell it still existed. And as a warning of what it could do; everyone who saw that fire remarked how the house was aflame from end to end in a moment. If there was an enquiry, that would come out. Imagine how the king would react.'

Barak gave me a look of horror. 'But if you're right, there can never be another demonstration. The earl will have to tell the king anyway.'

'Yes, yes. But he can tell him the whole thing was a plot by his enemies, that the king was deceived as well. Cromwell could still turn it to his advantage. If we can find who's behind it, if he can give the king a name.'

Barak ran a hand over his shaven skull. 'Marchamount? But Marchamount may be only a victim.'

'Yes,' I agreed. 'He may.' My enthusiasm started to wane.

Barak looked at me eagerly. 'If we can uncover who the earl's enemy is, they may still have some Greek Fire. Surely they'd keep at least a little back. If that were given to the king, he could set a troop of alchemists to make it and he might have it after all.'

I had forgotten that possibility. Of course they would keep some back. I cursed inwardly, then took a deep breath.

'Why does nobody think of the death and destruction this thing could wreak? You most of all, Barak – you've seen it, you were nearly killed by it! How can you be so disturbed by what was down that well, yet face the death of thousands by fire without a second thought?'

My appeal fell on deaf ears. 'They would be soldiers. Soldiers expect to fight and die for their country.' He looked at me fixedly. 'If it will save my master, he shall have it.'

I said nothing. Fortunately he was too excited to notice the depth of my concern. 'You should write a letter to the earl at once,' he urged. 'I'll take it to Grey. He should know about this.'

I hesitated. 'Very well. It's too late to go to Lincoln's Inn now, but we'll go tomorrow and see what we can find in Marchamount's rooms.'

'If it turns out he's behind it, and we can bring proof, the earl is safe.' He smiled eagerly.

I nodded. But if we find more Greek Fire, I said to myself, Cromwell shall not have it. If I have to, I will prevent Barak from giving it to him.

# Chapter Forty-one

DESPITE EVERYTHING, I slept peacefully that night. I woke towards six refreshed, although my back ached when I got up. I changed the bandage on my arm, pleased to see it had almost healed, then for the first time in days I did Guy's exercises, carefully lest I do more harm than good. It was the eighth of June; we had two days left now.

After breakfast Barak and I walked up to Lincoln's Inn, where the lawyers' day was just beginning. A carousing student lay collapsed on the bench where I had met Lady Honor. He sat up and winced at the light; barristers walking past with papers under their arms gave him disapproving scowls. We passed my rooms and headed for Marchamount's chambers.

The two clerks in his outer office were agitated. One was anxiously explaining a case where Marchamount was due to appear that morning to another serjeant. The other clerk was leafing frantically through a pile of papers; he gave a groan and sped across to Marchamount's room, the door of which was open. We followed him in. He glanced up from searching through another pile of papers and gave us a harassed look.

'This room is private. If you're here about one of Serjeant Marchamount's cases, please wait. We have to find the papers for this morning.'

'We're here on Lord Cromwell's orders.' I said. 'To investigate his disappearance. And make a search.' Barak produced his seal. The man looked at it, hesitated, then shook his head in despair. 'The serjeant will be angry, he has private things in here.' The clerk found the paper he was looking for, grasped it and hurried out. Barak shut the door behind him.

'What are we looking for?' he asked.

'I don't know. Anything. We'll search his living quarters after.'

'If he's gone of his own will, he won't have left anything incriminating behind.'

'*If* he has. Look in those drawers, I'll search the desk.'

It felt strange to be rifling through Marchamount's possessions. A locked drawer roused our hopes but when Barak prised it open we found nothing inside but a genealogical chart. It traced Marchamount's family back two hundred years. Occupations were scribbled under the names; fishmonger, bell-founder, and worst of all 'villein'. Under one name from a hundred years back Marchamount had scrawled '*This man was of* Norman *descent!*'

Barak laughed. 'How he lusted after that title.'

'Ay. He was always a vain man. Come, let's try his living quarters.'

But there was nothing there either, only clothes, more legal papers and some money, which we left. We quizzed the clerks but all they could tell us was that they had come in to work the day before to find Marchamount gone, with no message and a hundred jobs waiting. Defeated, we left and crossed the courtyard to my chambers.

'I'd hoped there would be something,' Barak said.

I shook my head. 'The people involved in this wouldn't leave evidence of Greek Fire in their homes. Even the Gristwoods kept that apparatus out at Lothbury.'

'They kept the formula at home.'

'And look what happened to them. No, everything's hidden away somewhere.'

'But where, if not in a house?'

I stopped dead. 'What about a warehouse?'

'That's possible. But there are dozens along the river bank.'

'There was a warehouse conveyancing among the cases I lost. Near Salt Wharf. It struck me at the time that the transaction was conducted in the name of people who looked like nominees and I wondered who would want to keep ownership of a warehouse secret.'

'But it was Rich who took those cases away from you.'

I paused a moment, then hastened into chambers. Skelly was sharpening a quill into a nib; he squinted up at me.

'John,' I asked. 'Is Master Godfrey in?'

'No, sir.' He shook his head sadly. 'He has another hearing before the committee.'

'Will you do something for me? You know a number of cases have been taken away from me recently – half a dozen or so. Would you make a list for me now? The names, what they were about and the parties.'

'Yes, sir.'

'Wait.' I looked into his red eyes. 'I have wondered, John, if you see as well as you might.' And then I was filled with guilt, for he looked mortally afraid.

'Perhaps not, sir,' he murmured, shifting from foot to foot.

I made my voice cheerful. 'I have an apothecary friend who is experimenting with spectacles. He is looking for subjects. If you would go to him he may be able to help your sight, and as you would be aiding his work there would be no fee.'

I saw hope in his face. 'I'll be glad to see him, sir.'

'Good. I'll arrange it. Now, go and make the list.'

He scurried away.

'Do you think that warehouse could really be where they are storing the Dark Fire and the apparatus?' Barak asked.

'It seems a long shot, I know. But it's a possibility; we have to follow it up.' I looked into his sceptical face. 'Unless you have a better suggestion.'

Barak nodded. 'All right, then.'

'I've never heard of a warehouse bought through a nominee before. It stayed in my mind, it was so unusual. Could that be the explanation? It was the last of my cases to go – just after I took Cromwell's assignment.'

'Anything's worth a try.' Barak had crossed to the open window. 'What's going on out there?' he asked suddenly.

I joined him. A small crowd of people, servants and barristers and clerks, had gathered round one of the students, a stocky young fellow with fair hair. He stood gesticulating wildly in the middle of the crowd, his eyes wide with shock. 'It's murder,' I heard him say.

Exchanging a look, Barak and I hurried outside. We shouldered our way through the crowd and I grasped the young fellow by the arm. 'What's going on?' I asked. 'Who's murdered?'

'I don't know, sir. I was going rabbit hunting, up by Coney Garth, and in the orchard I found – a foot. A foot in a shoe, cut off. And blood everywhere.'

'Take us there,' I said. He hesitated a moment, then turned and led us towards the gate to the orchard on the north side of Gatehouse Court. Part of the crowd followed us, nosy as sparrows.

'Stay back,' I said. 'This is official.' People grumbled, but they remained outside as we passed through to the orchard. The apple and pear trees were in full leaf and a carpet of long-fallen blossom lay all around. The student led the way through the trees.

'What's your name, fellow?' I asked.

'Francis Gregory, sir. I wanted some rabbits for the pot. I came out early, but I ran back when I saw that – thing.' I studied his face. He seemed none too bright and very frightened.

'All right, Francis. There's nothing to fear, but a man is missing and we have been ordered to find him.'

Reluctantly young Gregory led us on into the trees. In the middle of the orchard, on the blossom-covered ground, we found a gruesome chaos. A wide patch of ground was covered with blood, black and sticky-looking. One tree had had a branch hacked off and a great gouge cut in its side. The mark of an axe, Wright's weapon of choice. And, lying at the bottom of the tree, was a shoe with an inch of white leg visible above.

I stepped on to the bloody ground to look at the severed foot, my stomach churning a little at the sight. It had been shorn off like a pig's trotter. Flies were buzzing around it.

'That's a gentleman's shoe,' Barak observed.

'Ay.' I saw something else among the blossom and, taking my dagger, brushed the delicate petals aside. Then I jerked upright in disgust. Three fingers from a man's hand lay there, sliced off like the foot, little black hairs standing out against the waxy skin. And on one of them a large emerald ring.

'What is it?' Barak called. He stepped across to my side. I had been steeling myself to pick up the finger, but Barak did it without flinching. 'That is Marchamount's ring,' I said, in a low voice so the student could not hear. He had not ventured onto the patch of bloody ground.

'Shit,' Barak breathed.

'He must have come to meet somebody by arrangement and they went for him with an axe.' I took a deep breath.

'Toky and Wright.'

'Ay. He must have struggled, tried to escape. They probably swung at his foot to bring him down. Then he tried to defend himself with his hands. Poor Marchamount.'

'Why did they take the body away and leave these remains?'

'If it was dark, they may not have noticed the fingers or the ring.'

'I thought this place was patrolled to keep the lawyers and their gold safe.'

'Only the inner court, not the gardens or the orchard. There are ways in here over the wall from Lincoln's Inn Fields.'

His back to the student, Barak pulled the ring from the severed finger and slipped it in his pocket, letting the finger fall to the ground again. We walked over to the boy.

'There's no saying who this is, lad.' I said. 'Best report to the authorities. Go on now.'

He was happy to run from the place. Barak and I followed more slowly. I was glad I had sent a note to Lady Honor last night, warning her not to go out without servants.

'So Marchamount *was* involved with Toky and Wright,' Barak said.

'So it appears. Perhaps he was worried I was going to have him before Cromwell and told his master. Who decided to stop his mouth.' I stopped on the path. 'God's death, he should have known the risk he ran, enough mouths have been stopped already. The two Gristwoods, the founder, Bathsheba and her brother. And now him.'

'Perhaps he was the master,' Barak said.

'What?'

'Perhaps he had been running the whole thing with Toky and Wright, told them things were getting hot and they decided to kill him and make off with the Greek Fire.'

'You could be right,' I said. 'In that case, they're the ones we need to find.'

'Toky knows how things work. An education from the monks and years soldiering. He could arrange to sell Greek Fire to the highest bidder. Perhaps a foreigner.'

'But where are they? Where have they taken Marchamount's body? Where are the apparatus and the formula? Come, let us see if Skelly has done that list.'

By the time we reached the courtyard young Gregory was back at the centre of a crowd, declaiming about what we had found.

'They're bound to connect this to Marchamount soon,' Barak said.

'They won't be able to prove it's him, not without the ring.' I saw Bealknap on the fringe of the crowd, his eyes wide, and wondered if he had guessed who it was that had been killed.

Back in chambers Skelly was waiting for us, a paper in his hand. 'It's all done, sir.'

'Thank you.' I laid it on the table and Barak and I looked over his untidy scrawl. Four pieces of litigation over land, one over a will, and the warehouse conveyancing. Pelican Warehouse, off Salt Wharf.

'What's a pelican?' Barak asked.

'A bird from the Indies. It has a huge pouch in its beak, to hold fish. Or secrets.' I looked out of the window. 'Ask Bealknap to step in here, would you? Tell him, quietly, that we believe the dead man is Marchamount.' A thought occurred to me. 'John, would you add a couple of cases to the bottom of this list. Any cases of mine, choose them at random. Then bring it to me.'

Skelly, who had been standing open-mouthed, nodded and went into my office. A minute later Barak returned, Bealknap beside him. The rogue's eyes were full of fear.

'Is this true? Serjeant Marchamount is murdered? I feared it when I heard—'

'It is, Bealknap, though you'll say nothing, I order you by Lord Cromwell's authority. But I think no one who has any association with Greek Fire is safe any more.'

He waved his hands in angry desperation. 'But I've told you a dozen times, Shardlake, I've had nothing to do with it! It's over the priory matter that Sir Richard's been putting pressure on your cases, it's not about Greek Fire! I had nothing to do with the pestilential stuff beyond being a messenger!' Between fear and anger he was almost dancing; I had him worried now.

'You told Rich nothing about Greek Fire, I hope?'

'And get on the wrong side of the earl? Of course not!'

I handed him the list. 'Here, these are the cases I've lost recently. Can you confirm these are the ones Rich took from me?'

Bealknap ran his eye down the paper, then shook his head. 'I don't know. Sir Richard only told me he was going to damage your trade as a warning, he didn't say which cases he'd take!' He paused, running a hand through his wiry blond hair. 'Listen, if I'm in danger I need protection,' he said fiercely. 'I won't be struck down like Marchamount!'

'Why not?' Barak asked. 'Who'd miss you?'

'Bealknap,' I said quietly, 'I need to see Sir Richard Rich with this list. I need to know which cases he took away. It has a bearing on the other matter. Do you know where he is?'

'He should be at St Paul's at noon to hear Archbishop Cranmer preach. The archbishop is giving the lunchtime sermons this week, as Bishop Sampson's in the Tower. Half the king's council will be there.'

'I'd forgotten. Barak, we'd better go there. I need to show him this list.' I turned to Bealknap. 'Thank you. As for protection, perhaps you should lock yourself in your chambers the next few days with your chest of gold.'

'But – but I've business.'

I shrugged. Bealknap set his jaw, then turned and went out, slamming the door behind him. Through the window we saw him scurrying back to his chambers, glancing nervously around as he went. 'I doubt anyone will be after him,' I said. 'He knows nothing. Like Lady Honor.'

'You're sure he's telling the truth? He really knows nothing about Greek Fire?'

'Oh, yes. He's so scared for his skin he'd have thrown himself on our mercy if he thought he might meet Marchamount's fate. Now come, Barak, we must see Rich and find out whether he put that warehouse on the list.'

'What if he didn't?'

'Then we investigate the place.'

Barak nodded. 'And meet Toky and Wright with surprise on our side for once.'

# Chapter Forty-two

A s we rode down Fleet Street and into the City I noticed the
bank of cloud was spreading, filling the whole western sky.

'Probably the heavens will just tease us with a half-hour's rain like
last time,' Barak said.

I remembered the night of the banquet. Returning home to fetch
the horses, I had found a short note from Lady Honor – *Thank you
for your care for my safety. I am always watchful.* I had smiled and folded
it into my pocket. I sighed, wondering if my idea about the warehouse
had anything in it. It had fired Barak up, and me too, but that was
only for lack of any other leads.

We rode up Warwick Street, the great Norman cathedral looming
above us. I could see little dots moving on the flat roof under the giant
wooden spire. Londoners often went for a stroll up there to enjoy the
views of the City, and it had been crowded in the hot weather: like
the river, the roof was a place to catch a little breeze and escape the
City smells.

'Let's hope we get somewhere with Rich,' Barak said. 'Only two
days left, my master's enemies circling everywhere.'

'That warehouse was taken out of my hands at the end of May,' I
said. 'Just after Cromwell instructed me. The conveyance was almost
complete.'

'But who would have known then that you were acting in this?'

'Toky and Wright could have been watching us from the first day
we went to the Gristwoods and told their master I had been set on to
the matter. Yet—'

'What?'

'As I said yesterday, so many times they've been just ahead of us. As though someone close by was telling them our every move. But who?'

He laughed wryly. 'Joan Woode?'

'Hardly.'

'But who else has been near from the start?' He frowned. 'Only Joseph.'

'About as likely as Joan, I'd say. Even if Joseph wasn't a supporter of Cromwell.'

'And the earl has told nobody but Grey. He's been with the earl longer than Joan has with you. And he's as reformist as they come.'

I nodded. 'Then perhaps I am imagining it after all.' I wiped my brow; the air was distinctly clammy. I turned to Barak. 'I must visit the Wentworths' home today, confront the family with what we found. Will you come with me? I scent danger.'

He nodded. 'Ay. I'll come, if time allows.'

I felt a surge of relief. 'Thank you, Barak,' I said. He nodded gruffly, awkward as ever with praise. 'If we find Rich,' he said, 'you shouldn't let him know you're concerned particularly with the ware⁄house. He could have added it to his list to keep you clear of the place.'

'I know. That's why I got Skelly to add the names of a couple of cases that *haven't* been taken away. I'm going to ask Rich which ones he took away and observe how he reacts.'

'He may lie.'

'I know. He's good at dissembling, no lawyer does it better. And he's brutal enough to strike down anyone who gets in his way like a fly.' I bit my lip. It would take boldness to confront Richard Rich, privy councillor and, still, possible murderer.

'And if he satisfies you it wasn't him that took the warehouse out of your hands?'

'Then it was someone else. Either way, we go there today.' And if we found Greek Fire and Barak wanted to take it for Cromwell, I thought, what then? We were directly under the cathedral now, its great bulk shutting out the sky. 'Come,' I said, 'we can leave the horses at that inn.'

We stabled the animals and passed through the gate into St Paul's churchyard. I expected to see a great crowd round St Paul's Cross, where the preachers always stood, but the cobbled yard was deserted save for a few people waiting at the staircase leading to the roof. A couple of flower sellers stood by the door, doing a good trade in nosegays. They at least had done well out of the hot weather.

'Are we too early?' I asked Barak.

'No, it's nearly twelve.'

I accosted a passer-by. 'Pardon me sir, is the archbishop not preaching here this lunchtime?'

The man shook his head. 'He's preaching inside. On account of the hanging this morning.' He nodded to the wall behind me. I turned and saw a temporary gallows had been erected; sometimes people whose crimes had particularly sinful implications were hanged in the churchyard. 'A dirty sodomite,' the man said. 'The archbishop shouldn't be polluted by his presence.' He went to join the queue for the roof. I glanced at the figure hanging from the rope, then quickly looked away again. A young man in a cheap jerkin: no one had come to pull on his legs and he had strangled slowly, his face purple and hideous. He had died in terror. For a moment I felt surrounded by death. I took a deep breath and followed Barak, who was already at the cathedral door.

St Paul's Walk, the huge central nave with its vaulted stone ceilings, was the greatest marvel in London and normally visitors from the country would have been walking to and fro, gazing up in wonder while the cutpurses and bawdy women circled around the pillars waiting for their chance. But today the nave was almost empty. Further up the cathedral, though, a large crowd stood around the pulpit. There, under the brightly coloured painting of the Last Judgement showing death leading the estates of the realm to heaven and hell, which Cromwell had not yet removed, a man in a white cleric's robe and black stole stood preaching. Barak took a chair and stood on it, peering over the heads of the crowd and drawing disapproving glances from those nearest him.

'Can you see Rich?' I asked.

'No, there's too many folk. He's likely near the front. Come on.' He began jostling his way through the crowd, ignoring murmurs of protest, and I followed in his wake. There were several hundred people come to see the great archbishop, who together with his friend Cromwell had supervised all the religious changes since the break with Rome.

We reached the front, where robed merchants and courtiers stood with their heads lifted to the speaker. Even Barak dared not barge his way in among these people. He stood on tiptoe, looking out for Rich. I studied Cranmer, for I had never seen him before. He was surprisingly unimpressive, short and stocky with a long oval face and large brown eyes that seemed fuller of sadness than authority. A copy of the English Bible lay before him on the lectern. He touched the edges lovingly as he preached.

'God's Word,' he proclaimed in a ringing voice. 'All one needs to understand it is to be able to read and write, nay, even to listen may be enough. And thus one has access to the word of God himself direct, with no priest, no Latin mummery, to stand between. As it is said in Proverbs, chapter thirty: "Every word of God is pure, he is a shield to them that trust him—"'

It was strong reformist stuff; if the conservative Bishop Sampson had been preaching this week as planned, the emphasis would have been on obedience and tradition. Sampson, like Cranmer, would have had a stock of quotes culled from the vastness of the Bible to back his own position; I had heard some printers were even producing indexes of quotations for use in argument. I thought of Elizabeth's patient study, which had turned into fanatic rage against God, and turned away. Where is my own faith? I thought. Where did it go? How did it slip away?

'There he is,' Barak whispered in my ear. He began weaving through the crowd again, excusing himself politely. So he can be polite when he wants, I thought, as I followed him. At the very front, a small group of retainers round them, stood two richly robed figures; Richard Rich and Thomas Audley, the lord chancellor. Rich's handsome face was composed into a bland expression; it was impossible to tell if he approved of the sermon or not. He would be hedging his bets, for if Cromwell fell Cranmer would go too, probably to the fire. I saw Audley lean close and make a comment to Rich, smiling sarcastically, but Rich only nodded expressionlessly.

Barak took the earl's seal from his pocket and handed it to me. 'Here, you take this. It'll get you past those retainers.' I nodded. My heart was beating fast and I took a moment to compose myself before going over to the two privy councillors. One of the retainers turned, alert, as I approached, his hand going to his sword hilt. I showed him the seal.

'I need to speak to Sir Richard urgently. On Lord Cromwell's business.'

Rich had seen me. A frown crossed his face for a moment, then he smiled sardonically and stepped towards me.

'Well, Brother Shardlake again. God's death, you follow me everywhere. I thought I had settled our business when I spoke to the earl.'

'This is another matter, Sir Richard. Another matter of the earl's I need to discuss with you.'

He looked at me curiously. 'Well?'

'May we go somewhere a little quieter?'

He gathered his robe around him. With a sign to his retainers to stay where they were, he waved an arm to indicate I should lead the way through the crowd. I led him across to the far wall, out of earshot of the preaching. Barak followed, keeping at a little distance.

'Well?' Rich asked again.

I took the list from my robe. 'I need to know, Sir Richard, which of these cases are the ones you persuaded my clients to take away from me.'

He eyed me sharply. Those cold grey eyes were as empty of feeling as the sea. 'What has that to do with the earl?'

'I can only tell you he has an interest in one of the matters.'

'Which?' he asked sharply.

'I may not say.'

He tightened his hard mouth. 'One day, Shardlake . . .' he said quietly. He snatched the list and ran his eyes down it. 'The first, second, fourth and fifth,' he said. 'Not the third, sixth or seventh.'

The third was the warehouse. I studied his face intently, but could read nothing. Surely he would have paused, or blinked, if he had recognized Salt Wharf.

He thrust the list back at me. 'Well, is that all?'

'It is. Thank you, Sir Richard.'

'God's death,' he said with a mocking laugh, 'how you stare at one. And now, if I may, I shall return to the archbishop's sermon.' He turned away without a bow, shoving his way back through the crowd. Barak appeared at my side.

'What did he say?'

'He said the warehouse wasn't one of the ones he'd had taken.'

'D'you believe him?'

'He didn't pause for a second as he read the list. But he's so clever.' I was seized by uncertainty. 'I don't know. I don't know.'

But Barak did not reply. He was looking down the hall. Then he turned slowly and said to me quietly, 'Wright's here, I saw him. He's dodged behind that pillar. I don't think he saw me looking. He's watching us.'

Instinctively I backed against the wall. 'What's he doing here?'

'I don't know. Maybe he's after us again.'

'Maybe he's here with Rich. Can you see Toky?'

'No.' Barak's face set. 'This is our chance to catch him. Have you your dagger?'

I put a hand to my belt. 'These days, always.'

'Then will you help me?'

I nodded, though my heart raced at the thought of facing that monstrous creature again. It was only hours ago that he had struck Marchamount down. I tried not to look at the pillars. 'Is he armed?'

'He's a sword at his belt. Even he wouldn't bring an axe into St Paul's.' Barak spoke quickly and quietly, a casual smile on his face. 'We'll walk down the nave as though nothing is the matter. When we reach that pillar I'll rush round to one side. You go the other way and cut him off.' He looked at me intently. 'Can you do it?'

I nodded again. Barak began to move down St Paul's Walk, his stance casual. On the far side of the cathedral Cranmer's voice could be heard still rising and falling, a distant noise.

We reached the pillar; then, fast as a cat, Barak unsheathed his sword and leaped round the side. I heard a sharp ring of metal on metal; Wright must have had his own sword drawn already. He had been waiting there to kill us.

I ran round the other side of the pillar to see him and Barak with swords raised against each other, circling, Wright moving quickly and fluidly for such a big man. All around people stopped and flattened themselves against the wall. A woman screamed.

I drew my dagger. Wright had not seen me yet. If I could stab him in the arm or leg, disable him, we should have him. I had never attacked a man in cold blood before but my brain was clear, every nerve alert, my fear gone. I stepped forward. Wright heard me and turned, even as he parried a thrust from Barak. His expression was as it had been at the priory: brutish, inhuman, though intent on escape now, not murder.

He bounded to one side and ran down the nave, his sword flashing in the light from the stained-glass windows. 'Shit!' Barak said. 'Come on.' He ran after Wright and I followed, as fast as I could, down St Paul's Walk. Wright had paused, his way was blocked by a large family party heading for the door to the roof. Even if he slashed his way through them, Barak would have time to reach him and strike him down.

Wright turned and ran for the door. An elderly couple had just reached the bottom of the stairs; the woman yelled as Wright thrust her aside and began running up, Barak at his heels. I ran after them, my robe billowing around me. By the time I neared the top of the staircase I could scarcely breathe, my throat was burning as it had after the fire and for a second I tasted smoke. I saw the open door to the roof ahead, a rectangle of sky.

I raced up the last few steps. The breeze, colder and stronger here, struck my burning face. Ahead of me was the broad flat roof, the great wooden spire thrusting five hundred feet into the sky. Over the low parapet I saw all London laid out before me, the river curling like a snake, dark grey clouds looming right overhead now. Frightened strollers stood crouched against the parapet, staring at Barak. He had Wright at bay, his back against the steeple, sword held up as Barak circled. Wright was big and fast, but Barak was younger and faster. I ran over to join him, standing between Wright and the door to the stairs, holding my dagger just beyond reach of Wright's sword. Behind me, people began running for the door.

A mocking smile appeared on Barak's face. He waved a beckoning hand at Wright.

'Come on, bully, it's all up now. You shouldn't have left your mate Toky at home. Drop the sword and come quietly. We don't want you dead, just got some questions Lord Cromwell wants answered. Answer him nicely and he'll make you rich.'

'No, he won't.' Wright's voice was deep and heavy. 'He'll make me dead.' His eyes darted between Barak and me; I could see he was calculating whether he could rush me and get to the door. My stomach clenched with fear at that thought. But I would not let him escape, not now, no matter what the cost. I took a firm stance. Wright saw my resolution and his eyes roved between us wildly; he knew he was trapped.

'Come on,' Barak said. 'If you tell Lord Cromwell all, you may be spared the rack, eh?'

Then Wright jumped away from the steeple; not at me but away from us both, further out on the roof. The move took us by surprise. Barak jumped after him and I followed, helping him edge the big man towards the parapet to trap him again. Wright looked over his shoulder at the dizzying drop. He ran his tongue over his lips, swallowed, then spoke again, his voice suddenly high-pitched with fear.

'I always vowed I'd never hang! I vowed it again when I saw that man in the yard.'

'What?' Barak paused, his sword held in mid-air. I guessed what Wright meant before Barak and made a grab for his arm but he had already leapt onto the parapet. I believe he would have jumped anyway, but in glancing round at me he lost his balance and fell over. He vanished into the great void without even a cry. We ran to the parapet, but by then Wright had already hit the ground. He lay there a hundred feet below, his face a white blob, blood from his smashed body spreading slowly out across the yard.

# Chapter Forty-three

BARAK PULLED ME FROM the roof and hustled me down the stairs. At the cathedral entrance a number of people who had already run down were talking excitedly to some cathedral officials; as we neared the door a woman ran in screaming that a man was fallen from the roof. The officials raised their hands and bade them speak quietly, concerned above all with not interrupting the archbishop's sermon. We slipped out unnoticed.

Barak led me at a half-run into the maze of alleys round Foster Lane. He stopped at last near the Goldsmiths' Hall, leaning against the wall of a candlemaker's shop where a moon-faced apprentice stood in the doorway calling out, 'Tallow candles, farthing a dozen!' over and again. I collapsed against the wall, gasping for breath.

'Take off your robe,' Barak said. 'They'll be looking for a man in lawyer's garb.'

I pulled it off, bundling it under my arm. Barak straightened his doublet and looked around. The apprentice ignored us, calling his master's wares and occasionally pushing a lock of sweat-soaked hair back from his face.

'Come on,' Barak said. 'There'll be a hue and cry out soon. Bishop Bonner will be furious, a sword fight in the cathedral while the archbishop himself was preaching.'

'It'll be a murder hunt. And I'll be identified — a hunchback lawyer will be easily remembered. They'll be looking for a bald young man too. Here.' I gave him my cap — his own had fallen off during the struggle in the cathedral. He put it on.

'Thanks. I have the earl's seal, but we haven't time to argue with thick-headed constables.'

I wiped my brow. Over the roofs I could see the upper storeys of the Guildhall. Was it really only a fortnight since I had stood there as a respected barrister? Before Joseph came and set me on this dreadful, frantic journey?

'What now?' I asked wearily. 'The warehouse?'

'Ay, we should do it now.' He looked at me. 'God's nails, you're sweating.'

'I'm not used to fighting for my life, Barak. And it is so close.' I looked at the sky. The cloud had covered it completely and was thickening, darkening.

'We'll go by the back ways. Come on.'

I followed him through the lanes, jostling people and animals, squelching through the stinking channels. To reach the river we had to cross Cheapside, and as we crossed to the southern side someone called my name. I spun round, fearing to see a constable, but it was only Jephson, an alderman I knew, striding towards us with an attendant in tow. I bowed hastily.

'Master Shardlake, good morning. I must speak with you.' The expression on his round, clean-shaven face was serious. I cursed inwardly. If he had heard the news from St Paul's he might call the constable or even order passing citizens to arrest us. I did not relish a melee in the street. Already Barak's hand was slipping to his sword.

'I must tell you, sir. The Common Council wishes to thank you—'

'What?'

'For ordering those old stones from Ludgate to be brought to our attention. The Hebrew shows they were indeed from an ancient synagogue. Why, we have no other such examples of Hebrew writing in all London.'

My heart lurched with relief. I swallowed. 'I am glad I have been of service, sir. Now, urgent business awaits—'

'We shall arrange for the stones to be displayed at the Guildhall.

The Jews are only a memory, but still these stones are a part of our City's history and should be preserved.'

'Thank you, Master Jephson. But now, you must excuse me—' I bowed quickly and turned into the lanes before he could say more.

'Arsehole,' Barak said as soon as we were out of earshot. 'I'd've liked to knock him down, just to prove I'm no memory.'

'I'm glad you didn't.'

He pointed to where a man was selling small ale from a barrel. 'I'm thirsty.'

I needed a drink too and we each bought a half-pint, quaffing it down from the man's wooden cups. As we drank I looked down the lane leading to the river; I felt for a moment someone was watching, but I could identify no one among the sweating, bustling crowds.

✝

SALT WHARF WAS a wide triangular inlet which had been carved into the river bank to allow small boats to unload. There was a street of warehouses running along one side of Queenhithe dock. We walked round the dock, where two sea-going ships were unloading oranges, and began to look for Pelican Warehouse.

It was the last of the buildings, hard by the river and solidly constructed of brick, four storeys high. A faded sign showing a bird with a huge beak hung outside. The windows were well shuttered and barred against thieves and the door was secured with a big padlock. Although people were working in the adjacent buildings, Pelican Warehouse seemed deserted.

We walked to the far end of the building, where its south end dropped directly into the river. I looked down at the brown water. The tide was low, revealing green slime on the bottom of the wall. Peering up, I saw an open hatchway at the first-storey level, with a winch to draw goods from boats below projecting from it. A rope hung from the winch, swinging lightly in the cool breeze from the river.

'No sign of life,' Barak said at my elbow. 'I've knocked but there's no reply. There's a hollow echoing sound, like nothing's stored here. Shall I try and break in?'

I nodded and he produced his little metal tool and bent to pick the lock as he had at the Wentworths' well. I looked uneasily across the dock at the men unloading the boat, but they paid us no attention.

'I hope the bastards haven't gone,' he muttered. 'They might move the stuff regularly to avoid being found.'

'There may only be Toky left.' Even alone, I thought, he would be a dangerous adversary.

There was a click and the padlock fell open. 'There!' Barak said. 'Let's see what's inside.'

The door opened smoothly on well-greased hinges. Barak shoved it back against the wall lest anyone was concealed there. It made a hollow, echoing bang. A dark interior was revealed, lit only by one glassed window high up. The warehouse was as wide as the nave of a church and, I saw, quite empty. There was a musty smell of cloth and the stone floor was littered with tiny pieces of wool fibre. Drawing his sword, Barak stepped in. I followed.

'Empty as an old nun's womb,' he said.

I looked up at the end of the warehouse. A flight of wooden steps led up to an upper floor, which was merely a wooden platform running round the wall except for a room next to the stairs, its door closed.

'That must be the office,' I said.

'Shall we go up?'

I nodded, my heart beating fast. We climbed the rickety wooden staircase carefully. I looked at the door, afraid that it might open and that Toky might fly out at us. Barak held his drawn sword in front of him and I clutched the dagger at my belt. But we reached the platform safely. I saw that the door to the office was also secured by a padlock. It seemed darker now; glancing up at the high window, I saw the sky was dark as a winter dusk. I heard a faint rumble of thunder.

Barak bent to the padlock. I coughed at the fibre dust our feet had stirred up. The place looked as though it had not been used for months. I cast my eye along the platform. There was a bale of cloth in one corner. Barak grunted with satisfaction; he had the padlock off. He stepped back and kicked the door open.

The room was empty, there was nothing at all in there, just the big open hatchway giving a view of the lowering sky, the end of the winch secured to the floor with bolts. Then I saw a door to a second room. I nudged Barak and he threw it open, then whistled at what was inside.

A table stood in the middle of the room. There was a beer jug and three plates, an unlit tallow candle and a hunk of bread. Another bale of cloth by the table served as a seat. We stepped inside.

'Someone's been here very recently,' I said.

Then Barak stopped as he saw what was stacked against the far wall. A long metal pipe with a wick at one end, a complicated-looking pumping machine, and a metal tripod, all bundled together beside a large metal tank.

'The Greek Fire apparatus,' he breathed. 'And look at this.'

I saw, beside the ugly tangle of metal, a tall, narrow porcelain vase about two feet high. It was the type that might be used to plant a bush for display in a courtyard. I had seen ones like it at the House of Glass. I approached and, very carefully, lifted the little lid. Inside I saw a dark viscous liquid. The familiar vile stench of Greek Fire set the hairs at the back of my neck prickling.

I felt Barak's hot breath on my cheek as he stood beside me, peering into the vase. He dipped a finger into the stuff and lifted it to his nose. 'We've got it,' he breathed. 'God's blood, we've got it!' He stepped back, his face alight, gripping his sword handle hard in his excitement.

'It's probably all they have left,' I said. 'It would barely cover the bottom of that tank. Nowhere near enough to burn a ship.'

'I know.' Barak sniffed his finger, held it from him and sniffed again, as though the dreadful stuff were some wonderful perfume. 'But there's enough to show the king, enough for him to give to his alchemists. This could save the earl—'

There was a laugh behind us, loud and triumphant. We froze, then turned slowly. Toky stood there, a broad grin on his ravaged face. Two others were with him, a short stocky fellow with a straggly beard and a younger man, less rough-looking than the others. Him I had seen somewhere before. All three had swords raised.

'Drop the weapon, baldy,' Toky said in his sharp voice. 'You're outnumbered.' Barak hesitated a moment, then let his sword fall to the floor with a clatter.

Toky grinned again. 'Well, my beauties, we've been waiting for you. By God, you're hard to kill, but we've got you now.' He nodded at his younger confederate. 'Master Jackson here saw you drinking beer in Potter's Lane and hurried back to warn us. We padlocked the door so you wouldn't think we were here, hid round the corner, then came back once you'd broken in.' The bright catlike eyes fairly danced with delight. 'We thought you'd come up here and we guessed what you'd be looking for. You were so intent on the Dark Fire you never heard us creep across the boards.'

'Dark Fire,' I repeated. 'So you know that old name.'

'Ay, it's a better one than Greek Fire, for this is English Fire now and it will bring a mighty darkness to our enemies. And gold to us.' His smile broadened. I wondered if he knew Wright was dead – Barak said they had worked together for years. Perhaps he did not care. He laughed, an eager breathy laugh, then nodded at his confederates. '*Cadit quaestio.* The discussion is over. See, I know some lawyers' Latin.'

'So I heard. When you were a novice.'

'You know that, eh? Ay. Before they threw me out for charging the monks to grope me. I was pretty once.' He smiled. 'Kill them both,' he said.

Barak set his jaw. I stepped back, pointing to the jar. 'This is all you have left, isn't it?' I said hurriedly, talking for my life. 'You don't know how to make more – you failed. The barrel from Barty's was nearly used up in the demonstrations. It was all a trick to disgrace Cromwell. We know that and so does the earl.'

Toky's eyes narrowed. 'Then why are you here? Why not a troop of soldiers?'

'It was only a guess brought us. We didn't know where the stuff was. But others will follow soon, you'd do best to turn yourself over to the earl's mercy now.'

'Oh, shit,' the bearded man said, but Toky silenced him with a glare. Toky was frowning now, his ebullience gone. He ran a hand over his pockmarked face, eyes glittering between me and Barak.

'Do you know who our masters are?' he asked.

'Yes; they will be under arrest soon.' So there was more than one.

'Name them,' Toky snapped.

I hesitated. 'Richard Rich,' I said.

Toky smiled slowly. 'Rich. My arse. You don't know – this is bluff.'

'Kill them,' young Jackson said nervously. 'Get them out of the way while there's still time.'

'Not yet, don't be a fool,' Toky rasped. 'Our masters will need to hear how much they know. Fetch them here, they will have to decide what's to be done.'

'Both?' The young man's accent had some effort at cultivation; the accent of someone who served a rich master. Where had I seen him before?

'Ay. Tie them up first.' He nodded at some coils of rope in the corner. 'Use what we tied the founder with.'

Our hands were grasped roughly and pinned behind us. I felt a damp, greasy rope passed round them. We were manhandled into a corner and shoved down roughly onto the boards.

'Hurry, Jackson,' Toky urged.

With a last worried look at us, the young man left the room. I heard his footsteps descending the stairs. Toky sat on the bale of cloth, looking at us thoughtfully. The bearded fellow sat on the table, bit off a hunk of bread and washed it down with a swig of beer. He smiled at us, yellow teeth like a rat's dimly visible in the gloom.

'You're a scarecrow-looking pair to have caused so much trouble. Ain't they, Toky?'

Toky grunted; his ebullience had evaporated.

'Who are you, anyway?' Barak asked. 'I know who Toky is, but not you.'

'Jed Fletcher, out of Essex, at your service. Old friend of Master Toky's.' He gave a mocking bow and turned to Toky. 'Can we have the candle lit? It's getting black as night.' Outside I heard thunder again; the storm could not be far off.

Toky nodded at the vase of Greek Fire. 'No. You know it's not safe, not with that stuff here.'

'Who are they, then,' I asked, 'these masters of yours?'

Toky smiled evilly. 'You'll know them. You that's gone dining with the aristocracy.'

I felt suddenly cold. The only aristocrat I knew was Lady Honor. And now I remembered where I had seen the young man who was trying to improve his accent. He had been serving at Lady Honor's banquet. I stared at Toky. 'The House of Glass,' I whispered.

Toky looked at me through the deepening gloom. 'You'll see,' he said. 'Have patience.' He reached for the bread. There was silence for a minute. Then I heard a loud hissing sound from outside. I could not work out what it was at first, then drips began falling from the ceiling and I realized it was raining. Thunder sounded again, a mighty crack right overhead.

'It's come, then,' Fletcher said.

'Ay,' Toky agreed. 'God's bones, it is dark. We'll have that candle lit after all, but keep it on the far side of the table.' Fletcher set the candle on a plate, there was a struggle with a tinderbox and a yellow glow spread over the room. Our captors sat back, waiting.

'Listen,' Barak said. 'You know we work for Lord Cromwell. If we're killed there'll be a hunt up for you like you've never seen.'

Toky smiled sardonically. 'Piss the tavern keeper's son. He's finished.'

'If you let us go you'll be richly rewarded.'

'Too late for any of that, matey.' Toky sat looking at Barak, his eyes twin glinting points in the candlelight. 'I don't like the way you've led me such a dance,' he said.

'More of a dance than you think,' Barak said. 'Your mate Wright was killed this morning. Took a dive off the roof of St Paul's.'

'What?' Toky leaned forward.

'Join us, bully, before you join him.'

'You've killed Sam?' Toky's voice was a horrified croak. 'You've killed Sam!' Fletcher looked at him uneasily. Barak had made a bad mistake. Toky half-rose, then sat down again.

'By God,' he said, 'I'll see you two die slowly for this. You'll learn the tricks I know with my knife—' The look in his eyes chilled me.

Barak leaned back, brushing against me as he did so. He still stared at Toky, but I felt fingers brushing against my belt and realized he was trying to reach my dagger with his bound hands. They had not thought I might be carrying a weapon too. Taking care not to look at Barak, I edged slightly towards him. I felt the dagger withdrawn. Toky had put his head in his hands, Wright's death had affected him badly. Fletcher was still watching him anxiously.

Barak began sawing at my bonds, then lay still again as Fletcher rose and opened the door. Through the hatchway I could see rain sheeting down from the dark sky, a million tiny waterspouts dancing on the brown river. He closed the door again and returned to the table. Toky sat up. His face was paler than ever, a white oval, the candlelight making tiny pinpoint shadows in the pits of his face.

'Any sign of them?' His voice was composed, but I could sense the pain and fury behind it.

'No. It'll be a hard ride in this weather.'

Toky nodded, then sat looking down at his hands. He seemed not to want to look at us now. Barak recommenced sawing my bonds, slowly and carefully so that his movements should not attract attention. I bit back a cry as the sharp dagger sliced into my skin, then felt the rope fall away. It was hard not to follow the instinct to pull my chafed hands apart. I flexed my fingers carefully, then palmed the dagger from Barak and began sawing at his ropes in turn, all the while watching our captors. Toky was still absorbed in his thoughts, and Fletcher passed us only an occasional glance. He was restless, jumpy.

Then I heard feet on the stairs. Fletcher got up. I stopped sawing at Barak's bonds – surely I was almost through now? I risked a glance at him, but Barak kept his face impassive as Fletcher opened the door.

Serjeant Marchamount came in, shaking the water from a heavy coat. He looked down at us. There was a cold brutality I had never seen before in his face, the urbane mask quite fallen away.

'You did get out of your depth, didn't you?'

We stared at him open-mouthed. Barak was the first to recover his wits. 'You're supposed to be dead,' he said.

Marchamount smiled. 'You were getting too close, so I decided I'd better disappear. Just as well we'd kept that founder alive here. Toky and Wright took him to Lincoln's Inn orchard and hacked the life out of the fool. Then they put my ring on his finger and took the body away on a cart. That hatch is useful for throwing things into the Thames. You'll be leaving that way.'

'Wright's dead,' Toky said with a grim look at me. 'They threw him off the roof of St Paul's. I want my revenge with them.'

'So it's him they're all talking about all over the City,' Marcha-mount answered casually. He took off his coat, revealing a fine doublet embroidered with little diamonds. 'People were talking of some plot to kill Cranmer.' He looked at Toky. 'All right,' he said quietly. 'Do what you like with them later. I've sent Jackson on, by the way. We'll have to wait a little for a full house: this rain is turn-ing the streets into rivers.' He sat on the edge of the table, folding his plump hands together. He looked thoughtful. 'So. Cromwell knows we haven't been able to make any more Dark Fire, does he? But not our names?'

'No,' I said. There was no point in denying that now.

'Was the alchemy too hard for you?' Barak asked scoffingly.

For answer Marchamount crossed and struck him savagely across the face. 'I'm a serjeant, churl, you'll take a respectful tone when you talk to me.'

Barak stared boldly back at him. 'That didn't stop you conjuring up a common fraud. That's all this is.'

'No, it is not,' an aristocratic voice said from the doorway.

# Chapter Forty-four

MARCHAMOUNT AND THE two villains bowed deeply as the Duke of Norfolk entered, rain falling from his fur-lined coat, young Jackson following him. I realized he must have been at the banquet as Norfolk's servant, not Lady Honor's, and felt relief as well as horror as I understood just how high the plot reached.

Norfolk threw his coat to Fletcher, then stared at me with that cold haughty look of his. There would be no mercy from him, I knew. He walked over to the bale of cloth. Fletcher hastily rose to allow him to sit down.

'Well, Master Shardlake,' he said, 'I've had a wet trip across the river in the pissing rain thanks to you.' He smiled coldly. 'Yet you did well, considering the forces against you.' He laughed. 'More forces than you guessed. I wouldn't have minded a man like you on my side. But you've different loyalties, eh? Now, what does Cromwell know?'

'He knows by now that the Gristwoods were unable to make Greek Fire,' I lied.

'And how did you discover that?' His tone was conversational.

'By going back to how it began.'

'Ah yes, the monk Kytchyn. I expect he's squirrelled away in one of Cromwell's safe houses by now?'

'Yes, he's safe. Then I delved into the old sources. I realized there was a missing element that's needed to make Greek Fire, something that can't be found in England. But perhaps you have travelled the same path. Is that why Marchamount took the books from Lincoln's Inn?'

Marchamount nodded. 'Ay. And threatened the librarian with the duke's retribution if he asked any questions. It seems we have been following the same path, Shardlake. I have driven my mind to aching with those books. But I know we shall never be able to make Greek Fire in England.'

Norfolk nodded. 'But you didn't know I was behind the plot, or that Marchamount here was my man?'

'No, they didn't.' Toky said.

'Let the crookback answer.'

'No.'

Norfolk nodded slowly. 'Did you guess what our first plan was?'

'I think you planned to give Greek Fire to the king yourself, but when Sepultus Gristwood failed to make it you decided to turn it into a fraud to get Cromwell into worse odour with the king.'

Norfolk gave a bark of laughter. 'Why's the crookback not a serjeant, eh, Gabriel? He could outwit you in court any day.' Marchamount scowled.

'By God,' the duke continued, 'Sepultus Gristwood and his brother angered me. Going to Gabriel and promising they could make Greek Fire, him running to me saying we had the last nail for Cromwell's coffin. Then every week they said it would take a little longer, said there was another element they needed to find – it was months before they finally confessed they'd failed. It was Gabriel's idea to turn it against Cromwell, he's a clever fellow after all. And to make sure we dealt through intermediaries to give the story credence. He'll have his knighthood when Cromwell's gone, eh?' He clapped the serjeant on the shoulder; Marchamount reddened with embarrassment.

'So, no Greek Fire for the king. You should see him when he is in a rage. It is – spectacular!' Norfolk threw back his head and gave a bark of laughter. Marchamount and Fletcher joined in sycophantically, though Toky sat glaring at us, fingering the dagger he had pulled from his belt.

'Cromwell is tottering,' the duke said more quietly. 'This failure will bring him down. Then, when I step into his shoes, after a few months Greek Fire will be mysteriously found again. His alchemists shall have this vase and I shall be celebrated as the one who rediscovered it.'

'You can't make more,' I said.

'No? You have the formula safe, Marchamount?'

The serjeant patted his doublet. 'Yes, your grace. It never leaves my person now.'

The duke nodded, then turned back to me. 'We shall find the stuff the formula calls naphtha, Master Shardlake. We will make a voyage to where some can be found.'

'All those places are under the Turks.'

'Are they? Well, I am not short of gold.' Norfolk narrowed his eyes. 'This will be my triumph. The king tires of reform, he sees now the chaos it brings. In the end he will be persuaded back to Rome and, who knows, perhaps Catherine will give him another son. A Howard heir, in case anything should happen to the little Seymour prince.' He smiled again and raised his eyebrows.

'And you killed all those people to make it so.'

He nodded seriously. 'Yes. Does that offend your legal sensibilities, lawyer? They were common churls. Rogues and a whore, a common founder. They were nothing, chaff before the wind. I seek to change the future of England, save three million souls from the heresy of the reformists.' The duke stood up, walked over and kicked me, casually but painfully, on the shin. Then he nodded at Toky. 'I'll leave you to deal with them. Have what sport you wish, but before the lawyer's dead I want all the details of what Shardlake found in those old books. The bodies can go out of the hatchway afterwards. Marcha-mount, stay and help question him. Note what he says.'

The serjeant wrinkled his nose. 'Is that really necessary? It will be an unedifying spectacle—'

'Yes, it is,' the duke answered shortly. 'You're a bookish lawyer like the crookback. These fellows will know no more of old Roman writers than I do.'

Marchamount sighed. 'Very well.'

'And now I am going back to Bishop Gardiner's house to dine with Catherine. Inform me when it's done.' The duke inclined his head to me. 'You'll find there are more painful things than burning, lawyer, if I know Master Toky.' He snapped his fingers at young Jackson and the boy helped him back into his coat, then opened the door to the outer room. Through the hatchway I saw the sheeting rain and the river surging by, the tide nearly high now. Fletcher and Toky bowed as the duke swept through the doorway, followed by Jackson.

There was silence for a moment, save for the hissing of the rain and their footsteps descending the stairs. Toky pulled out a long, sharp dagger. He smiled. 'Each cut will be for Sam Wright.' He stood up. 'Here we go, crookback, we'll start with your ears—'

Marchamount gave me an apologetic smile. 'This will be an unusual type of discourse for lawyers, I am afraid.'

I felt Barak tense beside me. His hands, untied, shot down to the floor. Balancing on them, he launched a high kick at Fletcher. It was brilliantly done. He caught him in the stomach and sent him crashing back against the wall. His head hit it with a bang that shook the whole room and he slid down the wall, unconscious.

Barak leaped to his feet and lunged for the corner where his sword had been thrown. I hauled myself up, almost screaming at the pain from my back and my cut wrist, as Toky dropped his knife and pulled out his sword. Barak reached his weapon, but half-stumbled as he rose. Toky would have stuck him had I not grabbed my dagger and stabbed him in the thigh. As he let out a bellow of pain and fury Barak slashed at his hand, half severing it. Toky's sword clanged to the floor.

Marchamount reached to his belt and produced a dagger of his own. Breathing heavily, he lunged at me, but Barak kicked out again and knocked the big man's legs from under him. He landed on the floor with a thump. I winced as Barak lunged with his sword, burying it in Toky's heart. Toky looked down, stared round at us with those savage eyes, unbelieving, then their strange light seemed to go out and he crumpled slowly to the floor. Barak and I stood for a second, scarcely able to believe the savage force which had dogged our steps these last weeks was gone.

'There's a new face in hell,' Barak said.

There was a moan from the corner as Fletcher came to. Marcha-mount hauled himself up with the aid of the table, dusty and red in the face. Barak turned and held the sword at his throat. 'Now, you big old toad, you're going to come with us and croak to the earl.'

Marchamount swayed. 'Please,' he said. 'Listen. The duke will pay—'

Barak laughed. 'Not us, he won't. You'll have to do better than that, you fat toad. Whose ancestors were all fishmongers and serfs,' he added with pleasure.

Marchamount hung his head. I almost felt sorry for him. Fletcher was struggling to his feet. He stood groggily against the wall for a moment, taking in Toky's body and Marchamount pinned against the table. Then he jumped to the door, threw it open and ran. I made to follow but Barak held me back.

'Let him go. We've got our prize.'

'Please,' Marchamount groaned, 'let me sit. I feel faint.'

Barak gestured to the bale of wool. 'Go on, then, you great bag of guts.' He watched contemptuously as Marchamount half-fell onto it, then turned to me. 'Get that vase.'

'What?'

'We're taking that to the earl as well.'

I picked up the vase. At least it was in my hands. It was very heavy, almost full. 'I am not sure about this, Barak,' I said. 'We have Marchamount, we know about the duke. That's enough to save Cromwell and damn the Howards.'

He looked at me seriously. 'I must have that vase,' he said quietly.

'But Jack, you know what it can do—'

'I must have it. I—'

Barak broke off with a yell. Marchamount, moving faster than I would have thought possible, had bent and grabbed at Toky's sword, then jumped up and thrust at Barak's neck. Barak twisted just in time to deflect the blow, but it caught his sword arm. He grabbed at his bicep, blood welling between his fingers. He dropped the sword, his arm useless. Marchamount hefted Barak's sword and glanced at me standing with the vase. He gave me a triumphant look as he drew back his sword arm to give Barak a killing blow.

I threw the contents of the vase at him. A great spout of thick black liquid shot out, its stink filling the room as it drenched Marchamount. He howled, staggered back, and slipped in some of the stuff that had fallen to the floor. He overbalanced, falling back against the table. The candle overturned. The flame touched his sleeve and before my unbelieving eyes Marchamount's whole body erupted into a pillar of fire. I jumped back in horror as he screamed, a mass of flame from head to toe. He beat his hands against his sides, frantically, uselessly. Already there was an awful smell of burning flesh. I saw the table was burning too, and the floor where some of the stuff had fallen.

Marchamount ran for the open door, his legs swirling with flames, and staggered into the other room. I followed. I shall never forget the sight of him howling and writhing, a living torch of red and yellow flame, his white teeth bared in agony, his face already blackening, his hair on fire. He made a howling animal noise as he stumbled across to the hatchway, pieces of burning clothing falling from his body. An awful sizzling sound was coming from him. He leapt through the hatchway, still howling as he fell, a pillar of fire, into the river. He hit the water with a tremendous splash and disappeared. The horrible inhuman roaring was cut off and then nothing was left of him, only rags of his serjeants's robe still burning on the floor.

I heard Barak shout and turned back. The other room was an inferno, the vase that had held Greek Fire lying smashed in the centre of the flames, fire licking over the projection apparatus. Barak made a step towards it, bleeding copiously though he was. I grasped his shoulder.

'It's too late now. Come, or we'll go up with the warehouse.'

He gave me an angry, anguished look, but followed me as I ran for the stairs. We ran down into the body of the warehouse; looking up, we saw flames already licking round the walls of the office. Barak paused, blinked, collected himself.

'We must get to the earl,' he said. 'We must leave the fire to burn.'

I nodded. We ran outside into the rain. I gasped at the cold water lashing into my face. The ships were still being unloaded; the dock-hands, heads bowed, had not yet noticed the smoke that was starting to pour from the hatchway over the river. I looked down at the water; I thought I saw something black surface for a moment before it was swept upriver on the tide; it might have been a log of wood, or the remains of Marchamount, Greek Fire's last victim.

# Chapter Forty-five

WE WALKED SLOWLY BACK along Cheapside then down to the river, through lanes that the rain had already turned into trails of filthy, clinging mud. There can be something pitiless about rain when it pounds, hard, on exhausted heads, as though cast from heaven by an angry hand. This was a real storm, no half-hour cloudburst as before. Everywhere drenched Londoners, their thin summer clothes clinging to them, ran to get out of the rain.

Barak paused and leaned against a wall. He clasped his wounded arm and I saw a trickle of blood welling between his fingers.

'You need that seen to,' I said. 'We can walk to Guy's, it's not far.'

He shook his head. 'We must get to Whitehall. I'll be all right.' He looked at my wrist. 'How's your hand?'

'It's fine, it wasn't a deep cut.' I pulled a handkerchief from my pocket. 'Here, let me bind your arm up.' I tied the handkerchief round his arm, pulling it tight; there was a little spurt of blood and then, to my relief, the trickle stopped.

'Thank you.' Barak took a deep breath. 'Come, let's get a wherry.' He heaved himself away from the wall. 'We've won,' he said as we struggled on to the river stairs. 'It will be Norfolk who suffers, not Cromwell. Norfolk tried to gull the king and that won't ever be forgiven.'

'If the earl is believed. We've no proof now Marchamount is dead and everything destroyed in that fire.'

'Norfolk will be interrogated. And we'll get Fletcher picked up.' He whistled. 'Shit, the earl may have us appear before the king himself and tell our story.'

'I hope not. Whoever he believes, he'll be furious if there's no Greek Fire for him.'

Barak gave me a searching look. 'You saved my life by throwing that vase at Marchamount.'

'I did it without thinking – it was instinct. I'd not have had even Marchamount die like that.'

'But what if he hadn't attacked us? Would I have had to take that vase from you by force?'

I met his gaze. 'It's all one now,' I said. 'Past mattering.'

Barak said no more. There was a wherry waiting at the stairs, and soon a surging tide was carrying us rapidly upriver to Whitehall. The rain lashed down, churning up the river, rumbles of thunder still sounding overhead. A world of fire turned to a world of water, I thought. I could not help glancing into the river, fearing Marcha-mount's blackened corpse might reappear, but it must have long since sunk or been washed beyond the City by the tide. I hoped the people at Salt Wharf had managed to stop the warehouse fire from spreading; thank God the building was brick.

I huddled into my soaked clothes, watching the rain bouncing from the heads of Barak and the boatman. I saw from a church clock that it was almost three. I remembered I should have gone to the Wentworths today; I had only tomorrow left now. Joseph would be fretting and worrying.

'What did Norfolk mean when he said he's had more help than we guessed?' Barak asked suddenly.

I frowned. 'It sounds as though I was right earlier – someone close to us has been acting as a spy.'

'But who? The man I use to send messages is someone I trust.' He frowned. 'That old Moor knows much of what's been going on.'

I shook my head impatiently. 'Guy would never have any truck with murder.'

He grunted. 'Not even for the papist cause?'

'Believe me. I know him.'

'Or Joseph?'

'Come, Barak, can you see Joseph Wentworth acting as anyone's spy? Besides, he's a reformer.'

'Then who? Grey?'

'He's been at Cromwell's side these fifteen years.'

'Well, who then?'

'I don't know.'

The boat bumped into Whitehall steps. While I paid the boatman, Barak showed his seal to one of the guards and we were waved on into the palace. Climbing the stairs, I found it hard to get my breath, little white flashes danced in front of my eyes and I had to pause at the top. Barak was breathing hard too. I looked through the veil of tumbling water at the grand buildings, shivering, for a sudden cold had come with the rain. Barak blew out his cheeks and plodded on, and I followed him wearily.

Once again we made our way to the Privy Gallery and on to Cromwell's quarters. The guard admitted us to the outer office, where Grey sat over his papers. He was checking some documents with a clerk and looked up in surprise at our drenched, muddy forms.

'Master Grey,' I said, 'we have a message for Lord Cromwell. It is of the greatest urgency.'

He looked at us a moment, then bade the clerk leave. He came round his desk, fluttering his arms anxiously. 'What has happened, Master Shardlake? Barak, your arm—'

'We have the answer to Greek Fire,' I said. 'It was all a fraud, planned by Norfolk to discredit Cromwell.' I quickly told him what had happened at the warehouse, my words tumbling over each other. He sat with his mouth open.

'Please,' I concluded urgently, 'we must tell the earl at once.'

He glanced at Cromwell's closed door. 'He's not here. He had a message to go to Hampton Court, Queen Anne is there and sent for him. He left by boat an hour ago. He's due back at Westminster this evening, some parliamentary business—'

'Where is the king?'

'At Greenwich.'

'Then we'll go to Hampton Court.' Barak stepped away from the
table, then groaned. He staggered and would have fallen had I not
caught him and sat him on a chair. Grey's eyes widened.

'What ails him? Look, his arm is bleeding.'

I saw the tourniquet had loosened and Barak was bleeding again.
He was deathly pale and there was sweat on his face. 'God's teeth,
I'm cold.' He shivered, plucking at his soaked doublet.

'You're in no state to go to Hampton Court,' I said. I turned to
Grey. 'Is the king's physician here?'

Grey shook his head, hovering fussily over Barak. 'The king
ordered Dr Butts and his assistant away yesterday. They wanted to
open the ulcer on his leg again and he ordered them out with a volley
of oaths. Threw his cushions at them.'

'Then you should see Guy, Barak,' I said. 'I'll take you.'

'No. You must go to Hampton Court. Leave me here.'

'I'm half-fainting myself.' I turned to the secretary. 'Master Grey,
can you have a message taken to Hampton Court at once? By someone
you can trust, someone who is loyal to the earl?'

He nodded. 'If you think that best. Young Hanfold is here.'

'I remember him.' I smiled wryly. 'He brought me a message from
the Tower once that sealed the fate of a monastery. Yes, send him.'
I took a quill and scribbled a note to Cromwell. Grey impressed
Cromwell's seal on the letter and bustled from the room with it,
calling for Hanfold. I looked out over the sodden garden.

'What will Norfolk do now?' I asked pensively.

'He still thinks he's safe. It'll be hours before he starts to worry
because no message has come from the warehouse.'

I studied him; he was still very pale. 'Can you make it to Guy's?
We can come back after, or Cromwell can send for us there.'

'All right.' He got up slowly. 'Maybe I'd better, before I bleed to
death over Master Grey's fine chair.'

The secretary returned to say the message was on its way and a
boat was waiting to take us back downriver. I gave him the address of
Guy's shop and we hurried away. Another half-hour in the rain and

we disembarked. Barak was stumbling now and I helped him through the lanes to Guy's shop, staggering along the alleys like a pair of scarecrows.

Guy answered the door and let us in with little more than raised eyebrows; he was becoming used to this. We sat down in the shop; Barak removed his shirt and Guy examined his arm. It was a horrible gash, very deep. Barak clutched at his mezuzah as Guy's fingers probed.

'I think I should sew your arm, Master Barak,' Guy said. 'Can you bear some pain?'

Barak screwed up his face. 'Have I any choice?'

'Not much, I fear, unless you would bleed to death.'

I waited in the shop while Guy took Barak through to his workshop, after coating my wrist with some stinging oil. He brought dry clothes and I changed in the shop, glad there was no one to see. I wondered again what Lady Honor might make of my bent form if she saw it. Well, she knew what to expect and did not seem to find me so bad. As I transferred my belt and purse to my borrowed hose, wincing at another stifled cry from Barak in the other room, I felt a spurt of irritation at my long preoccupation over how I looked. It was a sort of dark vanity, almost, I thought, a sort of martyrdom. Well, my path was free to make friends with Lady Honor now and I would not miss my chance. My heart had plummeted when, in the warehouse, it had seemed for a while that she could be the one behind the Greek Fire plot after all. Plummeted far enough to make me realize the depth of my feeling for her.

I went across to the window and looked out; the rain seemed to be lessening. The window had steamed up and I leaned my head on the cool glass, shutting my eyes for a moment. The door opened behind me and Guy entered, flecks of blood on his robe.

'There,' he said quietly, 'that's done. I've told him to rest an hour. He's a brave young fellow.'

'Ay, he's hard as nails.' I smiled tiredly. 'We've won, Guy. There will be no Greek Fire. It's all burned up.'

He sat down on a stool. 'Praise God.'

'Did you destroy what was in that pot?'

'It's in the Thames.'

I told him what had happened at the warehouse. 'All that's left is to get that message to Cromwell.'

'Well, you have won, Matthew, fulfilled your mission and destroyed Greek Fire as well.'

'Ay, though that last was by strange chance. If Marchamount hadn't lunged at Barak—'

Guy smiled. 'Perhaps that was the hand of God, answering your prayers and mine.'

'God's hand struck Marchamount hard, then.' I looked at him seriously. 'I have hardly prayed at all these last days. What they did, Marchamount and Norfolk, all those people killed – they did it with the aim of restoring the pope, you do realize that?'

'As Cromwell too has done many evil things.'

I shook my head sadly. 'Once I did believe the world could be perfected. I don't think that any more. But I believe I've defended the bad side against the worse.' I frowned. 'Yet—'

'What?'

'Why does faith bring out the worst in so many, Guy?' I blurted out. 'How is it that it can turn men, papist and reformer both, into brutes?'

'Man is an angry, savage being. Sometimes faith becomes an excuse for battle. It is no real faith then. In justifying their positions in the name of God, men silence God.'

'But have the comfortable belief that, having read the Bible and prayed, they cannot be wrong.'

'I fear so.'

From within, I heard Barak call out for water. Guy rose. 'There, your friend is thirsty. I thought he would not lie quiet for long.' He smiled. 'I think he is no man of faith, but he has an earthy honesty.'

✝

THERE HAD BEEN NO message from Cromwell by the time we left Guy's an hour later. Nor was there any news at home. I sent Simon to retrieve the horses from the inn near St Paul's. Then Barak and I ate lunch and waited in my parlour as afternoon turned slowly to evening. We were too exhausted to do more than sit half-dozing.

'I must go to bed,' Barak said at length.

'Ay, I need rest too.' I frowned. 'Why hasn't Cromwell contacted us?'

'He's probably waiting for a chance to see the king,' Barak said. 'Likely he will do that first, then fetch us later if we're needed. We'll hear something in the morning.'

I heaved myself upright. 'Barak, do you think you are fit enough to come to the Wentworths tomorrow? It will be our last chance.'

He nodded, getting to his feet. 'Ay. It takes more than a sword thrust to lay me low. And what's to fear from a greasy steward, a fat old merchant and a brood of women? I'll come. The business started there after all, didn't it?'

'Ay, and it must end there, before Elizabeth comes back before Forbizer.'

✝

NORMALLY JOAN WOULD have woken us for breakfast, but after seeing the state in which Barak and I had returned home the good woman must have decided to let us sleep. Neither of us woke until nearly midday. I felt much better, though my wrist still hurt, and Barak seemed almost restored to his usual self, though still a trifle pale. It had stopped raining, but the sky was dark and heavy. To my surprise there was no word from Cromwell, only a plaintive note from Joseph begging for news.

'He must have seen the king by now,' I said. 'Surely he'd at least let us know.'

Barak shrugged. 'We're small fry, you and me.'

'Maybe we should send another message?'

'Demanding news? That would be a mighty insolence.'

'At least we can send a message saying if we're not here we'll be at the Wentworths, and ask him if he needs us.' I looked at him. 'Are you fit to go to Walbrook?'

'Fit as a fly. You look better too.' He laughed. 'You're not as weakly as you pretend.'

'It's all right for you to say that at your age. I'm going to write a note, then we ought to go. I'll send Simon, get him to put it into Master Grey's hands himself. That'll be an adventure for him, going to Whitehall. I'll borrow your seal, if I may, so I can stamp it in the wax.' I hesitated. 'I ought to go myself, but there's no time. We should not have slept so long, it is less than twenty-four hours before Elizabeth returns to court.'

✝

WE TOOK A BOAT into the City, then walked up to Walbrook. I had dressed in my robe and my best doublet and urged Barak to borrow my second-best robe to conceal his bandaged arm.

A maid answered the door. 'Is Sir Edwin in?' I asked. 'I am Master Shardlake.'

Her eyes widened a little; she recognized my name. I wondered how much the servants knew of what had happened here.

'He's at the Mercers' Hall, sir.'

'Goodwife Wentworth, then?' The girl hesitated. 'Come,' I said briskly, 'we have business with Lord Cromwell at Whitehall today. Is your mistress in?'

Her eyes widened further at Cromwell's name. 'I'll see, sir. Please wait.' She left us at the door and scurried off into the house. Minutes passed.

'What's keeping her?' Barak asked irritably. 'Let's go in.'

I held him back. 'She's coming.'

The girl reappeared, looking flustered. She took us upstairs, and once again we were led into the parlour with its tapestries and cushioned chairs, its view of the garden and the well. The room was cold today. This time the old woman was the only member of the

family present. She was still dressed in black, her dark hood highlight-
ing the paleness of her lined face. The young steward Needler stood
behind her, his broad features impassive but his eyes watchful. The
old woman had evidently just eaten, for a tray stood on a table at her
elbow, with the remains of a dish of spring vegetables and a hunk of
cold beef. I saw that the empty plate, the mustard pot and the little
salt cellar were all of silver.

Goodwife Wentworth did not get up. 'You will forgive me if my
steward stays, Master Shardlake. There are no other members of the
family at home just now.' She smiled. 'He can be my eyes. Tell me,
David, who is it that accompanies him? He has the steps of a young
man.'

'A bald young fellow,' Needler said insolently. 'Though he dresses
well enough.'

Barak gave him a steely look.

'He is my assistant,' I told her.

'Then we each have a chaperon,' Goodwife Wentworth said with
another smile, showing her horrible false teeth and wooden gums.
'Now, what may I do for you? I understand the business is urgent.
Elizabeth returns to court tomorrow, does she not?'

'She does indeed, madam, unless fresh evidence can be brought.
Evidence, for example, of what lies at the bottom of yonder well in
the garden.'

'Our well?' she asked quietly. 'Whatever can you mean, sir?' Her
composure was remarkable.

'The bodies of the animals your grandson Ralph tortured and
killed for sport are there. Including Elizabeth's cat that Sabine and
Avice brought to him. And a tortured child, a little beggar boy.
Whom Needler must have seen, but which you said nothing of at the
inquest.' I looked from one to the other of them. They were silent,
their faces expressionless.

'The boy had things done to him that would make a hangman
sick,' Barak added.

The old woman laughed then, a shrill cackle. 'Are they mad,

David? Are they frothing at the mouth, plucking straws from their hair?'

I spoke evenly. 'It must have been hard, these last weeks, for your granddaughters to keep such a secret.'

'Elizabeth is my granddaughter too,' the old woman said.

'Sir Edwin's children are all you have ever cared for. Them and their advancement.'

She was silent for a long moment. Then her lips set hard. 'I see you have learned much.' She sighed. 'It seems I must tell you all. David, I would like a glass of wine. Master Shardlake, you and your assistant will have one?'

I did not answer, surprised by the speed of her capitulation. I looked at the steward.

His face was tense, anxious.

'Get some wine, David,' the old woman said quietly.

Needler went over to the buffet, then turned to his mistress. 'The family had the last of it yesterday, madam. Shall I fetch another bottle from the cellar?'

'Ay, do that. I will be safe enough, I think.'

'Quite safe,' I replied grimly. Needler left the room. The old woman worked her hands in her lap, playing with her gnarled, beringed fingers. 'Elizabeth has spoken, then?'

'Reluctantly, yes. To us and to your son Joseph.'

She pursed her lips again. 'My family has come far,' she said quietly. 'If Edwin had been like Joseph we would all still be country clods, working at that dreary farm. But Edwin has brought us advancement, wealth, the chance for his children to mix with the highest in London. It has been a great consolation to me in my blindness. Now that Ralph is gone our hopes rest on good marriages for Sabine and Avice. It is all we have left.'

'Are they safe for a young man to marry? After what they have done?'

She shrugged. 'They only need a strong lusty fellow to take them in hand.'

Needler returned with a bottle of red wine and three silver goblets on a tray. He laid it on a table and gave a goblet to the old woman, then passed the others to Barak and me. His face was expressionless as he returned to his place behind his mistress's chair. Why were they both so calm? I wondered. I took a sip of the wine. It was sweet and sickly. Barak took a large draught.

'The truth, then,' Goodwife Wentworth said decisively.

'Yes, madam, the truth. If not here, then in court tomorrow morning.'

'Elizabeth will speak for herself?'

'Whether she does or not I shall bring forward the evidence I have. This is your chance to tell me the truth, madam. Perhaps –' I paused, taking another sip – 'something may be done.'

'Where is Joseph?' she asked.

'At his lodgings.'

She nodded then paused, gathering her thoughts. 'David saw it all,' she said. 'From this window. He was cleaning the tapestries; it is a task I trust only to him.' She hesitated a moment, as though listening for something, then continued.

'Elizabeth was in the garden alone that afternoon, sulking as usual. She would have done better to stand up for herself, the way she used to cower in corners like a pissing woman only encouraged the children to be cruel. And children are cruel, are they not? As a hunchback you will know that.'

'Yes they are. Which is why adults must correct them. And they were three against one, were they not?'

'Elizabeth was almost an adult. A great girl of eighteen afraid of a twelve-year-old boy.' She gave a snort of contempt. 'The day Ralph died he had gone down to the garden, to Elizabeth. He sat on the edge of the well and spoke to her. You could not hear what he said, could you, David, through the window?'

'No, madam.' He looked at us and shrugged. 'He was probably tormenting her, perhaps talking about that cat of hers he killed. She just sat under the tree and took it as usual, her head bowed.'

The old woman nodded. 'If she'd any courage she would have got up and boxed his ears.'

'The favoured son?' I said. 'Sir Edwin would not have been pleased.'

Goodwife Wentworth inclined her head. 'Perhaps not.'

'Did you know your grandson had killed a little boy, madam?' I asked. The steward laid a warning hand on her arm, but she shrugged it off.

'We heard the boy had disappeared. I wondered. I knew the things Ralph did and I was waiting for a chance to speak to him about it – I feared he was placing himself in danger. My son Edwin knows nothing,' she added. 'He believed Ralph could do no wrong and I thought it better he kept that belief. He has enough to worry about with his business.'

'You did not fear Ralph was growing into a monster?' I coughed. My throat was suddenly dry.

She shrugged. 'If Ralph did not grow out of his cruelties he would have learned to conceal them. People do.' She sighed. 'You go on, David, this is tiring me. Tell them what happened next.'

The steward looked at us intently. 'After a while Sabine and Avice came outside and sat with Ralph on the edge of the well. They joined in baiting Elizabeth, I think. But then Ralph said something to Sabine. Something she did not like.'

The steward reddened.

'He referred perhaps to her feelings for you?' I asked.

The old woman raised a hand. 'It's all right, David. Sabine developed a girlish fancy for David. He did not encourage her: he is loyal, he has served my son and me for ten years. He would do anything for us. Tell them what you saw next, David. From the window.'

'Sabine grabbed at Ralph. He twisted away from her, fell backwards and then he was gone. Down the well.'

Goodwife Wentworth sighed. 'Sabine says she did not mean to throw him in, she only lashed out in anger. I think at law that would be manslaughter, eh lawyer? Not murder?'

'It would be for the jury to decide on the facts.'

'Either way Sabine might hang, for all her status. We could try for a king's pardon, but that would bankrupt us. Of course, if Elizabeth had not been there Sabine and Avice could have said Ralph merely slipped, but Elizabeth saw everything. And she has no love for us.' She spread her hands and smiled. 'You see, that was our problem.'

'So she had to be silenced. By being accused.' My voice came out as a croak and speaking hurt my dry throat. I wondered whether I was sickening for something.

'When I saw Ralph go down the well,' Needler went on, 'I ran downstairs to the garden. Sabine and Avice were screaming, howling. I looked down the well. I could just make out Ralph's body.'

'Poor boy,' the old woman whispered.

'Elizabeth just sat there under the tree, gawping. Then, not knowing I had been looking from the window, Sabine pointed at Elizabeth and said, "She's killed Ralph. She put him in the well! We saw her!" Elizabeth just sat there, like a stone, saying nothing. Then Avice joined in, pointing at Elizabeth, accusing her.'

Goodwife Wentworth nodded. 'Then I came down, I had heard the screaming. I found Sabine and Avice howling that Elizabeth had killed Ralph. Elizabeth would not answer when I spoke to her. I thought at first that was what had really happened, I ordered Edwin fetched and he had the constable take Elizabeth away. It was only afterwards that David told me the truth. I questioned the girls and they admitted all. They knew about the beggar boy; they have been very frightened, Master Shardlake, but they know how to control themselves as young ladies should. They will make fine gentlewomen one day.'

'They'll make devilish monsters, like their brother,' Barak said.

The old woman ignored him. 'We waited a day, two days, to see if Elizabeth would tell her story, but she kept her silence. Joseph came and told us she was refusing to plead. So we decided, if Elizabeth was prepared to go to her death, let her.' She spoke calmly, as though of a business arrangement.

I coughed drily. 'Well, madam, you have told us all. What do you expect to happen now?'

She said nothing, only smiled. I was aware my heart was pounding very fast. I could not understand why. I heard voices from the hall, then the closing of the front door.

'Shit,' Barak said. 'My eyes. I'm seeing double.'

I looked at him. The pupils of his staring eyes were enlarged, enormous. I remembered Sabine's eyes on the day of my first visit and that nightshade was extremely poisonous. I had seen its effects before, at Scarnsea monastery.

'They've poisoned us,' I breathed.

'It's working quickly,' the old woman said quietly. Needler crossed quickly to the door and locked it. He stood against it and looked at us, a grim set to his fleshy jaw.

'The servants have all gone?' Goodwife Wentworth asked.

'I told them there's nothing more to do this morning, to go out and enjoy the air while it's fresh after the storm.' He turned to me. 'You thought you were unseen that night you went down the well, but my mistress heard someone in the orchard. She told me to wait at a window and see what happened. I saw the pair of you sneak in, saw baldy there go down the well.'

The old woman laughed, a brutal, ugly cackle. 'The blind have wondrous hearing, Master Shardlake, After that we feared the constable would come for us. When nothing happened we realized Elizabeth must still be refusing to plead.'

Barak tried to get to his feet but fell back, his eyes staring wildly. 'I can't see,' he said. His head began to shake. Whatever this stuff was, he had drunk more of it than me.

I tried to say something, but my voice would not come. I remembered standing by the nightshade bush at Scarnsea, Guy telling me about the poison. The only way to counteract it, if taken quickly enough, was an emetic.

Needler returned to his place behind the beldame. 'We knew you would come here,' she continued. 'It was all you could do.' She smiled evilly as I took deep breaths, trying to ease my pounding heart. 'The well, is empty now, by the way, the carcasses in the river. It's ready for you. Then we will deal with Joseph.' Her voice was low, a whisper, she was listening for us to fall on the floor. 'An old countrywoman knows many poisonous plants and we have a large herb garden. They are weakening, David. Kill them now.'

The steward swallowed hard. His face grim, he drew a dagger and came round the chair slowly, deliberately.

And then I remembered the mustard, what Guy had said about its emetic properties the day I first told him about the Wentworth case. Knowing it was my last chance, I hauled myself to my feet. I was shaking from head to foot. Barak too managed with a herculean effort to rise unsteadily and fumble for his sword. He seemed unable to focus. Needler, looking between us, appeared suddenly uncertain. I reached out for the mustard pot and, before Needler's astonished eyes, grasped it and thrust a big spoonful into my mouth. I swallowed, my throat on fire.

The old woman called out, a note of fear in her voice. 'What's happened, David? What have they done?'

Barak made an uncertain lunge with his sword. He cut only air, but Needler retreated quickly behind the chair.

I felt my stomach turn, then leaned over and vomited its contents onto the floor with a horrible retching sound. 'Jack!' I cried. 'Here, take this!'

He grabbed the pot and swallowed what was left. He gasped and leaned back against his chair, sword still raised at Needler. I put a hand on the back of my chair, my head spinning.

'Stay up, sir!' Barak shouted. 'We must stay up!'

I took long, deep breaths. It was horribly frightening, knowing if we allowed ourselves to pass out now it could be the end of us. But my heartbeat was steadying a little. I pulled out my dagger. The old woman stood too, trembling, hands stretched out before her. 'David!' she called in a shrill howl. 'David! What is happening?'

Needler's nerve broke. He stepped away from his mistress and ran to the door. Barak started to follow, but staggered. The old woman turned to the sound of Needler's footsteps, her hands waving helplessly. 'David! David! Where are you? What's happening?'

Needler unlocked the door and threw it open. He ran down the steps and out of the house just as Barak leaned forward and vomited as spectactularly as I had. He sank to his knees, gasping.

The old woman turned towards the noise, panicky now. 'Where are you?' she shouted. 'David! David!' She stumbled, lost her balance and fell with a cry. Her head struck the wall and she collapsed to the floor with a moan.

I staggered to the open door of the parlour, down the stairs and through the front door which Needler had left open. I leaned on it for support and called 'Help!' in a cracked voice, making heads turn along the crowded street. 'Murder! Call the constable! Help!' Then my legs seemed to disappear beneath me and I fell into blackness.

# Chapter Forty-six

I CAME TO WITH A START, jerking away from a vile smell under my nose. I gasped and looked round in confusion.

I was back in the Wentworths' parlour, but sitting in a chair now. A thickset man in a constable's jerkin stood watching me. Beside me stood Guy, holding the bottle he had just thrust under my nose. I stared around – the constable and Guy in his apothecary's robe both looked completely out of place amid the luxurious domesticity of the room. Barak sat sprawled in another chair, looking pale – but alive, the pupils of his eyes reduced to their normal size.

'The old woman—' I croaked.

'It's all right,' Guy said. 'She has been taken away. And her granddaughters. It was quick thinking to use the mustard to make you sick or you and Barak would both be dead by now. You've been unconscious nearly an hour. I was worried.'

I took a deep breath, aware that I had a mighty headache. 'It was you that told me about vomiting and poison.'

'I remember. You always had the best memory I know.'

'By Jesu.' I managed a hoarse laugh. 'I dread to think of the bill I will have for all you have done this last month.'

'You can afford it. Can you move your arms and legs?'

'Yes. I feel weak.'

'That should pass soon.' Guy reached to a bowl covered with a cloth on the table. He lifted the cloth and a sharp smell filled the room. 'I want you to drink this now,' he said. 'It will act against any poisonous humours remaining in your system.'

I looked at it warily, but suffered him to take my head and tip the stuff gently into my mouth. It was bitter. 'There,' he said, 'sit back now.' I did so, gasping.

The door opened and Joseph came in, his face ashen. But he smiled when he saw I had come to. 'Ah, sir, you are recovered. Thank God.'

I clasped Guy's arm. 'Did Needler get away?' I asked.

'Yes. There's a hue and cry out for him.'

'How did you get here?'

'You called for the constable.'

'Yes, I remember that. But nothing else till just now.'

'The constable found you, Barak and the old woman all unconscious. But you came round for a moment and asked for me.'

'I don't remember. Jesu, is my mind going?'

Guy laid a hand on my arm. 'It will come back to you. But you and Barak are both weak. You must rest.'

The constable spoke up. 'David Needler's been taken, sir, that's what I came to tell you. He tried to ride out through Cripplegate, but the gatekeeper took him. He didn't put up much of a struggle. He's in Newgate now.'

Barak looked at me seriously. 'Sabine and Avice have been taken there already with the old woman, though she hurt her head badly in the fall. The girls were hiding upstairs in their room; the constables had to pull them screaming from under the beds. I told the magistrate everything when I came round. They scratched like cats when they realized the game was up, but they've gone. Not to the Hole, though,' he croaked bitterly. 'The better quarters.'

I looked out of the window. The well was dimly visible in the dull late afternoon. 'Jesu,' I muttered. 'If Needler and the old bitch had had their way, we'd be down there too.' I turned to Joseph. 'I'm sorry. She is your mother—'

He shook his head. 'Always it was Edwin she loved; she had naught but contempt for the rest of us.'

'Barak,' I said, 'you must swear a statement, and the magistrate and constables. They must appear before Forbizer tomorrow . . .' I tried to stand, but fell back groggily. A thought struck me. 'What has happened to Sir Edwin?'

'He is in his room opposite,' Joseph said quietly. 'Poor Edwin, he's been hard hit. His son dead, his mother and daughters taken—'

I took a deep breath. 'Does Elizabeth know?'

'Yes. She set to weeping when I told her.' A ghost of a smile crossed his face. 'But she held my hand when I left. I will look after her now, sir. But I had to come here,' he added simply. 'My brother needs me.'

I looked at him. I saw clearly the reason I first took the horrible case on at all: it was for his goodness, such natural goodness and charity as few men have.

'I should go to Edwin,' he said.

The constable raised a hand. 'The magistrate's still with him, sir.'

Things kept floating into my mind. 'Cromwell!' I exclaimed. 'It's been hours, is there word from Grey?'

Barak nodded. 'This arrived here a short while ago.' He took a note with the earl's seal from his pocket and handed it to me. I read, in Grey's precise hand: *Lord Cromwell has your message. He is seeing the king today and will contact you should you be needed. He thanks you mightily.*

'Then it's done,' I breathed. I leant back, relieved. 'He sends us thanks too.'

Guy came over to me. He looked in my mouth and eyes, then did the same to Barak.

'You're both all right,' he said. 'But you should go home, sleep. You will be very tired and shaky for some days.'

'I'll not argue with you, sir,' Barak said.

'And now I ought to return to my shop. I have patients.' He bowed to us and turned for the door, exotic-looking as ever in his long hooded robe, with his oak-brown face, his curly grey-black hair.

'Thank you, old friend,' I said quietly.

He raised a hand and smiled, then went out.

'Odd-looking fellow,' the constable observed. 'When I came here I thought it was him I had to arrest.'

I did not reply.

The door opened again and a tall, thin man I recognized as Magistrate Parsloe entered. He was normally full of cheerful self-importance, but today he looked sombre. He bowed, then turned to Joseph. 'Master Wentworth, I think perhaps you should go to your brother.'

Joseph stood eagerly. 'I was going to, sir. Has he asked for me?'

Parsloe hesitated. 'No, but he needs someone with him, I think.' He looked at me. 'Master Shardlake, I am glad to see you are recovered. It was quite a scene that met my eyes when the constable called me here.'

'I can imagine. You have questioned Sir Edwin?'

'Yes. He says he knew nothing of his family's doings. I believe him; he is a stricken man.' Parsloe shook his head. 'Strange, though, that the old woman should work so closely with a mere steward.'

'Needler was her eyes, she said so herself. She needed him, she was vulnerable in that way if in no other.'

'We found this in the wine cellar.' Parsloe passed a little glass phial to me. 'Your apothecary friend says it is a very strong concentration of belladonna.'

I handed it back to him, suppressing a shudder.

'Can you come to the Old Bailey tomorrow, sir?' he asked. 'Elizabeth Wentworth is up before Judge Forbizer. It would help if you could give evidence.'

'I will. Do you think she will speak now?'

'Yes.'

I looked wryly at Barak. 'Now the facts are known, there will be no martyrdom for her, whether she wishes it or not.' I turned to Joseph. 'Can you be at court at ten tomorrow as well? Then Elizabeth can be discharged into your care.'

He nodded. 'Yes. And thank you, sir, thank you for everything.'

We followed him to the door. Opposite, we could see into a well-appointed bedroom. In a chair by the bed Sir Edwin sat still as a stone, his face white and puffy. Joseph knocked and went in. His brother looked up with dull unseeing eyes. Joseph sat on the bed and reached for his hand, but Sir Edwin flinched away.

'Come, Edwin,' Joseph said gently. 'I am here. I will help you if I can.' He reached out again, and this time his brother let him take his hand.

'Let us go, Barak,' I said quietly, nudging him to the front door.

✟

WE WENT HOME. Though I felt light-headed and kept having to pause I prepared a statement for Forbizer and had Barak, who was in little better case, do the same. Reading his statement over, I was surprised at how neatly and fluently he wrote; the monks' school had taught him well and no doubt he had needed writing for all the reports he must have sent to Cromwell. Afterwards we ate and then, for a second night, went wearily up to bed to sleep like stones.

✟

NEXT MORNING there was no further word from Cromwell. It was the tenth of June, the day of reckoning. As we breakfasted I looked out of the window. It was still cloudy and a little misty. The demonstration before the king would have been today. Greek Fire would have made a more extraordinary spectacle than ever on such a grey, wet morning.

'Time to go,' Barak said. 'Are you fit?'

'Just about. A little trembling and dryness of the throat is all.' I forced myself to my feet. 'Come on. We don't want to be late today of all days.'

At the Old Bailey everything was ready. Parsloe, the constable and three anxious-looking Wentworth servants were waiting in the outer hall; Parsloe had a collection of statements for me to look over.

Joseph stood next to him, still pale though more composed than yesterday. For him, this was indeed a Pyrrhic victory.

I took his arm. 'Are you ready, Joseph?'

'Ay. Edwin was unable to come, he is in a bad state.'

'I understand. And he was not there yesterday, he has no direct evidence to give.'

'I stayed with him last night. I think he will forgive me. I am all he has now.'

I nodded. 'He could have no greater support.'

'I may see if I can get him to come to the farm with me. I shall go back there with Elizabeth. It will be a familiar place for both of them, with some happy associations at least.'

'Yes. And it may be better to leave London. The pamphleteers will be busy again once this news is out, pox on their jeering cruelty.' I turned to Parsloe. 'Are we in open court with the rest of the cases?'

He shook his head. 'No. I have seen the judge. As it is simply a matter of Elizabeth's discharge he will see us in his chambers when we are all here.'

I took a deep breath. 'Then let's get it over. There's his clerk.' I looked over to where Forbizer's plump assistant was bustling about. I remembered the day he had brought me the news of the judge's change of mind, just before Barak had shouldered his way into my life.

Parsloe, Joseph and Barak accompanied me to the judge's chambers. Forbizer sat, already swathed in his red robe, behind a desk stacked neatly with papers. He looked at us coldly, his eyes lingering on Barak for a moment, then reached out and snapped his fingers.

'The statements.'

I handed them to him. Forbizer read them though, his face expressionless, occasionally pausing to frown and check something. It was all a charade, I knew, he had already heard the story from Parsloe and there was no alternative but to release Elizabeth now. At length he laid down the statements, straightening them so the edges were all in line, and grunted.

'So she was innocent after all,' he said.

'Yes,' I replied.

'She should still have been pressed,' he said coldly. 'That was the correct sentence for a refusal to plead, that would have been justice.' He stroked his grey beard reflectively. 'I have been considering whether to sentence her to some more time in the Hole for her contempt of court.' He looked at Joseph, whom I saw pale. I could not suppress a frown; this was sheer cruelty, revenge for the pressure Barak had put on him. Forbizer shrugged. 'But I have a busy enough assize this morning without bringing her back into court. I will let her go. At least until the rest of her family are tried – she will need to be a witness then.'

'Thank you, your honour,' I said quietly.

Forbizer drew a paper to him and I saw an order of release had already been drawn. He signed it, his lip curling over his beard again in that revolting gesture of contempt, then flicked it across the table to me.

'There you are, Brother Shardlake.' I reached to take it but he placed two fingers on the edge. I looked into his eyes. They were cold and angry.

'Do not cross me again, Brother,' he said quietly, 'or, whatever political connections you might have, I shall make your life a very hell.' He lifted his fingers and I took the order, rose and bowed. We filed silently out of the room.

Outside, Parsloe shook his head wonderingly. 'You'd think he would be glad to see an injustice righted, a girl saved from a cruel death. But he's an odd fellow.'

'The arsehole didn't like having his authority overruled,' Barak said. He had sat down on a bench. He still looked weak and pale. I was glad to sit beside him.

'How overruled?' Parsloe frowned at us. 'And what did he mean by political connections?'

'Jesu knows,' I said hastily. 'Well, Master Parsloe, I am most grateful for your help. We must not keep you.'

The magistrate turned away. I gave Barak a look. 'You nearly had me in trouble there. Parsloe's an old gossip, if you'd told him you'd brought an order from Cromwell to save Elizabeth, that story would be on a hundred pamphlets by tomorrow and Forbizer would be making my life hell as he promised. Though he'll do his best to achieve that anyway if I ever come before him again,' I added gloomily.

'Not my fault lawyers are all such gossips. Besides, I'm knackered. I should be in bed.'

'But sir,' Joseph asked, frowning, 'what *did* he mean about political influence?'

I hesitated. But Joseph had a right to know, if anyone did. 'Barak and I have been involved in a – a case for Lord Cromwell. It was very important, that was why I had so little time to give Elizabeth. It was his influence made Forbizer grant Elizabeth that stay. But, please, you must tell no one.'

He nodded. 'I will not, sir.' He shook his head. 'The earl. God bless him, God bless all the reforms he has brought.'

I handed him the order. 'There, take that to Newgate and Elizabeth will be released. Would you like us to come with you?'

He smiled. 'This is something I would rather do alone, sir. If you do not mind.'

'I understand.'

Barak and I watched as he left the Bailey, the precious document held carefully in his hand.

'Well,' I said, 'it's all over. What do you want to do now? I must go to Lincoln's Inn, to catch up on business.' I studied him, realizing, now that the parting of our ways was near, that for all his innumerable annoying habits I should miss him.

'Might I come with you to Chancery Lane?' he asked diffidently. 'I won't be able to sleep again, or settle to anything, until I hear from the earl.'

'Very well. I feel the same.'

'I wish there was some news.'

'Maybe there is a letter at Lincoln's Inn. We should go and see.'

He studied me. 'You *did* want the earl to win, didn't you? Always you call him Cromwell, and with such an edge on your voice sometimes.'

'Yes. I didn't want him to have Greek Fire but I don't want him overthrown. Norfolk would be a worse master. So I'm not quite like Lady Honor, who doesn't much care either way.' I hesitated. 'I suspected her, you know, there in the warehouse. When they mentioned an aristocrat being behind all this. When Norfolk came in it was almost a relief.' I sighed. 'I wish I could have found the answer sooner. Saved some of those lives.'

'Two of us against those ravening beasts of Norfolk's? It's a wonder we're even alive. You should take more credit. For that and for bringing justice to Elizabeth.'

'Perhaps.'

We both looked round at the chilling sound of chains scraping along the floor. Another trail of ragged felons was led across the hall, dirty and trembling, accompanied by frowning constables. We smelt the gaol's reek as they passed, then the courthouse door closed behind them. We stood silently a moment. I thought of the hanging cart, of justice and injustice and how the two were not always easy to tell apart. Then we turned and went slowly out to the street, glad to be out of that place.

☦

At Chancery Lane there was no message from Cromwell. Skelly was at his copying, still peering painfully at his papers but with less of an anxious air now. Godfrey, though, was gone. I went into his office to find a pile of papers stacked neatly on his desk, a note addressed to me on top.

*Please take custody of my cases, I know you will serve my clients well. I will send to you telling where to remit such fees as are due to me. Some friends and I are going to preach the Word of God in the towns, though we must take care of the magistrates; I had better not say where for now. Your brother, in the law and in Christ,*
*Godfrey Wheelwright*

I sighed. 'So that's that,' I said. I looked through the cases. Every-thing was meticulously in order, notes left for me summarizing what needed to be done. Then I went through to the outer office. Barak was sitting looking out of the window, his face gloomy. I sat beside him; my legs were still tired. I felt a spurt of irritation at Cromwell for keeping us waiting. But Barak was right, we were small fry.

'That arsehole's here,' he said, nodding to where Stephen Bealknap was crossing the quadrangle. He looked tense, his thin shoulders hunched. He stopped at some noise, casting a fearful glance around him.

I laughed. 'Let us put him out of his misery.'

Barak accompanied me into the courtyard. Seeing us, Bealknap hastened over. 'Brother Shardlake, is there any news?' There was a look of appeal in the rogue's pale eyes.

'You need fear no more, Bealknap,' I said with a smile. 'The issue of Greek Fire is settled. You are quite safe.'

His shoulders relaxed and he sighed with relief. 'What happened?' he asked, his eyes suddenly eager with curiosity. 'Who was behind it all? Does Lord Cromwell have Greek Fire?'

I raised a hand. 'Those matters remain confidential, Brother. All I can say is that you may resume your normal life in safety.'

His eyes narrowed. 'And the case about my houses? You'll be dropping that now you know of Sir Richard's interest?' I reflected it had taken no more than a minute for Bealknap's predatory instincts to reassert themselves.

'Why, no,' I replied. 'I am still instructed by the Common Council. I shall be going to Chancery.' And Cromwell, I gambled, would not stand in my way. He owed me too much.

Bealknap drew himself up, frowning. 'You would take a fellow barrister to court! That is dishonourable – I shall make sure it is known. Brother, you do not need to do this,' he added in sudden exasperation. 'The system works to all our advantage and there is much gold to be made with little effort if one chooses the easy path.'

I thought of those hovels, the people made to use that stinking cesspit, the neighbouring houses spoiled. And all the houses like it, mushrooming all over London from the shells of the old monasteries.

'You are a son of sin and death, Bealknap,' I said. 'And I shall fight you every way I can.'

I turned as Barak nudged my arm. A man was running towards us from the gate, red-faced. It was Joseph. He reached us and stopped, taking deep whooping breaths. I felt a terrible apprehension.

'Elizabeth—' I asked.

He shook his head. 'She is safe at my lodgings. But in the City, I heard—'

'What?'

He took a shuddering breath. 'Lord Cromwell has fallen!'

'What!'

'It has just been announced. He was arrested at the council table early this morning, for treason. He is taken to the Tower. They say his goods have been seized, you know what that means.'

'Attainder,' I said. My lips felt heavy, bloodless. 'He'll be condemned unheard.'

'They say the Duke of Norfolk himself ripped the seal of office from his neck. Arrested at the council table itself! All his associates are being arrested too, Wyatt's been taken!'

I took Joseph's shoulder and led him away. Bealknap stood goggle-eyed for a moment, then turned and hastened to the hall to spread the news.

'I thought you should know at once, sir.' Joseph said. 'After what you told me this morning, I thought – you may be in danger—'

I turned to Barak. 'But our message! Grey said he had it. It should be Norfolk that's arrested—'

'Master Grey?' Joseph asked. 'The earl's secretary?'

'Yes. What of him?'

'They're saying he's turned his coat, given evidence against the earl. Half his people have. And no one stood in his favour at the council, not even Cranmer.' He clenched his fists. 'The rogues.'

'Grey!' Barak whispered. 'The bastard. He never even gave the message to Hanfold. It was him all along, feeding news of our doings to our enemies.'

'I've known Grey years.' I laughed bitterly. 'I thought it couldn't possibly be him, but oh, Barak, when we were wondering who was working against us we should have thought of someone at the court, someone in that great cesspit.' I leaned against the wall, overcome. 'We've failed after all. And Norfolk's won.'

Barak looked at me intently. 'And we're in the shit.'

# Chapter Forty-seven

'ARE YOU QUITE SURE of this?' I asked Joseph. My heart was racing almost as hard as when I had taken the poison.

'Yes. It was the talk of the streets when I left Newgate.' He bit his lip. 'It is terrible.'

'What was the mood?'

'Most seemed pleased, saying they were glad the earl had gone. After all he has done for true religion. But others were frightened, wondering what would happen now.'

'Any word of the Duke of Norfolk?'

'No, none.'

I looked at Barak. 'So he hasn't been given Cromwell's place, or not yet.'

'Treason,' Joseph said incredulously. 'What could that mean, treason? No one could have served the king more faithfully—'

'It's just an excuse,' I said bitterly. 'An excuse to get him out of the way, bundle him into the Tower. If he's attainted before parliament there won't need to be a trial.'

'He's fallen off the tightrope of the king's pleasure at last,' Barak said, more slowly and seriously than I had ever heard him speak. 'He always feared he would. But he didn't see the end coming; in the end that little shit Grey saw how the wind was blowing more clearly than my master.' He looked at me seriously. His face was pale, he was shocked, but he kept a clear mind. 'We have to get out of here,' he said quickly, 'both of us. If they're arresting the earl's associates, it would be the ideal opportunity for Norfolk to put us out of the way before we tell any tales.'

'Tales?' Joseph asked. 'What tales?'

'Better you don't know,' I replied. I stared out of the window at the gatehouse, imagining riders coming through the gates and leading us away too, to the Tower. But more likely it would be a knife thrust in the dark from some ruffian like Toky. I turned back to Barak.

'You're right, Jack, it's not safe for us in London. Grey. By God – he started as a lawyer.'

'And learned to dissemble.' Barak frowned. 'Why didn't he kill Kytchyn and Goodwife Gristwood? He knew where they were.'

'He was almost the only one who did. If they'd been killed the trail would have led back to him. Besides, they'd told us all they knew. I hope they will be safe now, given what they know too.'

Barak shook his head. 'We can't hang around to find out.'

'But where will you both go?' Joseph asked.

'I've got people who'll keep me safe over in Essex,' Barak replied. He turned to me. 'You could go to your father's place – at Lichfield isn't it?'

I nodded. 'Yes, that's safest. It looks like I will have a sojourn in the country after all. Joseph, you should leave. Better you are not seen with us.'

Joseph was looking at the gate, where a messenger in the king's livery was dismounting. He ran across the courtyard to the hall. 'They're bringing the news to the lawyers,' I said.

'I'm off,' Barak said.

'Are you fit enough?'

'Ay.'

He stared at me with those keen dark eyes, then reached out and shook my hand. To my surprise his eyes were moist. 'We gave them a good run, eh?' he said. 'We did all we could?'

I returned his grip. 'Yes. We did. Thank you, Barak, for everything.'

He nodded, then turned and walked rapidly away across the yard, pulling his cap down low. The messenger had disappeared into the chapel. I felt alone, unprotected. I sat down again.

'Are you truly in danger, Master Shardlake?' Joseph asked quietly.

'I could be. I shall leave now, go home and pack some things, then ride out. There is just one visit I have to make before I go.' I shook his hand. 'Go, Joseph, now. Take Elizabeth and your brother to Essex.'

He shook my hand firmly. 'Thank you, sir, for everything. I shall never forget what you have done.'

I nodded. I could think of no words.

'If anyone asks, I'll say I don't know where you've gone.'

'That would be best. Thank you, Joseph.'

A bell began ringing through the misty morning, calling the members of the Inn to hear the news. A puzzled throng of lawyers appeared, crossing to the chapel. I saw Bealknap darting among them, announcing the news, his face flushed with pleasure at knowing before everyone else. I stood a moment, gathering all the reserves of strength I had left, then went back to my chambers.

✝

I LEFT SKELLY SOME money and instructions to refer Godfrey's and my cases to barristers I trusted with the work. I told him I did not know how long I would be away. Then I slipped out while everyone was in the chapel and walked quickly home. Joan was out; she had taken Simon with her on some errand. The house was still and empty in the quiet morning. I was glad I did not have to explain this latest disruption to her.

I took some money from the store in my room, leaving the rest for her with a note. Then I went out to the stable. Barak's mare Sukey was already gone, but Genesis was standing quietly in his stall. I patted him. 'Well, I think we may be stuck with each other. Lord Cromwell will not be wanting you back.'

And then, quite suddenly, it all overwhelmed me. I thought of my first meeting with Cromwell, at a dinner for reformers more than fifteen years before. I remembered his keenness for reform, his powerful

mind, the forcefulness and energy that had held me in thrall. Then the
years of power, his patronage of my work and afterwards my disillusion
with his ruthlessness and brutality. My break with him three years
before and now my failure to save him at the end. Perhaps no one
could have saved him after the Cleves debacle, but I laid my head
against the horse's flank and wept for him. I thought of that great man
of power, now locked in the Tower, where he had sent so many of
his foes.

'I am sorry,' I said aloud. 'I am sorry.'

I must leave, I told myself, I must pull myself together. I dried my
face as best I could on my sleeve, then rode out into the City. I had
one more thing to do.

✝

AS JOSEPH HAD SAID, people everywhere were discussing Cromwell's fall. Looking at their faces, the expression I saw most frequently
was fear. For all his brutality, Cromwell had provided stability in
uncertain times. And London was a reformist city: if there was to be
anything like a return to the old religion it would be unpopular here.
I heard someone say, 'The king is to marry Catherine Howard!' and
whirled round, but it was only some apprentice shooting his mouth
off, he could not know anything. A silent crowd watched as a
clergyman, a reformer no doubt, was manhandled down the steps of
his church by a squad of the king's guard. I turned quickly away. I
realized that, having once been ardent for reform, I had always taken
it for granted that London was a safe place for me, even after my
enthusiasm evaporated. Now I felt suddenly vulnerable. I realized how
Guy must feel most of the time in this city.

I found a hubbub outside the House of Glass. A black carriage
with four horses in the shafts was pulled up at the door and servants
were piling it high with trunks and boxes. I dismounted and asked
one of them whether Lady Honor was indoors.

'Who should I say – hey, you can't just go in!' But I had, tying

Genesis to the rail and stepping inside, dodging a lady attendant struggling with an armful of voluminous silk dresses. I ran upstairs to the parlour.

Lady Honor stood before the fireplace, checking items from a long list as a pair of servants manhandled another box out of the door. She wore a light dress such as might be used for travelling in summer.

'Lady Honor,' I said quietly.

She looked taken aback for a moment, then reddened.

'Matthew. I did not expect—'

'You are leaving?'

'Yes, for the country, today. Have you not heard—'

'I know. Lord Cromwell has fallen.'

'One of my friends at court has sent word the duke is displeased about my part in helping him over the Greek Fire business. And helping *you*,' she added with sudden asperity.

'You have done nothing—'

She laughed bitterly. 'Come, Matthew, we know better than that. When did anyone need to *do* something to be in danger? Several of my dinner guests have been arrested, and my friend says it might be a good thing for me to disappear for a while, go to my estates until the new dispensation is clearer.'

'So Norfolk's in the saddle.'

'The Cleves divorce and the Howard marriage are likely to be announced in the next few days.'

'My God.'

'I wish I'd never let you involve me in that matter!' she said with sudden anger. 'Now I am going to have to rot in Lincolnshire, for good for all I know.'

I must have looked as stricken as I felt, for her face softened. 'I am sorry, I hate all this hurry. There is so much to organize.' She looked at my bandaged wrist. 'What happened there?'

'It is nothing. I am leaving too. For the Midlands.'

She studied my face, then nodded. 'I see. Yes, you must go too. What happened with the Wentworth girl?'

'She is free.' I sighed. 'And I found the answer to Greek Fire, but too late to save Cromwell.'

She raised a hand. 'No, Matthew, you must not tell me any more.'

'Of course, I am sorry. Honor—'

She gave that wry smile of hers. 'Am I not a lady any more?'

'Always. But—' Although I had not planned the words, they came tumbling out. 'We are both going to the Midlands. Perhaps we could ride together as far as Northampton. And we will not be so very far apart. It is summer, the roads will not be too bad. Perhaps we could meet—'

Her face flushed. She was standing three paces away, and I stepped towards her. I should not want for courage now. But she raised her hand.

'No, Matthew,' she said gently. 'No. I am sorry.'

I gave a long, sad sigh. 'My appearance—'

Then she did close the distance between us and took my arm. I looked into her face.

'Is most pleasing to me. And always has been. Your features are as fine as any lord's. I tried to tell you so, that day by the river. But—' She paused, choosing her words carefully. 'Do you remember also I said once that some men, some exceptional men only, were fitted to rise above their class?'

'Class,' I said impatiently. 'What is class? If you want me—'

She shook her head. 'Class is everything. I am a Vaughan. Once I would have been happy to know you, you are one of those fit to be raised up, as my husband was. But not now, given your past loyalties and who the new powers are in the land. And I will not be lowered to your status, Matthew.' She shook her head again.

'Then you did not love me,' I said.

Her smile was sad. 'Love is a child's romantic dream.'

'Is it?'

'Yes, it is. I admired you, I liked you, yes. But my family's place is what matters in the end. If you came from noble lineage, you would understand.' She gave me a last, affectionate look. 'But you don't.

Goodbye, Matthew, keep safe.' And then, with a rustle of skirts, she was gone.

✝

I RODE OUT OF Cripplegate an hour later. A throng of people was queuing to pass through, some looking fearful. A group of the king's guard was posted there and I was afraid I might be stopped but I was allowed to pass through. I rode away through the dull afternoon, past Shoreditch and the windmills that turn endlessly on Finsbury Green, and did not pause till I reached Hampstead Heath. There I stopped. I rode off the track into the long grass and looked back at the City. I could make out the bulk of the Tower, where Thomas Cromwell lay now, the river flowing past. London looked strangely peaceful from up there, a tableau rather than a city on the edge of panic as old scores were settled among high-born and low. I felt utterly weary. I would have liked to lie down in the grass and sleep. But I could not. I took a deep breath and patted Genesis. 'We've far to go, good horse,' I said, then turned and rode away, fast, to the north.

# *Epilogue*

## 30 JULY 1540

I walked down from Chancery Lane to the Temple Stairs, looking keenly about me to see what changes might have occurred, for I had been away nearly two months. In truth people were going about their business much as ever, though there were fewer than usual for there were rumours of plague in the eastern suburbs and many lawyers had left the City. And for those who remained there was a double spectacle today, at Tyburn and at Smithfield.

The letter from Barak has come a few days before. It was brief and to the point.

> *Master Shardlake,*
>
> *I am back in London: I still have friends in the king's service and have had word that you and I may safely return to the City. Lord Cromwell is to die, but none of his supporters are to suffer unless they misbehave. Wyatt and other friends of his are free; only the most obstinate reformers remain in prison. If you wish to return to London and meet me, I shall be pleased to tell you more. I hope you are recovered now from the assault upon your person you had in that enterprise.*
>
> *JB*

His words tied in with other news that had reached the Midlands. The expected persecution of reformers had been milder than feared, though there were ever stronger warnings against Lutheranism from the pulpit and three Protestant preachers, including Cromwell's friend Barnes, were to be burned that day at Smithfield. But three papists were to be hanged, drawn and quartered at Tyburn at the same time: a message from the king that neither side had the upper hand now and there would, after all, be no return to Rome. Archbishop Cranmer, to everyone's surprise, had kept his place. And though a speedy divorce from Anne of Cleves had been approved by the Church, and everyone awaited the announcement of the king's betrothal to Catherine Howard, neither Norfolk nor anyone else had been appointed to Cromwell's place; his offices were being shared out among the courtiers. The word was that for the first time in nearly thirty years Henry intended to govern himself, without a chief minister. What a disappointment that must be to the duke.

I had arrived that morning and, to my relief, found everything quiet and normal at home. Joan had not been happy at my prolonged absence and I could see that, after the alarms of the weeks before I left, the poor woman had been frightened to be left in the house alone. I promised her faithfully that my life would now resume its quiet course.

The previous evening, over dinner in the inn at Berkhamsted where I had stayed overnight, I heard the news of Cromwell's execution. The man who brought it from London said the executioner had bungled the job and needed several blows to strike off his head. 'But it's off now, that's the main thing,' someone called out and people laughed. I rose and went quietly upstairs.

As I reached the river, I took off my cap and rubbed sweat from my brow. The blazing heat had returned in the days after Cromwell's fall and given no respite since. I scanned the stairs. Barak was waiting at the spot where I had asked him to meet me in my reply. His hair had grown again and he looked well set up in his best green doublet. His sword swung at his belt as usual. He was standing a little apart from the people waiting for boats, leaning over the parapet and staring pensively at the busy river. I tapped his shoulder and he turned, his sober look replaced by a broad grin. He extended a hand.

'You are well?' he asked.

'Quite recovered, Barak. I have been having a quiet time. You?'

'Ay, I'm back at the Old Barge and glad to be. Essex is too quiet for me. All that countryside, that wide horizon, gives you a headache to look at it.'

'I know what you mean.' And indeed my sojourn at Lichfield had cured me of the desire for a country life. Walking around the parched countryside, listening as my father and his steward endlessly bemoaned the weather, had begun to grate on my nerves. And as Barak said, there was something in those wide horizons that was unsettling to the eye.

'Our old master died two days ago. Did you know?' His expression was sombre again.

'Ay.' I lowered my voice. 'I heard the execution was bungled.'

'It was. I saw it.' His face darkened. 'His head's boiled and on a spike on London Bridge now, pointed away from the City so he cannot look on the king any more. But he died bravely, refusing to admit any fault.'

'Yes, he would.' I shook my head. 'Those charges were ridiculous. Conspiring to make war on the king? If there was one thing Thomas Cromwell did faithfully all his life it was serve Henry Tudor.'

'It's not the first time treason charges have been cooked up when the king wanted rid of someone. When they arrested Lord Cromwell at the council table he cried out, "I am no traitor," and threw his cap to the floor. Then Norfolk tore the Order of the Garter from his chest.'

'And what of Norfolk?' I asked. 'Are you sure we are safe?'

'Ay. I have friends in some of the less public parts of the king's service. I've had word from Norfolk himself we won't be touched. He's terrified of a single word getting out about Greek Fire. I've dropped a hint that if anything happened to either of us there might be others who knew the tale.'

I looked at him askance. 'That was a risky thing to do. For both of us.'

'It's insurance for us. Trust me, I know how these things work.'

'Did you hear anything of Kytchyn? Or Madam Gristwood and her son?'

'They are safe. They fled with the man who guarded their house as soon as they heard of Cromwell's fall. I don't know where they are.'

I nodded. 'So I may resume practice.'

He nodded. 'If that's what you wish.'

I went and leaned on the parapet, for my back hurt after my long ride. He joined me and we looked over the river. I tried to avoid looking down towards London Bridge.

'There hasn't been the purge I expected,' I said, 'though Robert Barnes is to be burned today. I haven't heard anything from Godfrey – I fear for him.' I looked at Barak. 'And three Catholics to die at Tyburn.'

Barak grunted. 'The king will never go back to Rome, whatever Norfolk wants. He likes being head of the Church too much. The old arsehole,' he added quietly. He looked at me with sudden intensity. 'Could we have saved Lord Cromwell, do you think? If we'd guessed Grey was a traitor?'

I sighed deeply. 'That question has tormented me night and day. I think he was so deep in trouble over the Cleves marriage he would have fallen in the end. Unless he'd agreed to abandon Queen Anne and reform, and he wouldn't do that.' I smiled sadly. 'At least that's what I tell myself, to comfort myself perhaps.'

'I think you're right,' Barak said. 'His principles killed him in the end.'

'He killed many others for those principles.'

Barak shook his head, but did not reply. We leaned there in silence for a moment. Then I saw a boat turning in to the stairs, two faces I recognized. I nudged Barak. 'I've arranged for some others to meet us here. They wished to see you.'

'Who?' Puzzled, he followed my gaze to the wherry. It pulled up and Joseph Wentworth stepped out. He gave his hand to a young woman in a dark dress and hood to help her out of the boat.

'Is that—'

I nodded. 'Elizabeth.'

She walked a little unsteadily, her head bowed low, and Joseph had to help her up the steps. I went to the head of the stairs and Barak followed.

Joseph took my hand warmly and bowed to Barak. 'Master Barak, I am glad you are here. My niece wished to thank you both.'

Barak shuffled awkwardly. 'I did nothing, really.'

Elizabeth raised her head. Her hair had grown again too, a few curly strands escaping beneath her hood. For the first time I saw her face properly, clean of dirt and marks. It was pretty but full of character too. There was none of the indrawn blankness or sudden ferocious anger I had seen before in her eyes, her gaze was full and clear though infinitely sad.

'Yes, sir, you did.' Her voice trembled and she clung tightly to her uncle's hand but she spoke clearly. 'You went down into that terrible well, you nearly died at my grandmother's hands.' She looked at Barak. 'And when you spoke to me that day in the gaol, sir, you showed me how my silent suffering did no good, for me or my poor uncle. You made me begin to see things I had not seen before.'

Barak bowed deeply. 'If I helped save you, I count it a great honour.'

'I owe you both so much. You and Uncle Joseph, you never wavered in your support, however wickedly I treated you.' Her lip trembled and she lowered her head again, still clutching her uncle's hand tightly.

'Suffering does not ennoble people,' I said. 'They turn and bite and so, perhaps, they should. Do not become guilty, Elizabeth, for that is only another form of martyrdom.' She looked at me and I smiled sadly. 'It does no good.'

'No, sir.' She nodded tremulously. Joseph patted her hand.

'Elizabeth is still sore tired and troubled,' he said. 'The peace of the countryside is a balm to her, she finds London a trial. But she insisted on coming up with me today to thank you.'

'And we are grateful.' I hesitated. 'How is your brother?'

'Sore afflicted since Sabine was found guilty of manslaughter and she and Avice imprisoned. Though he has paid for good lodgings for them. He is selling his house to try and buy a royal pardon. I come up each week. He needs me.' He hesitated. 'My mother died, did you know?'

'I had not heard.'

'In Newgate, a week after her arrest.'

'Was it the fall?'

'No.' He sighed. 'It was as though, with the family in total disgrace, she did not want to live any more.'

I nodded sadly. Joseph smiled at Elizabeth. 'I think we should go on now. But thank you again.'

He and Elizabeth shook our hands. Elizabeth's felt as delicate as a bird's. Then Joseph guided her away, up to Temple Walk. Looking after them, I saw how desperately thin she was.

'Will she recover, do you think?' Barak asked.

'I don't know. At least now she will have a chance.'

'Have you seen Lady Honor?' He looked at me with frank curiosity. 'I heard she's left London.'

I laughed. 'You hear everything. No, I shall not see Lady Honor again.'

'I am sorry.'

'It was a matter of status,' I said heavily. 'That means everything to her, you know. As it did to old Madam Wentworth.' I frowned. 'No, that was bitterness talking. But all those formal banquets and receptions would have bored me; I am better off as a mere jobbing lawyer.' I sighed. 'I shall go back to the Inns and pick up my cases; burrow into my books again.' I stood up. 'Get Bealknap into Chancery.'

'Watch out for Richard Rich. You've made an enemy there.'

'I can deal with that. In fact,' I took a deep breath, 'I rather enjoy that side of things, using the law to right wrongs. Where one can.'

'How is Master Skelly?'

'I saw him this morning. Fine with his glasses. Though still rather slow.' I looked out over the water. 'How easy it is to make victims of people,' I said quietly. 'How humanity is addicted to that sin. I made a victim of Skelly, Elizabeth's family made a far worse victim of her. Reformers have made victims of papists, and now the reformers are being victimized in their turn. Will it never end?' I stared north, towards Smithfield, where the fires would be lit now. The smoke would be visible from Chancery Lane; it takes much fuel to burn a living man to ashes. How they would suffer.

'People shouldn't let themselves be made victims,' Barak said.

'They cannot always help themselves. Not if they are ground down too far, or too often.'

'Perhaps.'

I looked at him. There was an idea I had been turning over in my mind for several days. I was not at all sure it was a good one.

'I have Godfrey's cases now as well as my own. I have a great deal of work to catch up on and more will come in. The population of London grows increasingly litigious by the day. I need more help than Skelly can give; I need an assistant, someone to exchange ideas with, do some of the investigative work. I suppose you are unemployed now?'

He looked at me in surprise. I was not taken in; I had guessed from the beginning he had not suggested this meeting entirely out of good will.

'I'll not get work with the government again. I'm known too well as Lord Cromwell's man.'

'Do you think you could work for me? Is that dog Latin of yours up to it?'

'I should think so.'

'Are you sure you want to stay in London? There are rumours of plague out at Islington.'

He shrugged contemptuously. 'There's always plague.'

'The work will be boring sometimes. You will have to get used to legal language, learn to understand it rather than mock it. You'll have to knock off some of your rough edges, learn to address barristers and judges with respect. And stop calling everyone you don't like arseholes.'

'Even Bealknap?'

'I'll make an exception there. And you'll have to call me sir.'

Barak bit his lip and wrinkled his nose, as though in an agony of indecision. It was all pretence, of course; I had come to know his ways too well to be taken in. I had to prevent myself from laughing.

'I will be happy to serve you, sir,' he said at last. And then he did something he had never done before. He bowed.

'Very well,' I said. 'Come, then, let's go to Chancery Lane. See if we can bring a little order into this wicked world. A tiny bit.'

We walked through Temple Gardens. Ahead lay Chancery Lane. Beyond that Smithfield, where the fires would be lit now. Behind us the river, flowing to London Bridge where Cromwell's head stood fixed on its stake. Between Smithfield and the river the roiling city, ever in need of justice and absolution.

# HISTORICAL NOTE

By the summer of 1540, the hottest of the sixteenth century, Thomas Cromwell's position as Henry VIII's chief minister was under threat. The king had repudiated Rome and declared himself head of the Church eight years before and had at first welcomed reformist measures. The dissolution of the monasteries, masterminded by Cromwell, had brought him vast wealth and Henry had allowed Cromwell and Archbishop Cranmer much latitude in ending Latin ceremonies and printing the Bible in English for the first time.

By the late 1530s, however, the tide was turning. Henry's innate religious conservatism was reasserting itself and he was afraid that the overturning of the old religious hierarchy might turn into a challenge to the secular class structure, as had happened in parts of Germany. The religious edicts of 1539 began a process of doctrinal backpedalling.

England, moreover, was now isolated in Europe and the pope was urging the main Catholic powers, France and Spain, to unite and reconquer the heretical island for Roman Catholicism. There was genuine fear of invasion and huge sums were spent in training young men in arms, fortifying the south coast, and building up the navy.

Cromwell sought to strengthen both reform at home and England's military position abroad by marrying the king (a widower since his third wife Jane Seymour's death in childbirth in 1537) to a princess from one of the states associated with the German Protestant League. However, his choice, Anne of Cleves, was a disaster. The king disliked her on sight and declared himself unable to have carnal relations with her. Although he had approved the match, Henry VIII always sought someone else to blame for his problems and now he blamed Cromwell. To make matters worse for the chief minister, an incipient Franco-Spanish alliance broke down as the two Catholic powers resumed their traditional hostilities and the threat of invasion receded.

Meanwhile the king, aged nearly fifty, had become infatuated with Catherine Howard, the teenage niece of the Duke of Norfolk. Norfolk headed the religious conservatives at court and had long been Cromwell's most dangerous enemy. When the king sought to divorce the newly married Anne of Cleves and take Catherine for a fifth wife, Cromwell was caught in a trap. He had previously helped the king rid himself of Catherine of Aragon and Anne Boleyn, but a Howard queen would inevitably mean a challenge both to his power and to reform. Perhaps, as Shardlake speculates, if Cromwell had helped the king to a divorce he might, just, have saved himself – he had escaped from tight corners before – but he tried to keep the Cleves marriage alive and this was probably the final straw for the king.

Nonetheless, the dramatic suddenness of his arrest at the council table on 10 June 1540 on obviously trumped-up charges of treason surprised contemporaries and has puzzled historians. My story of the Greek Fire fraud as a final nail in Cromwell's coffin is, of course, entirely imaginary, but it fills a gap. Everybody, including Sir Richard Rich, turned their coats; Secretary Grey is a fictitious character, but there must have been many like him.

Thomas Cromwell was executed on 28 July 1540. Henry divorced Anne of Cleves, who was happy enough to escape marriage to her terrifying husband, and married Catherine Howard in secret the day after Cromwell's execution – a marriage that only a year later was to end in yet another gruesome tragedy.

The return to Rome, however, did not happen. For the rest of his reign Henry governed without a chief minister, playing one faction off against another. A year after Cromwell's execution he was complaining that he had been tricked into sacrificing 'the most faithful councillor I ever had'. In time the Duke of Norfolk too fell from grace.

\*

Greek Fire was, it is believed, a compound of petroleum and certain wood resins. This primitive flame-thrower was discovered, as related in the book, in seventh-century Constantinople and was used to great effect by the Byzantines against the Arab navies. The secret of its construction was passed down from one Byzantine emperor to another and in due course was lost, though the memory of this astounding weapon lingered on among scholars.

Of course, even if the method of construction and propulsion had been rediscovered in Renaissance Europe, it is unlikely it could ever have been used since petroleum was an unknown substance there and all potential sources, from the Black Sea to the Middle East and North Africa, were under the control of the expanding Ottoman empire, with which Europe, weakened by political and now religious disunity, was in a state of internecine warfare throughout the sixteenth century. In time Western Europe recovered and rose to a new pre-eminence; together with America it developed weapons compared to which Greek Fire is a mere plaything.

# ACKNOWLEDGEMENTS

The research for *Dark Fire* took me to some widely varied sources. While I was in the early stages of writing this book, by great good fortune Channel 4 Television showed a documentary, *Machines Time Forgot, Fireship* (2003) in which Professor John Haldon of Birmingham University successfully re-created Greek Fire and the apparatus that fired it. I have modelled the apparatus and the formula in *Dark Fire* on his reconstruction, and I am grateful to him and to the programme.

I am indebted to a number of books on Tudor London, most especially Liza Picard's *Elizabeth's London* (Weidenfeld & Nicolson, 2003) as well as Gamini Salgado's *The Elizabethan Underworld* (Sovereign, 1977). John Schofield's *Medieval London Houses* (Yale University Press, 1995) and John Stow's *Survey of London* (first published 1598; reprinted 1999, Guernsey Press Co.) took me back to the houses and streets of the Tudor City. *The A–Z of Elizabethan London* (Harry Margary, 1979) enabled me to follow my characters from place to place.

Sir John H. Baker's monumental *Introduction to English Legal History* (Butterworths, 1971) was invaluable on the legal side; Adrienne Mayor's *Greek Fire, Poison Arrows and Scorpion Bombs – Biological and Chemical Warfare in the Ancient World* (Overlook Press, 2003) was very helpful on the history of Greek Fire, and Allan G. Debus's *Man and Nature in the Renaissance* (Cambridge University Press, 1978) opened up the world of medieval alchemy to me. Rena Gardiner's stunningly illustrated *The Story of St Bartholomew the Great* (Workshop Press, 1990) was a mine of information on St Bartholomew's Priory, one of the best survivals from the dissolution in England. I have invented the tradition of burying people with some items associated with their early lives.

I am grateful to James Dewar of the Lincoln's Inn treasurer's office for showing me round the Great Hall, to Mrs Bernstein of the Jewish Museum, London, for guiding me to sources on the history of English Jewry and English Jewish names, and to Victor Tunkel of the Selden Society for the Study of Legal History for his help on sources for legal studies of the period. Needless to say, any errors are my own.

While I was in the early stages of researching this book I was involved in a serious road accident. My heartfelt thanks go to a number of people without whose help and encouragement I doubt the book would have been finished anything like on time. First of all to Mike Holmes and Tony Macaulay for their advice to a scientific illiterate on how the fraud on Cromwell could actually have been carried out. Without their aid I would have been completely at sea. Thanks particularly to Mike for guiding me to the conclusion that there was nothing around at the time that would have made a credible substitute for petroleum, and to Tony for the idea of the vodka.

Thanks again to Mike and Tony, and also to Roz Brody, Jan King and William Shaw for reading the book in draft and making valuable comments. Thanks also to my agent, Antony Topping, for his comments and all his help generally, to my editors Maria Rejt and Kathryn Court, to Liz Cowen for her excellent copy-editing, and last but not least to Frankie Lawrence for her typing and for going to London to find books for me while I was housebound.